Melabeth

Book 2

Forgive Me,
For I Am Sin

This book is dedicated to my brother Nick Hood. Wish you were here bro. R.I.P 4-12-1978 to 11-18-2009.

Melabeth Forgive Me For I Am Sin (Melabeth Series, Book 2)

(www.melabeth.com)

Copyright © 2013 by Eric B Hood.
(melabeththevampire@gmail.com)

Alley Cat Publishing
alleycatpublishing@gmail.com

ISBN 978-0-9884100-2-2
Paperback V.4

Editing by: Bill Stanton

Cover: photography by Wendy Hood.

Cover Art By: Mirella Santana
Digital artist and genius, Thanks for all your hard work!
You can find Mirella Santana at
https://www.facebook.com/mirellasantana.digitalartist

Contents

Acknowledgments

Special Thanks to my wife, she has become part of my marketing team, an editor and moral support. It's tough to do all that needs to be done, without the love and support she offers.

Also, very special thanks to my test subjects –who have read every chapter after I had written it, and before they had been edited - they gave input and the motivation to keep writing. So, thank you Mom, Dad, and Joyce.

To my oldest son Tyler, who is serving our great country in Afghanistan. I wish he was here and cannot wait until his safe return. I am so proud of him for his service and bravery. Hope he is in back in time for the big release party!

To my second son Cory, who happens to be my biggest fan. Not only does he read his dad's writing, but he has been my sounding board; he allows me to speak my story out loud for hours, refining the details of the story. Cory has gone word to word with me on the final rewrite. What a trooper!

Thank you Sonja, my youngest, only six. She has brought so much fun to the process of writing. She has provided relief and joy when a break is needed.

To Bill Stanton, has devoted countless hours editing my book. Bill is my father-in-law, and a professor of English at Clemson University. Bill's input has been great and encouraging. His wife, Debbie has also put countless hours into editing my book. They are an amazing team and great parents. Thanks, from the bottom of my heart.

To my sister in-law Wendy, and my older brother Donny, who own and operate their photography studio; Wendy edited all of the book art. She is very talented in her skills and it is eye opening to see her work, from beginning to end. Wendy and my brother have brought a very personal touch, and face with my book, so thank you, for all your help.

It has been heartwarming to receive so much support from so many great people. Since the last book it would be hard to list all of the individuals that help me, or encourage me. Still, I'll have to try.

Susan, thank you, for all your hard work. Susan is new to my editorial team and volunteered to participate in the final edit. She was under the gun for launch date. Thanks for your hard work and not giving up.

Maryanne also stepped up in helping with final edits. I appreciated all that she has done. It is more work than I ever could have imagined, producing a piece of literature. Thanks for your help and being a fan.

In closing, Mom, Dad, for not only for everything, but also for everything! They helped with editing, re-reading, marketing, book distribution and even financial support. How do you say thanks to all that? I guess by saying, Thanks!!!

Aaron, Erica, Mark and Bridget without friends and support I would be lonely. Thank you fans, for without my fans, I would be talking to myself

Chapter 1 The Pyramid
角錐

March 10th, 1990, it has been three days since the fight in the cemetery. Yet it feels so long ago.

Charlotte interrupted my thoughts, "Are you ready yet?" She yelled through the door.

I yelled back, "Ready for what?"

Can't a girl bathe in peace? I have been in this stupid hotel for two days and was told to stay put. Then Charlotte showed up unannounced and was in a hurry, no less.

Charlotte barked, "We have stuff to do; get a move on girl."

Irritated, I replied, "Let me get dressed, I wouldn't want to be late for whatever the hell we're doing."

A few minutes later I came out of the bathroom with my hair in a towel. I was only wearing my undergarments; my clothes were in the room. Just as well because Charlotte had an outfit laid out on the bed. It was a red skirt with a black blouse.

I mocked, "Great, you're here to help, I have a fear of dressing myself."

Charlotte gave me a half smile, "You have never been able to dress yourself, but don't worry; I don't mind helping."

My tone was nastier than I meant it to be, "So, where are we going?"

"You're grumpy; have you eaten?" Charlotte asked, but she knew the answer.

I had been told not to leave this room, and I was starving.

I snapped, "Have you noticed any missing room service? Or perhaps, the smell of a rotting corpse? No, well that must mean that in the last two days I haven't…"

She held her hands up in surrender. "Okay, okay don't get so excited. You're in Vegas now, and there is plenty of blood in this town."

"Could have fooled me, I haven't even seen a bag of blood."

She became stern. "Stop with the unpleasantness. We've had problems to deal with… ones you created. This city is a safe place for vampires, but you have to know the rules. There are plenty of people to feed off. Why bother with importing blood bags? Once I give you a tour, you'll love it here, trust me."

Charlotte pulled the towel off of my head and started to brush my hair. It was still dyed black and I hadn't grown it out blonde again. David and I were still going with the Goth look.

We didn't exchange words as she fixed my hair into a braid. Then I got dressed. After two days stuck in that room, I didn't care where we were going. As long as there was blood, I would be happy. My stomach ached for nourishment, and for the first time since I had become a vampire, I felt weaker.

As we headed out the door, Charlotte remarked, "You look weak, like you haven't fed for two days."

"I haven't fed for two days. I keep hearing a lot of remarks on my strength from you, Alice and Ezra. What does it mean?"

Charlotte looked thoughtful, looking back and forth down the hall checking if anyone was in earshot, "Let's talk about this another time, another place. I will say that in Vegas, blood will be the only source of power. Let's go."

I didn't understand what Charlotte was going on about, but I knew better than to have this conversation out in the open. Whatever it was, it had something to do with Las Vegas, being one of the dead places of the world.

Years ago, some gangster came out here to set up some legal gambling. Apparently, lots of gangs had magic users, vampires and other supernatural creatures working with them. I also found out that the government hires supernatural beings. The supernatural are like humans in the respect that they can be on either side of the law.

I guess after Vegas established it didn't take long for a couple of things to happen. First, the power that most magic users draw from being very weak here. The magic users call the energy of their power manna, and from what I understand it comes from life. There is not much life here, so there's not much manna, but there is more to it than just that. I do understand that hunters who normally use magic against us, why they cannot do it here. Something about where Vegas is located happens to be where the veil between life and death is thinnest. The closer magic users get to these dead spots, the more they became powerless.

I guess that's why vampires love the dead places of the world, and this one especially. Unlike other locations, this one doesn't have a strong governmental influence. Gangsters control the local government with all the money they are making. That's why no one pays state taxes in Vegas; the casinos do, and therefore they control the local government. Blood and money comes from all over the world here. To make vampires more at home, you will not find a window in a casino; all the stores are open twenty-four hours a day. You can even do your banking at night. This city will drain your wallet, as well as your body.

There are large tunnels under the casinos. Most believe that they are for service employees, but there is a lot more to the tunnels than that. In fact, there is an entire city underground; that's where my room is now. David and I were moved into the underground dwellings after the first night. It was so strange seeing other vampires walk around like it was nothing. Ezra said that one reason for free drinks were served to the humans. Too drunk and mesmerized by all the lights to notice us. It's these reasons that Las Vegas is perfect for vampires and a safe place for us to live, but there are different rules here, and I needed to learn them.

I walked over to the next room where David was staying. It was still daytime and Carrie wouldn't be around. It never felt like daytime here, but I know that is the way it was designed.

"What are you doing? Does David need blood too?" Charlotte asked mocking me.

"What, he's not allowed to go?" I snapped back.

"It doesn't matter because no one's home." Charlotte turned to me as she started walking toward the elevators.

"What do you mean? Where is he?" I demanded, as I flashed up next to her. She didn't answer me. We came to the elevators and she reached for the button. I stepped in front of her, "What, bad vampire ears? Where is he?"

Charlotte gave me a disapproving look. "You are so pushy, we don't need another Alice." I stared her down, "OK, OK, I will tell you."

"Ready," I said with impatience.

"About an hour ago I saw David leave the hotel."

I looked at Charlotte waiting for her to finish her story when I realized what she was doing. "That's it? You saw him leave; that is the extent of your information?"

Charlotte tossed her arms out as if I were asking her for the secrets of the universe. "See, this is why I didn't want to tell you! Look, I'm not, *or anyone else for that matter*, keeping track of your Necromancer. In a city of vampires, it's like bringing a cop to a speakeasy. Sure, he might drink and party with everyone, but no one really trusts him. Never quite sure if he would turn you in to save his job."

I crossed my arms over my chest. "What you just said doesn't make any sense, but I doubt you care. I am too hungry to think straight. Let's just get some food."

Charlotte laughed, "*You're* the one blocking the elevator, dear."

I spun around and mashed the button. I took some deep breaths and attempted to calm my nerves. My temper was bad. It seemed like it was always around the corner, just waiting for a reason to beat someone up. I guess being raped and killed had that effect on me. Charlotte didn't help, she likes to play mom. It infuriates me, sometimes I like it; most days I don't.

Charlotte, picking up on my mood said, with a softer, kinder voice, "Darling, you will feel better after you eat. After that you... we can figure out where your friend ran off to. In fact, when we're done, I am sure he will come out from whatever rock he is under. We can even start looking at the mall for him!"

"You're probably right," I half heartily agreed. Her kindness or at least her version of kindness helped reel in my temper.   "Thanks, but I doubt he is at the mall."

As we stepped inside the elevator, Charlotte lectured, "Now you need to control yourself. We let you go too long without eating, but I know you can handle yourself. Just do what I tell you, okay?"

"Aye, aye, captain," I responded with a salute.

In the elevator Charlotte started filling me in on the basics. They weren't that difficult; first rule, don't make a mess while feeding on someone, not even in the hotel rooms. Blood was hard to clean up. Second, don't let others see you feeding, which I considered it to be a no brainer.

The only time these rules didn't apply, was if you were underground in a vampire bar. They were secret and you could feed in the open; a lot of people in Vegas were blood whores. It feels good to be fed on by vampires, but that's only half the reason. If you have a gambling habit, vampires pay to bite, but you need to be careful not to kill these people. The bars charged a lot of money, if they had to get rid of evidence. I found that the druggies are no fun to feed on, unless you want to be high and out of your head. Once I fed from a drunken kid, I was drunk for almost an hour.

Third, you had to check that whoever you were about to feed on was not wearing a necklace or a ring with a vampire symbol. This was the hard part for me because I didn't know all the different symbols. There were dozens of different symbols in existence for different vampire families that lived in Vegas. They gave the jewelry to their human families for protection. If you fed off the humans with those marks, you may be hunted down and killed.

Of course the real problem from feeding in Vegas, was the same problem I had everywhere, I couldn't mesmerize people. Drunken people should have been easy. It only took a few words out of Charlotte's mouth and some drunk man in the midst of gambling would stop what he was doing and follow me anywhere.

 I fed on three men before my belly was satisfied. I have only been that hungry since the day I had awoken. Charlotte wasn't ready to introduce me to a vampire bar yet. It was good to feel my strength return, my mood greatly improved too.

Charlotte and I had a great time gambling, drinking and we even went dancing. When we went dancing, we were joined by Ezra. It was about ten in the evening when I broke away from Ezra and Charlotte to go check on David. David was still mourning about the loss of his parents, so it was no great surprise that Carrie was bothering him. Last night she hung out with me to give the poor guy some space. I figured that he wouldn't be out much past dark. Hopefully he was waiting for me.

I didn't even have to knock. Carrie was out in the hall waiting for me. She gave me a big hug, "Where you been sweetie? David told me to keep a sharp eye out for you. I don't know why I had to wait in the hall. Do you think he wanted me to wait out here to get rid of me?"

I smiled, "Give me a moment with him, if you don't mind?"

"No problem sugar, y'all take your time now," Carrie added with a wink.

"Thanks," and I slipped into David's room. I didn't even knock, but unlucky for me, David was dressed. He was sitting quietly, propped up on two pillows, reading a book. "Hey, you up for a little company?" I whispered in a sexy voice.

David marked his spot in the book, looked up at me and gave me a smile. "Yes... yes I am. In fact, I was waiting for you." He then gestured for me to sit with him.

His hair hung down just below his shoulders, it appeared wild and was always in his face concealing his eyes. His overall demeanor had changed... darker, maybe? That wasn't it... he was tougher looking now than when I had first met him. The way he moved, the way he looked, it all said he was tougher now, dangerous even.

I slid right into the bed, curling my body next to his. "So, what have you been up to today?"

I looked across at David's face. I couldn't read what he was thinking, but I waited patiently while he worked up an answer. David took in a breath as he admitted, "Don't get upset, but I buried Lizzie today."

I did get upset, "WHAT? I would have liked to have been with you." Then I paused, "I understand if you didn't want me there."

"Can I please tell you the whole story first, before you jump to conclusions? I know you wanted to be there. I would have liked for you to be there. Lizzie would have liked you to be there too, but I do have reasons."

"Okay, before I kill you, tell me your silly excuses," I teased.

A small smile and a little relief washed across David's face. "Let's go for a walk."

"I like that idea; I am *so* sick of these hotel rooms." I tried not to whine when I said this, but I missed the mark.

David grabbed his hoodie and threw it over his shoulder. Then he looked over at me and gestured for me to walk with him. As we headed out of his room and toward the elevator door, David started talking. "I made some phone calls this morning when you were sleeping. I got hold of my stepdad's friend Alex McDonald. Alex is not just an old friend, he's also a human detective. He is famous for working with the supernatural. My stepdad and Alex would help each other solve crimes in the supernatural world. They worked together for years on many cases."

"I know this detective; he called me after the incident at the mall," I recalled.

David laughed as the elevator doors closed and we made our ascent. David continued, "Incident? Is that what we're calling it now?"

"That's what I'm calling it," I smirked.

David started to explain. "Well, no matter what you call it, yes, that is the same detective. He helped cover up the incident with the help of my stepdad. They believed it was in our best interest to keep The Order from getting involved. To make a long story shorter, he's still helping us out. Leaving the other tapes behind was a good idea, because he's already put together a lot of the pieces of the puzzle. He has issues with The Order, and in his words, he's had *enough*."

As we got out of the elevator and headed into the casino, it was too crowded to talk, so we just walked hand in hand. I couldn't help but think it was a good thing that we still had people in our corner. I liked Alex, I liked him when I first talked to him. He was a man with morals which made me wonder if he really would be on our side when he realized what kind of revenge David and I would be after.

We walked through Caesars Palace, it was a beautiful casino. We walked through the mall and when you looked up, you saw the sky. Not the real sky, but a blue sky with moving clouds. The roof looked like this day or night. It made complete sense when Charlotte explained that a vampire who missed the daytime designed this area. This was my favorite casino that I had been in, with its old Roman statues and stone walls. It made you think you were in Rome from long ago. We headed through the gambling area and toward the doors to outside.

Once we got outside, the air felt warm and dry; David wasn't going to need his hoodie. As soon as we were on the main street, I could talk again. "How can Alex help us?"

"He's a detective in the supernatural world. How could he not help us?" David went on to say, "He knows everyone, and our best bet for finding leads on the biker gang. He will know how and where we can attack The Order. We need this kind of direction to take on The Order. In fact, he has already given me information about two important groups."

"What groups?" I asked.

"One is the local Necromancers," When David spoke, he did this with a strange sense of reverence. It was like he found his people. He went on, "That is the reason I didn't have time to invite you to Lizzie's burial. I don't think the other Necromancers would have welcomed you."

"And why not? Why would you have them bury Lizzie?" I was trying not to be pissed. I knew David had been through a lot in the last few days, but I didn't know who these people were. I didn't like being left out on such an important occasion.

Carrie jumped into the conversation, "I asked, but he wouldn't answer my questions, then again no one does."

I just about jumped out of my pants as I let out a little yelp.

Carrie went on, "Good God, honey, calm yourself. That's right, I'm still here, third wheel, did ya forget that? You know I have to tag along, I ain't got no choice, you know that right? Y'all know I don't mind giving space, but if you're going to drag me all over town..."

"Okay... okay," I interrupted. "Enough already and before you start in on the long haul of questions, let David finish telling us the story."

Carrie gave me a bright smile, "That's all I was sayin', that I asked those questions, and I would like to know the answers too. It happened during the day so I didn't get to meet these Necromancers. So, who are they?"

David was looking at some lights on the side of a casino, then he looked at us and went on speaking as if our conversation had never happened. "Do you know anything about dead spots?"

I answered David, "Just what Charlotte and Ezra have told me. They told me that there was a place where the curtain between life and death is the thinnest. It means there is little or no manna for a magic user to draw their magic from."

David gave my hand a little squeeze and then interjected. "And to think how little time we have had in this world, a world within the backdrop of reality; so much for us to learn."

Carrie added, "You can say that again; I wasn't much for learnin' when I was alive. And now that I'm dead... and still don't like learnin'."

I looked over at Carrie, "Don't worry dear, in life and death, you still don't know shit."

 David chuckled while Carrie stuck her tongue out at me.

"We're almost there," David announced.

"Where?" Carrie and I asked in stereo.

We were walking past the Excalibur. It was a casino that looked like a castle surrounded by giant hotels. Beyond Excalibur, there was nothing but empty desert. David stopped and stared at the empty land. Then I saw something I have never seen before. It looked as if the sky was ripped and through the rip, was light. There were spirits all around just walking. They looked lost or they were seeing something different than what I was seeing. They didn't seem to know we were there.

Carrie's eyes were wide, "There's a lot of ghosts over there. We're not getting any closer, are we? I don't think that would be a good idea. What ya'll think?"

David looked over at Carrie and shook his head. "Over there is where we buried Lizzie."

"A field of ghosts next to a vampire city. Who wouldn't want to be buried there?" I teased David.

David laughed, "You two are impossible! I can't take you anywhere."

"And yet you do," I replied as me and Carrie giggled. I added, "So, what's so special about this field, I mean besides the ghosts?"

"Two things: First, this is the center of the dead spot. The second thing is, this is where the Necromancers are going to build their temple." David said this with a strange look in his eyes that I can only describe as pride.

"Okay fill in the blanks already!" I said with impatience.

"I reckon that I still wouldn't understand what's going on," Carrie added with a huff of frustration.

David stopped walking as we moved to the edge of the sidewalk. He then started to tell me what I missed out on while I was sleeping. "See when I talked to Alex, he told me where the local Necromancers meet. I couldn't wait to meet some people… you know, like me. I went there this morning before you got up. I talked to the lead Necromancer, and I told him what happened. He explained to me that it was really important to get my sister into the earth; he offered to let me bury her in their sacred ground. This is where their temple is going to be built. That's why I did it during the day, when the ghosts are away and so are the vampires. That's when the Necromancers lay their dead to rest in the ground."

"I understand what you're sayin'; this is goin' to be a pyramid for the Necromancers," Carrie stated like it all made sense.

David and I looked at Carrie, then in stereo said, "What?"

Carrie looked confused while she said, "You know, a pyramid. My grandma told me all about Necromancers. She was a witch I reckon; that's why she had the necklace. She told me not to wear it, but I did, and now I'm trapped as a ghost. When she was alive, she told me all kinds of stories. Back then I used to think they were just stories, but now I reckon she knows." She came to realize that we were staring at her funny. "What are you 'all lookin' at? I mean y'all staring at me like I have crawdad's cumin' out of my ears."

I snickered, "Sorry, I didn't mean to be so surprised at the fact you knew something."

Carrie's face had a hurt look on it, "I'm not a dumb ass… do you think I'm a dumb ass?"

David said matter-of-fact, "No, just ignorant."

I quickly added, "But, ignorance can be corrected by the introduction of knowledge. Unlike asshole here," I pointed my thumb at David, "You can't fix rude. How did you know they're building a pyramid? And what does that have to do with Necromancers?"

David added with a nicer tone, "I don't know about the pyramids, but I would like to." I must have been giving him a look, so he added… "What… you're rude to her all the time and now I'm the bad guy?"

I turned and faced him, "I tease her; I don't hurt her feelings."

Carrie jumped between us. "Excuse the hell out of me; I have a story that needs some tellin'. And you both hurt my feelings, on a regular basis… I might add. As my grandma used to say, shut it, so I can talk."

"Go ahead, all ears girl," I urged.

David let out a huff, and then said, "Listening."

Carrie smiled, she loved it when she had the floor, "Okay, so here's what my Grammy told me. She said that Necromancers were known to go to the dark places of the world. Y'all call them dead places, but my granny called them dark places."

I interrupted, "Just tell the story."

Carrie waved her hand at me, "I am! Where was I? Oh yeah, the dark spots, that's where the entrance to the land of the dead is the thinnest. No one knows why, but my grandma said it was probably where the dead traveled through when it was time to go to heaven or hell I guess. Now the Necromancers, unlike any other magic users draw their power from the dead. So, it's on these spots that they build their temples. All over the world dead places exist and that's where the Necromancers build their temples. I also know this because I'm a ghost and when I look over to the spot on where they're going to build, well, I see… I'm not sure if I can explain it, but it scares me. And there are lots ghosts over there."

"I guess that explains why there are so many vampires here," I said.

David looked thoughtful for a second, then disagreed, "No. I don't believe that's why vampires are here. Manna or magic comes from life and vampires get their power from stealing life. I think they come here because their enemies can't fight them here; also it works well for the Necromancers. You know, my enemies of my enemies are my friends."

David, Carrie and I headed back towards the casinos. We went into several different casinos laughing, drinking and we even did a little bit of gambling. They were really strict about ages here, but as soon as they saw me and realized what I was, the security would give me a head tilt. They also would take two fingers to their foreheads and then give me a small salute, letting me know they recognized me and everything was good. It didn't take me long to figure out all the security needed was to see my large eyes and they left me alone. When I noticed them heading over, all I had to do was make eye contact.

I didn't have to wear contacts to change my eyes here in Vegas. People were too drunk and let's face it, people see what they want to see and believe what they will. You can see aliens, Bigfoot all day long, but good luck making someone believe that you're not crazy.

We got back to our rooms right before the morning light. I went into David's room with my bags in hand. Of course I had done a little bit of shopping, but not too much. I picked up a bottle of wine that David didn't waste any time opening. Carrie and I made ourselves at home on the bed. The room wasn't very big. It had a bathroom and a king-size bed. In front of the bed there was a dresser with a TV on it. In the corner of the room there was a table with two seats; there were also two night stands with lamps on them, and I am sure there would be a bible in one of the drawers.

Carrie was looking at some of my purchases. I picked up some cheap jewelry and a couple of blouses. I also bought a deck of cards. Carrie looked over at me, "It's been fun hangin' with y'all, but the sun is about to rise. See 'ya tomorrow night," and she disappeared.

David and I were alone at last. He came over and sat next to me handing me a glass of wine. Then he held his glass up saying, "Cheers, to the future success of our endeavors against the assholes who have done us wrong."

"Here, here!" We clinked our glasses together. I took a sip and added, "Good, I will have to get this kind again."

While swirling his wine around in his glass, "Yeah, it's good, but I like my wine dry. This is a little sweet for me."

I laughed and David trying to act suficated.Finsishing my glass of wine and set it down on the nightstand. I turned and faced David. We were now staring into each other's eyes.

David with an unsure voice asked, "What do you want to do now?"

I didn't answer him, well, I did answer him, just not with words. I moved forward and started kissing him. His lips were like fire and I could almost taste his blood right below the surface. My teeth and nails extended, as my tongue explored his mouth.

David was still trying to balance his glass of wine. I stopped kissing him and he emptied the glass, then threw it against the wall. We laughed as we pulled each other closer.

I ripped his shirt off like it had been made of paper. In one quick motion I slipped my shirt off as we rolled together into a horizontal position.

I made love, it was wonderful, but different than I had imagined. One thing was that I was much stronger than David, but I knew that helped me. It helped me because with David I wouldn't feel trapped again.

David had fallen asleep next to me. In some ways sleeping with him seemed unavoidable, but in others, I might have rushed it. Still, I deeply cared about David and was glad he was there by my side. I would sleep better knowing he was with me.

I closed my eyes, I knew the morning sun had risen. Soon, I would find sleep.

Chapter 2 Dreams
甘夢

I knew it was a dream…

I'm in my bed and surrounded by books. Carefully pushing some books aside, I check the time… 7:12 in the morning. Moving over to the window, I lift the curtain just a little bit and take a peek. Through the window I can see the kids in the neighborhood lining up at the bus stop waiting for the school bus. Dropping the curtain, I fall back onto my bed.

I don't go to school, no need to get up, but I'm not tired. I pick up a book that I had been reading the night before I fell asleep. Basic car mechanics, my dad's Ford Escort broke a timing belt. Now we had to walk or ride the bus. I found out that the car has a non interference motor; which means that if I could fix it, the only cost would be the timing belt. I borrowed some tools from the neighbor last night, my father picked up a timing belt from the auto store.

After a bit I got up and got dressed. Then, I make myself some cereal and headed out to the garage. I have several books to help me, plus a manual for this model car. According to the book with a non interference motor, the pistons didn't hit the valves. Basically, the motor was fine as long as I correctly install the timing belt and timed the motor correctly.

I like working, it keeps my mind busy. I had been hard at work when I felt my stomach growl. The clock on the wall said it was a little after 4:00, but I was putting the car back together and was too excited to see if the car would start.

My father and one of his buddies joined me. I can't seem to remember my dad's friend's name, but it doesn't really matter to me anyways.

My father, full of smiles, says, "She's fourteen, and a genius. I bet she'll have this car running in no time."

My father's friend spoke with too much enthusiasm, "Wow, like where did she learn how to work on cars, man?"

"Books," I said with a little bit of an attitude. I didn't like my dad's friends, and I learned that if I was nice to them, it only encouraged them to speak to me.

My dad's friend went on like he didn't understand my hostility, "Books, *wow man*, to be able to pick up a book… and then like, wow. And then just do it, man!"

My dad, sweetly as possible asked me, "Sweetheart, I made you a sandwich. Would you like me to just bring it out here?"

He knew I was still pissed off at him. We could have paid a mechanic to fix the car if he hadn't spent his money on drugs and alcohol.

"Sure Dad… thanks," I answered him, but didn't make eye contact. I just kept on working.

My dad started talking to his buddy again, "See, my girl doesn't need no school. She needs to know something, then she goes to the library, reads a book."

"Yeah, man, it's *amazing*. I wish I could do that kind of shit, I can't even remember what day it is."

I couldn't help myself, "Wow, *man*, I am so surprised that you can even speak."

My father laughed uneasily, and then scolded, "Mel, be nice now."

My father's buddy just laughed, "No man, it's cool, she's a tough chick, I get it."

They both headed back into the house with my dad saying, "I'll be right back with some food Mel."

I guess my father had to fight off wild Indians to get the sandwich. It was an hour before he returned, his dumb ass friend still in tow. At least he was making himself useful by carrying a soda for me. My dad cleared a spot off one of the work benches and laid my sandwich down. His buddy announced what he did for me, "Dude, I got this drink for you... I'm going to put it next to your sandwich, okay."

"Thanks dad," Ignoring his buddy, kind of rude of me, after all he did carry my drink all the way to the garage.

My dad asked, "So how is it going? Can I help you, or do you think you got it?"

I put it back together and was just finishing some small details before seeing if it would run. My dad didn't want to help. It's probably why he took so long to get my sandwich. "No dad, I'm about done. Give me one more minute, and we'll see if this works."

Dad's buddy said, "Man, I am totally stoked, man it will be cool if she fixes it. You know what I am sayin, dude?" as he elbowed my father.

"Oh man I do, I really could use a car." My father added back.

I hate the word dude, but here in California everyone's a dude, even the girls. Mockingly I added, "*Dude*, because we could use some groceries, *dude!*"

My dad's face went slack, because that's not what he had in mind at all. In fact, he was probably planning on some kind of drug run, but if I wanted food in the house, I had to put my foot down, "Food first... *DUDE*."

"Of course Mel," My dad said acting as if that was what he was planning the whole time.

I walked around the car, reached in the driver's window, and turned over the motor. It spun a few times, and then it started. Everyone cheered, as I jumped up and down in excitement.

I had grease all over me, but it didn't matter; my dad grabbed me and pulled me into a hug.

I'm awake…

These dreams of my life before becoming a vampire, I wish they would stop.

The dreams had been increasing, both in clarity and length. I felt as if my past would haunt me until I killed all who had done me wrong. Killing Devon had not brought me peace. Of course the death of David's family was too high of a price to pay. Especially Lizzie, I had grown close to her. I would have never traded her life for Devon's. I felt indebted to David as if I had stolen his family away from him in order to have a piece of my revenge.

Chapter 3 Hunting
狩猟

June 3rd, 1990

The wind blew through my hair as I gently swayed back and forth upon a branch.

The air was cool and crisp. Sitting up in the tree; waiting for the attack to begin leaving me with time to think. The last two and a half months had been crazy. David and I have already attacked and or destroyed over a dozen different locations. Each one had been full of Order members and each time, we wiped them out. David was getting a name for himself, not only that, but he had mastered more tricks with raising the dead.

Tonight was special because the group we were attacking was important to The Order. The members in this group gathered information and created weapons. One member, Aaron Reite was the key player in making their weapons. David came across information that Reite was a gifted magic user that was unparalleled in making magical items. Among the many weapons he crafted were guns and crosses that were used to destroy vampires.

We were in a small town somewhere outside of New York, New York. It was a suburb of the city, full of middle class homes. I was sitting atop of a large Oak tree on one of the uppermost branches. I was at least a one hundred fifty feet above the ground. I was able to see the house where the Order members were meeting. I watched each figure below as they filed in the home. The meeting was starting and so were we. I could see the shadows of the dead coming through the trees.

David raised a graveyard not too far from here. Now a small army of the undead slowly marched through the forest. They worked through the wooded area around the home, encircling it. The attack would start any moment.

I was forbidden to go into the home because it was protected. I knew they wouldn't invite me in, but the walking dead needed no invitation. If any of The Order members tried to escape, they would have more than undead to worry about. They would have me.

I noticed a man coming down the street. He was still a few houses away. The lights in the homes went out, because David had cut the power. The undead were now moving toward the house. The attack had begun.

The man that had been moving toward the house came to a stop out front. He looked around and he must have noticed that the power had gone off. He headed toward the house. My attention was diverted to the back of the house. The undead were now breaking in the back door and crowding their way in.

There was also a sliding glass door set further down the house. A group of undead reached the door and smashed the glass in, as they rushed into the home.

An explosion went off at the side of the house. Pieces of the wall flew across the neighbor's yard as some men rushed out of the hole in the wall. It was time for me to intervene.

Two men ran into the wooded area, shouting and casting spells. They were forcing their way through the undead. I was about to drop down to take them on, when I heard a small explosion. The man who had been approaching the house was now shooting the undead. When he shot them, they exploded into pieces.

A giant man crashed out of the house behind the man with the gun. The giant started throwing the undead around like children. He began to run while the armed man followed through the giants wake. He fired off a few more shots, blowing up the corpses as they retreated.

Now that I had four men fleeing the scene, I decided to go after the first two. The giant looked like he might take longer to deal with, so I will chase him down later.

I dropped to the ground, making myself weightless before I hit the ground. I landed without a noise, then flashed forward behind the two men.

I came upon them quickly as they were fighting off more of the undead. They were about to break free from the crowd of corpses so that they would have a clear path to run from the chaos.

My hands were so fast that I slashed him three or four times in his neck before he could even react. With one final quick slice, I took his head off. By this time his friend had taken notice of me, I had turned to face him.

He held a short sword in his hand, covered with blood from the dead. He cast a spell, then the blade lit on fire. He attacked, but his moves were slow and clumsy.

I easily moved around him and slashed his skin with my claws. He cried out in pain, but kept on attacking me.

Magic users and wizards can be powerful foes, but there're more like canons than fighters. If you let them stand back and cast spells they will destroy everything in sight. But up close and personal, vampires rule.

I grabbed his wrist that held the sword and easily broke it. The sword fell to the ground. The wizard mumbled something under his breath; then shoved his free arm towards me.

I flashed to the side as a burst of air came forth from his hand. I stood to one side and smiled at him, "Missed me, missed me, now you have to kiss me."

Anger was his dominant facial expression. He stepped back, holding his broken wrist with his good hand. He held his arms apart and started to cast a circle.

I laughed, but did not move forward. His look went from anger to confusion. About the same time his face registered the fact that he was still surrounded by undead, two of the foul corpses grabbed him from behind.

I turned and walked away while listening to the screams of a man being ripped in half.

It was hard to be smug. I still had a giant and a man with a magic gun to deal with. I flew into the air, jumping off a rooftop to the tree top. I heard a crashing noise and then headed toward the sound of screams.

I flew through the air and landed on a roof of a two story house. The home is set high upon a hill overlooking a park. The park was surrounded by woods. Across the street, I could see fresh broken limbs where someone had crashed through the forest. The limbs were huge. It must have been the giant and that means the other man was right behind him.

As I listened, there was a distinct sound of a man gasping for breath. I floated down to the wooded area and followed the trail. The man with the gun was now in full sight. He had fallen and I watched as he struggled to stand. It looked as if he might have hurt himself, but he still had that gun.

Instead of following the trail of the giant, the man turned to his left and headed for the park. The best idea was to deal with him before the giant. I flashed over to the playground and took cover behind the jungle gym. The man sneaked across the field looking all round him. It was obvious that he was winded from running, one thing I don't miss about being human.

I decided to have some fun with him. I flashed over to the swing set and gave it a hard push. I flashed behind the man just as his head swung toward the sound of the swing. He stared at it for a second and his heart accelerated.

He spun around and he stopped cold when his eyes met mine. He lifted his gun hand, it shook with his nerves. He took aim… I flashed right before he pulled the trigger. His human reaction time was too slow to register the fact that I had already moved.

The gun fired and the bullet found no target as it flew across the field and into the forest. There it found a tree or a branch and exploded. The gun slide was wide open, he had fired his last bullet.

I came up behind him."You missed," I whispered in his ear. "It's okay. Everything is just fine," as I wrapped my arms around his chest from behind him.

I nibbled the bottom of his ear. I could feel his panic. With a calming voice, "Shhh… it's okay, I'm not going to hurt you, in fact… you'll like it."

He begged, "Please…"

"It's okay, you're okay," I purred into his ear. Kissing his ear, I worked my way down his neck.

He asked, "Who are you?"

I whispered, "Melabeth."

Then I bit down into his neck, and the blood gushed into my mouth. The warmth of his life slid down my throat and warmed my whole body. His life was over and I let his body hit the ground.

"It looks like he's playin' possum," Carrie's voice rang from behind me.

It startled me. I tried to keep the irritation out of my voice, "What do you need Carrie?"

She laughed, "Just ate and still as grumpy, as a one tooth crocodile. David just asked me to check up on you. He ended up at the house, but he still hasn't found Reite. What's you think? Have you seen Reite? Do you know what Reite looks like? Is that Reite?" Carrie continued to rattle on.

I just shook my head in disbelief. She would never change. Before she could ask another ten questions, I interrupted, "Did David see the two men I killed outside of the house?"

Carrie answered, "He sure did and they ain't who he was looking for. Y'all sure made a mess of the place."

I looked down at the man I just killed. I picked up his body and tossed it over my shoulder. "I will take this body back to the house... is David still there?"

"Sure is," Carrie answered.

"Let him know that I'm coming with a body. This guy might be Reite for all I know." Carrie nodded her head then disappeared. It looked as if the giant would get away, but I doubted very seriously that he was Reite.

When I got back, David had pulled a truck into the driveway of the house. The undead were loading up the dead Order members. I knew that David had cast a spell around this area. The spell not only made the lights go out, but also kept the sleeping neighbors from hearing anything. Even knowing all this, it was still strange to see David standing out on the lawn overseeing the undead moving the dead into a truck.

I dropped the body at David's feet, he looked down at it. He smiled, "You got him, that's Reite. Good job sweetheart!"

With that, he pulled me into his arms and kissed me deeply. I sighed breathlessly, "Let's get out of here."

David spoke like a general, "First, I need to finish cleaning up, but why don't you go head. I will catch up with you in Vegas."

I felt a little put off; I wanted to be with him. My voice didn't hide my feelings, "You'll be missing out. What could be more important than a night in my arms?"

David looked into my eyes and gave me his award winning smile. With a soft voice, "I need to talk to my contacts. Also, don't you think I should return all the corpses to the graveyard? The less evidence we leave behind, the better."

"And why can't I go with you?" I didn't mean to sound whiny, but I did.

David chuckled, "You scare my contacts. I am getting closer all the time to the men who killed you. You do want me to track them down, don't you?"

Carrie spoke up for me, "Oh, yeah, she sure does."

I hid the pain in my voice, "Yes... I do. Hurry back, I'll miss you."

David took me into his arms and held me tight, then kissed me deeply. With hunger in his eyes, "I will hurry... promise."

Chapter 4 Nightmares
悪夢

I arrived back in Vegas by aircraft. The flight arrived early in the morning, I hurried to grab a cab. I wanted to make it back to my room before the sunrise. The sun bothered me and I was tired.

I arrived at the hotel and made it into my room in record time. Sitting on the edge of my bed and staring at the wall. I didn't know where any of the other White's were. I suddenly felt alone and wished that Carrie was here.

Rather than mope around, I decided to get some sleep. Sometimes I dreaded sleep, I didn't like the dreams. The dreams of my past haunt me.

*   *   *

I am late.

"Good night sweetheart," I said to my daughter. I closed the door, leaving a crack so the light of the hallway would make her feel safe.

"Aaron, how long will you be out tonight?" my wife whispered into my ear. I could hear the worry in her voice.

I walked down the hallway toward the front door, with my wife in tow. I spoke in hushed tones, "A couple of hours. I will be five houses down. Just call my beeper if you need me."

My wife said in an authoritative way, "Listen here, Mr. Aaron Reite," her voice softened, "Hurry home, love."

"Don't worry! This is the last meeting I will be attending. Love you, be back soon." I held my wife as I kissed her and after a few moments, I went out the front door. I checked to make sure I had everything. Wallet check, keys, checks and gun safely slid into the back of my pants, check. I started walking slowly toward the Dexter's house.

I was never much of a sorcerer. I happen to have a really unique ability to make magical items, like the gun that rested on my back. It had twelve rounds in it. I had spent eight hours on each bullet. Making the symbols at the end of the bullet and pouring my magic into each one, so that when the bullet hit its target, the target would explode. Not bad for a small 9mm.

Still, I don't have much to do with the magic community. All I ever did was help make the magical weapons that The Order used to help keep peace. Now it's all gone haywire.

Instead of us hunting down the criminals, we are the ones being hunted down. No one even knows who or why; actually, there are a lot of reasons why. The Order never has had any real order. It's always been small groups of magical citizens trying to keep our life's secret, free of government involvement and trying to keep magic users and magic creatures from running amuck. But, like all things that start out with good, it only takes a few bad individuals to take down the whole organization.

I have a wife and two children. I will not be killed for this shit. I am going to tell Mark that I quit.

As I came up to Mark Dexter's house, I was lost in thought, but something felt wrong. I stopped walking and looked around.

It took me a minute to figure out what was wrong, it was too dark. The street lights were all out and normally Mark left his porch light on, especially the nights we were having a meeting. As I looked around, I noticed that all the houses in the neighborhood were dark, I let out a small laugh… wow, I really need to get out of this. A power outage had me scared.

I walked up the driveway leading to Mark's garage door, when I heard a loud bang. It was quickly followed by the sounds of smashing glass, walls and wood.

Whatever was going on, it was happening in the back of the house. It didn't take a genius to figure out there was a fight. I pulled my gun out and froze.

What do I do, rescue my friends or make a break for home? All I could tell was that I was frozen between fright and indecision.

A new sound, this one from behind me. A snapping noise with the sound of dead leaves being crushed underfoot. Spinning around, I pointed the gun into the dark.

"Who's there?" I sounded brave, but I felt my heart in my throat.

No one answered.

I heard more noise and realized that more than one person was coming at me through the dark. I grabbed my keys out of my pocket with one hand while holding my gun toward the approaching sounds with the other.

I was sure glad I brought my keys. One of the first enchantments my father taught me was how to make objects emit light. It was one of my favorite things to turn the keys into flashlights. That way I could see the lock and try to get the key into it.

I rubbed my thumb against the key. The light came out, and I could see who was approaching. I wish I hadn't… in front of me were a dozen rotting corpses were heading straight for me and the lead one was only ten feet away. I fired right into the chest of the first undead. The corpse barely moved back and then he started forward again.

Now I knew to kill a undead walker you should shoot them in the head, but these were my bullets. I watched as my bullet detonated and the corpse blew apart. Blood and guts sprayed everywhere, all over me as well. The only thing left were the legs of the undead and they fell to the ground. It was time to get out of here. I turned and headed away from the undead and toward my house only to find that another group of undead was heading toward me… I was surrounded.

Not sure what to do, I decided to shoot my way through; cutting a path and then make a run for it. I took aim and shot two of the undead and watched them explode. Before I could make my way to the gap, it was quickly filled with more walking corpses. Despite being fired at, they just kept walking forward.

A large, smashing noise came from behind me; I had to look. I turned around to see my good friend Mark smashing down the garage door. Mark was a half-giant, and why, when humans met him, they didn't know this, always amazed me.

"This way, Mark," I yelled. With my friend, I felt like I might get out of this alive.

Mark looked over at me, "Aaron, we've got to get out of here."

"Just thinking the same thing," I fired two more rounds and blew up three undead.

"Two for one, nice shooting," Mark yelled this as he rushed in front of me.

Mark ran toward the gap that I had made. I quickly followed him as the undead poured in behind me. I ran behind Mark as he smashed the undead out of his way. I fired two more rounds behind us and took down some of them chasing us.

If I counted right, there was one bullet left in my gun. The thought was starting to worry me, but we broke through the crowd. I ran behind Mark as we headed down the street, but we were heading in the opposite direction of my house.

I never thought of Mark as being fast before, but with his long legs, he flew across the ground. He was such a big guy with short brown hair and a goatee. He always wore glasses that looked too small for his face, but, despite his size, he was the friendliest guy I knew. Even his appearance seemed non threatening, but to watch him toss the undead out of his way was something else to behold.

He headed straight into a local park and then continued into the forest. I tried to follow, but the branches and trees grabbed at my clothes. As Mark ran, the tree branches snapped loudly as he pushed his way through.

Out of breath, I said, "Mark… wait! Wait up!"

I didn't have enough air. I had been running full out and could not yell above a whisper. I felt my foot catch a tree root and I landed on my knee hard. "AAaaaa!!" I put my hand over my mouth and winced in pain.

Mark was crashing through the forest. It would take a mighty sound for him to hear me over the racket he was already making. Then the sounds quickly became quieter as he moved away from me. I stood up and listened.

I heard nothing. Hopefully I had gotten away; I better make a large circle back to my house. I started to pray that my family was okay.

I limped out of the woods and into the quiet park. I decided to cross the park and work my way down a block or so, then circle my way back to my house. I only had one bullet left and couldn't afford to run into another group of undead.

I just passed the play set when I heard the sound of a swing. When I turned and looked, an empty swing moved up and down. The air was still, and so were all the other swings.

I spun around, behind me stood a girl.

I lifted my gun at her, and took in the sight in front of me. There stood a pretty young lady with long black hair. Wearing a long overcoat with tall boots. The edges of her black dress hung below the overcoat with a red pattern around the bottom of the dress. Her makeup was hard to make out in the light, but appeared to be black eyeliner with red lipstick. It was the eyes; the eyes told me what she was.

Her eyes were as blue as the sky, but too large to be human. I have never met or seen a vampire before, but I knew what to look for. If I stared into the eyes, she would hypnotize me; I had to kill her fast. I fired my last bullet.

The slide of my gun was now in the open position, showing me I was out of bullets. My target was gone.

"You missed," stated a voice from behind me. Her voice was gentle and inviting. She was close enough for me to feel her cold breath. I have heard how fast vampires were, but I had no appreciation, until now.

"It's okay. Everything is just fine," she wrapped her arms around my chest from behind me.

I felt her mouth nibble the bottom of my ear. I could feel my heart trying to break free from my rib cage as the panic set in; once again, she tried calming me with her voice. "Shh… it's okay, I'm not going to hurt you in fact… you'll like it."

I found a small piece of my voice, "Please…"

"It's okay, you're okay," She purred into my ear. Then she kissed my ear and worked her way down to my neck.

"Who are you?"

She whispered a strange name into my ear, "Melabeth."

Her mouth found my neck.

It felt good whatever she was doing, it felt really good. Then it felt like sex, I couldn't help but moan in pleasure. I reached my climax, but she didn't stop.

All she had been doing was… what had she been doing? Draining me, I realized. I started to feel the pain, followed by weakness and dizziness. If she hadn't been holding me up, I was sure that I would fall. I heard a sound and then realized it was my gun that hit the ground.

I was dying; Oh man... she was killing me. The world went black...

*   *   *

I awoke screaming... it was the worst dream I had ever had.

The dream of being Aaron Reite felt so real, I felt his emotions. I didn't even feel like I was there. It was truly the most horrifying out of body experience. This was no dream of my past, it wasn't even me.

I had to go see Alice, something was wrong, very wrong.

Chapter 5 Candy Land
お伽の国

I was waiting outside Alice's room for the third time this evening. The horrible dream awoke me about three in the afternoon. Alice was a late sleeper. She normally didn't bother to get out of bed until six. It was five o'clock and I was pounding on her door.

I heard the lock turn so I stopped pounding. The door opened and there stood Alice in her pink nightgown. Her black hair was all over the place and the look on her face was to kill.

In a very annoyed tone Alice asked, "Who died?"

I barged in talking as I invited myself in, "I had a bad dream. A dream of a man I killed. No, that's not it; I dreamed I *was* the man I killed."

Alice slammed the door and followed me into the living area. Alice had a very nice penthouse, complete with two bedrooms, a kitchen and a living room.

Alice tossed herself on the couch. "Since your shrink was unavailable to hear this life changing dream of yours… I have to rise early to hear it?"

I sat across from her, holding back tears, "Yes… it was awful, it was the worst dream… or the second worst dream I have ever had. I just don't understand, it felt so real, but it wasn't me."

Alice let out a breath. She sounded put out, "Okay, I get it, you had a nightmare. How can I help?"

I jumped over and gave her a big hug, "Thanks Alice."

Not able to hold back a smile, Alice gave in, "Well, let's hear it. Tell me the dream and leave nothing out. In fact, start from the very beginning. Start where you killed this man."

It was dark before my story was finished in its entirety. She interrupted with a lot of questions. After I finished, Alice sat there quietly, thinking. A few minutes I lost my patience, "Well… what you think? I mean have you ever had dreams like that? Does it have something to do with being a vampire, or am I just feeling guilt?"

Alice had been staring off into space. She looked at me and smiled, "Let's go out and play."

With a little bit of anger, "You're not going to answer my question?"

Alice giggled, "Of course I will… that is why we must go out and play. I am hungry, try to be patient with me. I will answer your question before the night is through."

I tried not to sound too disappointed, "Okay, where are we going?"

Alice jumped to her feet, and with a big smile she blurted out, "Candy Land."

She ran into her room to get dressed. She called for me to follow her. I had no idea what she was talking about, but I was sure the night was about to get interesting.

*   *   *

Alice still had not let me in on where we were going. She dressed us like we were twelve years old. Then she put my hair into ponytails and with her expert hands, she applied makeup that not only made me look younger, but alive.

We were driving across town in a Cadillac. I quietly watched the lights go by. The lights of the strip were replaced by the lights of homes and street lamps. The further we drove, the more shady the neighborhood became.

"Come on… where are we going? What is Candy Land?"

Alice snickered, "You sound whiny and needy, you're really getting into your role."

"And what role is that?"

Alice laughed, "A young, lost little girl, full of questions and unsure of what to do."

I stopped looking out the window and looked over at Alice driving. "Let me get this straight, you want me to act like you?"

She glanced over at me before returning her eyes back to the road. Full of mischief, "Oh just you wait. You have no idea what the night has in store for you. We are creatures of the night, we are killers. There is so much you don't know about being a vampire. Like the fact that we can steal more than just life; we can steal memories. Oh the fun we will have, little sister!"

It took me a moment for her words to register. Did she say we could steal memories? If so, was that really a dream? I yelled without meaning to, "What? We can steal memories, HOW?"

Alice chuckled darkly, "I will show you… tonight… in Candy Land."

Alice pulled the Cadillac into a parking lot. It was a casino, but not like one on the strip. There were lots of small casinos spread around Las Vegas that didn't worry about the big lights. They were casinos for locals, the odds were slightly better, but that was just to keep you coming back. One sign stood out. It hung over the front door with a couple of the letters black out. The sign said, *Candy Land Casino*.

"Oh whoopee a Casino," I mocked.

Alice grunted, "You wouldn't know a good time if it hit you between the legs."

I answered her, "I thought you *were* the good time." We both got out of the car and headed toward the front door. "We do look young, can we get in?"

As we opened the door to go inside, one of the security guards looked right at us and nodded as we passed by. I looked over at Alice and asked, "What did he see when we came in the door?"

Alice grinned, "A beautiful middle age woman, and an old hag."

I laughed, "Let me guess which one I was."

Alice retorted, "You have to guess?"

I came right back with, "What about the cameras? You can't hypnotize someone through a camera."

She looked at me as if she was tired of this, "Melabeth, this is a vampire city. This is a vampire owned and operated Casino. Don't you think they know who I am?"

I conceded, "Okay, Alice... what now?"

Alice led me over to the far side of the Casino, then explained. "We are hunting my favorite food tonight."

I looked around the Casino and commented, "All I see are old people and overweight middle age men. The women look as rough as an old carpet. This place is nothing like the Casinos uptown, where everything looks shiny and new. This place looked like a warehouse that had been closed by the health inspectors and reopened as a Casino. What kind of people do you like to eat?"

Alice gave me a dirty look, "I like to kill. You like to kill. It is why we are here. If I must kill then I chose to kill hunters like myself. They hunt children, girls and boys alike. They are foul, and worthy of nothing but a painful death. They make victims of the weak and innocent. The devils of this world protect them, but not from me, not from us. Let us hunt to kill tonight and I will show you how to steal the memories of the slain. Then you may see them as the monsters that they are and you will sleep without foul dreams."

I was taken back, but excited at the prospect of killing. That excitement scared me. I asked, "You always kill... *monsters*?"

Alice looked at me and for the first time ever... I saw something in her face: sadness, age, and the weight of a long life. She spoke as if her words carried weight, "We don't always choose well. And sometimes we choose the ones we love, for we are creatures of passion. Sometimes I kill good, so I can remember what good looks like through their memories."

I was struck into silence; we both looked away. After a few minutes Alice's eyes meet mine. Her face was that of a child's, she grinned as if nothing happened. She spoke carefree, "Let's go find some perverts. Come on Melabeth follow me, this is going to rock."

"Right behind you," I followed up behind her. I couldn't help but think that for the first time ever, I had witnessed the true Alice. I was in for one hell of a night.

The Casino ended up being a dead end. It was a slow night and apparently none of the child molesters were gambling. This did not bother Alice in the least. We left Candy Land and went by foot, walking straight out of the Casino and right into a shitty neighborhood. And yet again, no one bothered us.

Walking next to Alice, I announced in a mocking tone, "This is scary, what should we do?"

Alice laughed and replied, "See, this is why vampires eat good people, they are so much easier to find. This is WAY more effort than I thought it would be."

I noticed we were heading into a commercial area, but all the stores were closed. There were also a lot of warehouses. I looked around and couldn't see a soul. Barely a car, one passed by every twenty minutes or so. I then related my new theory to Alice, "I know why we haven't found any bad men. It's because this area has been over hunted. I watched this show on hunting. When you hunt too heavily in the same area you can wipe a species out."

Alice was flustered, "Ha ha, very funny. Let's go back. Maybe we will have time to swing by the Doll Shop before it closes."

I shook my head, "Nope, can't do it, not tonight, no dolls."

Alice moaned, "Why not?"

At that moment a car passed by us, and then made a right. With excitement, "Did you see that?"

Alice was still pouting, "See what? I bet it wasn't a doll."

I shook my head in disbelief, "That was the second time that Oldsmobile passed us. I think they're circling and I counted three heads in that car."

Alice smiled, she spoke fast and excited, "Alright, get your scared face on. Remember, we're lost and scared. Oh yeah, our very drunk, and Dad dropped us off in the middle of nowhere. Also, no one is looking for us."

I put my arm around Alice in mock horror, "Hold me… I'm scared."

Alice shook me off, "You suck at acting. Just be quiet and let me do all the talking."

I mumbled, "What's it matter? They will see and hear what you want them to anyways."

Alice snapped back, "Get ready I can hear their car coming. Side note, I don't like using my power… it takes all the fun out of it."

"Oh great, now I have to play little girl for a bunch of perverts. This night is turning out to be a barrel of laughs. Maybe I should just go home and have a good nightmare." The car circled the block and was approaching us from behind. I could hear the squeal of squeaky brakes as they slowed behind us.

The car came up slowly, matching our speed. The passenger window was next to me. The window was already down and a large arm hung out of it. He looked a little overweight, but he was also very muscular. He would have been intimidating, if I were human. The driver was a medium built man while the man in the back seat was small and skinny. They all looked to be in their late thirties or early forties.

The passenger started talking first, "Hey girls, you two all right?"

I answered without making eye contact and with less volume, "Yeah, we're *okay*." I knew that my response wasn't going to make them leave.

The driver started talking, "You both know this isn't a safe neighborhood. I got kids your age. I wouldn't feel right just leaving you two out here all alone. Can we give you a ride somewhere?"

Alice spoke up, "We don't have anywhere to go. Our father dumped us out here all alone, we don't know what to do."

I kind of thought Alice laid it on a little thick, but the men just looked as if they hit the jackpot. The car stopped and the passenger hopped out. He opened the back door of the car for us. He said with a commanding voice, "Hop in girls, you can stay with me. I can't leave you two out here in the cold, so hurry up and get in."

We did what he asked and the car sped away. Of course I couldn't help but thinking, it was close to ninety degrees out; in the cold my ass.

We didn't have to ride very long with them. They took us straight to the passenger's house. He lived with some creepy guy and the next thing we knew, we had four men surrounding us, they were asking inappropriate questions. Alice was funny as she played the part. I just acted nervous and shy.

They slowly separated us. I had the driver and the passenger's roommate. Alice took the skinny guy and the passenger. I don't even recall their names, I bet they had told us.

One of the men was trying to put his hand up my dress. The other man was trying to kiss me. I didn't open my mouth because my fangs were already out. I was ready to eat. If they weren't such perverts they might have noticed mine and Alice's hands. We both now had long, sharp fingernails, and our fingers were unnaturally long.

I heard Alice tell one of the men, "I don't know, I've never been with a man before. Before we… you know… have sex. Can I show you something?"

One of the men asked in an eager voice, "What? What do you want to show us?"

Alice smiled without opening her mouth, then whispered real quiet, "My teeth."

The man asked, "What did you say? Did you say your teeth?"

Alice nodded her head. The man laughed and the other one said, "We don't care if your teeth are a little messed up, hell, I didn't even notice. Let me see, open up."

Alice opened wide.

"What the hell... they look like fangs," one of the men said.

This caught the attention of the man trying to kiss me, "She has fangs?" Then he laughed, looking back at me, "What about you, do you have fangs?"

I smiled tight lipped, and then opened wide. I could hear the man's heart speed up. He let out a tight whisper, "What the hell?"

The man next to me was too busy trying to get up my skirt, but his friend's reaction made him look up. He moved away with, "What the fu..." He never finished that sentence.

The next half an hour was like a roller coaster ride. It was full of fun, excitement, terror and satisfaction. Not sure how it was for the four guys in the house, but from their screams I was sure they were enjoying it too.

Alice and I bit, clawed and drained three men. The last man just ran around in a circle trapped in one of Alice's nightmares.

I leaned against the couch covered head to toe with blood. I hated myself. I hated myself because I loved it. Where was my humanity? The man ran past me screaming... nope, not there.

Chapter 6 Blood Memories
血思い出

Alice interrupted my internal debate, "Are you ready to learn how to steal the memories of the living?"

I looked at the man we had left alive. He had been begging for his life, but now he sat upon the floor with an empty look upon his face. His eyes swept the floor, looking at all the different scenes of carnage. Blood was splattered everywhere, along with pieces of his friends. In front of him lay a severed hand. I vaguely remember cutting it off.

I licked some blood off my finger as I lazily told Alice, "Sure, I'm all ears."

Alice got up and floated over to the man. The man was on his knees and froze at the sight of Alice eerie approach. She slowly walked around him. She sat Indian style next to the man. I followed her lead and sat down on the other side of him. The man was now shaking and making strange noises. He was trying to speak, but the only thing that came out was gibberish.

Alice began, "First, you need a great emotion out of your host to transfer his memory from his blood. The second thing you need to know is that adrenaline blocks this process. This is why it's best to let them run it out."

I asked, "Why, does the adrenaline stop it?"

Alice snidely responded, "What... do I look like a doctor? I don't know, it doesn't matter. I can't explain why our memories are always in the blood, or why it happens during extreme emotions. Before you ask, fear is just one of the emotions." A wicked smile crossed Alice's face as she looked at the man who was as still as a statue. She asked him, "What is your name?"

He didn't answer, he just stuttered something unintelligible. I answered for him, "He says his name is Bob... Bob's a nice name."

Alice giggled in delight, "Bob it is. So Bob, do you think you could remember some past memory for us. Like something evil you have done... and I prefer it to be resent."

Bob found his voice, "I... I don't want to, die. My name is Ralph."

I pulled his face to mine and lifted my lip and growled low and menacing. I said real slowly, "I said your name is Bob... understand?"

He couldn't answer for a second. He nodded his head as he made the world, "Yes," came from his lips.

Alice was rocking back and forth laughing. She calmed herself, "I think Bob is ready. You see, his adrenaline has run low. He is in shock, but he is still gripped with fear."

I did my best Yoda, "Fear, is the path to the dark side."

Alice and I giggled, that is when Bob tried to make a break for it. We pulled him onto the floor, he could hardly move. Alice held one arm and I the other.

Alice spoke calmly and softly to the man, "Remember your crimes, remember your sins." Then Alice spoke to me, "Ready?"

I was hesitant, I was not sure if I wanted more memories that were not my own. Reluctantly, I answered, "Ready."

With excitement Alice ordered, "Feed until his death."

We both bit into the man. I bit into one wrist, while Alice bit into the other. He struggled under us, but it was to no avail. The pleasure of feeding soon made me forget the life and the memories I was stealing.

After I finished, I dropped the man's limp arm to the ground and then hopped up onto the couch. Alice sat down on a chair across from me and closed her eyes. She sat quietly for a moment, then opened her eyes wide and smiled.

Alice looked at me and with delight, "We did it, we acquired some of his memories. Boy, oh boy, this guy was a piece of shit."

I was surprised, "We don't have to sleep to see them?"

Alice explained, "No silly, but that is the easiest way to access the memories. It took me decades to learn to access the memories by will alone. At the rate you do things, you will probably be able to do it by the end of the week. I get so jealous of you, but then I remember you are a mental mute."

Alice was referring to my inability to control minds or use any mind powers for that matter. She likes to tease me, but she knew it didn't bother me and I hardly even responded to her jabs. I looked down at my blood soaked clothes, "Ugh, I need a bath and will need to burn this dress."

Alice answered with a neutral tone, "We will need to burn this house, but first there is a bathroom we can use to wash up."

With that Alice undressed and tossed her clothes onto the floor. She headed off to the only bathroom and started the water. A few minutes passed as I lay back lazily on the couch allowing my mind to wander. The sound of the water filling the tub echoed in my ears.

I heard Alice get in the tub and once again, my mind was wandering, trying to catch a glimpse of the memories I had stolen.

A noise erupted from the bathroom. Without a thought I flashed to the bathroom door, only to see Alice in a large bath tub, full of bubbles. She added so many bubbles, it was overflowing onto the floor. Alice was making a high pitch squeal of delight as she played.

I could not help but laugh, this caught Alice's attention. She looked over me and gave me a look of disapproval. "Oh come on, get in already. You are not that grown up, play with me."

I shook my head at her.

Michael slowly rose from the water in the tub. He was smiling at me as the soapy water fell from his upper body. I knew this was Alice's illusion, but I couldn't turn away. He kept rising out of the tub. He lifted one hand and motioned for me to come to him. His body was amazing and the water made his tight chest look soft and inviting.

He rose high enough that I should be able to see the goods, but instead all I could see was a cloud of sudsy soap. I looked over at Alice. She had the biggest shit eating grin I had ever seen. "How is it that the soap is not falling from just that one spot?"

Alice giggled as I turned my eyes back to the image of Michael. I was so hot for him, he was stunning. Unfair I thought, in the illusion I could hear Michael ask me in a seductive voice, "Why don't you take off that dirty dress? Come over here and join me."

He sank back into the water and I sighed. "Okay, you win, you're such a brat."

I would be lying if I told myself that I wasn't enjoying playing with bubbles in the bathtub. Here I was with a four hundred year old vampire playing like I was ten; it was wonderful. Four men lay dead, torn apart… and I was happy.

We burned the house and then flew back to the casino. It was not a problem being naked, we moved too fast for anyone to see. Of course, Alice could make you see anything. Alice had extra clothes in the car and before I knew it, we were heading back to our casino before the sunrise.

Alice showing me how I could steal memories didn't really resolve anything. The night I had with her just made me question myself more than ever. I'm making excuses for the darkness in me. So many questions, so few answers.

Alice drove as she hummed to herself. I interrupted her humming and asked her, "Why did we do that? Not why did we kill those men. I mean, why steal memories on purpose? I'm not sure I want those memories. I didn't want Reite's."

Alice was quiet for a minute, she began to answer me, "Why? Why not silly? It is a power that vampires have. You need to understand what you are and what you can do. You are a special vampire in so many ways."

Frustrated, I asked, "In what ways? I know I am more powerful, as if I have been alive for hundred of years. I know I have a gift that other vampires do not. I have none of the mind power that all other vampires do. I still don't understand why stealing others memories is something I need to do."

Alice laughed, "Where to begin with you. Yes, you're right, you are more powerful than your age should allow. You have a power, that no other vampire possesses. A most annoying power that allows you to see around my illusions. And to answer your question, why steal memories? Because we can. You will find it useful to know your enemy's mind. You will also find it easier to control your power so that you do not take memories that you do not wish to have. These things you know of, are not what make you special."

I retorted, "Enlighten me."

Alice turned her head from the road long enough to stick her tongue out at me. She asked, "Who was the first person you killed?"

I was taken by surprise, "What... What does that have to do with me being special?"

Alice answered with a seldom used tone, she sounded serious. "Most people that turn to vampires react in a couple of different ways. Some feel such guilt from killing that they kill themselves. Some become mindless killers, and at some point someone has to put them down. Unfortunately the mindless killer is the most common; one good reason legends speak *so* highly of us." Alice chuckled darkly before continuing. "You my dear are special because you have been raised without love. And that has given you the strength to kill without regret."

I quickly corrected Alice, "You're wrong, I do regret killing. Well, not all of them, but I do regret killing. Also, I was raised with love, it was just that it was taken away from me."

Alice with her playful voice, "If you say so, you still haven't answered my question. Who was the first man you killed?"

I defensively answered, "I told you. The first night I was turned. I snuck into his house and killed him while he watched TV. I almost killed his wife too."

Alice pulled into the underground parking lot and parked the car. She put the car in park but made no move to get out. She looked over at me like she was trying to make a decision. After a few seconds she must have made up her mind. "Okay sister, let's talk openly. I am not Charlotte, who can tell when you are lying with her power, but I am old and with age, there is knowledge. First, you can see around my power with sound."

My mind raced, I had no idea that she understood my power. I told my father Nicks that I would not tell Alice, but somehow she knew. I asked, "How did you figure that out?"

A little smile spread on her face as she whispered, "Fairies."

I didn't understand, "Fairies told you?"

She narrowed her eyes, "Ask your true master, Nicks."

I let out a gasp, "How did... you know? I don't understand?"

A very wicked smile spread across her face, "I feed on you when you slept. All your memories are in your blood."

I almost let out a scream as I covered my mouth. "How could you?"

"Well, it was easy. I waited until you fell asleep, then I snuck..."

I interrupted, this time rage rang in my voice, "That is an invasion of privacy Alice! You had no right!"

Alice giggled with wicked pleasure, "I know the first man you killed wasn't the man watching TV. And before you get all pissed off, you should know one other thing."

I was seeing red, I felt betrayed. Trying not to scream, "What is that?"

Alice smiled ruefully, "I will pay for feeding upon you. If I would have understood what you were before I fed on you, I wouldn't have done it. You are only a half vampire, and I have no idea who Nicks is, but I fear him. Your blood does not die, I feel it at all times. I am afraid of it, I am afraid of you. I have always taken blood from vampires and watched their memories, for our memories are always in the blood. No emotion is required, just drink, but after time other vampire's blood fades away. I feel you now and your blood is alive in me."

My anger fell away as I realized what she was saying, "Why would you fear me? Even if I could, I would never hurt you. We are sisters after all."

Alice smiled tightly, "I know. I hate to admit it, but I am afraid of the unknown. You are the first person in over four hundred years that I can't control. And now by feeding on you... I don't know what it means, but I can feel you."

I let out an empty chuckle, "Well, at least you are in good company. I don't like to admit it, but now days I am always afraid. Still the hatred inside of me will not die, not until these men do. Alice, if I haven't said this to you, I am glad you are my friend."

Surprise crossed her face, "You really mean it? I normally just make people like me, but you like me all on your own. You even like playing dolls with me."

I narrowed my eyes at her, "Don't push it. Plus, you should know by now, you do have all of my memories."

Alice smiled at me. Her large eyes looked at me with some new found joy. Then, with a sheepish grin, "Well, you haven't been paying close attention."

"What's that mean?"

Alice explained, "When you take someone's blood, you steal some memories, but not all of them. And after taking blood twice, I knew better than to take anymore. I remember some of your meetings with your master Nicks, but not all the details. I also learned how you were able to see past my illusions. And for whatever reason I can now tell when you are hiding things from me. It's like I know how you feel."

I moaned, "Great, it was bad enough that I couldn't lie to Charlotte. I guess it's a good thing that you don't know everything about me."

Alice laughed, "We are truly sisters and this moment I feel closer to you than I have ever felt to anyone. Let's go to my room, I wish to hear about the first man you killed."

As we got out of the car I complained to Alice, "I don't like telling that story. In fact, I have never told anyone... *ever*."

Alice's face lit up with delight, "Oh, I love being the first."

With that, she hurried toward the elevator. I was not looking forward to telling her, but wasn't sure how I could get out of it. Then again, I don't think the little thief could make me tell her. By the time we reached her room, I decided that if anyone would understand, she would.

It didn't take long before me and Alice were on her bed in our pajamas. Alice was literally jumping up and down waiting for me to start. "Settle down already."

Alice stopped bouncing then said really fast, "Okay, ready!"

I laughed, "It's not that great of a story. Okay, let me begin, you may not know how my mother died. She died when I was twelve by overdosing on heroin. I found her, dead on the floor with a needle sticking out of her arm. I went to live with my grandparents after that. My father was supposed to clean up before he could have me back. He ended up kidnapping me and taking me to California. He opened up business as a drug dealer. He sold cocaine mostly, but he also dealt in marijuana and heroin.

We had been there six months when I meet Chris. A lot of people came in and out of my Dad's house. I only meet the drug heads that my Dad let into our home. I wasn't allowed to go to school or hang out with anyone 'cause my dad was worried that I would get caught. Chris was a beer drinking, pot head, surfer dude. He was also twenty-nine and hot. He hung out with a younger crowd, so when I met him I thought he was so cool. It didn't take long before I developed quite a crush on him.

He came around often to buy or sell pot with my Dad. He often stayed and got high and passed out on the couch. One night I was in my room when I heard a knock on the door. I opened it to find Chris standing there. Everyone else had gone to sleep and he was bored. I invited him in and we hung out.

That night I kissed my first guy. It was harmless enough, we made out and afterwards he left. This went on for a little while until we progressed sexually. I was head over heels for him, writing his name in my notebook with lots of hearts, x's and o's.

Early one morning, he came in my room. We had been making out and touching each other for a week, so I was excited to see him. That morning was different, he was... more demanding. I said no, but he did it anyway."

Alice's head cocked to one side, "Did what?"

I let out a breath and clarified, "Sex. It was my first time."

Alice's face tightened, "If you said no, then he raped you."

"I know, let me finish." Alice nodded and I went on. "After that night, I made excuses for him. I was in love with him, so I told myself it was okay that we had made love. I would have probably been willing to do it again. I was young and foolish. Now we were lovers, it would seem natural that we did it again; that's what I told myself.

"It didn't work out that way. I didn't see him for at least a week. He had never stayed away so long before. It didn't take long before I was blaming myself. Thinking that I should have said yes, and that I was so bad in bed he didn't want me anymore. He finally came over, but he didn't come alone.

"He brought his girlfriend and introduced her to me. I remember fleeing the room, shutting my door and crying through the night. No one ever came into check on me. Chris came around off and on with his new girlfriend in tow. After a couple of weeks of heartbreak, I hated him.

"While sleeping one night, I was awoken by a man in my bed. I could smell the alcohol. Screaming, I tried to push him out. The man said, *Don't worry, it's me, Chris.* As if that made it better somehow.

"I screamed at him to get out. When he finally got out of the bed, there was no way not to notice that he was naked and hard as a rock. He tried to shove it in my face and I screamed. Angry at all the noise I was making. He left, while cursing at me.

Alice asked, "That's when you killed him, right?"

I shook my head, "No, I told my Dad. Dad sat me down and explained that I needed to lock my door at night. He excused Chris because he was drunk. In a week's time, he was hanging around the house again.

"I was mean to him, and I did my best to make him go away, but he didn't. His girlfriend had left him. Now he had more free time to hang out. Every night that he stayed over, I slept like shit, jumping at every little sound in the house. I would freak out every time someone walked down the hall to use the bathroom.

"Finally, all my fears came true. One night he came into my room. I hadn't locked the door because I hadn't known he was over. I had been staying up late reading that night. He came into the room and locked the door behind him. I yelled at him to get out and then he slapped me.

"Every time I tried to yell, he hit me. He hadn't gotten very far when someone knocked on my door. He got off of me, and pulled his pants up then straightened his clothes. He answered the door like it was his house. My father stood on the other side of it.

"He explained to my father that we were just talking. My Dad was so high he could barely stand up straight. Dad laughed with him and they both went into the living room and started smoking pot."

Alice grinned, "Now you killed him."

I nodded my head with a small smile, "After sitting in my room and thinking about it… I had had enough. I sneaked into my Dad's room. I knew where he kept the drugs. Knowing full-well what I was doing, I prepared a needle. The dose was three times what anyone should take. It would have killed a horse.

Later that night I went out into the living room. Dad had gone to bed in his room. Chris was sleeping on the couch. I walked up and tied his arm with a rubber hose. My mother taught me, so I could help her shoot up. Chris had already taken too many drugs and alcohol to wake up. I stuck the needle into his vein and let him have it.

I watched him… I watched him shake. I watched him foam at the mouth. I watched him die.

I went back to bed and waited. The next morning my father found him with a needle sticking out of his arm, dead. He called some of his friends to move Chris to his own apartment before calling 911. Can't have overdose calls at the drug dealer's own house. He was the first person I murdered."

Alice shook her head, "Murder, no. Killed, yes, he had it coming. Self defense if you ask me. It explains your inner strength and how you cope with killing so fast. You have been dealing with this shit for years. You are independent and self reliant. You will do well as a vampire."

I smiled, "We both are, we are sisters."

Chapter 7 Michael
美い

DEC 15, 1990

Eight months just flew by. David joined the local Necromancers so he could learn how to tap into his powers. While I was still training with Ezra and Charlotte. Alice too was also instructing me on how to fight, but mostly wanted to have tea parties. Still, Alice and I went hunting at least once a week, just two helpless little girls.

My power increased as well. David and I continued hunting down The Order members. We went out at least once a week, sometimes more. The bodies were really piling up.

I was having terrible dreams, reliving Aaron's death. Ezra and Charlotte were not very helpful. Alice just repeated, "If you keep your eyes open I will give you something that will really keep you up every night."

I tried to talk to David, but he was always with the Necromancers, when he wasn't hunting down The Order with me. I was finding my bed to be a lonely place. Finally, we had a night together and I told him about my nightmares. He was cold and indifferent, "In war, not all soldiers were bad, but we had to destroy them to win." Wow, that didn't make me feel better or make the dreams stop.

Later, when I told him I wasn't in the mood to make love. He told me that I needed to separate my feelings if I wanted my revenge. He kissed me on the forehead, "I don't understand you Melabeth. Look, I need to go back to the temple. I'm working on a new spell. You'll be alright... you'll see, we're close to finding your killers."

He left, and once again I was alone. I could go see Alice, but she would just want to have a tea party. She didn't really care about my problems with David. Ezra and Charlotte were sent on a mission by Alice. Their flight had left this morning.

Frustrated, I went to see Michael. He hadn't really spoken to me since the death of Lizzie. It made me wonder, was he that mad that I got David's family killed or was he in love with Lizzie? Gee, only I would get jealous of someone I indirectly killed. When I knocked on his door, it didn't surprise me that Lea answered. As soon as she laid eyes upon me her eyes narrowed. "What do you want?"

"To kick your ass," Keeping eye contact with her, I put one hand on the door so she couldn't shut it.

Her attitude went from, put off, too scared, as she stammered out, "Why... what did I do?"

I pushed the door open as she stepped back into the room, then I smiled really big, "Just kidding... is Michael in?"

Her face went from scared to angry, "No, and he doesn't want to talk to you."

Michael came into the living space from the adjoining room, "I'm here, what do you want Melabeth?"

I felt ashamed, but I needed someone to talk to. I was hoping that Michael wouldn't judge me too hard. "I need to talk."

Lea spit out, "Talk then."

"*Privately*," I responded, giving her a threatening look.

She snapped back, "Michael tells me everything, so you may as well talk in front of me."

I felt myself losing my cool, "Then he can fill you in later. For now you need to take a walk sister."

In a very commanding voice Micheal spoke, "Lea, I am going out with Melabeth, and Melabeth, do not bully Lea." I started to argue with Michael, but he cut me off. "I will meet you downstairs at the bar, near the front lobby."

"Okay," I answered. I didn't even give Lea a backward glance as I shut the door. I could hear Lea whining at Michael. Why he ever put up with her is a mystery to me.

I hadn't been at the bar long before Michael approached me. He gently took me by the shoulder as he led me away from the bar stool I had been sitting upon. "Let's go for a walk, it's a beautiful night."

"Okay," I respond as I let him lead me. He was a dazzling night. He was wearing khaki slacks with a light blue colored shirt. And the way his clothes hung off him, showed just enough of his curves to remind me of just how many he had.

As we worked our way through the casino, we ran into a sizable crowd. It was one of those crowds where everyone was trying to move in different directions, all at the same time. I was pushed by some large man into a lady. The man was saying, "Sorry," but then again, he could have been talking to half the crowd. Being large had its drawbacks, moving through a crowd was one of them.

The woman I ran into spun around, "Watch where you're going klutz."

The woman was a young looking blonde. She was about my height and build. It only took me a second after seeing her huge brown eyes to know that she was a vampire. I spoke before I even thought about it, "I was watching, that's why I ran into you. You were in my way."

She had already been mad, but now she looked furious. She was not alone. She was traveling with at least four more vampires. "Who do you think you are?" she practically spat it at me.

Michael grabbed my shoulders as he wrapped his arm around me, "Not here Melabeth. Don't start a fight."

The girl took a step back. Her face went from mad, too unsure. Her friends looked apprehensive. They all stepped aside and one of the male vampires said, "Please, we meant no harm... pass through."

Michael pushed me through the gap while adding an unnecessary, "Thank you."

I grumbled, "They should be thanking you... you just saved their asses." I made sure I was loud enough for them to hear me.

As soon as we came out of the Casino, Michael disapprovingly scolded me, "Melabeth, you never know who you're dealing with. Yes, you could of beaten *those* vampires, but you're not the most powerful vampire by far. Please be careful."

"Why do you care?" I was full of anger and I didn't mean to direct it at Michael, but I did.

Michael gave me a reassuring smile, "I will always care. The real question is... why don't you care?"

Still sounding like a childish brat, "I care... why don't you think I care?"

Michael gave me a concerned look, "What's going on? You wanted to talk. I can tell you're upset, so tell me what's bothering you."

I didn't answer him at first, we just walked for a bit. Michael walked quietly and didn't say a word. Then he broke the silence with, "I think I'm getting used to the black hair."

"What, you don't like it?" I quickly retorted.

He only got a little defensive, "I didn't say that. I thought you looked better as a blonde, but you're still beautiful. You have always been beautiful."

The way he said beautiful, it made my stomach twist. I wanted to be mad, but it was hard to stay mad at Michael, "Yeah right."

Michael put his arm around me. We came to a stop around a beautiful fountain in front of Caesars Palace. There we stood, in front of a white statue of a woman's body with wings and no head.

Michael spoke softly, "Your temper scares me. I didn't come here for a fight about your hair color. I came here to listen."

I was taken aback, "Why would I scare you?"

Michael's voice softly spoke into my ear, "You don't scare me, your temper scares me. Did you see how those other vampires reacted when they heard your name?"

I was puzzled, "I did, but why did they act in such a way?"

Michael chuckled, "Why indeed? David and you have made a name for yourselves. Him, more than you. It's no secret that you do the killing. You're quick, powerful, fearless and care about no one. It scares people... and vampires. You work with a powerful necromancer, it makes vampires nervous."

I gave Michael a hard look. I could feel my face tighten and my anger boiling, but I didn't want to prove him right by losing my temper. "So… you don't think I care about anyone?"

Michael answered softly, "If the shoe fits…"

Okay, I was mad. Pulling free from his arm, I vocalized my frustrations, "For someone who is afraid of my temper, you sure act like you would like to see it."

Michael put his hands up like I was pointing a gun at him. His voice was still kind, "I am just stating the obvious, and it's what makes you unstoppable. You have one goal, and no one to slow you down. Are you looking for love and relationships? From my point of view, you will not start your life until you end others."

He was half right and I knew it, "I do care." Great, now I felt like crying.

Michael gave me a worried look, "Enough to put others before your revenge?"

What was he asking? I was almost shouting, "Should I allow those men to get away with rape and murder?"

Michael looked over at the fountain, then back at me, "I don't have your answers, all I was saying was that at this point of your life others are not your concern. I'm sorry if I upset you… look, let's start over. For what it's worth, I don't think you're heartless, you just have different priorities. You didn't call me out here so I could tell you how you don't care. What did you want to talk about?"

His tone and the way his eyes pleaded for me to understand, it softened me, "Yes, you're right, I would rather talk about my hair."

Michael's body relaxed and he laughed out loud, "Don't kill me, but you're still prettier as a blonde."

I laughed as I lost eye contact with him and looked at the fountain. I wasn't sure how I felt about Michael; except for the fact he was the sexiest man on earth. In a much softer voice, "I will spare you this once."

Michael once again moved closer to me, and then put his arm around my waist. I don't know why he touched me, but I found it comforting and didn't complain as I laid my head on his shoulder.

I watched the water fall from the fountain and tried to find peace in it. After a minute of silence, I broke the silence by blurting out, "I loved David, and I still love David." I paused, before saying, "I don't know how I feel about him. I don't know how he feels about me. I believe us to be lovers, but he makes me feel like his weapon. Something's changed, I don't know what. If I don't know what has changed, how do I fix it?"

Michael looked thoughtful for a second, "I can't say that I understand your relationship with him. Let us try to figure it out, together. How does that sound?"

I looked up at Michael and asked, "Where do I begin?"

A big, goofy smile crossed his face, "I have an idea. How about the beginning?"

"I can still hurt you," I was smiling.

Michael changed the subject, "Have I ever told you about my tattoo?"

"No, what tattoo? I've never seen it." I had seen Michael in a bathing suit before, so I believe I had an idea where it might be.

Michael moved away from me, he then lifted his shirt showing me his back. There on his back was a large tattoo of many Celtic patterns. On the top of the tattoo, the name McCloud was woven across his shoulder blades and between the patterns.

"McCloud?" I wondered out loud.

"My name before I became a White," Michael answered.

I traced my fingers around the tattoo, it was beautiful. I had no idea this much detail could be painted onto a human body. "When did you get this done?" I asked.

Michael lowered his shirt, grabbed my hand and we started to walk. As we did, he answered my question. "This is the second time I have had this tattoo. Do you remember the story that Ezra told you when we first met? The tale of when I was on fire after being hit with tracer rounds."

"Vaguely," I didn't remember the story in detail. "Where are you taking me?"

"To the tattoo parlor, there's someone there I would like you to meet." Michael answered me and then went on by saying, "Ezra had explained tracer rounds to you. Remember how he told you that I had been hit and almost burned up before he put me out? He then killed the men who had shot me. What he hadn't told you was that I had been burned from head to toe. My skin, eyes, everything, I was a complete mess."

I stated the obvious by saying, "That must have hurt?"

Michael went on, "Only for a minute, one of the great things about being a vampire. Our pain never goes on too long. If I were human, of course, I would have never survived. It had taken me two weeks to completely recover. Charlotte and Lea had taken care of me, but when all my skin grew back, my tattoos didn't. That happened about six months before you came to live with us."

"I remember that story now. That reminds me. I remember when I first came to live with the Whites. You were less than happy about it. I was remembering they said something about you going to school, here in Vegas. What school were they talking about? And are you going?"

Michael smiled at me as he answered me, "Yes, and you should be going to. It would be good for you to understand how to survive the decades."

Wondering about what he was learning, I inquired, "What do you mean? What are they teaching you?"

He held up his pointer finger, signaling to give him one minute while he organized his thoughts. He began, "How best to summarize. I know, they are teaching us how to survive as a vampire in a human world. And the number one thing you have to do is learn how to manage money. It's not like you would think, being a vampire is a unique issue when it comes to owning anything. Humans live much shorter lives, but in that life they spend much of it on the collection of wealth or material items. If they're not earning it, they're stealing it, or waiting for someone else to die so they can have it. Vampires live long lives and the collection of wealth or material possessions, attract attention from humans. Have you ever known anyone wealthy?"

"My grandparents, both my mother and father came from money. I grew up as a poor hippie."

He went on, "Well, I don't know how much experience you have with people and with wealth, but others notice. They notice they age, and they also pay attention to who will benefit from their death. It would be hard, if not impossible to keep inheriting your own money. There are three basic ways we make it in this world. One, use your mind powers to take what others have; let's face it who needs wealth when you have power."

I made a big lower lip, "What if you have no mind powers?"

Michael laughed at me, "No worries, there's still two more ways to survive. Second, live wild like an animal and just kill the people in their houses, but don't stay too long, someone is bound to notice the smell. You have to keep moving, but you can have whatever you can take."

I put my finger to my lip, "Hmm, I can do that, but it might get old. I bet it would feel like you were always stealing your life. I also bet it is a good way to be put on a hunter's list."

Michael nodded in agreement, "I believe you're right, but then again what *you're* doing, could put you on some hunter's list."

I gave Michael a sharp look, "Don't start."

Michael gave me a chuckle, "Of course, there's my favorite way of surviving. The Alice way, there's lots of rich families and businesses that will hire vampires for various reasons. The pay is good, if not great, depending on what job you take. All the groups that hire our kind also know how to get us I.D.'s, houses, and even blood. Didn't you ever wonder how Alice keeps the fridge stocked with fresh blood?"

This made me wonder, "So, Alice works for someone, who?"

Michael continued, "Long ago, before this was even a country, Alice was involved in shipping. She was involved with pirates in the seventeen hundreds. One of these pirates became rich and opened a shipping business. Alice started off working for him, and then his son and the son after that. After a long time the family business became incorporated; and Alice worked for the corporation. With the help of Ezra, Alice trains vampires that work around the globe in service of this international shipping company. In fact Alice works directly for members of Congress. You will find that little girl is more powerful than most could imagine. This is why no one has really come against David and you."

I never knew that, or even came close to guessing. I knew that Alice was powerful, but I assumed it was because of her physical power. Now I realize she was much more. I should know better than to read a book by its cover. I asked Michael, "What is the name of the company she works for?"

Michael answered with, "I don't know, I don't know if she works for just one company anymore. There is more of a need for global security across international waters. I do believe that Alice is in service to most all U.S. shipping companies, in one form or another."

"Do you work for her as well?" I asked.

Michael said with pride, "Yes, in fact, that's how I caught on fire. Ezra and I were on a mission for Alice. You never know when she might need me or Ezra to go abroad and deal with issues."

Before I asked anymore questions about the family business, we came to a stop in front of a little building. There in neon lights were the words *Ed's Tattoos*. We had walked for a while now and gotten some distance from the strip. In fact, this side of Vegas was somewhat run down and scary looking. The only people on the street looked haggard and hard up. Three black men, dressed like thugs, passed by Michael and me giving us a hard look. They acted as if this was their neighborhood.

I couldn't help myself, I started to sing, "Because I'm bad, I'm bad- Come On You Know- I'm Bad, I'm Bad- You Know It." I always had a thing for Michael Jackson, but behold my new friends didn't take the same appreciation for music.

The three men stopped and turned around.

Michael shook his head back and forth, "Come on Melabeth, really... you could just let them pass."

I smiled bigger, "I have no idea what you're talking about, and I love to sing." I felt my teeth get longer as I became excited about my future meal.

Before Michael could say another word, one of the men walked up to me and looked me straight into the eyes. He said with a deep voice, "Girl, you can sing, damn, I haven't heard anything that pretty since Whitney Houston."

One of the men behind him joined in, "She sure sings like an angel, she sure does, yes indeed."

I covered my mouth as I said, "Thank you." The three men went on for a little bit and gave me a chance to get control of myself. These men were really nice.

After talking with them for a minute, one of the men told me that I should try out down the street at this lounge. The other two men thought that I should go to some blue's music bar. I kind of like the idea. I never thought of pursuing a carrier as a singer. After a few more minutes of going back and forth, the men took their leave, I waved them off, "See you guys later… and thanks."

I turned to look at Michael, who was just staring at me, "What?" he didn't answer. "They were nice. Don't you think so?"

Michael cracked a grin, "Disappointed?"

I could feel the mischievous grin spread across my face, "I was a little bit hungry, who would have guessed… nice guys."

Michael took my hand, "You're about to meet my oldest friend. Try your hardest not to start a fight, so what I am saying is, don't be yourself."

"Hey," I tried to sound indigent, but I wasn't really pulling it off.

The tattoo parlor was much nicer on the inside than the out. Michael introduced me to his buddy Ed. Ed was a forty-five year old vampire that had a tattoo on every inch of skin. He was also a black man, tall and good looking. His head was shaven and he had an infectious smile. On top of all that, he was one of the most talented artists that I have ever laid my eyes upon.

Michael and I hung out at the parlor for a couple of hours laughing and joking, Ed was full of jokes. I spent a lot of this time looking at the different drawings for tattoos. There were some really cool pieces that I thought would look good, but they weren't perfect.

Ed worked on editing some of the pictures. He finished his drawing and slid it over to me, "Now, that would go all over your upper back. Then this pattern would follow down your spine and flare out into this pattern right above your ass. What do you think?"

"I'm in, that would look slick. How long for you to finish it, and can you add some words?" I asked all excited.

Ed smiled, "Four hours angel, not including words. What do you want it to say? Wait, I know, jackpot, because that's what a guy would be thinking if he got your shirt off."

I laughed, and then took a piece of paper, "I want you to add this right across the top of my back, above the pattern."

"Right across here?" Ed pointed out on his sketch.

"Yep," then I wrote down, *Death From Every Direction*. "What do you think about that?"

Michael spoke up, "Figures, but I like it." I looked over at him. He was comfortable sitting in a chair, he looked relaxed. His smile was soft and so was the way he was looking at me.

Ed broke the moment, "I love it, and now the moment I have been waiting for." Ed started making a drum roll, "Off with the shirt."

Ed was wild and he made me laugh. I knew he was kidding, I could take off my shirt in private and lay down on the table, but I figured what the hell. I pulled off my dress and removed my bra. Michael's eyes widened, he did not turn away. Flipping my hair around over my chest, then I laid upon my chest so Ed could start my tattoo.

Ed was hooting and hollering, "Hell yeah, that's my kind of girl." Looking over at Michael, "She's hot and spicy, shit… I do believe this girl is too much for you my friend."

Michael shook his head back and forth laughing at the same time. Ed could make anyone laugh. "Believe me, she's too much for both of us. The words you are going to tattoo across her back are not for show, she's an action star."

Ed laughed and the two men went back and forth while Ed started tattooing on my back. As I lay upon the table, Michael's eyes kept falling on me. Maybe I was just being silly, but the way he looked at me, it made my stomach feel funny. I was also feeling anxious. I lay there wondering what he thought of my breasts, and maybe I shouldn't have undressed in front of him. What if he didn't like what I looked like? I had known that I was trying to be wild and sexy for Michael, but I've never felt sexy and comfortable at the same time.

I need to stop thinking like this, what about David? I looked over at Michael and he was positively the most beautiful man ever, with a body that commanded more study.

David who?

Michael was staring at me from his seat. He was no longer looking at Ed working on my back. His eyes were full of kindness, it made me feel comfortable enough to start to talk again. "I don't know if me and David changed, or if that it was more David. When I first met him, he was kind and sensitive. Even after his family was killed there was still something about David. He was understanding, and his laugh… I had forgotten about his laugh."

Ed was quiet. Michael's face went serious, "What was so special about his laugh?"

It took a moment to find the right words, "It filled me with happiness. When he laughed, I felt great joy, it was one of the first things that made me take notice of him. It was more than understandable that I didn't hear that laugh after his family was murdered, but I still heard it on occasions."

Michael inquired, "Do you hear it now?"

Once again, I found myself searching for the answer, deep down I felt like this should be an easy question. "It's not the same, I don't know when it changed. Maybe it changed slowly, and I hadn't noticed, but it's different. Now when he laughs, it fills me with hate… I'm being silly, it's just a laugh."

Michael's look didn't change as he asked, "Is it?" There was no judgment in the way he asked.

Ed interjected while he continued tattooing on my back, "I don't know if this is true, but a witch once told me that you could see souls through people's eyes. She also said that you could feel their emotions through the sound of their voice and you could know where they have been from the lines on their hands."

I couldn't tell if he was joking, so I asked, "Is that true?"

Ed laughed, "Once a guy told me you could tell what someone had eaten by tasting their shit, those are the kind of things you have to take at face value."

It was hard to hold still because he made me laugh. Once I stopped laughing, I looked at Michael real serious, "Michael, what should I do?"

Michael put his hands together, "What does your heart say?"

I lay quiet for a moment listen to the buzzing of the tattoo gun. Then I answered honestly, "I cannot hear it over the sound of revenge."

Michael sat back in his chair, and in a concerned voice, "That's too bad, but if you were to ask me, and I know you didn't; you cannot have revenge, forgive, and find peace all at the same time."

This is where me and Michael did not see eye to eye, "What, and let them get away with it?"

Michael just simply said, "Justice is best served cold."

I had nothing else to say, we sat quietly as Ed worked on my tattoo.

*   *   *

Michael and I were walking back from the tattoo parlor. He reached down and once again took my hand. In the past, I didn't read anything into this or I didn't want to read anything into it. His hand was soft in mine and the same temperature. Our hands didn't sweat, so it felt good to hold tight. It also helped he was a vampire, I didn't have to worry about squeezing too tight. Still, when he held my hand, I mostly felt like a woman.

We didn't say much as we walked back to the Casino. We mostly talked about tattoos and art. I didn't mention David, and Michael didn't bring it back up. I couldn't help but feel that I was betraying David. I looked over at Michael, well at least it was with a Greek God of a man.

Michael let go of my hand right before we reached his room. I knew he did this to spare Lea's feelings, that really bothered me. Not that I have any right to him, I just wanted her to realize he was mine anyways, because I am a selfish bitch. I can't help it, even if I were to try.

Michael barely started opening his door when Lea yanked it open. She looked disheveled, like she had been having rough sex and just pulled her clothes back on. Lea in a shrieked voice, "Michael, thank God you're back. What the hell have you been doing?"

Michael, with concern asked, "What's wrong Lea? What's going on?"

I quickly added before Lea could answer him, "And what's his name?"

Lea gave me a funny look, it took a second for what I said to sink in. Between being upset and angry, "There's no man... Michael, Alice is here! She has been waiting for Melabeth. She wouldn't stop screwing with me... she's being a fu..."

Michael pulled her into his arms, "Calm down Lea. It's alright I'm here, you're going to be fine." He looked over his shoulder at me, "Would you go find out what she wants?"

I nodded my head, "Yeah, no problem. I'll check on the little monster."

I slipped around Michael and Lea and went inside. There, sitting snuggled on the couch was Alice. She had a wicked grin, so I knew that she had been screwing with Lea while she waited for us. Alice was wearing modern clothes. She had been since coming to Vegas. When we were all living in that mountain house in California, Alice had worn these really old dresses. Now that she was in Vegas she dressed more modern than me. Today she was wearing tight blue jeans and a white blouse. I had come to find out that Alice's hair was not white, that is the way she wanted me to see her. In truth, her hair was black and today she had it pulled up in pigtails.

I spoke first, "Why don't you just kill her?"

Alice smiled, and then she tried to put on an innocent face, "Oh, she's over excited, that's all."

I laughed. Alice rose swiftly and came over to me to give me a hug. I was already whistling and half closing my eyes. Alice giggled, "Afraid of seeing the truth?"

Grinning to myself, "Is that what you're calling it these days? Lea makes it sound like you were looking for me, not just coming over to brighten up her night."

Alice twirled and spun across the room to where the radio was, "Music?"

I nodded my head, "Sounds good to me."

Alice spoke up as she turned on the stereo, "Would you be a dear, and dance with me?"

I smiled, "No problem." Michael came in the room with Lea under his arm, comforting her. I watched him move toward the bedroom as I danced with Alice, I yelled out, "Michael," then motioned for him to join us.

Michael stopped and with a grumpy voice, "No thanks, Lea and I are going out."

Alice danced over to Michael and in a childlike tone, "Afraid not, dear, I need you." She pointed at Michael, then she pointed at me, "And her." Then she pointed at Lea, "But not her."

Lea quickly added with a shaky voice, "I'm fine Michael, don't worry, I have places to go."

With that Lea hurried away, Michael chased after her. The front door shut and they were both gone.

Alice beamed at me, with confidence and announced, "He'll be back soon, but until then, tea time?"

I had a love/hate relationship with Alice's tea time ritual. It was magical, funny and scary all rolled into one. It ended up being short lived, because Michael was only gone for a few minutes.

When Michael returned, I could tell he was really put out by Alice's badgering of Lea. Michael was upset and started scolding Alice like she was a child, "She's going to snap one of these days and it will be your doing. What's so important that you feel the need to hang out at my place and torture Lea?"

Alice answered with a sweet voice, "It doesn't have to be important to torture Lea."

As she spoke, Michael's clothes melted off his body.

He was standing before me naked, but his dick was so small I could barely see it. I knew that this was just Alice is screwing with me, but I couldn't help myself when I burst out into an uncontrollable laughter.

Michael looked at me angrily, "What… what is so funny, is it funny that she is torturing Lea? I know you don't like her, but you…"

I waved my arm back and forth trying to stop him as I was having a fit of laughter, "No… no, that's not what I'm laughing at. Alice made you naked in front of me, but she made your junk about this big." I held my thumb and my pointer finger about a half inch apart to illustrate.

I started to laugh again, and I could tell Michael was holding back a smile. I looked over at Alice, "I know it's bigger than that!"

Alice's mouth fell open and she went into mock horror, "You do! When did this happen? And how long did it happen for?"

I quickly defended myself, "That's NOT what I meant! I've never seen it before, but I know it would be bigger than that."

Michael loudly cleared his throat, "Enough already. Stop trying to change the subject Alice."

Alice got serious, it wasn't something she did often, but I noticed that people who knew her best reacted like soldiers when she spoke this way. "You're right Michael, we have a real problem to deal with. Ezra and Charlotte are on a field trip for me. They are on a plane to New York as we speak. We do not have time to wait for them. I need to make arrangements, but you need to get Melabeth ready. I have a feeling we will need someone of her skill set, once we get there."

Michael's anger faded away, as he became serious, "I will take care of it."

Alice just simply responded with a, "Good."

I didn't have the foggiest idea of what they were talking about. "Where are we going? What problem?"

Alice smiled, "Don't worry. Michael will explain, and Melabeth…"

"Yes?"

"Bring a nice dress. There will be time for tea and dancing." Alice skipped out of the room at a high rate of speed.

I looked over at Michael, who had a thoughtful look on his face. Here we were all alone. And a few steps away there was a bedroom, with a bed. David, I kept reminding myself to remember David, it's not like I had broken it off with him.

Chapter 8 Atlantic Sun
太陽

I went to my room to pack, and then went over to see David and Carrie. After a long kiss goodbye, a very worried David finally let me go. He didn't want me to go without him. I wasn't sure if it was because he would miss me, or that he didn't want me alone with Michael. Most likely both reasons, at this point of my relationship with David, things had been stressed.

I remembered the long flight over and how tired I had been. The flight was during the day, and it would be unsafe for us to sleep on the plane. Michael, Alice and I spent most of the flight planning.

I found out that what had been stolen was a book… not any book, of course, but a magical one. The government had kept this book under lock and key. Fifteen years ago the book had been stolen.

Alice was talking about evidence the CIA had found that a wizard going by the name Shbam was behind it. Of course I couldn't help but think… how could someone with such a stupid name, pull off such a heist?

Alice's information indicated that this wizard, who had stolen the book, was in Jamaica. He was traveling with at least two vampires, a boy and a girl. No names or photos, just descriptions. The C I A believed they were in Montego Bay, Jamaica. Alice was being called in a hurry; they needed her expertise right away. They needed someone who could handle a wizard and two vampires. Alice sounded wary of our new foes. She didn't like not knowing who she was up against. Vampires' range of power and ability was only second to wizards. You could never tell how powerful or well equipped a wizard was until it was too late.

Michael and Alice came up with a theory on how the wizard may get out of Jamaica unnoticed. They believed that he would board the cruise ship and slip away in the crowd. Alice came up with the great idea of Michael and I going as newlyweds. My fake ID said that I was twenty one, and my name was Melabeth White. I asked her how we would explain her. She simply said, "Your little sis, that you couldn't leave at home."

I snorted, "No one will buy that. I'm supposed to tell people that I brought my little sister on my honeymoon?"

Alice giggled, "No, silly, I don't want anyone but you two to know I'm aboard. The Wizard we're looking for is most likely trying to sneak this book back into the states. They may also know what I look like. We are boarding in broad daylight, so my powers are very weak in the sun. Plus there will be hundreds of passengers. Even I have my limits as to how many people I can hypnotize at once."

Michael added, "To answer your question, Melabeth, Alice will be hiding in the luggage. We have a second room on the other end of the ship where the luggage will be delivered. I will make sure that all goes well on that end. This way we can search the ship at night, and if all goes right, we will spot this wizard before he spots us."

I shrugged my shoulders, "Sounds like a plan. Just point out who you want me to kill."

Alice laughed, but Michael gave me a disapproving look as he shook his head. I couldn't help but feel a little uneasy. I would be facing an unknown wizard with unknown vampires… I would also be sharing a room with the hottest man alive. I could see myself heading for disaster… and I could be killed too.

I was walking up the gangplank with Michael. It was only seventy five degrees, it felt like a hundred. Wearing black from head to toe, I wore dark sunglasses and a big black hat with a large brim. Still the sun felt as if it might kill me at any moment. Michael was struggling as well. He was wearing tight blue jeans with sneakers. He wore a white turtleneck sweater and, with the big sunglasses and a ball cap. He looked like he was on the run. Then again, we both probably looked like we were wanted.

Michael reached over and pulled me to his side. In a grumpy voice I barked, "Hey, what's the big idea? Not enough room for you?"

Michael whispered in my ear, "We're supposed to be newlyweds. We stand out enough without you acting like I'm a stranger trying to grope you."

"Whatever," I bitched. I was in such a mood. All I wanted was to get to our room. I would take a shower and get some sleep, and then we could start searching for this wizard and our book.

My mood improved as we headed inside the boat and into the lower levels. Once on the boat, the air was cool and best of all there was no sun. One of the over the top, happy stewards showed us to our cabin. I threw myself on the bed. As I did, I could hear the girl saying to us, "Enjoy your cruise aboard the Atlantic Sun."

I think she was about to say more, but Michael shuts the door on her. He plopped onto the bed next to me and gave me a little shove. He commented, "For such a small thing, you sure do hog the bed."

"What? I didn't leave enough room for your ego?" I quipped.

For the next few minutes Michael and I lay quietly upon the bed. The sun had wiped us out. Michael had taken a chance of bursting into flames. He couldn't handle as much sun as I could. Our blood was like kerosene and would burn if subjected to flame or sunlight. Still, we were creatures of the night, and the sun took a lot of our strength away. We couldn't fly or flash and the sun was so bright, vampires couldn't see if it weren't for really good sunglasses.

In many ways I have still not come to terms with being a vampire. I had only been a vampire for less than a year. In that time I spent most of it with David, who was a Necromancer, not dead and a ghost named Carrie, who disappeared during the day. I didn't spend a lot of time with my undead family, and, when I did, they were awake. Staring at Michael's unmoving body, I felt like crying. I felt like he was dead… what does that make me?

I got up and took a shower and put on fresh clothes. My choice of attire was black tights with a blue dress over them. Black boots that came up just a few inches above my ankle completed the look. I had a knife in each boot as well as a leg holster holding my 40 caliber Glock. On the other leg, I had a holster to hold two more magazines. Wrapping a thin cable around my waist, and, to top it off, I put a small revolver in my little black purse. I worked my hair into a tight ponytail, leaving two loose strands hanging from the sides of my forehead.

Our cabin was below sea level so there was no porthole, yet I knew it was almost night time. In fact, I could tell that the sun was starting to sink into the ocean that very moment. I don't know how I knew, but I did. My stomach always knew, too, even if I didn't really need to eat. Wherever I pull this separate power from, it does nothing to help with the blood lust. I may not need to eat, I felt strong and had fed the night before, but still, the call for blood is great. Michael would awaken soon, then we would get out of our room. I would get a chance to hunt. The thought alone brought excitement to me, like addicts waiting to get high.

Michael woke with a start. When his eyes found me, he became calm. With a smile he said, "You look good, I better get ready too."

I gave him a small smile, "Don't keep me waiting."

He slipped into the bathroom and started the water for a shower. I didn't mind looking at him now that he was awake and moving. In fact, I could stand looking at him all night long… bad girl, we're with David. The fact I was arguing with myself was a bad sign.

Half an hour later I was tapping my foot against the floor impatiently waiting for him. He finally came out, and I discovered the wait was worth it. His blond hair hung around his head to perfection. He was wearing a pair of khaki colored slacks that somehow made his ass the highlight of the show. But not to be undone, he wore a charcoal colored shirt. The shirt was a button up with long sleeves and a collar. The fabric clung to his chest and around his waist, reminding me of what he looked like without a shirt on.

I had been staring too long. With an arrogant smile, Michael teased, "I am glad that the wait was worth it."

Embarrassed for getting caught checking him out, I stammered over my words. "I… I wasn't impatient… you look okay, I guess. Are you ready?"

Michael smiled, then gently took me by the shoulder, "Oh, my misunderstanding. I thought the foot tapping was your way of saying hurry up."

Still embarrassed and a little defensive, "I wasn't staring."

Michael laughed as we headed out the door and into the hall. He took my hand and I let him lead me down the hall. If I could blush I would have, because even though he had not called me out on it, he had never accused me of staring. I hated the fact that when I looked at him I lost control of my wits.

The next few hours felt like a date. I fell into my role, pretending to be his new wife with ease and a little bit of guilt. We wandered the ship, went to the casino, the bar and then to the disco. We danced, we danced like professionals. David didn't like to dance. The way I danced with Michael, the way I rubbed against him, yes I was in trouble. After we finished dancing, we went to a restaurant and sat down to eat. Of course, all we ordered were drinks. I kept forgetting we were looking for a wizard. Michael thought we should at least check out the restaurants because wizards need to eat too.

I sat across from Michael. Empty plates with a bottle of wine and two half empty glasses sat between us. His eyes wandered the restaurant looking for our bandits, but I was looking at Michael, maybe for the first time. In front of me was a level headed man, calm, loving and forgiving. He was also hot as hell, but there was so much more to him than that.

In that moment I realized something… I needed more wine. As I drank, I remembered my David. I remembered David on the bus. I recalled when he was an innocent boy trying to help a very lost girl. If not for me, his family would be alive. I stopped looking at Michael, and started looking for the bandits. It was time to get serious.

We moved on from the dining area and went to the casino. There we found some slot machines that overlooked most of the casinos and the main hallway. I knew Alice was also searching, but I had not seen her. The ship had hundreds of people on it and there was a good chance that the wizard was sleeping in his quarters. I sat quietly staring at the slot machine wheels, as they spun around landing on different fruits.

"Are you winning?"

I realized Michael was talking to me, "Oh, yeah… I mean no, not really. Sorry I was daydreaming."

Michael flashed his award winning smile, "I noticed, you have been staring at your machine for ten minutes. What's up? Can you talk about it?"

"Not really," I admitted.

He elbowed me, "Cheer up, we're newlyweds after all."

I laughed, then I got serious, "I know why I fight. I fight for revenge. I fight to put The Order in its place. I owe Alice, she has taken care of me, so now I fight for her. Why do you fight? Don't get me wrong, I'm glad you're here. It's just that Alice has many warriors she can call on… do you *have* to fight for her?"

Michael's face was thoughtful. He was quiet for a second, then in a serious tone he spoke. "I do not have to fight, not for Alice, not for anyone. I'm helping Alice… well, because it's what's right. Alice is wicked, and so are you, but I am no better. You see, we are vampires. We will never be "good". I believe that, but I also believe that as long as I still exist that I should try to do some good. Balance… I try for balance, I strive to be better. And maybe, just maybe, if I save hundreds, it will make up for some of the humans I have killed."

I was quiet for a second. Not looking at him, I asked, "Do you believe that? Do you really believe that if we do things for the greater good, it will undo our past sins?"

A weak smile crossed Michael's face. For the first time I could see a great pain in him. He answered in hushed tones, "No, I do not believe it will undo our past sins, but it couldn't hurt."

Michael started to gamble, but I wasn't finished, "What we're doing now, it's for the greater good?"

A dark chuckle came from Michael, "A book of dark magic was taken. It was under lock and key, taken by God knows who. The book itself is a weapon, that much is obvious. It is also obvious that whoever took the book did it with the purpose of using it."

I simply responded, "Oh."

Michael went back to gambling. Have I become such a blind follower that I have not even stopped long enough to find out what the quest is? Alice says, *come along* and I do, but I never asked why. I trust my friends. I sneaked a peak at Michael. He was still busy gambling. Have I become such a killer that I don't even care why?

This line of thought was depressing. I need some blood, "Michael, I'm going to grab a bite, be back in a few."

Michael didn't look at me as he answered, "I'll be here. Be discreet and hurry back."

"Of course," I replied as I walked away.

Lost in thought, I found that I had walked away from the crowds on the ship. I was heading toward the bow moving along the deck. I walked past a boy and a girl bickering about football teams. I only glanced at them for a second. They were teenagers. I headed to the very crest of the bow, then looked over the railing. There I could see the ship cut its way through the ocean. The sound of the water mixed with the wind, and the smell of the ocean, it was hypnotizing.

Someone approached me. I turned my head to see an old man walking slowly toward me. He wore a round little hat and a long raincoat. He was carrying a long umbrella cane. It was too dark to make out all of his features, but he had a long beard and wore round glasses. He wasn't looking at me. He was watching the ocean as he slowly walked. I went back to look over the railing. With my second sight I knew that he passed behind me and kept walking. He stopped a few feet away and looked out over the ocean.

I ignored the old man and went back to enjoying my moment of peace and tranquility. The stars were bright with wisps of clouds and no moon in sight. I let that peace come over me and tried my hardest not to think about anything.

I realized as time slipped by that Michael may be coming to look for me. I had not yet found a victim to feed on. It would probably be wise to check in with Michael and then resume hunting. I'll check in, in a few more minutes.

"Beautiful night, wouldn't you say, dear?" The old man was speaking to me.

I didn't raise my head or look at him as I replied, "Yes, most magical."

The old man spoke again. This time there was an edge to his voice, "It feels awfully cool out here. When I passed the thermometer it was hovering at forty degrees, not counting wind chill."

I raised my head and I used my second sight, but there was no one there except for the teenagers I passed earlier. They were sitting on a bench behind me, sitting quietly. I answered the old man and tried to play off his concerns. "I hadn't really noticed, must have gotten overheated from dancing."

The old man said thoughtfully, "Well, one does get hot and sweaty from dancing."

I quickly agreed, "Must have been it."

I turned and looked at the old man. He was about eight feet away, and looked familiar.

The old man started talking again, like he was trying to solve a mystery. "Um, the thing is, you are wearing a thin dress. If you did get all sweaty in it, then it would be wet and you would have become cold faster than if you had not sweated at all. You've been out here for twenty minutes and not one chill, not even steamy breath."

I hadn't noticed until he said that, but it was cold outside and steam rose out of his mouth every time he exhaled. Oh great, I've really screwed up, we're supposed to be undercover and I've allowed some human to see me. If it weren't for the teenagers I could drain him and throw him off the ship. Still, I knew this guy… how did I know him and from where?

My curiosity got the better of me. I ignored his inquiries about how I was staying warm. Instead, I asked him, "Do I know you from somewhere?"

The old man cocked his head to one side. Then, rubbing his beard as he spoke, "Funny thing is, I always remember faces. It's a little gift of mine." He stopped rubbing his beard as his facial expression changed from wonder to surprise. "I do know you... well, well, look what we've got here."

I didn't like how he said that. "Where do you know me from? I can't place your face."

He laughed a deep laugh, "Don't worry, you'll remember... give it some time."

I had noticed the teenagers had gotten up and walked over to us. They quietly moved to the old man's side. In fact, they had made no noise at all as they walked over. No cloud of steam came from their mouths. I looked at the two teenagers. The boy looked like he was in his early twenties, older than I had originally thought. He had short brown hair and brown eyes. The girl looked younger, with Hispanic features and straight black hair. Her eyes were dark black coals. Both their eyes were oversized. I was truly a fool.

The old man's eyes were what I remembered first. He had aged since last I had seen him. Green eyes, cruel eyes... those eyes, his name slipped from my mouth, "Alex."

Alex clapped his hands together in delight, "She does remember me. So the legends are true. You do walk the earth again. I would love to know how someone brought you back from the other side."

I was frozen in shock. My expectations had not been my killer, the man who raped me and murdered me with his own hands. Now he stood before me with vampires protecting him on both sides. I could feel my revenge, so close, so far away. I prayed a small prayer, for revenge. Of course I needed to be careful. Alex was the wizard we had been looking for. He had been going by Shbam, but who knew what his real name was.

Without emotion, Alex announced, "It looks like we have been discovering my friends. Peter, come with me." Then he looked over at the girl. "I'll leave her in your capable hands."

The vampire girl just nodded as Alex turned his back on me and walked off. He was flanked by the male vampire, he had called Peter. The nameless girl stood between me and Alex. She let her claws come out along with her teeth, her face no longer resembling a young girl. It was sharper, the eyes were wide, and her mouth was enlarged. We must have looked the same as I let out a hiss.

She snarled back and gave me a wicked smile. I returned the smile, then flashed forward and attacked.

I clawed at her and kicked at her, but my hands and feet found nothing but air. She moved between my attacks as if I were the slowest thing on earth. She flashed sideways, forwards and back again. I couldn't seem to make contact with her.

She retaliated, and I received some pretty good scratches and hits. I healed quickly, but this fight was costing me time. I needed to warn Alice and Michael.

The thought of Michael made me move faster. Time to take her out. I swung at her head, but she ducked. She spun against the ground and did a spin kick. Taking my feet right out from under me.

She was a little surprised when I didn't fall, instead I went weightless. I flew up into the air did a back flip and landed back on the deck a few feet away from her.

Her surprise was short-lived as she flashed the distance, and we continued our dance. It felt as if we were at some kind of draw; she knew better than to let me get a hold on her, and she was too fast for me to hit.

Still, she didn't know about my second sight, and I came up with a plan. She moved in and attacked again, but this time I let my guard down. She hit me, and I pretended it hurt more than it did.

She then kicked me, my face slid down across the deck of the ship. Faking injury, I started to get up slowly, holding one hand on my stomach where she had made contact. I had my back turned to her, but I could see her perfectly with my second sight.

She flashed in for the kill and several things happened at the same time. She grabbed my neck with both her hands to rip my head off. My right hand that had been holding my stomach was really holding one end of the metal wire I had put around my waist.

As soon as she flashed, my hand had whipped out the wire like a lasso. When she grabbed my neck, she didn't even see the cable until it hit her neck. It wrapped one time around before I caught the other end of the cable with my left hand.

I then pulled my arms apart. There was a sound of a dull thud behind me. Her head fell against the deck, shortly followed by her body.

I tossed the bloody cable off the ship. Throwing her head overboard, waited a few minutes, and then tossed the body. No one would find her before her blood died; she would never put back together. One down, two to go; I hurried back.

I was in a hurry to get back to the casino before Alex and his vampire spotted Michael. I knew I was moving a little too fast for humans as I weaved in out of the crowds and headed toward the entrance of the casino.

I calmed down as soon as I laid eyes upon him. Michael was still sitting in front of the same slot machine with a concerned look about him. As soon as his eyes reached mine, he relaxed, but not for long. I rushed to his side, and he knew immediately something was wrong.

In hushed tones, Michael asked, "What happened? Did you spot them?"

"Yes…" I started hesitantly. I knew that Alice wanted us to spot them first, then we could lure them into a trap.

Michael's face tightened, "And?"

I stuttered out, "And they spotted me… then I had to defend myself."

Michael was now upset, "Just tell me what happened."

I quickly told him what went down, but before I could tell him about the Wizard being Alex, he was pulling me across the ship. He tugged me along by the hand through the crowd. We descended down a staircase toward the lower levels.

I blurted out, "Does this mean that the honeymoon is over?"

Michael ignored my remark as he pulled me down the hallway faster. "Melabeth, we need to get to Alice, instead of telling jokes. This is serious, and surprise is no longer on our side. We need to get Alice and find these two fast, before they can get off this boat."

That made me think of something, "Can't Wizards just teleport?"

He looked at me funny, "If he could teleport, he wouldn't have bothered to get on this boat in the first place. The fact is, he can teleport, but the book cannot. It is common practice with magical items to cast spells so they cannot be teleported."

This kind of bothered me; I knew the mission was to get the book, but that wasn't my mission anymore. My mission was to kill Alex… I better not tell Michael or Alice. They don't need to know what's important to me.

Michael was knocking on a cabin door. Alice opened the door wearing quite the get up. She had a dress that looked to be from the eighteen hundreds or older, but yet there have been some more modern cuts. It was black with white trim. She had large knives attached front and back, and, to top it off, she was wearing a black witch's hat.

I took one look at her, "I didn't know it was Halloween."

Alice snorted at me, "Ha, some things never go out of style. I have struck fear into the hearts of men for hundreds of years dressed like this."

I laughed, "And women, I know I am afraid, but you don't need an outfit to do it."

Michael's voice was impatient, "We don't have time for this. Alice, Melabeth has already made contact with our prey. She was recognized; they left one of the vampires to cover their retreat. Melabeth killed the unknown vampire, then found me. This means the Wizard knows we're here for him and is most likely getting ready for us."

I thought Alice might get upset as Michael, but, instead, she smiled. "Leave it to Melabeth to announce our arrival; well at least we outnumber them now." Michael looked as if he was going to interrupt her, but she put a hand up and said, "Relax Michael. Melabeth, tell me the name of the vampire you killed."

I shrugged my shoulders, "I don't know."

Alice giggled, "You're such a killer; why take names? Tell me what you do know, and describe what they all looked like."

I sneered at her remark about being a killer, but I didn't comment on it. Instead, I told her everything that had happened. I could describe Alex in great detail, but didn't tell her who he was to me. When it came to the other vampire, Peter, I couldn't really recall what he looked like. In fact, the more I thought about it, the less I could remember. I had thought he was a teenager when I had passed him on deck, but, when he stood next to Alex, he seemed to look older and much taller. The memory wasn't very clear.

After listening to me try to describe the vampire, Alice spoke very thoughtfully. "Well, I hope this isn't the vampire I think it might be. No matter, we do know that he is powerful and most likely blurred Melabeth's memory."

I inquired, "How do you know he is powerful?"

Michael answered, "It takes a lot of skill to blur a memory, and your mind is hard to reach."

Alice added with a giggle, "You could say that again."

Michael and Alice both laughed at my expense. I interrupted their little joke, "What now then… if you two are done?"

Alice smiled, "We will stick together. Let's go hunt these two down and boil them in their own pudding."

With that, Alice shut the door to her room and started heading down the hall. I, followed by Michael taking up the rear.

I asked Alice, "How do we find them? There must be hundreds of rooms, and where will we find that much pudding?"

Alice explained, "They know we are after them. They will have to assume that we know what room they are in. We don't know what room they are in, but they can't count on that. If I were them, I would have a backup plan just in case this very thing happened. It would have to be a place away from the passengers and crew where they could set up defenses. Also, I am assuming that they brought their own pudding."

Michael was so serious and grumbled just loud enough for us to hear him, "Enough with the pudding already." Me and Alice ignored him.

I asked, "And where would that be?"

Alice turned her head and looked at me, then gave me a wink, "Ask Michael."

Still following Alice, I redirected my question, "And where would that be, Michael?"

Michael sounded a little grumpy as he answered, "Well, if either of you would have done a little investigation before we boarded, you might know."

Alice piped in with a pleasant voice, "I don't need to do homework; I brought you. So try your hardest to make yourself useful dear."

Michael gave a dark chuckle, "Yes, I wouldn't want to be useless. Well, there is a dining hall that is in the middle of being refurbished. The ship is just over half full, they have enough room in the main dining hall. The secondary dining hall is located towards the stern of the ship. It happens to be surrounded by empty cabins."

"Well, let's go see how the remodeling is going," I said with excitement. I couldn't wait until we caught up with Alex. Alice and Michael should be able to take care of the vampire, and I'll take care of Alex.

Alice stopped suddenly, and I almost ran into her. She turned, then faced me, "What's going on dear?"

I answered like I had no idea what she could be talking about, "What do you mean?"

Alice scrutinized me for a second, she now knew me through my blood. She let it go, "My mistake, I thought you might be up to something. Here's the plan; Michael and I will search the rooms. Melabeth, you go check out the dining hall. Don't go in; just make sure no one comes out. I am positive the Wizard will set up in there. Michael and I need to flush out the vampire first… everyone ready to go play?"

I answered quickly, "Ready."

Michael's answer was hesitant, "Ready… after you Alice."

Alice and Michael left me in front of a set of double doors as they headed down the hall together. I watched them as they rounded the first corner. I looked at the doors with a paper sign hanging on them that said this area was closed for future improvements. I had no intention of waiting for those two to get back; this Wizard was mine.

I opened one of the doors and went in quietly. The room was large and dark. There were rows of chairs stacked up in one corner of the room. Next to that, they had metal carts full of round tables that were stacked up like a deck of cards. On the other side of the room they had built scaffolding against the wall. The carpet had been ripped up in one corner there was a pile of old carpet. I walked slowly into the room using my second site.

The boy vampire called Peter came causally out from behind a stack of chairs. He walked up to me, slowly, silently with a lazy look on his face. Now that he wasn't standing next to Alex, I looked at him for the first time. He was young looking with brown hair. His hair was short and neat; he was taller than I remembered. He stood at least six foot, but was built like a runner. All in all I would have called him good looking.

He reached behind him; I prepared myself for battle. He noticed me reading myself, and a thin smile crossed his face. His hand slowly came out, and, in is hand was the book. It wasn't very big, six by nine, a hardback and very old looking. An old metal clasp held the book shut, and the clasp looked as if might need a key.

He spoke very pleasantly to me, "I have what you want. Here it is; all you have to do is take it. It appears that we both have choices. You have made yours, but what about me. Should I fight for this old book or just give it to you? What should I do?"

Wow, this guy is something, I about laughed when I answered him. "What, stalling for time? You don't look as if you're thinking about it."

He smiled, but it was false. He spoke like a car salesman, "Well, I can see you mean to get down to business. And you're right; by now I should know what I mean to do. And I have decided… to give you the book."

With his outstretched hand, he held out the book for me. All I had to do was to take four steps forward and grab it. I was still using my second sight, and, so far, it was just me and him, but there was no book in his hand. I didn't care to play games with this man, "That's nice, but save it. I don't want the book, where is the Wizard?"

The smile fell from his lips, and he looked at me with wonder in his eyes. He spoke again, but this time he spoke seriously without the game, "Why do you seek the Wizard?"

His question was straightforward, and I felt obliged to answer him. "Well, it's kind of a long story. I will give you the short version… he raped and killed me, and now I want revenge. And I was told he knows how to get back to Kansas."

His eyes widened a bit; he spoke with a careful tone. "Oh, I see. Well, I had no idea. That really was the short version. I'm sure there is more to it, but first I would like to ask you something."

"What?" I spit it out. I was in a hurry.

"The girl vampire on deck, where is she?" His eyes narrowed as he finished his question.

It's impossible to lie to some vampires, and, knowing my luck, this would be one of them. I was in a hurry so I hoped they're right when they say that the truth will set you free. I needed to get a move on. Fighting with this guy would only delay things even longer. With a cold voice I answered, "Fish food."

His face was full of rage. He was almost screaming when he spoke, "Why?… why would you do that? How could you do that? You were no match for her. I was a fool; I should have stayed." He calmed down as he spoke as his anger turned to remorse. "She was my dearest friend for over two hundred years, and in a blink of an eye, some nobody kills her."

Well, so much for not fighting him, but, after calling me a nobody, he needed to die. He dropped the book on the ground, and it disappeared. I was still looking at his eyes when my second sight noticed movement. He was using his mind powers; he had flashed to the right of me. He was working his way around behind me. I pretended that I still thought he was standing in front of me. At the same time, my right hand was playing with my dress. In truth, it was loosening the strap that held my pistol.

He flashed up behind me, but I saw him coming. I dropped to the floor and rolled away. I came up on my feet with my gun pointing at him. If he thought he was surprised by that, he would really be surprised by my ammunition. It was special bullets that burst into flames when they hit something, a gift from one of Alice's friends.

I fired, but this time I was in for the shock. He flashed and moved like nothing I have ever seen before. By the time the slide locked open on the thirteenth round, he was still standing in front of me with a smile on his face. The bullets did burst into flames, but harmlessly against the far wall where they burned for a minute before going out.

He laughed, and then held one hand forward; his hand in a fist. He opened his hand, and there inside were one of my bullets. He tossed it behind him where it smacked against the wall, making another small fire.

With mocking tones he spoke, "I am Peter the Lionheart. I have walked this world for over eight hundred years. Know this, girl; you have brought a smile to my face. Now prepare to die."

I threw the gun at him; he moved his head with ease as it flew by harmlessly. With no fear in my voice, I said, "We'll see about that, Lionheart, let's see what you're made of."

The next ten minutes I got to see what Peter was made of, and he was made of pure badass. He was faster, and stronger. If that would have been it, I could have beaten him, but it wasn't. He was a better fighter; even with my second sight, I couldn't out fight this guy. He could have shown Ezra some moves. He cut me and broke bones in every move, lucky for me I healed quickly.

I had been attempting to kick him when he grabbed my leg and tossed me into the wall. Contacting with the wall I heard and felt my collarbone snap. I landed on my feet and shook it off, then pulled my shoulder straight. It started to heal right away. Peter was not following up on his attack, lucky for me.

Instead, he watched me with curious eyes. This gave me time for my shoulder to heal, but I wasn't sure what good that did me. The time fighting this guy gave Alex more time to get away, and, of course, it gave more time for me to get killed.

He spoke with a commanding voice, "What manner of vampire are you?"

I was a little taken aback by his question, "What do you mean? I am just a vampire."

At this he laughed, "You don't believe that; I can hear it in your voice. You fight with a second sight, and you heal fast, even for a vampire."

I hadn't noticed that I had healed any faster than normal vampires, but then again, I had never really paid attention. What he said made me ask a question without thinking about it, "I thought vampires healed faster the more powerful they were. And what do you know about my second sight?"

It was probably best if I kept him talking, I would need Alice and Michael to bail me out of this one. Lucky for me, I intrigued him. Peter answered, mildly amused, "I am stronger than you, but I would be lucky to heal that fast. I don't know anything about your second sight, girl, but I know you have one. You fight with your eyes closed, and none of my illusions work. You react from attacks from behind you as if you had eyes in the back of your head. I tell how you killed, my friend on the deck. I can also tell that you're young, too young for all the power which you possess. Who is your master, girl?"

I answered, trying not to sound too bitchy, "First, my name is not a girl; it is Melabeth. Second, I have no master that I can remember. I awoke alone, in the state that I am in."

He considered my words, "It will be a shame to kill you."

I laughed nervously, "It will be a shame to die."

He looked as if he were about to attack, then something caught his eye. The walls were bleeding; blood poured down the walls and puddles formed on the floor. The light became darker and more menacing.

The room filled with a dark smoke, Peter spun around looking for the source. "What magic is this? Come out little Wizard and meet Peter the Lionheart."

People started to come out of the smoke filled room. They were dressed in very old clothes and some of them looked to be knights. I recognized some of their outfits from pictures in books I had read; they were Templar Knights from the Crusades. They were thin and looked starved, nothing but skin and bones.

Peter yelled out in rage and anger, "What is this black magic? Why do you show me these things? Oh Lord, show thy mercy."

Peter grabbed his head and fell to his knees in self inflicted pain. I had known as soon as it all started this was nothing but one of Alice's illusions. I had no idea how powerful she was until this very moment as she spit out nightmares of this man's past.

With my second sight I flashed over to where I knew Alice was. I spoke my gratitude for saving me, "Thank you…"

Alice didn't let me finish. "You're a bad girl. I had hoped to help you with this Wizard, but now I must deal with him myself."

I felt bad, "What now?"

Alice lifted the brim of her hat so she could look up at me. With her childlike voice she asked, "Are you dense? Go get the book… and Melabeth, be careful. This Wizard has had a lot of time to prepare. He'll be ready for you; Michael's waiting... hurry."

As I headed for the door, I could see Peter standing. There was the rage on his face as he screamed, "I know you're in here; I will kill you for *this*."

He may have been blind, but I would have been blind thinking he was not dangerous. As I shut the door, I saw Michael standing at the end of the hall waiting for me. His face said it all, disapproving; I had not followed Alice's instructions. As I flashed over to join him, I couldn't help but think, I hope my actions, my need for revenge doesn't get Alice hurt or killed.

Michael's voice was tight, "Later you will need to explain to me why you can't follow directions."

I snapped back, "I don't need to explain shit to you. Let's get a move on before this Wizard escapes."

Michael growled, "After you, your highness."

I was moving through the corridors with Michael right behind me. I stopped at every door and listened. My hearing was good enough to hear a man breathing, but no one was supposed to be in these cabins. I came to a T-section, and came to a halt; it was so sudden that Michael almost ran into me. The hallway to the T-section was a bridge between the rooms and two different staircases. The door to one of the staircases now lay behind me, and the other staircase was down the hall, between me and a surprised Wizard. He had been heading towards us until I had stepped out in front of him.

He didn't pause for a second; he cast some kind of spell; not waiting to see what it was, I flashed forward.

I came to a halt ten feet away as my body was pulled to a sudden stop. I knew then that the Wizard had cast a protection spell from spirits. It was the same spell that the spell casters used to protect their homes. It was also where the legend of vampires needing to be invited in came from. If the house had this protection on it, we could not come in unless someone invited us. It would keep out or keep in the dead, and now Alex was using it to keep us out.

Michael was quick. He had flashed down halls and popped up behind Alex and in front of the door that led to the other set of staircases. Alex may have protected himself from my attack, but he also allowed us to trap him in the hall.

A slow, wicked smile spread across Alex's face. He spoke with contempt, "You are not ready to face me little one. Who is your master?"

I bared my teeth, and snarled out, "You will die."

Michael spoke with an even voice, "You don't have to die. Give us the book, and you can go free."

Alex had an old leather satchel in his hand. He reached in the bag and pulled out the book. It looked like the one Peter had shown me in the empty dining room. I didn't know if this was the book, but, then again, I didn't care.

Looking at Michael, Alex spits out, "I give you this and you'll let me go. Hah, Melabeth would never let me go; in fact, I don't even think she cares about this book." He turned and looked at me, "Do you?"

I yelled out, "The book means nothing; your death is what I need."

Michael looked back and forth at me and Alex. I could tell his confusion was leading into anger. Michael yelled out at me, "What's going on, Melabeth?"

Alex answered, "Oh, how rich. She didn't tell you... I am the one who raped and killed her. She was my little star; I just wonder who revived her. I watched her die."

I growled and tried my hardest to push forward so I could rip his head off, but my feet just slid against the ground. Alex laughed at my attempts. Michael now understood what was going on, and worry crossed over his face.

Michael tried to calm me down, "Melabeth, stop. His spell will not last forever, and he's not going anywhere. Save your energy, and I will help you kill him."

The fact that Michael was ready to help me kill him, calmed me down. I simply replied, "You're right. He will die soon enough."

Alex put the book back into his bag, but his hand did not come up empty. He pulled out an ornate brass plate. He held it out in front of him supporting it with one hand under the middle of the plate. His other hand sprinkled something onto the plate as he began to chant.

I really didn't want to wait to see what this spell was, and I no longer had my gun, but I did still have the knives stashed away in my boots. I pulled one out and threw it at Alex. Alex had seen what I was doing and tried to move, but he was too slow. The knife missed its mark, but still the blade drove into his shoulder. Alex dropped the plate as he let out a scream of pain.

Alex screamed at me in pain and anger, "Look what you've done."

The plate he had dropped now lay face down on the floor. Fire was bursting out from around the edges. Soon the plate flipped over and the fire grew. Alex was starting a new chant; I pulled out my last knife and aimed for his head.

My throw was right on, but the target was gone by the time the knife reached its destination. Alex had transported away. All that remained was a book, a knife stuck in the wall as a fire was getting bigger by the second.

The fire filled the hallway in front of me, and then did something I had not expected. The fire turned into some kind of creature made of flames.

Michael yelled out, "Fire element, *run… run!*"

I realized that I had been staring at the creature as it started to move forward. The creature was made of fire and even though it had shape, it was hard to make out within the ever moving flames. The creature's mouth opened and inside it was a fire so hot it was black. I could feel the heat like a desert wind, burning my skin. I did the only thing I could; I turned and ran as fast as my legs would carry me.

I felt the heat on my back and my second sight could not see this creature of flames, the sound didn't bounce off fire. I looked back as I ran, and what I saw chilled me to the bone. Behind me the creature had become a ball of fire rushing down the hall. When I darted down another hallway it turned and chased me. The noise this creature made was deafening, it sounded like a jet engine.

I had to get to the upper decks; it was my only chance; this creature was lighting all it touched burst into flames. I could not stay on the same deck for longer. Soon this whole floor would be in flames.

It felt like forever before I reached a door marked Stairway. I opened the door, then slammed it shut behind me. I ran up the first flight of stairs, and then stopped for a minute as my back healed. I had third degree burns all over my shoulder, and I could smell my dress. It hasn't caught on fire, but it had become so hot that the plastic polyester had started to melt. My hair had to grow back as well since it had burned away. My tattoo was ruined, the only small piece remained.

I looked down at the door that I had to shut to stop the fire element. The whole door was glowing red; it was made of metal, so it should hold I thought to myself.

It sounded like an explosion when the door burst open and a wall of flames came in. I didn't stand around; I flew as fast as I could up the staircase, and, once again, I could hear and feel the terrible fire racing up behind me.

I reached the top of the staircase and ran into the casino, the ball of fire right behind me. Smoke filled the air along with the screams of the passengers. The passengers were all crowding the exits all at the same time to save their asses. I was forced more than once to jump in between some casino machine, or slide under a table to keep away from the raging fire; its only purpose it seemed was to kill me.

With no way out of the small casino area, I was forced to run down another set of staircases, back down into the belly of the beast, as the fire rushed after me.

I slid through the door to one of the lower decks shutting the steel door behind me. I knew it wouldn't hold the fire element for long, but it would give me a head start. The fire had been spreading through the ship much faster than a normal fire would or could; even this area was full of smoke. It was two floors higher and fifty feet further toward the bow. The smoke seemed to be toxic. I knew that one of the great advantages of being a vampire was that a lot of things didn't kill us.

I was starting down one of the halls when I noticed a fire hose. That gave me an idea. I broke open the door and pulled the hose out at the same time I turned the knob so that the hose pressurized. Right away a stream of water shot out. I aimed it at the door to the stairwell. The door had already turned bright red and was about to burst. When the water hit the door, a mass of white steam filled the air.

Still the door had been weakened, and the creature burst through as the door as it gave way. I put the stream of water right on the fire element. The sound that burst forth was deafening as it roared. White steam filled the hallway and blinded me. I could see nothing through the clouds of white, and, even though my second sight was of no use in this situation, I could still feel the heat radiating from the fire element. I kept the hose pointed toward the source of heat, and the fire element raged on.

After what seemed to be hours, but was only minutes, the sound of the roar and fire quieted, until it was gone all together. The white smoke cleared the air, and the fire element was nowhere to be found. I don't know if I finished him off, but I bought some more time.

I looked up the staircase from where I had just come. It was ablaze. I would need to find another way out, without delay, I headed toward the bow, and hopefully there was another staircase to the deck of the ship that was not on fire.

As I worked my way down the hall, it was filled with smoke. It was so bad that I had to use my second sight to see where I was going. I heard a noise… it was the sound of weeping, a woman crying, and it was coming from the room just a few feet ahead of me and to the right. I wasn't sure if I should go in, but maybe I could help her.

I opened the door to the cabin, quickly shutting the door behind me to keep out as much of the smoke as I could. It did little good, for the room was already full of noxious gases. In the corner of the room there was a woman huddled face down. I went to her side and bent down to see if she was alright.

I tried not to speak too loudly and startle her, "Are you okay? Let me help you out of here."

The woman lifted her head in response to my voice. It was then that I could see that she was hunched over, two small children. They were both boys; one looked to be about two and the other about five years old. It took me a second, and then I realized… they were dead.

My eyes welled up with tears. I had never laid eyes upon dead children before… it chilled me to the bone. I felt myself shake with remorse and regret. I spoke with a shaky voice, "Let me help you out of here. We must hurry."

Her face turned to me, and her eyes met mine. Her stare was cold and icy and filled with pain. She said with strength and conviction, "Let me be. I will soon join my boys… save yourself if you must, but leave me alone."

She turned her head away from me and leaned over her dead children. She was coughing now from the smoke in the room, and soon she would be dead.

I would grant her wish, but she would die quickly and without pain. I leaned her head to one side, and before she could react, my fangs punctured her throat. I drained her quickly taking what life was left in her.

I laid her to rest next to her children. It took all I had not to cry; I said a little prayer then hurried to the door. I needed to get out, or I would be joining her sooner rather than later.

As I went out the cabin door and headed toward the front of the ship again, I saw a sign pointing toward a staircase. I went up the stairs as fast as possible. The staircase came out in the forward dining area. It was empty and full of smoke; how could the fire have engulfed this much of the ship, I wondered?

Moving as fast as I could I work my way up to the top of the staircase. There were tables everywhere, but no people. Some of the chairs lay on their sides, and half empty plates adorned the tables. This was the main dining area and was always packed. I saw a man in a uniform come towards me. He was one of the crew, and I could tell from the sweat and the look on his face that the ship was under full evacuation.

The crew member spoke in a hurried tone, trying to hide the panic in his voice, "Miss, miss. You can't be in here; it's not safe. Move out onto the deck please. There will be crew directing you to the nearest lifeboat."

I still needed to find Michael. Alice could handle herself, but still I would like to find both of them before abandoning ship. The crew member was trying his best to hurry me along. I looked him in the eye and spoke clearly, "I have to find someone first; I'll be fine."

The man spoke a clearly rehearsed line, "Your loved ones are most likely in line or on a lifeboat. Please move toward the deck."

He said please but I could tell the man was losing patience with me.

As I looked at the man, his face morphed, from worry and impatience, into a look I couldn't quite place. Then, like a bad B movie, his body fell to the ground while his head stayed in the air. It didn't take a second to realize his head was held by the vampire Peter.

He tossed the head across the room like an old glove. His clothes were ripped from head to toe; he looked like he had been attacked by a great cat. The tattered clothes that hung from his body were splattered with blood, but his cuts had all healed. He had a wild look on his face as he stared at me. I was in deep trouble if he was able to defeat Alice.

Peter spoke first; he almost sounded calm, "Where's Alice?"

The sound of his voice didn't match his face or body language. I answered in a little voice, "I don't know."

Of course, if he were looking for Alice, that meant he hadn't killed her. Well, little good that did me, because I was pretty sure this vampire was about to kill me. With half his clothes ripped off, he looked hot. I mean for a crazy psycho vampire, he was really good looking, in another different circumstances, I might have enjoyed looking at him half naked, but things being what they were…

Oh well, I thought… then I attacked.

My sudden attack and the fact I had just fed off that woman and having regained some of my strength, took him off guard. It only took a few seconds before he regained his composure, and I found myself defending against his attacks.

I had never even taken into consideration that maybe he had eaten a passenger and had recovered his strength as well. He was as strong and as fast as the first time I fought him. To top it off, he was also a better fighter; my second sight is the only reason I was able to stand my ground at all, but not for long.

He tossed me against a wall. After dodging a punch to the head, he punched me in the gut. Peter followed with a quick slice with his fingernails across my neck. I didn't need to breath, but it caused other problems. First and foremost was blood loss and that is where my strength lies. Second was I couldn't breathe which meant I couldn't whistle. Peter was fast and didn't make any noise; without my second sight I wasn't dodging the incoming punches.

After a few hard hits to the head and a few more cuts, things got a little blurry. My body healed fast, but only so fast. As my vision started to return, I realized I was staring at the carpet, and then I felt my body lifted off the ground.

I could feel Peter walking, and then he lifted me higher. He said in a cold voice, "Goodbye."

I felt my body being hurled through the air. The sudden impact of the wall brought pain to my legs and back. I fell down the wall and onto the ground, and my body worked to put it back together again. Peter left without a backward glance. Well, it could have been worse, I thought he could have killed me... what was that smell?

Chapter 9 Flames

I had been bleeding and now was covered in my own flammable blood. I had just barely stopped the bleeding and my wounds were closing up when I smelled smoke and burning fabric. The dining area was on fire. I could hardly move my neck, but with some effort I craned my neck to one side; only to see the flames coming down the wall towards me. Once the fire reached the pool of blood I lay in, it would be all over.

I was going to die.

This had been a really bad trip. I hadn't kissed Michael once, Alex got away. Michael most likely burned up. Alice was hiding from crazy Peter, and to top it off, we didn't even get that stupid ass book. Instead, I was about to get myself killed.

I started to feel my fingers and toes again. The fire was almost upon me. Forcing myself, with all the willpower I had, I started to crawl. Not fast enough, the fire was moving faster. I pulled my body slowly forward, leaving a streak of blood behind me, but the fire was getting closer.

As if a fuse was lit, the fire ignited the pool of blood that I had been in. The fire moved down the streak of blood toward me. First, it caught my boots on fire, then spread up my leg.

I screamed in pain and kept pulling myself away from the fire with my hands. The pain from my flesh was burning like nothing I had ever felt before.

Every time I crawled forward the flames burned further up my body. It would only take a few more seconds before it burned through my legs and then I would burn from the inside out.

I cried out, "God... why? Please help me. HELP ME!"

I knew God would not help me, but it was worth a try.

The pain of the fire stopped as cool water engulfed my body. A pair of hands grabbed hold of mine and pulled my body away from the flames. My legs had been burned so badly I couldn't even feel them, let alone use them.

My world spun around and the next thing I knew I was looking up at Michael's beautiful face. He carried me gracefully, cradling me tightly to his chest. He didn't look down at me as he ran; his face full of concentration. He was a man on a mission, and he was saving my life.

I had healed enough that I now understood Michael's rush. Behind us the ship was engulfed in flames. My legs didn't work, but other than that I felt good. Carrying me caused Michael to slow down, as he weaved through the hallways of the ship. Sometimes he had to run through a tunnel of flames. It burned both of us, but he was quick enough that it didn't catch us entirely.

An explosion came from behind us, I felt the blast wave. We were engulfed into a ball of flames.

It felt as if we were falling as my eyes first saw red, then saw nothing as they were melted from the heat. It would only be a few seconds more and Michael and I would burn to death.

For the second time in a short period, I felt my life ending under the pain of fire. It hurt everywhere, and all I could think of was the pain. I waited for death, at least the pain of burning would stop.

The pain did stopped without warning. My ears still worked, since I heard the sound of splashing into water. I could feel the cool water all around me as Michael and I held each other together. We slowly sunk into the ocean, with no need to breathe, we could heal.

Michael had saved my life, he was braver than I had ever known.

As my body healed, I could feel Michael giving me reassuring squeeze as our bodies came to rest upon the ocean floor.

There we would rest… and I would dream, of Michael.

*   *   *

I awoke to light and noise.

The sound was that of the ocean, the waves crashing upon the shore. I felt the hot sun upon my naked body as I lay upon the sand. My wounds had healed, but not my clothes. My hair was wet and matted, I soon found out why. Cool water rushed upon the shore, running over my body and up to my head. The water sped away, leaving me in a hole shaped like me. The sun was so bright and I had no sunglasses, it was nighttime for vampires. I could hardly make out my hands in front of my face, just blurring and bright light.

The sound of birds was barely audible over the roar of the waves. The sounds made my second sight come to life. My sight showed me outcrops of rocks on either side of the small beach on which I lay. Up further on shore there were palm trees swaying in the wind. I sat up and whipped my hair back. The air was cool and refreshing and even though I could not see the blue sky, I did not let it take away from my enjoyment of the beach. I was sure that no tattoo, it had burned away.

I noticed the shape sitting at the bottom of one of the palm trees. Remembering I was naked, my arm covered my breasts, since I was sure it was Michael. I remembered if I couldn't see, he couldn't see as well. As I paid more attention to the shape I could see that he was sitting up with his knees drawn toward his chest. His arms, sat upon the top of his knees as he appeared to be looking at me.

I said in a pleasant tone, "What are you doing all the way up there?"

He did not answer; I got up and moved to join him. Using both hands to cover myself, I fell on one knee in front of him. Even closer he was just a blur of light. I squinted my eyes, but could not make him out. I couldn't tell if he was mad, awake or what; all I knew was that he hadn't answered me yet. I had not followed orders on the ship; I had made a wreck of things. Alex got away, we lost the book and that other vampire, Peter kicked my ass.

I spoke first, "Look, I'm sorry, I know I screwed up."

He shifted his position, so I knew he was awake. He now sat Indian style in front of me. I waited for him to speak, to tell me I was a bitch, anything, but he was silent. How much worse, silence was, couldn't he just tell me off.

I tried pleading, "Okay, I know you hate me. I wish you didn't, I screwed up… again. I know you hate me for what happen to Lizzie. I know you blame me… well, okay, it was my fault. This mission, it was my fault, the book at the bottom of the sea, my fault."

In a strange rough voice he simply said, "Why?"

I fell down onto the sand so I was now sitting directly in front of him. My eyes were closed and I was pretty sure he could not see me, so I stopped covering myself. Trying to keep myself from crying, "Revenge! The wizard was Alex. The Alex, who raped and killed me, and just like with Lizzie my anger was all that mattered." I felt a tear slide down my cheek, it burned in the daylight, because of the blood in it. I knew he could not see the tear and I did nothing to wipe it away.

Michael did not answer me. Even the ocean wasn't loud enough to drown out the silence. I hated this, I felt like such a screw up. I was surprised when my second site showed movement; Michael was moving toward me. He pulled me in with his arms until our bare chests came together. He had half picked me off the ground as my legs instinctively wrapped around him. I came to a realization; he was wearing shorts, or what was left of his jeans.

His hand found my face, then slid back gently over my ear; pulling my face to his. I didn't fight this, I wanted this. Our lips met, slow and soft with the lightest of pressure. He tasted wonderful, like I knew he would. Our kiss, picked up speed and increased pressure. I felt our mouths open so that we could explore with our tongues.

His hands pulled at my body as if to bring me closer. I could have sworn he had four sets of hands as they searched my body. I could feel his excitement as he pressed against me.

I only stopped kissing him to moan in pleasure. His mouth was quick to find my neck, then my ear. He bit the end of my ear playfully, pulling just a little. His hands went to my chest; he brought down his head why his tongue explored my body.

I ran my hands through his short hair... I thought Michael had long hair?

I asked between gasps of pleasure, "Why haven't you grown all your hair out?"

He answered in a low a growly voice, "I like it short."

Oh well, I thought. He took me into his arms and pulled me back as he lay upon his back. I could explore his chest with my hands.

His chest was muscular... I don't mind some hair on the chest, but I never recalled Michael having any.

I froze, then started to pull away. He pulled me closer to him, he was so strong. He was stronger than me.

"Peter? What the hell? Let me GO!"

He laughed, and spoke deep and slow, "Why should I?"

I growled, "Because... I know, how about I don't like you for starters!"

His arms were like iron bars as he laughed. "Funny, even now you have no fear. Yet you are not suicidal, or are you? Maybe you like to get in fights?"

His laughter even upset me further, I tried to push free from his grip. Straining with effort, "I hold both in equal disdain... let me go."

His voice was hard, but calm, "I will not. You didn't give me adequate reason. And let us not forget, I saved your life."

I stopped struggling, the audacity of this man. My voice raised an octave, "Excuse me... you, you didn't save my life, you tried to kill me."

He was cocky with his response, "Incorrect. I was on a mission for an old friend, to see a magic book to safety. This friend was endangered on deck. My good friend Danielle was killed while protecting him; she had been a friend for over two hundred years. You are her killer. I am obligated to seek revenge for her death. Instead, I have spared it, therefore I have saved you."

In a tight voice I asked, "Why didn't you avenge Danielle?"

His voice was still full of good humor, "Good question, I haven't decided. At any rate, I saved your life."

His insistence on saving my life was infuriating me, "Michael pulled me from the fire. I saw his face... Oh, I see. Stupid illusions, you knew I would be calm if I thought it was Michael." My second sight had limitations, how did he figure them out.

He replied in a sinister tone, "I'm glad to see you have your wits about you."

I could hear my own defeat in my voice, "You still haven't saved my life; I don't care what you say. Let me go already."

His voice moved from sinister, too seductive, "I don't wish to let go of you... and sparing a life, is the same thing as saving one."

I was at a loss for words, "Really?"

He softly spoke to me, "Yes. Why do you fight me?"

I answered him reluctantly, "I don't know you. You think that I am going to sleep with you?"

In the same seductive voice, "Why not? We are vampires; we live our lives to the fullest. Right now I wish to make love to you." When I didn't answer him, he continued, "I must kiss as good as your lover, if you couldn't even tell us apart."

I replied angrily, "He is not my boyfriend, David is. And I have never kissed him, if I had, I would have known it was not him."

Peter chuckled darkly, "Oh, I see, you *are* young. You must want him…"

"Michael," I blurted out as if he needed to know is name.

He chuckled again, "Michael, you must want this, Michael."

"It's none of your business." He broke into laughter, "Stop laughing at me… I do not find it funny!"

He stopped and then kissed me, I fought a little, but he was strong and aggressive. When he stopped I was full of anger and fear. Men holding me against my will, why do they act like this? "Please, do not force me."

He was quiet a second before answering, "You want me. I don't need to force you; you just need to stop fighting me. I will be yours, and you shall be mine. Never have I met your equal, I must have you."

I remained calm, "Your act is not getting you laid. In fact, it is the biggest turn off ever, if you want to share my bed, first let me go!"

He sat up, I was now in his lap, "I see let's play this your way, but if you run, I will chase."

His voice was playful and threatening at the same time. I laughed, "Don't worry… I don't run." Then I lowered my mouth to his ear and whispered, "I like to be the boss." I smiled, but I realized he couldn't really see me, and that gave me an idea. I peered, "You know what I could do? Only if you weren't holding me so tight."

He spoke in an assured voice, "I am over eight hundred years old. I started as a Templar knight so long ago. After I was turned into a vampire, all women wanted me sexually: Queens, princesses, ladies and commoners. Why do you play me the fool? You have no desire for me?"

I hadn't fooled him for a second; he knew I was playing it nice. I dropped the act, "No, I don't. It's nothing with your looks, but I don't just sleep with any old men."

Having this conversation without being able to see his face was strange. He hadn't let me go. He then reveled, "I will respect you, I will not force you to have sex, but I will not let you go. You will be staying with me."

"Why?"

With longing and need, "Tonight I will feed from you, and you from me. And we will become one, together forever in our cursed lives. I have never wanted a woman, not in eight hundred years, but tonight you shall be mine. When you feed from me, you will understand my need of you."

"No thank you," but he just laughed. He was stronger than me, and so far he had outsmarted me. I hissed at him, "You can't hold me forever."

"When the sun sets, I will feed from you, stealing your power. Then you will feed from me, and take it back, and we will be together. I will have no need to hold you after that."

I was taken back, I had no idea vampires could do that. I could not have this man take my blood, somewhere deep down in me, screamed at this idea. I was desperate for escape, without thinking, I asked "Why wait until night?" That was a stupid question, why am I trying to hurry him up?

He laughed, "The sun is upon us." He spoke as if I should know.

It took me a second, I was an idiot. Our blood would burst into flames if the sun hits it directly. In fact, it felt as if it slowly boiled under my skin right now. It was like sweating without liquid. My claws elongated; my arms were still behind him as my hands lay flat on his back. He realized what I was about to do and yelled out, "No, you are a *fool*."

I pulled my claws down his back, and flames burst forth.

He screamed and threw me as he rolled in the sand to put himself out. Now that I was free from him, I had all the advantages, I could see. With my second sight I could see him just fine. He had stopped rolling around and now was screaming and cursing at me.

I attacked. He tried to claw me, but I simply moved or ducked under his swipes. I clawed anywhere I could, his arms, his side and his back. It had only taken a second and now there were so many flames coming off of him that my own hands had caught ablaze. I moved away from the now screaming fireball and shoved my own hands into the ocean.

The screams stopped as Peter collapsed onto the ground. In a few minutes he would burn away to a pile of ash. I ran up to him and grabbed his ankle; the lower halves of his legs were the only part of him that were not a flame. I quickly pulled him down the beach and into the ocean.

White smoke rose from the oceans as the hissing of the dying flames filled the air. I pushed his body under the waves so that he would not catch again.

When I pulled his body toward the surface of the water, he no longer looked human. His skin looked like a marshmallow held too close to the fire. His skin was black and full of cracks, and within the cracks pink and red flesh stood exposed. His hair was gone and the face was a black mess, but of course I was having a hard time seeing him. My eyes strained in the light, I still had to rely on my second sight. It is of no wonder vampires were not out during the day. Between the brightness of the day and the chances of being burned alive, I wouldn't have come out in the old days; not before sunglasses.

I put my head to him. I could make out the hole in his head, it was all that was left of his ear. I didn't know if he could hear me, I spoke loud and clear. "Remember this moment... for this is the moment that I Melabeth, SAVED YOUR LIFE." I dropped his limp, crusty ass back into the sea. The ocean waves drag him out to sea, to what end, I don't even care.

I walked up the beach for a while and found a nice shady place under a group of palm trees. There I sat, not tired, but full of thought. Like the fact that Peter's overwhelming desire for me, unnerved me. Not because he felt that way about me, because I responded, and even felt bad for almost killing him. That was only a side note of my troubling thoughts. I thought he was Michael, I would have... no doubt, no denying it anymore. I have always had feelings for Michael.

I thought about my night with him before we left for the cruise. The tattoo on my back, as he watched the artist's work with me. His green eyes; always in my dreams. I felt like I owed David my life for what he has done for me, what he had sacrificed for me. Yet, if it would have been Michael on this beach, I would have betrayed David.

A tear slipped from my eye, it burned down my face. Let it burn my face, the pain reminded me. It reminded me of what's truly important. Not David or Michael, but *revenge*. Let nothing get in my way, otherwise my pain shall live with me, eating me alive.

Time to worry about getting back... suddenly I knew two things. Alice was fine, how I knew that for sure, was unsettling. That little shit stealing my blood, I was sure I would regret it. The other thing I knew was, I had no idea if Michael had gotten off that ship alive. Terror shot through my body. The last time I had really seen him, was right before the fire element started chasing me. I hadn't really thought about it until now, I need to get back.

Chapter 10 Island

   I waited for the sun to drop below the horizon, and for my mind to calm.

   I had panicked when I realized I had no idea what had happened to Michael. To find out what happened, I would need to find Alice. To find Alice I would need to find out where I was. And the more I thought about it, the more I came to realize that I had become reliant to other people. I always had thought of myself to be an independent woman.

   I was not that independent, I relied on others for all kinds of things. I had no ID on me and no idea how to get one. I had no money; I would have to steal it. Alice, David, Ezra, it was always someone taking care of all those small details. Those details didn't feel so small now. I had a feeling I was on an island. The cruise ship had left Miami, and was heading for the Bahamas. There was no way I could jump across the ocean. I could swim, but it would have to be in one night, that wouldn't work either.

   I couldn't even picture swimming there, what if I lost my way? Swimming in circles would not get me home any faster. Still, I would handle this like I handle most things in my life; one foot in front of the other. I remember my grandfather telling me, "Worrying is like a rocking chair, it gives you something to do, but you won't get anywhere."

   I knew the big picture; I would start with the basics. First thing is first, clothes and food. Then I will find out where I am and then a way out. Finally, I will find Michael, and if he is alive, I will kiss him. That thought brought a smile to my face. Now all I had to do is wait for the sun to go away.

   The sunset was behind the beach, I now knew where west lies. The sun finished sinking behind the earth, the sky darkened, my eyesight cleared. I could now see the white sand and the topaz waters. The water was so clear I could see right down to the bottom. Black rocks jutted from the white sand. The tree line was not just palm trees, but various species of trees and plants. All with different shades of green, none of the trees stood very tall. The bushes were thick on the ground and made the land appear to be impassable past the beach. This area of the beach was not inhabited by people. I chose to walk south, right or wrong, it was a direction.

   It was a direction, the wrong direction. I had walked, flashed and walked and saw nothing, but empty beach. The beach curved and started heading west now, there was a real possibility I could be walking in a circle. And what would I do if there were no humans? I was starting to feel hungry.

My long walk gave me time to consider a mystery. I slowly recharged like a battery, in some cases, I didn't need to feed all the time. Vampires feed from humans to have power. In no other way could vampires get power. In Vegas I didn't recharge, I had to feed, but in most other places I have been, I don't need to feed if I don't want to. This beach was void of humans, and I couldn't feel that other power, that recharging. What on earth does the beach and Las Vegas have in common? Why is it that I don't recharge here or there?

I thought about it for a little bit. Vegas has this really crazy dead place, I could see all the spirits surrounding it. Maybe, it was eating all the energy of death and life. On this island there are no people, so that also means few people have died here. So there would be no energy from death or life.

I stopped dead in my tracks.

Wait, that means that my other source of power is from… death. I feed off death. That makes sense; it's also pretty damn weird and scary. Why do I feed from death? Why can I see ghosts? What the hell am I? A question I seldom like to think about.

I started walking again. Hunger ripped through my body; I didn't care if it was a cemetery or town, I needed to eat. I had used so much power fighting on the ship, fighting on the beach. Let me not forget all the power I have used to heal myself.

I had lots of time to think because the beach never ended. I had started to travel North, my heart sank; I was traveling in a circle. Then the beach ended, the trees and bushes grew all the way to the ocean leaving no beach. I noticed the water lay flat here, like a lake. This Island must wrap around and make a natural cove.

Now I have tracked through mangroves. A lot of the bushes had sharp thorns that cut on my bare skin. Just more pain, more energy to heal the cuts. Covered in mud and filth, I was so tired. Not just out of strength, but exhausted, I wouldn't be able to travel in the sun. Weak, I pushed on; it would be an hour or so before the sun broke over the horizon.

Just as the sun rose, I buried myself in the mud face first. The cool mud made me feel good and relaxed, there I found sleep. There I found dreamless sleep.

I awoke upon sunset and with a deep weariness I headed out again. Hope arouses in me when I saw the light, it was light from homes in the distance. They lay across a wide stretch of water. If I continued my way up the beach I would be heading north and parallel with the light. Either I wade my way through the rocky shallows, or go through the mangroves. I would swim; swimming was such a relief from the drudgery of that terrain. I felt clean as I cut through the water, towards the promise of food.

As soon as I hit the beach I felt dismay. The current had taken me off target. I didn't have the power to fly, but I could still climb a tree. I found out that I was only a few miles off, hopping down from the tree, I headed out.

It did not take long before I heard the sound of voices carried in the wind. The sky was full of stars and my eyesight became crystal clear as the starlit path was illuminated before me. I was passing an old beach house, the walls were an off white and full of cracks. The straw roof laid half collapsed inside the old structure. Bushes and small trees grew up the side and covered the windows. The front door hung by one hinge and was mostly rotted wood.

I could hear the voices clearly now and I realized they came from inside the structure itself. I heard the voices, but no other sounds to accompany it. It sounded happy, it sounded like children. Like the idiot I am, I investigated. Hunger drove me forward as I felt like there was food before me. Opening the old wooden door, it almost fell off in my hands. I walked inside, and as I did, the old door shut behind me.

They're playing on the wooden floor, were two children. A girl that looked to be about twelve, she had black hair and dark skin. The boy was about nine and shared the girl's features; they both stared at me with dark eyes.

I was annoyed, "Ghosts, why did I come here?"

The boy asked in a small voice, "Is it mother?"

The sister answered, "No… she's a stranger."

I shook my head back and forth, "How sad. Waiting for mom? Well bad news, she's not coming."

The girl's face went from surprised that I respond to angry. "What do you know?"

I was not in a good mood; I was harsh when I spoke, "I know you're a ghost, I know your mom is NOT coming. You'll wait night after night, until you fade away."

Both spirits rose up from the floor, floating. The children melted away until their bodies and faces stretched long and distorted. They screamed as they rushed toward me.

I reached out and grabbed each one by the throat. They tried to tear at my flesh, but their nails only made small scratches upon my skin. My claws were tearing into their skin, they had no blood. I squeezed tight.

I felt myself stealing their strength, their life force. Their faces were not full of rage now; it had been replaced by confusion and fear. Instead of trying to attack me, they were trying to pull away, but my grip was too much for them.

The smaller ghost started to dissipate as I drained his power. His white ghostly body fell away as black soot, which floated away in the air. Soon all that remained was his sister; I grabbed her with both hands. I squeezed her throat until she turned to ash.

It felt like I had fed, my strength returned and I felt whole again.

The house felt empty, the wood floor looked as if it had aged. Cracks started to spread across the walls. I walked to the front door and kicked it out of my way. The door hit the white sandy ground with a thud. I walked away from the old house. I could hear it falling to the ground. I turned to look, and only one white wall stood, surrounded by rumble.

If I had any doubt earlier, I couldn't doubt now. I was stealing life energy from spirits; I could drain them by touch alone. In fact, I could now feel that little trickle of power that I normally felt. Maybe it wasn't just ghost I thought as I headed toward the town. Maybe I could feed off of all forms of human life; alive, dead, it didn't matter. Nicks my father, the man who created me, he knew. I could visit him if I wanted. Suddenly I felt like a visit to Nicks was overdue. When I rested today, I would find a graveyard. I had noticed that it was easy to enter the library where Nicks was, when I sleep near or at places of death.

I still needed some clothes.

Chapter 11 Escape
脱出

It didn't take me long to find a nice sundress hanging on a clothes line. The houses were closely packed, and I found that I was in a small strip of land, only a few homes wide at some points. I crossed the strip of land, only to find the ocean again. I found a small store and it was open. I picked up a map from the counter top. I was on Bimini Islands; with map in hand, I could see where I had been. If I would have headed north, I would have arrived here twice as fast, and without having to go through the mangroves.

I realized the man behind the counter was trying to speak to me, "On vacation?"

I simply answered, "Yes." Satisfied that I could learn no more, I folded the map up. Returning it to its place, then headed to leave.

The man yelled out as I left, "Have a nice night." I didn't answer him; I just walked towards the beach.

I walked down the beach considering how I might escape this Island. On the map it showed there was an airport on an Island just south of here. Of course I didn't know how to fly a plane, nor did I have money or ID. There were plenty of boats, but I have never been on a boat in my life. And if it took more than one night to get back to the mainland, how could I drive during the day. Every plan I came up with had its challenges. Half of them required money that I must first steal. The worst part was that every plan I came up with, took too much time. Time, that I would not know if Michael had survived. I had already been on this Island for almost two days.

I walked down the beach; lost in thought. A smell hit my nose, a smell that made my senses come to life. It was the smell of blood, human blood. My eyes strained down the beach toward the direction of where the smell came from. My eyes could make out a lump on the sand. Closer examination, I could see it was a person lying lifeless upon the beach. I flashed closer, the smell, it intoxicated me.

I could see the body; the throat had been ripped out.

Panic sets in.

My eyes searched frantically for any movement, all my senses were now working overtime. I flashed up the beach and in-between some homes for cover.

How could have I been such a fool? To let him live... and then forget about him; Peter was here, I could smell him.

I moved without sound between the homes. A small road was before me, and across the road were more homes. I had no idea which way to go; I hadn't a clue where he was at. I peeked down the street; it was quiet with no movement. At the end of the street there was the corner grocery store. The man who spoke to me earlier came out and locked the door. He walked away in a different direction whistling.

I was half afraid to use my own whistle for my second sight. I was not a hundred percent sure that he couldn't hear it, and therefore give away my position. The shop owner had been helpful; the sound of his whistle carried through the air and gave me my second sight. With my sight I could see a man standing at the end of the street, the opposite direction of the grocery store. He stood there with arms crossed, still as a statue, staring at the houses I was hiding behind.

The sound of the wind made some chimes ring in the distance. Peter was downwind from me; as soon as I came up the beach he had known. I came out from between the homes and walked slowly into the middle of the street. The only part of him that moved was his head, it slowly followed me. He wore a pair of beach shorts and a T-shirt. He had been shopping on clothes lines as well.

We stood there quietly, staring at each other. There was no way one man on the shore would have brought his strength to what it once was. On the other hand, I had only had two ghosts, and had spent the last few days starving. I was nowhere near back to my full strength. He didn't know this, it might be the only reason he was hesitating.

His face was serious, and then he grinned at me like a funny thought came to mind. I spoke first, "I will have you know, I never run away."

His face didn't give an inch, with a voice of confidence, "I know. You've told me before. Your bravery my lady is truly second to none."

I grumped, "I'm no lady old man. You will not walk away... *what the...*" My voice raised an octave as it filled with excitement. I was now intensely looking over his shoulder.

He turned to see what was behind him; I wasted no time. I turned to flash as far down the road as I could see. Then shot between some homes, twisting and turning my body as I fled. Behind me, I could hear a deep laughter fading away. I had never run away before, this was true, but it didn't mean I couldn't give it a try. The man has beaten the hell out of me twice, and even with my pride, I knew he held back.

I ran like a mad woman, in-between houses, over houses through trees and bushes. I was whistling as I ran, using all my senses to move fast. I had no idea if he were behind me, or if he was catching up, but I wasn't going to slow down to find out.

I did have a plan; I had to double back to where I had seen the man leave the small grocery store. When I approached, the door was shut, but it had a large glass window in it. I ran straight through the glass, I went through so quickly, that I didn't even cut myself. I spied what I had come here for. Quickly grabbing a bag full of garlic I made a mad dash out the back of the store. Smashing the back door, then I ran outside into a small alley.

I jumped up on the roof of a house and this time ran north. Dropping in-between homes; dodging in and out of trees. The whole time I squeezed the garlic until the juice was everywhere. I wiped it on my clothes and pulled it through my hair.

 I could remember what garlic smelled like, but now it had no scent at all. It was so strange because I could smell everything, even the fabric softener that someone had used on this dress. Now I couldn't even smell that, I couldn't smell my hands. This was my only chance of losing Peter.

There was this nagging thought in my mind. How long could I evade him? How could I get off this Island while he was hunting me? And why haven't I stolen a bra, for all this running?

I came to rest in an empty house on the edge of this small village. Anymore north, and I would find nothing but beach, south I would find Peter. I would hide here tonight sleep, my day, hidden somewhere in the sand, and hopefully figure this out tomorrow night.

The house I had chosen had no furniture in it. It was a nice home that needed a little T.L.C. The realtor sign out front is what had led me to it. The home had a nice large window in the front of the house, overlooking the beach. The window had seating built into it, there I curled up and watched the waves.

I had been watching the ocean, not much time had passed. I never heard him, but I did smell him, I knew Peter was in the living room. He was standing right behind me.

I tried to hide the surrender in my voice, "I knew you would find me."

He spoke calmly, "I can see why you don't run. You're not very good at it."

I couldn't hide the indignity in my voice, "Hey, this isn't a very big island. I thought the garlic would work better."

He chuckled, "The garlic worked fine for hiding your scent, but when you squeezed the garlic so hard that small pieces of garlic fell upon the ground. All I had to do was follow the trail. You also left foot prints… Oh, you also went to the only empty house I could find."

Staring out the window, my voice shook with embarrassment, "Anything else I forgot to do."

He answered me in a surprisingly soft voice, "I have not come to kill you."

I turned and looked at him, then raised my eyebrows, but said nothing.

He couldn't make eye contact all of the sudden, "I came to apologize."

It was impossible for me to hide the hurt, "Apologize, for what? Trying to kill me?"

He shook his head, "No, for assuming that you would allow me to take you as my lover."

I was still embarrassed by my failure to get away. I was also angry at him, I was angry because he scared me, "I don't have time for you, if you're not going to…"

He interrupted me, his eyes narrowed, "Please, let me finish."

His intensity scared me; I softened my tone, "Okay… finish."

Peter explained, "I have made a fool of myself. I foolishly believed that you would be my bride. I am vain, I see this now. All my life I have never taken a bride and it is my right. My clan is powerful and well known; I have never met a lady who would not throw herself before me. I believed you would want me to take you; as I said, vanity. I have never met your equal, or seen your power. I believe you would be the prize I was looking for. Never did it cross my mind; you would be willing to destroy yourself and me to be free. It was that act… the act of no self regard; it showed me how free you are. Forgive me my lady; give me a chance to prove myself worthy of you."

Had he just declared himself to me? What the hell, did I land on Bizarro Island? My voice stuttered as I tried to take in Peter's behavior, "Are you serious?"

He smiled from my reaction, "Of course… your beauty is almost too much for me to behold."

What choice did I have, I quickly gathered myself, "You're forgiven… so I'll see you around then… bye."

His eyes narrowed at me dismissing him, "Can I tell you a secret?"

I wasn't ready to get all buddy, buddy with him, "No, I am bad at keeping secrets, I will tell everyone." He smiled, but it didn't reach his eyes. I caved, "Okay already. I will take the secret to the grave, the next grave that is."

His face lightened. He moved toward me, it took will power to not get into a protective fighting stance. He sat next to me by the window, looking out the window at the ocean. He told me, "For eight hundred years I have walked this earth. Two days ago I felt my death, never has it been so near. And for two days my mind has been lost. Had you out smarted me? How had you nearly brought the end of me? In the end, I figured it out. You are without a doubt the oddest person I have ever met. You are brave and ready to die for whatever cause that lies before you. And let us not forget your beauty, for it is something to behold."

I couldn't believe this guy, of course I really didn't mind being called beautiful, but odd. "Well, that's nice… but this odd bird needs to get going, thanks."

He turned his deep blue eyes upon me. The weight of his stare made me feel small and helpless. I wasn't responding the way he hoped, but he wasn't ready to give up. His voice was even when he asked, "Let me make it up to you?"

This should be good I thought, "How?"

"Let me help you off this island."

I felt defensive again, "I can get off... okay, how would you get me off the island? I'm not saying I'll go with you, I would just like to know how you plan on leaving."

He tried to hide his smile, "They have a small airport, and I will fly a plane back to the mainland."

I asked, "You know how to fly planes?"

He answered, "I have been around for a while."

He put his hand out for me to take it. I crossed my arms over my chest, "No biting, no hitting, and no holding me against my will. And I can leave at any time?"

His smile was triumphant, "Terms, well, well." With a grin he added, "I give you my word."

I narrowed my eyes, "I don't know if that's any good." I knew that I was pushing it, but that's what I'm good at.

He became serious, "I swear upon my clan's name, that no harm shall come to you. I will not bite unless invited and I will respect my lady's personal space."

I put my hand into his, "Deal."

He pulled me to him, "Shall we kiss on that?"

I pushed him away; he laughed and did not try to hold me. I realized he was joking, but I still scowled him, "Space, personal space. Damn men have short memories."

He pointed out the door, "After you."

I gave him a look, "Don't be watching my ass."

"My eyes will be over every inch of your body."

I laughed, "I'm riding in the back of the plane."

He asked, "If you do, how will you learn to fly?"

I like the idea of learning how to fly; it intrigued me, "Are you teaching me?"

He took me by the hand, "Of course."

Chapter 12 Flight Plan
飛行予定

Peter informed me that it was too close to sunrise to finish the flight. Plus both of us were hungry, so he suggested we hunt, then leave after sunset. We walked down the road quietly. Now Peter acts like he was taking me on a date. I was starting to get concerned. Why on earth would he be suddenly in love with me?

I didn't understand Peter's change of heart, therefore I don't trust him. I had no idea if he might fall out of love with me as quick as he fell in. The thought made me nervous, Peter was a perilous adversary.

We came to a house and Peter stopped walking. He stood quietly in front of it, studying the home and the surroundings. The home looked like the other houses we passed by. The real difference was it stood away from the other homes; it was separated from the other houses by trees and bushes.

Peter spoke, "This will do. I believe there is a man and a woman inside. Shall we eat?"

Apprehensively, "This house, are you sure? I just never randomly pick someone before."

Peter laughed with amusement, "Oh, and just how do you do it?"

I put a finger to my chin as I organized my thoughts. "I set traps; sometimes at bars, hitchhiking and overall acting stupid. Men come to pick me up, and I feed off them."

Peter looked back and forth dramatically while saying, "I see no bars. Nor do I see men hunting for women. It's almost sunrise on an island, I would venture that we are the only ones awake. How would you feed in this situation?"

"Well, I would… I think I could… hell I don't know." I was flustered; I didn't want to kill without reason. "Do we have to kill them?"

Peter laughed, "You must be joking. Of course we shall kill them, we are vampires, no?"

I tried to keep control of my emotions, "We are vampires, but it's still a choice. We don't have to kill to feed… not every time. Do we?"

Peter stared at me, his face was void of emotions. After what felt like forever, he answered, "It is a choice, I agree. Still, if we kill them, we can gain a lot more of our strength back, without feeding again. In my experience I have found it to be in my advantage to be well fed. I shall leave this decision in your fair hands."

I tried not to smile to big, I liked getting my way, "In that case, I say, let them live."

He didn't argue anymore, he gave me a nod as he told me, "As my Lady wishes." And with that he led me to the front door, and together we went inside.

The couple would awake tired and worn out. They would think that they got a bad flu, but in a few days time they would be as right as rain. After feeding I felt whole again, I could tell that Peter still wasn't satisfied. He would survive and I wouldn't lose sleep over killing random people. We returned to the empty house, there we would sleep.

*   *   *

I fell asleep only to wake in the library.

The library was a beautiful place. Full of books as far as the eye could see; I always felt like I was wandering through a great castle as I moved around the library. There was no ceiling, instead it was a night sky, full of stars. Torches hung from the walls, but even with torches and the light of stars, it was unnaturally bright.

It didn't take me long to find Nicks, from the look on his face, he had been waiting for me. He had been pacing back and forth in front of his fireplace. As soon as our eyes met he closed the distance between us and embraced me with a hug.

He offered me a seat, with a hot cup of Java. Pulling his own chair across from me, our knees were almost hitting he sat so close. With a twinkle in his eye, "Let me know everything. You don't come often enough. Staying in Vegas has kept us apart, I must know how you're doing."

I poured out, everything… talking to Nicks was always easy. For some reason I could not explain how I trusted him with my most inner thoughts. He was always quick to listen and slow to judge. His advice to me was full of wisdom, but he never forced it upon me. It was good to see my father and hear his voice, until this moment I had forgotten how much I had missed him.

When I had finished, Nicks took a deep swig of his coffee. He sat quietly for a moment, processing all I had told him. With a kind face, he asked, "Why do you think this Aaron Reite dream bothers you so bad?"

I searched for reasons, "I don't know, maybe because it is real."

Nicks brought up the question, "What about the memories of the man you and Alice killed, do they haunt your dreams?"

I laughed; I had barely even given thought to the man's memories. I answered, "No, he was a sick puppy. All he ever thought about was having sex with little girls."

Nicks voice was full of understanding and kindness, "It was real. So real, must not be the problem. What else might cause these nightmares?"

I didn't want to answer him, I had always known the answer, but until now I never had to face it. I spoke in hushed tones, "He wasn't evil. He was a good man, with a wife and children. My friends tell me it's the price of war. Are they right?"

Nicks looked thoughtful, "Yes, I do believe they are right. Fighting wars are awful affairs, and most all people who start them, never fight them. If you stopped and looked at the opposing army as humans and not monsters, it would be hard to kill them." He was quiet for a moment. I thought he was done speaking, but then he asked, "Are you in a war?"

What a strange question I thought. I start answering, "Yes, I'm in a war. I am at war with The Order." I stopped mid sentence and thought about it for a second. I was unsure of myself, "I don't know if I am at war. All I want to do is kill the men who raped and killed me. All I ever wanted was revenge; I don't need the fall of The Order for that."

Nicks simply stated, "Then you have your answer. The memory is a nightmare; because deep down inside yourself, it's not what you want. You must follow your own path."

I moaned, "Easier said than done."

Nicks chuckled, "Never has there been wiser words."

I didn't feel that Nicks understood. I tried to explain, "I owe David, and I need his help."

Nicks was guarded when he spoke, "Sometimes help is good… sometimes the price is too steep. And you owe David nothing. He knew the risks when he decided to help you. Even if he didn't understand them, you never meant to put him and his family in harm's way. You are not responsible for Devon's actions, nor could you have known what was to come."

Changing the subject, I asked, "What about this power of mine, to take the power from the dead. What do you know about it?"

Nicks was stern, "I realize you will discover your powers and gifts as time goes by. You are no mere vampire Melabeth, but you have no idea what you're asking. Let me try to make you understand. There are powers at work right now, and they mean to harm the world. You will do great things one day, I truly believe this, but for now worry about your justice. I will worry about what you are."

I was mad he wouldn't tell me. I spouted off the first thing in my head without really thinking about it. "You sure don't act like a father. Hiding secrets, you don't give a shit about what happens to me." Nicks sat with hands folded, just looking at me. He was not angry; he was just calmly waiting for me to calm down. His patience made me feel ashamed for my behavior, "Sorry."

Nicks eyes were full of sincerity, "It's okay… I know this has been hard on you. Believe me when I say, I would like nothing more than to tell you everything."

I asked, "What are you? Never mind, I know you will not answer me, but I know you are no vampire."

Nicks had a sheepish grin, "Well, that brings up something I should tell you. It's about your new friend Peter."

I felt a nervous twitch run through my body. Defensively, I asked, "What about him?"

Nicks spoke with a strange smirk on his face, "Well, earlier when you were telling me your story. You were wondering why Peter had fallen in love with you. You couldn't put your finger on what had made him change... so quickly."

The look on his face, "What... did you have something to do with it?"

He was trying not to laugh, "Yes, you see..."

I interrupted him with my outrage, "How could you? I don't mean how you did it, but why would you? I don't need some old... crazy vampire that could kill me at any moment; or worse, turn me into his wife. What were you thinking?"

Nicks explained, "I had no real time to think it out... spur of the moment. He was burning you to death, so I interfered in the only way I could."

Surprise rang in my voice, "You saved me by making him fall in love with me? Thanks, I guess... you couldn't have come up with something else?"

Nicks shook his head and once again looked as if he might laugh. He corrected me, "I didn't make him fall in love with you. Peter is a very old vampire, and in all his hundreds of years, he has never felt the need for another; or anything for that matter. I simply... well it wasn't simple, but I put need in to him. I put the need for you. I wouldn't go so far as to call it love."

I asked, "Now what?"

Nicks face and tone filled with worries, "That is where the real problem lies. The spell doesn't last long; in fact, it should have worn off already."

I echoed his concern, "Are you telling me when I awake, he is going to kill me?"

Nicks mused, "Not sure, I would have thought last night he would have been out for blood. I think that by awaking this emotion in him. That he believes that he is now in love with you."

I wondered out loud, "You think, you mean you don't know?"

Nicks chuckled darkly, "Well, how could I? I have never used this power on a vampire before, let alone one as old as Peter."

I asked with dismay, "What do I do now? I mean, if he doesn't kill me, or lock me into a dungeon until he works out his new found emotions."

Nicks shook his head, "If I were you, I would kill him or get away from him. I think the latter would be your best bet."

I throw my hands up in the air, "Great, I already tried that. And for your information, I'm not good at it."

Nicks asked, "You have flight plans with him, don't you?"

I answered his question by going into a rant, "Yes, like I told you earlier, he's going to help me off the island. Of course, that's before I found out my new stalker boyfriend is under a spell; that is most likely going to stop working. Changing him from romance, and love interest... to vengeful killer; are those the flight plans to which you refer?"

Nicks laughed at my rant, "Yes, those are the plans I am talking about."

"What about them?"

Nicks conspired, "That would be a time to escape."

I inquired, "Oh, do explain. How do they escape?"

He scolded me, "No need to be a smart ass. Do understand it could be a stalker boyfriend or permanent death. I chose stalker to save you... so I guess you'll have to be thankful."

"Okay, okay, the plan already."

He let out a breath, then explained, "Simple, when he's not looking... busy flying the plane that is. Hit him in the head... HARD. It will give you a few seconds to jump out of the plane. By the time he comes around, he will have traveled quite a few miles. It will give you a large head start. From there I bet you can escape."

I thought about it, with a laugh, I said, "It might work. No harm in trying; that's, of course, if he's still in love with me when I awake."

He took a drink of his coffee, "Well, yes, there's that."

"Other than that it sounds like a plan."

With a serious tone Nicks said, "I feel you will need your rest. Let us catch up at another time, shall we."

I agreed with him, "Sounds good Nicks... I will miss you."

Nicks rose to his feet as he spoke, "Me as well... and Melabeth."

"What?"

With a smile, "I love you... good luck."

We embraced, and as the library dissolved around me. I whispered into his ear, "Love you, and I will need all the luck I can get."

The visit had been a good one. He had left me lots to think about. Like, was I really into this war with The Order? Nicks was still holding back on me, but it didn't bother me, because I knew he had great faith in me. Also, he loved me as a daughter, and if you can't trust the ones you love, who can you trust?

Chapter 13 Falling
落下

I awoke, and I knew the sun had not yet set. Deciding the house was too empty, I went for a walk down the beach. The day was overcast with dark clouds in the sky. It was much easier on my eyes. I could at least make out what was in front of me.

Peter had yet to rise, but my aspersion of who he might be, had me full of worry. I had no weapons, if I ran now… what good would it do. No matter if he still is enthralled with me or just plain wants to kill me; there just wasn't anywhere to go on this small island. Even if he woke up still in love with me, for how much longer? And would Nicks escape plan work?

I walked down the beach and tried my hardest to escape my own thoughts and fears. The last few days had been so stressful. And the visions of Alex's face danced behind my eyes. The face he made when he choked me to death while in the act of… I can't keep thinking about this. His escape aboard the ship, I hadn't had time to really think it over. To think about my failure, and what that might mean. Alex can now warn all the others.

So much for escaping my thoughts, for the roar of the water did nothing to drown out the noise in my head.

I watched over the ocean as the waves churned with new found anger. I could feel the pressure in my head, a storm was approaching. As I looked down the beach from where I had come, I saw a man emerge from the tree line onto the beach. It was too far away to be sure, but I do believe it was Peter. When the man spotted me he headed straight towards me, I was about to find out.

When he became closer I could make him out, it was Peter. It took him a dozen more steps before I could make out his face. At that time I was tense, ready to fight, but trying to look relaxed. When I was able to see his face, he was calm and gave me a head nod.

I relaxed, as Peter came to a stop next to me, "Good afternoon."

I replied, "Yes, it is a nice afternoon, less sun."

Peter looked up at the sky, "Less sun because there is a storm. That may make flying a bad idea for tonight."

Panic set in, I could not be on this island with him another twenty four hours. I had already pushed my luck. I tried to hide the panic, "We must leave tonight. I have to check on my friends."

Peter retorted, "It can't wait one more day? Is it worth putting us in danger?"

I stood my ground, "Afraid I am heading back to the mainland, with or without you."

Peter didn't rise to the bait, he was calm. He argued, "It is unwise to put yourself in harm's way, unless there is no other option." He read my face, and then added. "I can see you don't care. I will take you tonight. Let us travel to the airport, maybe we can get a head start on the storm."

I tried not to be too victorious with my response, "Alright, let's go."

It didn't take us long to get to the airport. It was on the southernmost island, but Peter and I moved swiftly across the ground. By the time we arrived the sun was well on its way down. It would not have mattered because the sky had darkened, the storm was closing in. Sprinkles had started to fall as the wind became more fearsome. Peter said the storm was coming from the southeast. We were heading west, so the faster we took off, the better off we would be. He figured we would be in Florida before the brunt of the storm hit us.

The airport was nothing more than a short runway with some hangers on one end. We both figured we could grab a bite in Miami. We stole a little airplane that only sat four. Peter quickly hot-wired the aircraft. The tower was closed. I listened to Peter as he explained in detail about how to fly the plane, but it was way too much information to take in. Still, I like the idea of learning, I would like to know how to fly one of these someday.

The plane shook and rocked as we left the ground. It was a rough flight and it was not long before the rain started coming down by the bucket. It was hard to see anything out the window. Peter had stopped explaining on how to fly as he fought with the controls of the little plane. The thought did pass through my head; maybe Peter was right about flying tonight.

Peter asked me, "How are you doing over there?"

I moaned, "Other than wanting to puke my guts out, fine. How can you see where you're going? I can't see shit."

Peter responded, "I told you, you don't have to see to navigate. I am using the instruments on the plane. See the artificial horizon that lets me know if I am climbing or losing altitude. There is the v.o.r; that gives me…"

That was a stupid question. Peter droned on and on. I might have been more into what he was saying; if it wasn't for the fact I was getting sick from this rough flight. It didn't help that I had no idea what he was talking about. I couldn't keep up with all his pilot jargon. In short, how was I to know the time to hit him over the head and make a jump for it? It would not help me if I landed in the ocean.

After about ten minutes Peter got the idea I wasn't listening. He went back to flying the plane. The next hour or so we shook and rocked and we spoke little. Peter kept looking over at me, but I couldn't read his face. I couldn't help but worry every time he did. Like he would wake up from a bad dream, and realize he wanted to kill me.

Peter mumbled through the mic, "I do believe the storm is throwing us off course."

I chuckled, "Figures."

He quickly defended himself, "It's not a big deal. And remember who's idea it was to fly through a storm in the first place."

In a pleasant voice, "Let's try not to place blame… I am sure it will work out."

Peter laughed deeply, "You do make me smile. I do believe you will die right after your last joke."

"Ha, everyone knows that when I die it will be the final joke."

Peter confused, asked, "What do you mean by that?"

I didn't answer, "You'll understand after I die."

He shook his head, "You are strange."

The clouds broke enough that I could see lights below. They were moving, there were cars moving down a highway. Peter must have noticed at the same time. He announced, "Well, we made the land. I believe that we are North of Miami; the storm will be too strong to land there. I will turn to the North and fly us out of the storm before we land."

We crossed over the highway, and then Peter began to bank the plane to the right. The highway must run North and South. This was the moment I had been waiting for, I let my nails grow. I would have to act fast.

Peter's eyes were glued upon the instrument panel as he turned the plane. I struck with my left hand, nails out, right towards his temple.

Wow, how did he react so quickly? Blocking my right hand with his left, I wasted no time. I swung my right hand right for his head.

He tried to block me again, but this time I made contact. It was a clean hit, but Peter screamed, *"What the hell are you doing?"*

Blood rushed down from his forehead and covered his face. I tried to hit him again, but it was my turn to get hit. With no room to move, I took a direct hit and felt the full force of Peter's strength. His fist hit my left shoulder, breaking it. It then hit me square in the face and the world went black.

My head was spinning. I felt like I was being stung all over my body. After a few seconds of this I realized I was wet… the stinging was water. The spinning was not in my head, I was spinning through the air. He had hit me so hard that he knocked me right out of the plane.

I worked on righting myself and started to concentrate on being weightless… all for nothing.

My ears were filled with noise… the sound of breaking bones. My body was being twisted into a pretzel. All my joints were being bent in a way that God had never intended. The noise of snapping branches rang in my ear, that sound was the only reason I understood what was happing.

I do believe I found every branch on this tree. I blacked out for the second time. When I awoke the first thing I thought was, I do believe there was a joke in this. The second thing I thought was why was I underwater?

I could feel the water in my throat and lungs, lucky I didn't need to breathe, but still very uncomfortable. I felt my body begin the process of repair. Worry enter my brain as my mind cleared. I had no idea if I hit Peter hard enough to lose him. He could have jumped right behind me and if so, I better get a move on.

My left arm was bent backwards; I reached over with my good arm to straighten it. I found a piece of a branch was shoved through my elbow. I pulled it out gritting my teeth. Then, with reluctance I pulled my arm until it was bending the correct direction. Being underwater helped hide the tears and muffle the screams. It would take more time before I was finished healing.

It was amazing what kind of physical damage a vampire could take. It was also amazing how much it hurt every time I took it.

I had barely lifted my head when it broke free from the water, so much for swimming. I started to gag up all the water in my lungs. After clearing my throat a few times, I could take stock in where I was.

I was sitting in the middle of a swamp. The water was only a few feet deep and trees sprung right out of the water. The tree I sat next to was huge and looking up I could spy the broken branches where I had made my entrance. The sounds of the swamp filled my ears as bugs of all shapes and sizes flew by. The frogs were singing along with crickets. A snake glided by me as it swam through the water with a whip of its body. Not far off I could make out an alligator floating slowly through the water. It was still raining, but under the canopy of the trees it dripped on me. I could see, the world was alive in my eyes, but I knew a human would have a time seeing their hand in front of their face for it was very dark.

I stood up, some of my joints hurt, but I was almost done healing. I listened, but what good would that do? For I would not hear the sound of Peter until it was too late. My dress had somehow survived, it had tears in it and full of dirt, but for once I wasn't standing naked. I really needed to find more durable clothes for my life style.

I was ready; I floated out of the water and kick off against the base of a tree. I moved through the swamp as fast as I could go. Flying over the water, swinging off branches and flipping or spinning my way through the obstacles of the swamp. I loved the feeling of my body being under my control, with my second sight it was like seeing the world in a way I could not describe. My muscles never tired and I pushed myself as hard as I could go.

I hope to be traveling east, because we had passed over a highway. If I could get a car, it would be the easiest way to ditch Peter. He would not be able to smell my trail and cars were not slow. Also, there were lots of them, hard to track; I believe it to my best bet.

My sense of direction had not failed me, I came upon the highway. From a sign it was I 95 this was a major interstate that led north and south along the east side of Florida. I should be north of Miami, and decided I would head north. I jumped the interstate and floated easily to the other side. Now all I needed was a ride.

Chapter 14 Kidnapped
とら

The cars buzzed by while I stood in the shadows.

I didn't feel that I had time to hitchhike the old fashion way. I needed to stop a car and get out of here before Peter came out of nowhere. If the love spell wasn't broke, I'm sure I broke it. Next time I see him, he'll be out for blood.

I waited until there was a break in traffic; I didn't need to involve more than one car. I jumped out into the road waving my arms. The car came screeching to a halt. I wasted no time going to the passenger door, but it was locked. The window came down only a few inches. A middle aged woman was driving alone. I could see the panic in her eyes.

The women stammered out, "What's wrong… with you? I almost ran you over."

I was frantic, "I need a ride, let me in."

The women started to pull forward, at the same time she yelled, "Sorry, I don't pick up hitchhikers."

My panic turned to anger. How could she refuse a young girl, standing on the side of the highway in the middle of nowhere? I reached through the window to try to unlock the door. She was still pulling forward and I was now moving alongside the car. The bitch started to roll up the window with my arm in it.

I grabbed the window with my free hands. Then used both my arms to pry down the window, it groaned in disapproval; the window was ready to break. I was able to quickly reach in and unlock the door. In one quick move I opened the door and swung inside the car. I could see headlights now approaching us, sitting at a dead stop in the middle of the highway was going to get us in an accident.

I yelled at the lady, "Punch the gas."

"GET OUT OF MY CAR." She yelled.

I reached my foot over and shoved down the accelerator. The women screamed something at me as the car lurched forward spinning the front tires. The lady then started to push the brake, but I reached down and dug my claws into her knee cap. She screamed in pain, but stopped pressing the brake pedal.

I growled, "If you don't want to get hurt… *drive.*"

The women tested the last of my patience when she pulled a 38 revolver out. She pointed the gun at my head. The voice was full of strain, "You better let me stop this car, or I will…"

She never finished her sentence. I disarmed her so fast she couldn't react. Then I punched her; not hard, not hard for me. Her head still slammed into the driver side window as her body went limp. I pushed her back and was now steering the car with my left hand. Anyone behind us would have thought we were drunk, but now I controlled the car and kept it at an even speed, and in one lane.

The women had a purse; it was down on the passenger floorboard next to my feet. I picked it up and dumped it on my lap. She had sixty dollars cash and a few credit cards. The rest of her purse was full of makeup. Looking over at the lady her face was covered, she put on makeup like a clown. Her driver license said her name was Beverly Sutton, but who cared? I tossed all her crap on to the back seat, but kept the purse. I put the money and my newly acquired gun into it.

*   *   *

I lost track of time as I drove, when Beverly finally started to come to. I announced to her, "Here's the deal Beverly. You behave, you live… screw with me one more time and I'll make you wish you were dead."

She moaned a few times while holding her head. She was a heavy set woman, but it hadn't kept me from tossing her ass into the back seat. It took her a minute or two to sit up. She squeezed her temples moaning.

I barked, "Shut up, all ready. Moaning does not, will not, help with pain. Damn you're a pain in the ass."

She didn't shut up, she just moaned quieter. I didn't reach back and slap her, a true miracle. I was trying to keep in mind that I had super hearing and she probably didn't think I could hear her moaning. My hearing was good; I could keep time with her heartbeat.

Beverly finally spoke about a half hour after waking. She sounded like a nag, "Your dress is dirty. I just had this car shampooed. Do you know this is kidnapping?"

I hissed, "Don't worry about it, or I'll pick up a shovel and some lime. And then end this trip for you real fast."

She did show a little common sense when she went silent again, but it didn't last. She nagged again, "You're speeding and traveling in the left lane, when there is no one to pass."

With as much sarcasm I could muster, "Thanks, can't have a speeding ticket in the middle of a kidnapping. Can I?"

"Well, you're almost out of gas." She said with the same tone, as if she didn't even understand my sarcasm.

A sign was up ahead, it showed a gas station on the next exit. I informed Beverly, "Exit in two miles, will stop for gas… and a bite to eat."

I was hungry.

There were two gas stations at this exit. One was one of those big trucker stations, it was huge. The large building was surrounded by pumps and big rigs. On the other side of the highway was a normal little gas station. That would be all I needed, so I crossed the highway to the station. I pulled the Chevy Lumina up to one of the pumps. I got out of the car glad to stretch my legs.

I was surveying the area, I could hear other cars coming and going. This was a smaller station, but it was still busy. Then I heard the back door of the Lumina open and my meal jump out and start to run. It took me by complete surprise, a woman of such size and age could move that fast.

I moved around the pump to intercept Beverly, but then came to realize what she was running to. There sat a patrol car, just two pumps down and I hadn't even noticed it. I didn't have time to kill everyone in the gas station, so I quickly flashed in the shadows outside of the station's lights.

I figured it would not be wise to hang around here, and the station across the highway I could hitch a ride with a truck driver. With that thought and a hungry belly, I went weightless and jumped into the night sky. I easily crossed over the highway landing in a clearing just outside the parking lot of the trucker's gas station.

I noticed a sign that said showers, and I could see they sold clothes. Well this worked out better after all. Still, it would have been nice to have eaten Beverly.

It didn't take me long to purchase a new outfit and a shower. I purchased some blue jeans and a gray top with a root beer logo on it. I also picked up some flip flops; I didn't need people noticing I had no shoes. After my shower, I noticed that the ugly purse didn't match, so I put the cash into my pocket. The gun left a big bulge if I tried shoving it in my pants. I figured I really didn't need it anyways, so I cleaned off the gun and tossed it into the trash.

I had a little over twenty dollars left as I walked through the store. I noticed sunglasses on a rack for five dollars. I was trying them on while looking in the little mirror. There was a lot of movement behind me, the store was busy. I could see the shapes of people with my second sight, but I hadn't turned around for a little bit.

A man cleared his throat from behind me. With a deep voice he spoke with authority, "Ma'am, I need to speak with you."

I turned around to find myself standing face to face with a police officer. He was huge, tall and full of muscles. Standing behind him was another officer, of normal size. Standing behind the other officer stood Beverly, sneering at me.

I spoke as sweet as I could, "Yes, officer, how can I help you?"

He spoke sternly as he looked down upon me, "Ma'am, do you have any weapons that I should know about?"

I laughed, "None you should know about… I don't have any weapons."

He tried to stare through me. He barked, "This is not a joke. I need to know… do you have any weapons?"

I answered like I didn't care, mostly because I didn't, "No."

He was leaning over me, trying to intimidate me with his size. He then asked, "Your name?"

I snapped back, "Your name?"

He pointed to his name tag. He spoke slowly as if I were dumb, "Officer Clark. What is your name?"

"My name…"

Another officer had walked up, "Yes, your name, girl."

I sneered at this officer. The big officer has been just a bully, but this one was mean, I could see it in his eyes. Like poking a bear, I looked him the face, "Do we know each other?"

"No." he snapped with no hesitation.

I went on, "Oh, it's just that you called me by name, that's all. My name is Girl."

I noticed the new officer's name was Mac Holman. His face turned red with anger, "You think this is a game, do you? Do you have any I.D?"

I smiled bigger, "Nope."

The big officer spoke, "You have been accused of kidnapping. Can you account for your whereabouts?"

I wasn't sure what to do, but I knew where this was going. I answered with a straight face, "No, I can't."

Mac yelled in my face, "What is your name?"

I was getting angry, "Bite me."

Mac started to yell again but Clark interrupted him. He then he spoke as if he was doing me a favor. "Look, if you don't want to get arrested tonight, I would start to cooperate. Do you understand?"

I narrowed my eyes, "I think you need to get a female officer here."

They both looked confused as Clark asked, "Why?"

I stared him down, "Because neither of you are searching me during the arrest. I don't have any more to add."

Mac about spit in my face, "Have it your way. We will continue this conversation downtown."

Mac started barking in his radio as he walked away. He went over and started to lead Beverly out. Clark started the questioning over again. If I fought it would make it easy for Peter to track me. I was going to let them arrest me.

*   *   *

I sat handcuffed to a chair. There were police coming and going all around me. I was sitting in front of an empty desk. My arrested went quick, I had to listen to Mac go on and on while I rode in the back seat of the squad car. They asked me questions over and over again; the more they asked, the more I just made up shit. I had changed my name at least fifteen times, so at last they stopped asking it. They finger printed me then handcuffed me to this chair. The name tag on the desk said, detective Jamar Washington.

A slightly overweight black man sat down in the chair on the other side of the desk. He was middle aged and bald, with no facial hair. He had a no nonsense look. The detective spoke with a deep voice, "Hi, I'm detective Jamar Washington. I've been told you will not give your name."

He really didn't ask a question, so I didn't answer him. A long pause went by while he waited for me to respond. During that time we both stared at each other unblinking. He finally looked down as he picked up a yellow folder. He opened the file. "You are being accused of a very serious crime. I see here that you had no I.D. on you and less than twenty dollars cash. No credit cards or any other personal items. So where do we begin? How about, why were you at the gas station, and how did you get there?"

It was now three in the morning, I needed to get out of here. I couldn't stay here, I wondered if I had made a mistake letting the officers arrest me. Maybe I should have fought my way through, but something came over me. I don't know what it was, but I let them arrest me without a fight. Well, if I broke free by force, now it would be worse than earlier. I will follow my path and see where it takes me. I kind of felt like they don't have much to arrest me on; all they have is that crazy lady's story, maybe I could use that to my advantage. I decided to answer the detective questions, but carefully. "I was at the gas station to buy some beef jerky with my purchase of Playgirl magazine."

A smile almost broke loose on the detective's face, but he quickly cleared his throat. With a serious tone, "Where do you live?"

"Where ever I lay my head."

The detective said, "This is what we know so far. We know that you were hitchhiking along I 95. That you stopped Mrs. Sutton then forced your way into her car. Mrs. Sutton says at that point of entry, you rook control of the car in a reckless manner. In fear for her life she pulled a gun out, at this point you disarmed her. You proceeded to hit her until Mrs. Sutton passed out. When she came to, she found herself tied up in the back seat. When you stopped for gas, she escaped her bonds and ran for help. It is at that point that you fled the scene disposing of Mrs. Sutton's gun. You were later spotted at the truck station."

I couldn't believe she told them I had tied her up, what a bitch. I answered calmly, "That's a great story, wonderful really. I have no idea what you're talking about, can I go now?"

Jamar leaned back as he folded his hands over his lap. He stared at me, like he was trying to see what made me tick. He spoke with the same deep voice, "Melanie, I would like to help you. I'm on your side; I know there is more to the story. Like what drove you out to the highway? What was chasing you? Maybe you were trying to get away from someone."

I chuckled, "You really are a great story teller. You're on my side? Someone is chasing me? Who might that be?"

He shook his head, "I can't help you, not if you're not willing to help yourself."

I shook my head, "I guess we're done here."

Jamar never changed his tone; his eyes seemed to look right through me. He made me wiggle around in my chair. I was beginning to get upset, upset that I let myself get arrested and that this man understood to much about me. I had no idea how he understood, but he must have been a good detective. He announced to me, "Sorry Melanie, but I wasn't done asking the questions."

Wait, did he say, Melanie. He did, and I realized he had said it before. My body froze in shock and my eyes locked with Jamar's. I wasn't squirming in my chair anymore; I was alert and ready to fight. I demanded, "Where did you get that name from?"

His face changed, ever so slightly. He had been waiting for a reaction. He was intrigued by my response, "Why? Is it not your name? See I am a little confused myself. When they booked you, they took your fingerprints. Sometimes they are on file and sometimes not. Yours came up as, Melanie Dare, missing in 1975. And according to my records you were fifteen at the time. I have to say, you look good for someone that is three months from their thirty-first birthday."

"It's all in what you eat," I replied with a grin.

Jamar lightened his tone, trying to gain my trust, "You will have to tell me what that diet is; Lord knows in this job I look older every night. That's why I shave my head, it's all gray now. Three kids and a job like this, well, I'll be lucky to make it to fifty. You know, you have been missing for a long time now. Normally when I see someone as pale as you… I think, must be from the North visiting our beaches. How long have you been in Florida now? I wouldn't think long, unless you never went out during the day."

I shook my head, "Come on, charge me or let me go. You don't have any proof that I did anything wrong, other than a crazy lady."

He asked, "How do you know she's crazy?"

I laughed, then answered him, "Well, she didn't even know who kidnapped her."

Jamar mused, "Because you didn't have anything to do with it?"

I stated, "That's right."

"And you don't know anything about the gun found in the bathroom trash can. The same bathroom the video surveillance caught you go in and out of. The same video Mrs. Sutton was not on. So, how do you think that Mrs. Sutton's gun found its way into that bathroom?"

That caught me off guard, I stuttered out, "Surveillance at a gas station, really?"

Jamar looked surprised at my response. Then he added, "Almost all gas stations have them, these days."

Well, that did it, time to kill everyone. I had enough; I needed to get out of here. I had no idea why I let them arrest me in the first place. Jamar was about to say something when his phone rang. He looked at me and said, "Hold on one minute."

He answered the phone call and started talking. I wasn't listening; I was using my second sight to determine how many people were in the room. I couldn't wait much later; I needed as much night time to get away as possible. All I knew, was a lot of people were about to die.

My attention was pulled away from my plan when I realized that Jamar was now speaking angrily into the phone. His face was red from frustration, "They have no right, no right to take my suspect. How is this a federal case? I can't believe this shit." He slammed the phone down.

A female cop entered into the room, followed by two men. Jamar stared at the trio with daggers in his eyes. The whole situation gave me pause in attacking. The female officer was obviously showing the two men where to go. She stopped and pointed right at me. The men nodded and started over without her.

They both wore black suits with white shirts and black ties. And they both stood about six feet with the same dark hair and both kept in a buzz cut. That is where their stimulatory ended; they both had very different faces. One of the men was white, while the other looked to be Hispanic, with dark brown skin. They approached the desk and the white man spoke, "Detective Washington. I am special officer Spencer and this is my partner officer Lopez. We are with the FBI and are here to obtain Mrs. Dare for questioning."

Jamar deep voice boomed, "On what grounds? She is being charged with kidnapping."

Lopez spoke with a Hispanic accent, "We're not at liberty to discuss the case, but let me say this little senorita is bad news partner."

Jamar wasn't about to give this up, "I'm not your partner, poncho. And I will need a little bit more information than that."

Lopez's face tightened, but before he could speak Spencer said, "Call your superior; you will see she is already ours." He turned to speak to me, "You are coming with us."

Jamar was busy jamming his finger down on the phone when Lopez un-cuffed me from the chair. He un-cuffed my wrist, and left the cuffs dangling from the chair. I couldn't help but notice the speed in which he moved, he didn't want to be close to me. Jamar was now fighting with someone over the phone.

Spencer spoke to me, "Come along."

Leaving with two officers made for a much easier escape plan, but the fact that they were just letting me follow them out with no handcuffs, weird, yet the fact they both walked in front and let me follow; never once turning their heads my way. Uneasiness was setting in, as we walked out of the front doors of the police station.

I stopped walking, they kept going. I cleared my throat, they both turned and looked at me. Crossing my hands over my chest they got the idea and walked back to me. Lopez fussed, "What's the holdup senorita?"

I looked from one to the other, "You tell me."

Spencer snarled, "We know who you are. I mean what you are. Your friend Alice White sent us."

Lopez then added, "Works real simple bat girl, we take you to an airport. Your ass gets on a plane… then you leave. We don't need your nasty ass around here. Hurry up."

With that they both turned and started walking. I followed, but I was ready for anything. We arrived at the airport in less than thirty minutes. Lopez and Spencer walked me right up to the gate. They were making sure I got on the plane. Lopez made some remark about never seeing me again. I spit back, "What makes you think that any of my kind wants to come to the sunshine state?"

I got a dark chuckle, as I descended down the walkway and onto my plane. It was a straight flight to Las Vegas. I knew without a shadow of a doubt that Alice had wanted me to get arrested so she could send these men for me. How she knew was scary, this link between us had me full of worries. I didn't need Alice to be able to influence me from a distance.

I couldn't help myself on the flight from feeding from several passengers; it helped with the stress.

Chapter 15 My Heart
心臓

I was in a hurry to get off the plane. As soon as I got off the plane, my heart sank. There stood David smiling with Carrie right behind him. I immediately felt like a jerk; the look on his face was full of excitement to see me, and all I could do was think of was Michael.

David embraced me, "We were worried; glad you're back. I missed you."

Carrie added, "Yeah girl could have called us or somethin'. I was worried sick; where were you? Why didn't you call? And where did you get that shirt? I like root beer."

I laughed at her, "I had no idea how ugly this shirt was until right this moment."

Carrie was full of indignation, "Hey, just because I like it, don't mean it's bad or something."

David kissed me. He pulled back, and his eyes tightened. In a concerned voice he asked, "What's wrong?"

I couldn't tell him what was really wrong, that I was having feelings for another man. I shook my head and said, "Nothing."

His look said he wasn't buying it, but he wasn't about to go rounds with me in the middle of the airport. He smiled, but it didn't reach his eyes. Grabbing my hand, he announced, "Let's get out of here. Melabeth has a story for us; let's get back to the hotel so we can hear it."

Carrie thought that was a great idea, but it didn't keep her from asking questions all the way back to the hotel. Walking from where the taxi dropped us off, we crossed through the casino on the way to our room. Carrie stopped to take a breath, well not literally. It was more like a pause; David jumped in, "Do you think you will be ready to go Saturday morning?"

I was a little confused, "Where?"

David became a little agitated, "My Dad… for Christmas. Did you forget?"

I burst out, "Sorry David. I don't even know what day it is. Being chased around by a crazy vampire while being stuck on an island, was not my idea of a vacation."

David softened his tone, "Sorry, I didn't know. I haven't even let you explain what happened… sorry."

I softened my tone as well, "It's okay." It was hard keeping the guilt from eating me alive. I only got upset because I realized that I had promised to spend Christmas with David and his dad. How was I, going to break up with him days before Christmas? I couldn't even ask if Michael was okay; I was afraid he would see right through me. I was afraid he would see me for the monster I was.

Carrie laughed and tried her hardest to lighten the mood. "Can't wait to hear this story... I bet it will blow our socks off!"

It didn't take us, but a few more minutes to arrive at my room. As soon I entered the room, I announced, "Off to the showers. David, let Alice know that I am back."

David's tone was light and playful, "Yes, ma'am, right away."

I added, "Please."

Carrie moaned, "Great, she's going to take a long shower. I really wanted to hear what happened on the boat."

"Ship," I corrected.

After a nice long shower, I came out with a towel wrapped around me. Alice was sitting on the edge of the bed quietly waiting for me. David sat at the small table with a sour look on his face. Carrie was nowhere to be seen. "What's going on?"

David answered dryly, "Alice wants to play games. That's all."

A tight smile formed on Alice's face, "Good, you made it sister. Your boyfriend is no fun; did you know that?"

Before they could start, "Enough. I don't want to hear it." I noticed that Alice was not sitting empty handed. There in her arms was the book, the magic book that Alex dropped. "You got the book... and Michael?"

Alice smiled, "Michael's fine... and he's the one who got the book. It's about time he did something other than look pretty."

I could feel my whole body relax now that I knew Michael was okay. Of course now I could work myself up in knots over all my different problems. Like when would I get to see Michael? What about David? And how could I forget Carrie? She was pulling power from David, could I take that away? I didn't have much time to think about it; Alice interrupted my thoughts, "Well?"

"Well, what?" I responded.

David answered for her, "Story time."

"Oh yeah... where to begin?"

Carrie had not waited long after I started telling my story to join us. I started at the beginning when Michael and I first boarded the ship. This annoyed Alice because she knew this part; still it didn't take me long to get to the parts she didn't know about. I was only interrupted by a few questions from my friends. I got a look from Alice when I told them what happened on the beach. I left out some of the details. She would question me about them later, but I didn't think David caught the exchange of looks. Everyone was wowed over Nicks' involvement, and David wondered out loud what the extent, of his powers were.

We all fell into conversation afterwards; we were interrupted by the phone. Alice answered it like it was her room. She looked over at David, and none too nicely said, "Need to steal your girlfriend for a little bit. Don't worry; I might bring her back."

David just smiled and nodded his head. I asked Alice, "Where are we going?"

Alice just headed toward the door, "You will know when we get there."

I shook my head, and then waved my arm in front of my body, "Should I wear more than a towel?"

Alice's head tilted to one side, "Don't worry; I will make sure no one sees you in a towel. They will all see you in a beautiful dress."

I complained, "I don't have time to get dressed?"

Alice stomped her foot, "I told you, they will see you in a dress."

David wrapped me in his arms from behind, "Just do what she says and hurry back."

Reluctantly I agreed, and then I gave David a small kiss. I joined the impatient Alice in the hall; from there we walked toward the elevator. My guess was that we were heading toward her penthouse, where she could question me on what I had left out of my story.

We barely walked in her front door when she started in, "I felt the lust… and wow. Do you have the hots for this Peter or what?"

I laughed as I tossed myself on her couch, "Not exactly."

Alice, was bursting at the seams, "Exactly what then; did you have sex? It didn't feel like you did… or it didn't last very long. Some men, well they just don't last… it happens."

I shook my head, "No, nothing like that. Just let me tell you what happened and stop you guessing. It's way off the mark."

I started into the story of what happened on the beach. Alice was enthralled and gasped at the part where I thought Peter was Michael. She had never really wanted me to get together with Michael, but she still liked to hear all the details. Of course she liked to tease me about it more than anything. She had always known that I liked Michael; it was one thing she teased me about regularly.

"Well, I guess I knew that you might want to really get with Michael sooner or later," Alice mused.

I snapped back, "And you have a problem with that?"

Alice went into the kitchen to pour some wine. She yelled back at me, "I have a problem with David. You don't care what I think about that; why would you care what I thought about Michael?"

I answered her, "You're right; I don't care what you think." I sat quietly for a moment. I could hear Alice fixing us both something to drink. I continued, "Okay, I do care what you think. I know you don't like David because he is a Necromancer. You once told me that you were afraid I would break Michael's heart. Is that the only reason you don't want me to be with him?"

Alice came into the living room with glasses in her hands. She handed me one before she took a seat next to me on the couch. She spoke with a serious tone, something Alice seldom did. "Yes and no. Michael, does not do well with heartbreaks; that much is true. You are not ready for a serious relationship, not until you are done with this revenge business. The other thing... well, I just don't think you're right for each other. I don't feel I should stick my nose into your business anymore than I have, but I do not believe Michael will support you in your quest for revenge. In fact, I do believe David is the better choice for that."

I sipped some wine, and it was really good. It gave me a minute to calm down. I tried to hide the bitterness in my voice, "So, you think I should stay with David?"

Alice laughed, and then said playfully, "No silly. I think you should get rid of both of them and stick with me. Sisters are better than lovers, but if you must have one, Michael is so much hotter."

I shook my head, "I should know better than to talk to you about this. You change your mind every other time."

Alice laughed, but, before she could reply, the doorbell rang. Alice looked at the door, "That's funny; I didn't order anything."

I was immediately ready, using my second site. I set my glass of wine down and rose to my feet at the same time Alice did. Alice whispered, "Stay calm my pet; I will see who this is."

Alice walked to the door and looked out the peephole. She must have known the person because she opened the door right away. She stood aside and invited the man in. He was a tall man, older with gray hair. He had no facial hair, and his head had started balding. He had deep wrinkles; his eyes were a dark brown, but friendly. He wore a gray suit that looked as old as him.

Alice said in a sweet voice, "Hadn't expected you this soon. Please sit down."

His eyes cased the room, landing on me. They narrowed, and I could see his dislike of me. His voice was kind and did not match his eyes, "That is truly a beautiful dress. What is the occasion?"

I remembered that all I was wearing was a towel. Well, at least Alice kept her promise, and I was well dressed. I answered him, "No occasion; I'm Melabeth."

Alice introduced him, "Sorry, Melabeth this is Dan Caster. He is from the council of twelve; he is here to pick up the book."

Dan added, "Yes, and I am short on time. If you just give me the book, I can be on my way."

I could tell Dan was very uncomfortable being here. Alice looked around for a minute. "I forgot it in your room Melabeth. Be a dear and fetch it for me."

Dan sounded annoyed, "You don't have it on you?"

Alice's tone was direct, "You can take a seat. Melabeth will be back shortly with the book. Can I get you some wine while you wait?"

I walked toward the front door and excused myself. I could hear the old man grumbling about having to wait. He had not yet taken a seat when the door shut behind me. I headed over to the elevator and mashed the button for my floor. As the doors to the elevator shut, I remembered something. I was still wearing a towel, and Alice wasn't with me.

I made it back to my room with only a few looks. There I knocked on the door for at least five minutes before Carrie answered it. She looked angry as she stepped aside for me. I went into the room, but David was nowhere to be found. The door slammed behind me.

As I pulled out some clothes, I asked Carrie, "What's wrong with you? And where's David?"

I looked over at Carrie; she stood there with her arms crossing her chest staring at me. She was angry as she spoke, "David had to run. He didn't tell me what for, but he cast a spell which allows me to be away from him for a while."

"I didn't know he could do that."

She snapped back, "Well, he can."

"Cool, so we can hang out. Why are your panties in a wad?"

Carrie went into a tirade; she spoke really fast using her hands like they were guiding an aircraft. "I went up to Alice's room to see what y'all were doing. I overheard your little story about Peter, only you thought he was Michael. Now what, you have a thing for him now? How could you do that to David? His whole family died... died because he was help-in' you. All he does is help you. I'm with him all the time; you don't know what he's been doing... tracking your killers down and such. What have you been doing? I mean besides trying to get in Michael's pants."

I was shocked into silence. I started to say something, but my words didn't come out right. Carrie was now pacing in anger, she turned her rage upon me, "He deserves better, better than you! I should tell him... but I won't. You better not break his heart right before Christmas. You know he always spent Christmas with his mama and sisters. What the hell..." She stopped yelling and looked as if she might cry. "You know this sucks; I'm dead. I have one friend after a year of hiding in a cabin only to find myself hiding in the middle of a relationship. What happens to me if y'all break? I know you don't need me to be your friend, but I need you. You don't know what David might do. He could… I don't want to… Oh shoot, you just never mind."

The way she said the last part caught my attention. I asked, "What do you mean, what David might do?"

Her eyes didn't meet mine as she answered, "Nothin'."

I said with a gentle voice, "Sorry Carrie, I have been a shitty friend. I haven't seen you a lot and when I do, we don't really talk. I really don't want to put you in the middle of this, but it seems pretty hard not to. Let's talk about this later; I promise I won't break up with David until after the holidays… okay."

She nodded her head and simply said, "Okay."

I hurried and finished getting dressed. Throwing on a simple blue dress, I slipped on some shorts for modesty. I looked over at Carrie; she was full of worry. She had been right about one thing; she was in the middle. What a mess; if I break up with David, what about Carrie? She has to be attached to one of us. If she chooses me, then her power would be limited. She would not be able to take new forms, so she would be forever stuck in the same clothes. The distance she could travel would be half of what it is with David, and she wouldn't even have the power to be seen by anyone but me.

I couldn't help but think of how she drove me nuts in three days. On the other hand, if she chooses David, would he let me see her? If not, I would miss her. This whole magical world becomes really complicated really fast. When I was a little girl, I dreamed of magical kingdoms… what a let down.

My choices sucked; if I choose love, what of my revenge and my friend Carrie? If I stayed with David, I could have my revenge. I couldn't think about this anymore, and, besides, Alice is waiting, and I will do nothing until after Christmas.

I hugged Carrie and whispered in her ear, "I have to run this book up to Alice. Follow me if you like, but we will talk, I promise. I will let you know what I am doing before I do it. And Carrie, no matter what, you are my friend."

As she pulled away from my embrace, she smiled. She tried to sound cheerful, "Okay, ain't like worrying about it will change it. Alice can scare a flea off a dog. Do you mind if I stay real quiet like and just listen?"

I nodded, "I'm not hiding anything from you, come on."

I looked around the room and saw the book. I grabbed it off the night stand and headed out the door. Carrie followed me; on the way up to Alice's room we talked. She was scared, and I was confused, but we were friends. As much as she annoyed me, I was glad she was with me.

Chapter 16 Too Many Messes
多すぎる月

Dan was annoyed that I had taken so long to get the book.

Alice didn't seem to care and disregarded his anger. Dan snatched the book from me; I yelled at him, "HEY!"

He ignored me as he laid the book down on the bar that stood between the living room and kitchen. Then he started to chant some words while waving his hands above the book. Alice looked bored as the man worked. I should have known this man was a wizard.

The book suddenly changed. It went from an ancient looking book with a big hinge lock, to a Gideon's Bible. The mage slammed his hand on the counter. He turned and looked at both of us.

Dan bellowed out, "This is not the book. This is a fake… a cheap spell. You screwed up; you didn't get the right book."

Alice shrugged, and said nonchalantly, "Well, it looked right. You know we aren't wizards. If that's not the right one, how were we to know?"

He was beside himself with anger. His face was turning red as his voice fell right below a scream; "It was your JOB, to get *the book*."

Alice puts up one hand like she was signaling for a car to stop, and, with a child's voice, she asked, "Could you please calm down!"

Dan's face was fully red now as he barked out, "Why should I calm down?"

His anger was really putting me on edge. My voice was full of venom, "Because you want to walk out… not be dragged."

His eyes tried to bore holes in me, but, when he saw I had no fear of him, his eyes wandered the room in irritation.

Alice giggled, "Well put Melabeth." Then she spoke to Dan, "I think it's time you left. Report what you will to the Council, and, if you need our help in the future, just call."

The mage huffed something, but I couldn't make it out. He looked all around then stared at his feet, taking long breaths. After about a minute, he regained some control of himself. He spoke with anger, but with less fury and much quieter. "Sorry if I angered you. You have no idea how important that book is. It can't fall into the wrong hands. I was worried about it coming to Vegas in the first place, now only to find out I have no idea where it is. The wizard who stole it… I will be in touch."

The mage began chanting, and then disappeared. Alice looked over at me and said, "Oh dear, we have a lot of messes now, and I'm not talking about your love life."

"Then what are we talking about?"

Alice spoke fluently, "Where to start. Your boyfriend is starting a war, and you're helping him... not that people realize that. The Council of Twelve is looking to get involved, and now they are freaked over the disappearance of this book which could not be a good thing. This book must be bad, really bad for Dan to act like that. I have known him for many decades now, and, to top it all off, you have Peter Lionheart stalking you. You have no idea how bad that is... you my dear... how do I put this?"

I moaned, "A disaster?"

Alice giggled, "Well, yes that. But I believe the word I was looking for was... busy. Yes, you're very busy. I will give you this; you do liven things up around here. Dolly and I haven't been bored since you arrived."

I laughed darkly as I dropped down on the couch. I dreaded asking, "I think I need more information on my spilled milk... I mean milks. I will start on the scary one first; who is Peter Lionheart?"

A wicked smile spread across Alice's face. Then, like someone telling a bedtime story, she began, "Once upon a time, somewhere in the Twelfth century to be exact, there lived three brothers: Peter, Luke, and Matthew. They were also known as The Apostles. They were sons of a lord in England; all three brothers heeded the call from the church. They all joined a crusade to Jerusalem to help save the Holy Land. They were devoted followers of the church and great warriors. It didn't take long before they all joined the Templar knights and fought directly for the church. They did wonders for the church in the Holy Land, but it was on their return home that things became interesting.

"As the story goes, on their return to England they met four women on the road. It was late and they had just made camp. The women came asking if they may join them by their fire. Being men of the cross they said, "Yes."

"The men were of course separated and were intended to be a meal, but Peter was strong willed and did not fall for the vampires' tricks. When the brothers became aware of their predicament, they fought the women. Two brothers were badly injured, but not before beheading and killing one of the vampires. It was Peter who showed his worth, for he alone killed two.

"The last vampire was the strongest and stopped Peter, but she also saw greatness in him. That night, not only did she start the process of turning Peter, but his brothers as well. After they had been turned into vampires, it didn't take them long to free themselves from their new master. They overpowered the unknown vampire and killed her, thus freeing themselves. From thenceforth they continued to do the lord's work. They killed the unholy and unchristian, and, in their own right, became a scourge themselves, killing vampires and the un-baptized alike."

I interjected, "He was crazy, but he didn't seem that religious to me. He talked about marrying me, or some such thing. He also mentioned how powerful his clan was; do you think it was just his brothers he was referring to?"

Alice answered me, "Yes, he was talking about his brothers, but that's not all. The Apostles spent most of their existence killing all the unchristian, humans and vampires alike. They changed after the Great War. All of us did, really."

Without thinking, I asked "You mean World War I?"

Alice frowned, "Is there another Great War?"

I shook my head in embarrassment. I had read that World War I was called the Great War. It wasn't called World War I, until after World War II. Still, I had no idea from the history books as to how this war affected vampires. I asked, "What happened in the war?"

Alice got up and went over to a shelf. There were several books on it; she retrieved one and then tossed it to me like a Frisbee. I caught it easily. Then she said, "Read that book over; you will need to understand some of what happened to clearly understand what is about to happen."

I moaned, "Great... homework."

Alice laughed, "It will help explain some of the mess we are in. It will also tell you about the Council of Twelve. Your boyfriend is inviting disaster, but I think he knows this."

I defended David, "I don't believe that."

Alice simply said, "I know."

I left the room with my head spinning. I really needed to put my feelings on hold over Michael no matter how much it hurt. As I headed back toward my room, Carrie reappeared. I had hardly shut my door before her mouth went into overdrive.

The rest of the night I spent talking with Carrie. We did a lot of complaining, but, in the end, we worked out some things. She came to understand how I was feeling about Michael; I believe she understood. I also came to find out that she had not been doing so well herself. David had kept her wandering around the Necromancer temple while he was busy working. He spent all his time with his face in books and practicing his magic. The other ghost that lived at the temple was less than friendly, and she hadn't had anyone to talk to.

Morning came before I knew it, I said my goodbyes to Carrie. After she disappeared, I headed to bed myself. After some rest I would be better at making decisions. I was too tired to think straight and had too many things to think about.

*   *   *

I awoke with a start.

All that excitement on the island had kept the dreams at bay, but not tonight. Too upset over my dream to go back to bed, I grabbed the book Alice gave me. It was three in the afternoon; it was way too early to be up.

The book was written by a wizard named J.E. Dale. It was an overview of the last hundred years of magic community politics. It started off talking about the separation of magical creatures and humans. Everyone was fighting each other on different levels and different degrees. The humans were never considered anything to most magic folks until the late eighteen hundreds. With their numbers and their science they were a threat to all. A lot of magic creatures fled to the New World to get away from the humans who would destroy them on sight.

When the Great War broke out, many magical creatures took sides, and, as the war deepened, many more were forced to take sides. Many wizards and other magical creatures came from America where they had fled, to help their kind. Millions died… millions… it was hard to even imagine. How many of the millions were magical? Countries had made individual pacts with different groups of magic users and creatures alike, and, after the war ended, there were very few left.

The Council of Twelve was formed after the Great War. It was called that because a group of eleven wizards of the highest order and the last full blooded elf formed it. Even though it now has hundreds of members and dozens who sit on the council, it still remains the Council of Twelve to honor the founders. The book was written in 1984 so it was a little out of date.

The head of the council was the last remaining full blooded elf, Luna Longaeva. World War II broke out. The council was on the side of the allies. Still the Germans had wizards, shifters, werewolves and vampires at their disposal. After the war, vampires, who fought for the Germans, fled to the Americas or pledged their allegiance to stronger clans. There were many clan names listed in the book. The Lionheart was listed among them.

Magic diseases were listed in the back of the book; there were many according to the council. The council has never recognized werewolves or vampires as magical creatures. They are listed as diseases of humans. Shifters who could turn into animals were not a disease and known to work for the council in a police like status.

All this book did for me, is fill my head full of questions, like, how come a member of the council hired Alice? A vampire, to recover the book, and what, if anything, does the council and The Order have in common?

The author's writing was dull, and he droned on and on about council members and events that the council took part in. I flipped through the book, and, toward the end, I found the answer to one of my questions: the history of The Order and its dealings with the council.

After reading through it, I started to understand the concerns Alice was having. Basically The Council still looks upon America as the New World or the West. All the governments are represented in the council, including America. In the states, we came up with The Order, kind of America's version of its own council for regulating magic users and magical creatures. The Order is made up of volunteers, unlike the elected council. In short, David and I are attacking and killing volunteers. The writer of this book openly complains that there is not enough oversight in The Order allowing bad people to do evil in the name of good, kind of like Alex and Devon; I had never stopped and thought about it like this.

Now that we are putting the fear of God into anyone who dares to say they're in The Order, this will allow the council or government to step in. Magic users left Europe to get away from the oversight and to be free of The Council. I had never looked at it from the point of view of The Order members themselves. David and I killed dozens of Order members in the graveyard, but how many of them were bad. How would they have known that Devon was lying to them? All they would have seen was a vampire and a Necromancer with some other magic users' meeting in a graveyard. If they took Devon's word for it… Well, there it is in a nutshell, why The Order needs oversight. It needs judges and trials.

Then there is Alex, he stole a book from the council; they hired vampires to get it. I couldn't even fathom why they would hire us? In turn, I now have a very old vampire stalking me, and let it not be forgotten that I am still hunting members of The Order. Which means that the same council that hired Alice to get the book, may be my enemy? Or do they want The Order destroyed?

I tossed the book on the floor; Alice was right. Way too many messes!

And still, the constant nagging about what I really was. I got dressed, grabbed the book and went to the wall safe. There I pulled it out, the tin, simply marked Melanie. I looked at the time; it was close to eight and Alice would be up.

I arrived at Alice's door and knocked loudly. She answered with hair still unkempt and in her nightgown. In a grumpy tone, "You need to stop doing that. It's called a phone; try it."

Without waiting for her invite, I barged my way in. "Okay, I think I understand what you have been trying to tell me."

Alice slammed the door. She grumbled, "Oh goody."

I went on, "To sum it up, you don't care that I am killing my murderers. You just don't think I should be helping David on this crusade of madness, because it will never end. It will just start a war that I don't want anything to do with."

Alice screamed out so loud it startled me, "ALL I HAD TO DO WAS GIVE YOU A BOOK. I have approached you all wrong my dear... wait, I should say no more. Let me write it down, so you may hear me."

I chuckled at her goings on, "All right, all right, I get it; I don't listen. I am new..."

"Yeah, like yesterday," Alice quipped.

"To this life. Too much too fast, but I haven't ignored what you have said. Like the fact I am like no other vampire. Living in a city of vampires, I have witnessed first hand what you have said, but did not understand.

"Any vampire under a hundred, like Michael and Lea, would try to never go outside during the day. They wouldn't risk bursting into flames for they are not strong enough. And even the older vampires like Charlotte and Ezra don't take in the sun as easily as I do. When we first met, you remarked on my strength and speed, and I know I am faster and stronger than Ezra now."

Alice added, "I do believe you are as fast and strong as me. Of course, no matter how much you grow, you will never match my beauty."

"Oh, for sure," We both laughed.

After we stopped giggling, Alice took notice of my tin case. She inquired, "What have we brought with us?"

I went serious, "I think it's time I start investigating my own death and stop leaving it to others. I need to find out where and who these men are. I also need to know more about what I am... I know Nicks doesn't want me to know, but I will take my chances."

Alice grinned, "It's about time."

I continued, "This is a film case. In it, is a movie, a movie of my death. I have not let anyone watch it, not even myself. There could be clues in it; David thought so, but he understood my reasons for not allowing him or the detective to see it."

Alice's face went all slack, as she regarded the tin case. She had a look of horror as her eyes locked upon it. With a small voice, "You don't want me... to watch it?"

I shrugged, "I can't watch it by myself; if not you... there is no one else."

Alice's eyes moved from the tin case to my face, then back again. She fell onto the couch and with deep surrender in her eyes said, "I'll call room service for a projector. I better get a bottle of wine, scratch that, a case." She gave me one of her best devilish grins, "Why don't you be a dear and go pop some popcorn?"

I narrowed my eyes at her, "Shut the hell up." Alice just laughed.

Alice and chatted about the council and The Order. In moments like these you could really see Alice's true age. I had begun to notice that she was more and more like this, when it was just the two of us. The more I was with Alice, the more I trusted her. She was crazy, but loyal to no end.

A knock at the door, let us know that room service was here. A few minutes later Alice setup the projector. She chilled some of the wine and prepared us some glasses. Alice told me, "Not long after I met you, I started my own investigations into your murder. After you found and killed Devon I had more to go on. Still, I had never found a buyer."

I asked, "A buyer, for what?"

She shook her head slowly, "Your bad movie, silly. As far as I know, no one has bought this film. That means this is the only copy. If not for sale, then why make it?"

I didn't have an answer, but I guessed, "Maybe they did sell it, and we just haven't found out to whom."

Alice puts her finger to her chin, "Maybe." She then handed me a glass of wine and asked me. "If that were the case, if they just made the movie for sale... did they wear masks?"

"No."

Alice wondered out loud, "They all worked for The Order. They couldn't afford for a copy to get into the wrong hands. David had to watch some of the movies when he was stealing the tapes out of Devon's house. I remember him, saying he only watched a minute of it. At that time he clearly saw you and Devon. As much as I don't want to watch this, I will admit I am curious. We must watch it carefully, in the background and every word that is said."

I swigged a big drink of my wine. My voice rattled, "Okay... I'm ready."

Alice refilled my glass; then softly added, "Let's try to stay sober until after the movie."

My voice cracked a little, "Okay, but after we drink the whole case."

She sat next to me and gently rubbed my shoulder, "Are you sure?"

All I could do was nod. "Okay, but if you can't finish it... nothing to be ashamed of."

Alice got up and flipped the lights off, sat back down next to me. Putting one arm around me, she used her free hand to start the projector. The lights flickered to life as the white and black flashes came to life on the wall.

As the film began, my eyes stayed glued to the screen. The movie started with me on my knees, in the middle of the bed. My eyes were wide and my face was smeared with tears. As I looked upon my own eyes, they were devoid of emotion... broken, past fear. One of the Smith brothers came to the bed first and grabbed hold of me.

My eyes blurred as the tears began to fall down my cheek. My eyes were unblinking as the images passed in front of me, yet I could not make out what was on the screen as my own tears rolled off my face. The tears fell, some down my neck, while others escaped my face and fell to my shirt. My tears were blood. The thought passed somewhere in the back of my mind; my outfit was ruined.

My chest tightened, and, if I were to have a heart, I might have thought I was having a heart attack. I found it hard to breathe, but remembered I didn't need to. My screams filled my ears; they were coming from the film. I could feel the pain, my pain. I could also hear the men laughing and speaking, but what they said I could not make out in my grief.

The world tilted; it took me a few seconds to realize I could no longer see the screen. In front of my eyes just a few inches away, was a human hand. It took me a few more moments to realize it was not my hand, but Alice's. My tears now ran as freely as a river, and the sobs filled my ears. They were not sobs from the movie, but from me. The movie went on forever, and, as it did, I felt like I was having an out of body experience.

The movie stopped; Alice picked me up like I weighed nothing. She moved me into her room and gently laid me upon her bed. Laying a blanket on me, she left me without a word. I lay there, face stained with blood, but no more tears.

The hate slowly started to fill my heart and replace the pain.

After a while, I washed up and then joined Alice in the living room. She sat quietly sipping on a glass of wine, deep in thought. I broke the silence, "I missed everything. Did you see anything?"

Alice gently swirled the wine in her glass as she stared at the wall. I wasn't sure she heard me, but she hushed me when I began to repeat myself. After a few more seconds, Alice's eyes shifted to me, "You have to watch it."

I felt the horror rise in me. I protested, "I don't know if I can."

Alice shook her head, "You have to... not the whole thing, just the end."

My voice was weak, "If you say so."

Alice went over to the projector and started it. I didn't sit; I let my hate well up in me. It kept the tears at bay so that I could watch the film play. Alice started it at the end... my end that is. Alex was on top of me choking the life out of me. I watched myself die; what a strange thing to see.

My anger was a dam that held back the flood of pain. I watched as Alex rose off my dead body. The camera panned back, and, for the first time, I noticed something other than myself being destroyed. Under the bed were markings on the floor, symbols drawn in red. A red circle with hundreds of symbols all lay within the circle. I now looked at all the things in the background instead of the scene being played out on the bed. There were symbols on the walls, some in red, some in black. Some of the symbols appeared to be glowing.

Then one of the Smith brothers handed Alex a large knife. I watched in wonder as he plunged this huge knife into my dead chest. He proceeded to carve my body open. Being a vampire I was no longer bothered by the butchering of flesh, but my hand found its way to my chest. My eyes were glued to the screen. He cut and cut, then laid the knife off to one side. Reaching down into my chest, he pulled my heart out.

Jason came over with a large golden goblet; Alex squeezed the blood from my heart into the goblet. He then took the goblet from Jason; as Jason moved out of the camera's range, Alex began to chant. He held the goblet with both hands out in front of him. His chanting sped up. At the same time it increased in volume. The goblet started to overflow with blood as if it were being filled. I watched as the blood ran over the top of the goblet and onto the floor; the symbols were now ablaze with red light.

When Alex stopped chanting, the cup stopped overflowing. He then brought the goblet to his lips and began to drink.

Then one of the Smith brothers came over and drank. He was shortly followed by his brother, then Jason and finally Devon. They were all naked except for Devon as they formed a circle around the bed and my dead body. They began to chant, and I watched in horror as my body melted like wax. It looked as if someone took white and red wax and poured it upon the bed. The room darkened, and the symbols burned with light.

In the background my eyes caught something, but I was distracted by the screaming coming from the movie. All the men had broken from the circle and were writhing in pain. They were screaming, which was shortly followed by throwing up of blood.

Devon stood up and wiped his mouth with the back of his sleeve. With anger in his eyes, he growled, "Alex what have you done? How did you screw up the spell?"

I couldn't tell from the film who was talking, but one of the other men said, "Does that mean we're not immortal then?"

Alex growled with anger, "I did the spell right... I followed the book to the letter."

Jason, who looked less affected than the rest of them, mumbled, "You missed something."

Alex whipped his head toward Jason, then barked out, "What did you say?"

Devon, using a calmer voice said, "Stop it. He's right, we screwed something up. Was she a virgin?"

One of the Smith brothers joked, "She wasn't when I was done with her."

Alex said in a low voice, "She needed to be a virgin before we brought her into the circle. We believed she was."

Devon asked, "What will happen if she wasn't?"

Alex barked, "Turn off that camera."

Devon walked toward the screen the screen went black. The next sound was the projector slapping as the last of the film spun around. I looked over at Alice, "Rewind it."

Alice angled her head, "Why?"

My voice was empty, "I saw something. Take the film back right before I melted."

Alice nodded, "Not a problem."

I asked, "Can you move it one frame at a time?"

"Yes."

As she did, I watched in the background for the image I thought I saw. I yelled out, "Stop… that's it."

Alice asked, confused, "It… what? I don't see anything."

I explained, "Look into the background. Look where the red glowing symbols on the wall are. See where two red dots are; now look at the shadows around the dots."

Alice gasped, "It looks like a face of a man."

I shook my head, "Not a man… Nicks."

Alice added, "You weren't a virgin."

I nodded, "I know."

Chapter 17 Christmas
クリスマス

After watching the movie of my death, I had to get something to drink. Alice and I went down to the casino and lured a few men back to our rooms. We didn't kill them, but the casino still had to send men up to take them away.

We were both just sitting in Alice's living room. We hadn't really talked since the end of the movie. I announced, "I probably should get going. David and I are leaving for New York tomorrow night." I added with a hollow laugh, "I hope his dad doesn't mind vampires."

Alice was looking at a magazine. She didn't look at me when she remarked, "No worries there."

"What do you mean by that?"

Alice lowered her magazine as she made eye contact with me. She explained, "Well sweetie, you are no vampire." She went back to her magazine.

"Then what am I?"

She shrugged, "Hell if I know." I started to leave when she added. "I drank your blood."

I turned to look at her; she was staring at me with a blank expression, "And?"

"I do believe Dolly and I are in for the long haul. I've lived for long enough to know when trouble is starting. Don't worry… we are sisters. I will stand with you."

A small weight lifted off me. "You're right, I am not a vampire, but I am glad you are my sister."

Alice laughed, "Enough of this mushy shit. You know I just realized something."

"What?"

Alice got up and walked over to me, "I know how you feel, and I know where you are. I always do ever since I drank your blood. If you were to practice you should be able to do the same with me. What I realized was, that there are times I don't know where you are, or how you feel, like a few days ago when you were on the island; you disappeared from me. Did you go to that library, you told me about?"

"Yes."

Alice nodded her head, "Well, you better get ready. I am not sure what it means, but I bet you will find out, or die trying."

I smiled, then gave her a hug, "See you in a week or so. I will practice trying to find you."

Alice giggled, "Have time for a quick tea party?"

The room grew in size, with giant columns. We were now standing in the most magnificent cathedral with giant white walls decorated with hundreds of paintings and even more statues. Little animals scurried across the floor, and I came to realize the ground was made of grass. Plants and vines grew up the side of the building; the whole thing was breathtaking, and I found myself wearing a beautiful gown while Alice prepared the tea.

I smiled as the sun shown down far above me since there was no roof, just walls. There were hundreds of stained glass windows in the walls. I looked over at Alice in her beautiful dress as she glided toward me with tea in hand. I simply said, "I do believe I can spare a minute."

Alice smiled, "Tea?"

"Why thank you."

*   *   *

I slept well; for the first time in a long time I didn't have that same nightmare of Aaron. I did have a small nightmare of my murder, but I expected it. It was the same nightmare I had since I had been murdered, and I just watched the film of my killing; talk about pouring salt into a wound.

The question that was running through my head as I hurried through the airport with David was; did my nightmare of Aaron quit because of the reminder of my own death, or did it quit because I now knew I was no longer going to hunt The Order? Of course I dreaded that conversation with David. It seemed like I was a small ship being pushed by a large storm for it was no time at all before I was sitting next to David as the plane lifted off the ground.

One thing I always liked about David was that he respected for my silence. He said very little as my mind spun around and around. As the plane grew quiet and the roar of the engines filled my ears, my mind calmed. My path was easy; hunt down my killers, and kill them. I was not going to worry about Michael; I was going to deal with David. I did better when I had a plan and knew the direction I was heading in.

David asked, "Can we talk?"

"Sure, what's on your mind?"

David took my hand, "I could ask you the same thing. Look, I know you have a lot on your mind. I have an idea; let's take it all down a notch this Christmas. No magic, no Order, just Christmas. What do you think?"

I smiled and honestly answered, "That sounds like a good idea to me."

David went on, "I bought you a small gift for Christmas. No big deal, it's just something you can't open in front of my dad."

Remembering I hadn't bothered to buy him anything yet, "You really shouldn't have." And I really meant it; I was now having a small panic attack. What to get him, and when?

David laughed, and if I had a heart it would have stopped. I had forgotten how wonderful his laugh was to me, and I also realized how long it had been since I heard it. Being in this plane, sitting close to him… it brought back memories of our first night on the bus. David stopped laughing, "I can always tell when you are stressed. You forgot to get me a present, didn't you?"

I was defensive, "I got you something… I forgot it. I forgot it at the store, and as soon as I have time to find that store, I will retrieve it." David laughed again, and his happiness was infectious, for soon I was laughing too. I added, "I know, I am a jerk."

David stopped laughing and got serious, "Stop that. It's not Christmas yet, and you still have time to shop. I was only telling you about your gift… well the reason was that you need to understand that my dad can't see you open your real gift. In fact, I plan on giving it to you right now." David reached under his seat and pulled a large flat present. He handed it to me, it looked as if he had wrapped up a folder.

"You shouldn't have."

With a wink, David encouraged me, "Open it."

The wrapping paper was red with little green Christmas trees on it. The words Happy Holidays were under every tree. I opened the present… I was surprised. It was a folder, a brown folder. I opened it to find it stuffed with papers. Flipping the folder open on my lap, I thumbed through some of the paper when I came to a piece of paper with a small photo attached; my mind started to put it together.

There in the little photo was a picture of Jason Black. He was the large biker who raped me. I could see the folder was packed with information about the man. It had his current place of employment and his known friends and family. This was all I needed to hunt the bastard down; David's Christmas present was another piece of my revenge.

I looked up at him; he was grinning from ear to ear. "So, what do you think?"

I beamed at him, "This is the best present I could think of. When can we go get him?"

He shook his head, "Not so fast sweetheart. If you take a look at that file you will find out that Jason is no mere man… he's a troll."

I chuckled because I thought he was joking. Then I remembered I lived in a world where myths and legends were not stories to entertain us, but real and hidden in the shadows of what I called reality. I asked, "How do we kill him?"

David smiled; it was sinister in nature, "Trust me… I got this."

"I do trust you… What do you need of me?"

David mused, "I need you to kill him, and you will need a special weapon to do it. You should know that I have just figured out how to make soul weapons. Enchanters could make the weapon we need to kill him, but they won't help us."

I know David had been working on his magic, but it sounded like what he was making would be hard to do. I wondered, "It's not going to be dangerous for you to make this weapon?"

"No," David looked a little lost in thought, but I had to get his attention again, "I will have to hurt someone to make it."

"I don't care."

David nodded, "I didn't think you would. I'll sort out all the details. We'll get him after Christmas, okay?"

I smiled and put my arm around him, "Sounds like a date."

The thought did pass through my head; what about Michael? It hurt to think about it, now that I had admitted my feelings for him to myself... I felt like I was having an affair. I was doing it for reasons other than love. Alice was right; I must finish my revenge before I could love.

Hate and *Love*, they have the same goal... to devour another.

Chapter 18 Final Plan
最終案

We arrived in New York; by then, Carrie had talked my ear off. She had been really quiet at first, most likely because David had requested some time with me. After David gave me my gift, she was in full swing. The flight was a red eye; our plane was taxiing when the sun rose and Carrie disappeared.

We took a taxi to David's father's apartment. His father was the general manager in an apartment building near Central Park. David's dad was nice, but busy. I didn't see him much. David and I had a time in New York. Shopping was amazing, and the best part was that the city never slept. I found a really nice coat for David and bought it for him for Christmas. He wore it with pride as we walked around Central Park. I teased him not to get used to it, I still had to wrap it.

Christmas morning, and, for the first time, I was still awake. As a little girl I always got really excited for Christmas. I tried to stay up for it, but never made it. I got older, and, with my father, Christmas lost its meaning. It was just a day I slept in on. I hadn't slept, but it wasn't because I was excited about the magic of Christmas… it is the fact that I am a vampire.

Carrie had been great on the flight over. She was a real pain Christmas night. She had become really depressed… no presents and she would be gone by morning. I pointed out that we were both dead and no longer got to enjoy the gifts of life. Carrie was usually happy go lucky, so it was hard to see her so bummed out.

Christmas morning; it was fun opening presents with David and his father. I opened a little box and pulled out a beautiful heart shaped necklace. It was silver and sparkled as if it were encrusted with diamonds. David's father helped me put it around my neck. I reached over and gave David a big kiss. I was so happy.

Then, as soon as the necklace was around my neck, I felt different. I got up and went to the kitchen, and I started to have an out of body experience as I made some coffee. It really wasn't a big deal that I was making coffee; I just didn't know why I was. Then I brought it to David, "Here you go sweetheart. I hope I made it the way you like it."

David took a sip, "Perfect… just what I wanted, thanks."

It was the *just what he wanted* remark that made my mind stop in its tracks. I sat down across from David and his father. They were both engrossed in conversion. David broke away and looked at me, "Would you be a dear and make my father a cup, and I would enjoy another one."

His father objected, "Oh, she doesn't have to make one for me."

I spoke, but I wasn't sure it was me, "I would love to." And with that I headed to the kitchen.

I was once again sitting quietly across from David and his father as they talked. They both sipped on their coffee. It took all my willpower, all I had to pull the necklace from my neck. As soon as it was free, I felt free. David's will was gone as fast as it had come. I couldn't believe it; he tried to put a spell on me... to control me.

Now I sat there trying not to look like I was going to murder him in front of his father. It had taken a moment or two before he had noticed I was no longer wearing the necklace. He didn't say anything, but I could tell he was worried, and he should be.

I excused myself and told his father, I wasn't feeling well. I went to a room to sleep. That evening I told David I would like to go for a walk. Reluctantly, he agreed, and together we caught a cab to the park. There was snow on the ground and lights in the trees. There were a lot of couples taking a walk, some with their families. It was Christmas night; I would try to remember that so I didn't kill David. Carrie had reappeared and was clueless as she went on about how beautiful the lights were and asked fifty questions about what she had missed.

Carrie asked, "Come on Melabeth. Tell me what else you got... actually I know. I saw the pretty little necklace when he wrapped it. Why aren't you wearin' it? And why are you so quiet? What's the matter with y'all... it's Christmas."

We had finally walked deep enough into the park where there wasn't an audience. I looked over at David, trying my best to remain calm. I asked, "Answer Carrie's question. Why am I not wearing it?"

Carrie asked carefully, "You two fightin'?"

My eyes narrowed and with venom I asked, "How could you... try to control me?"

David shrugged his shoulders. His voice held no remorse, "I had to do something. Between you leaving me for Michael, and the fact you're not going to kill Order members anymore... what should I have done? I am losing you."

I was shocked, "How did you know? Carrie... that..."

Carried defended herself, "I didn't..."

David cut her off, "Don't blame her; she's stupid but loyal. Unlike you I might add. When I cast that spell for her to be away from me, she had no idea I could hear what she could hear."

Carrie said indignantly, "Stupid?"

I ignored her and asked, "You eavesdropped?"

David threw his arms out in frustration, "*Yes*, but I had no idea I shouldn't have. The spell I used is for Necromancers to send their ghost out, so they might spy for them. I used it so Carrie could hang out with you; I had no idea you were hiding so much. You want to screw Michael *so much*, that you would have at the beach… if it weren't for the fact it was the wrong man. Or how about the fact Alice has convinced you that you should stop killing The Order because… I don't even know why. Maybe it's because she works for them, or it will hurt your vampire morals too much."

I crossed my arms over my chest. I was mad at him, but I knew this was my fault, "Well, now you know the truth, now what?"

David's face hardened, "Nothing, it's over."

I am cold, inside and out for the only reason this bothered me came straight to my lips, "What about Jason?"

"Of course, you're all to precious revenge, how could I forget?" He walked up to me, nose to nose, as if he were looking for a fight. His voice was hollow, "I'll help you, for old times' sake… and one other thing."

"What?"

"Jason is in The Order, I want him dead. I need your help, but he's not the only Order member that hangs out at his work. You do this my way, we kill everyone, and then you kill Jason. One last mission, then we split."

I asked, "And Carrie?"

"She chooses," He said coolly.

"Deal," I held my hand out, but he just turned and walked away.

On the flight home, we didn't sit next to each other. Carrie sat next to me. Carrie kept on telling me everything was going to be all right. I do believe she was trying to convince herself of that.

"I'm sorry Carrie," Was the only response I had for her.

Carrie looked into her lap, "Don't be; if it weren't for my stupid ears…"

I squeezed her hand, "It's not your fault; it will all work out. You'll see."

After the flight, I didn't see Carrie or David. I ended up hanging out with Ezra, Charlotte and Alice. Michael and Lea took off for some Christmas getaway. Lea would have a much better Christmas if she got away from Charlotte and Alice. I was having mixed emotions about the breakup. I wanted to see Michael, but I was not ready.

I did exchange gifts with my vampire friends. They all went in on one gift for me, a dress. It was no ordinary dress, that's for sure. It had Alice's design input; it looked to be old. It had two layers, the outer layer being black, while the under layer was white. The dress hung right below the knees; it also came with boots that came up to my knees. The boots were black leather that fit tightly over my lower legs with buckles at the top and ankle. The dress had black strings that crisscrossed in the front. Below the black strings, the material was white. The dress had full length sleeves that went all the way down to my wrists. The shoulders were large and puffy.

What was really amazing about this dress was the fabric. It was magical as they told me, able to resist tears and even fire.

Alice said, "If you have to fight… you need to look good doing it."

I had a good time, but my mind was still full of worry for my friend. It was the next night when David called me. Over the phone he said, "I have sent your flight info and where you will be staying. We attack on January sixth; that's three days from now. Be ready."

I was excited about killing Jason, but not sure how I felt about dealing with David. He was so mad at me; I hated for things to end like this. I had really hurt him, and I had to find a way to make it right.

Or did I?

Chapter 19 Killing Jason Black
殺害

Looking over at the clock it was 7:00 pm, I had slept in. I needed to get ready and meet up with David; no doubt he was already waiting for me. Tonight I would have a small piece of my heart back. Tonight I would kill one of my killers.

I put on some black stockings, followed by my new dress. Alice had ordered it special for me; it was a Christmas present. I finished this outfit off with tall black boots. I looked a little old fashioned, but who cares? I wasn't going to make friends.

David had been waiting outside my door at the hotel where we had checked in. He was wearing his usual getup: black jeans, Doc Martens, black T-shirt and long overcoat. He looked me over, and then said, "Ready?"

"Yes, do I look nice?"

He didn't answer me; instead, he started walking off. I shut the hotel door, and then followed after David, "How far?" I yelled at him as I hurried to catch up.

"The club up the street, we will walk there. While you were sleeping, I took care of all the details… just follow my instructions, you'll know when to start killing."

"Okay."

I walked behind David as we entered the club. I couldn't let David's mood distract me from the task at hand. I had never been in a strip club before, and wasn't really excited about being in this one, but we had work to do. I felt my head spin from all the movement and different types of smells that were bombarding my senses. David moved over to a small booth; he guided me into my seat before taking his place across from me. At least he was showing some manners.

We both sat quietly across from each other scanning the room. The place was crazy busy; women danced on three different stages. There were women and men here of all ages, in all different stages of drunkenness. There were even male strippers for the ladies; none of them were on stage, but a couple of them were dancing for a group of women across from us.

I pushed my black hair out of my face; it had really grown on me. Plus, depending on what outfits and how much makeup we wore, it was hard to recognize us. Our eyes made contact; David gave me a reassuring head nod. He was sure that our plan would work, and tonight I would finally get another piece of my revenge.

The waitress came over to our table. She gave me a questionable look; they carded us at the door, but as David ordered two beers, she gave me a look that said you must have a fake ID. She left to get our drinks without a word. It was a good thing; I could use a drink to calm my nerves.

When the waitress came back with our drinks, David paid her. I picked up the cold beer; I felt the liquid slide down my throat. I leaned back in my seat and tried to relax. I looked around at all the faces as we sat in silence.

I pulled out a pack of cigarettes and lit one up. Everyone in Vegas smoked, and half the people in this bar were smoking, but, without even looking, I knew David was giving me that disapproving look. It's not like cigarettes can hurt me, in fact, I was pretty sure I did it just to annoy David because the nicotine did nothing for me. I healed too fast to even enjoy the chemical effects I was supposed to get from smoking. I was mad at him. I knew the smoking would bother him, and I knew that I was being petty.

An hour passed by, yet no sign of our prey. I sipped another drink of my second beer, and then lit up another smoke. The last hour had been educational, that's for sure. In my mind, I could classify everyone that went to strip bars in three different categories.

First, there were the younger crowds that came just to party and get drunk. I noticed that strippers didn't pay them as much attention as the others. Most likely, the reason for that, was that they liked to spend their money on booze more than shoving it in the strippers' pants.

The second kind of person I noticed wasn't having the same kind of fun. This customer gave more money to the strippers and spent a lot more time watching the girls dance as they slowly drank the night away. They didn't hoot and holler; instead they stared with hunger in their eyes. In a way, you can say they were here for the sex, unlike the first type of customer that was here for the booze and party.

The third kind of customer that I had noticed was sad. All of them were middle age men, and all of them had an empty look in their eyes; not necessarily craving sex, but seeking companionship.

The black light helped make the girls' skin look smoother and unblemished; the strong smell of cheap perfume hid the smell of sweat. These men searched for something they couldn't find. A dancer would dance for them, and they looked on with hope and need.

The women would come and sit at their table and talk with them, and would make them feel as if they really liked them for who they were and not what they looked like. I could hear all the conversations going on. All the Johns asked how their schooling was going. I guess all women who stripped, 'did it to get through school', yeah right. The women knew these men's lives in great detail as they absorbed their hard earned cash. How sad to play on their loneliness I thought, and to think, all I wanted was their blood. Who's really sucking the life out of them?

Finally, he walked in, Jason Black. I had forgotten how big he really was. He strolled into the bar from the employee entrance. He was wearing blue jeans with a gray T-shirt, with a black leather vest over it. His long blonde hair was tied in a ponytail; his hair was so much like mine in length, color and thickness. That's where the similarities ended. The man was built like a tree trunk. His arms were huge; he wasn't cut like some bodybuilder; in fact, he was overweight. Under all that fat was a powerful man.

Alex McDonald, a good friend of the late Tony Abbott, (David's stepfather) had been instrumental in locating Jason. Alex was human and as David and I found out, he was one hell of a detective. It had taken him over a year, but, he finally brought one of my killers into my sight. If he had not found out what Jason really was, we would be in serious trouble right about now. Now that I was looking at him, it wasn't so hard to believe that he was a troll.

Alex had some great leads on the Smith brothers; David told me that he would most likely know everything by the end of the month. Of course Alex still had little or no information on the biker gang's old leader, Alex. I never had found out what his last name was and the fact that he had shared names with the detective made conversations confusing. So now we all just referred to him as, the 'Evil' Alex. Of course after the ship, he would know that I was looking for him.

Looking at Jason reminded me of how I felt when I first sat down in Devon's class. My stomach hurt, and I felt like running away and crying, and when those emotions passed, a new emotion flooded in… rage. Soon, I would fill some of this emptiness in my heart, with the blood of this animal.

David had a plan, so I shoved all the emotions away. I worked best when I was calm. Over the last year and half David and I had successfully attacked and destroyed dozens of The Order's groups.

"Ready?" David asked.

"Oh yes, let's get this party started." I finished off my beer, and was ready for the show to begin.

A man in a dingy suit strolled in, and then took a seat at the bar, "Is that him?" I asked David, even though I was pretty sure that was our bait; it was obvious what he was, if you knew what to look for.

David finished his beer, "Yep, I'll go make the phone calls, and make sure the trucks are in position and ready."

"Alright," I responded as David got up. He headed to the back of the bar towards the restrooms, where the pay phones were. It wouldn't be long now. David returned to his seat; he didn't acknowledge me or look at me. My revenge is so close I could taste it. "It's time," David announced, "See you in a little bit."

David got up and left; my attention was now on the man with the dingy suit sitting at the bar. He had ordered a beer and had sat there quietly, taking small drinks now and then. He was the most lifelike Undead that David had ever made.

David had come up with some new death magic. What he ended up with were zombies, or at least that is what he called them. I hadn't even heard about this new ability until the flight to New York; before he was pissed off at me. He informed me that these new creatures were better than the undead, he had risen in the past.

The zombie started to yell at the bartender. I could hear the zombie perfectly from where I sat; he sounded like he was drunk because of all the slurring of words, but I knew that zombies always sounded like that.

He yelled at the surprised bartender, and then threw his beer bottle at him. The bartender moved fast, the bottle smashed against the back of the bar. One of the other customers moved in to stop the zombie, but the zombie tossed the customer onto the ground.

These zombies were made with vampire blood, so they were much stronger than humans; even if that wasn't the case, these creatures would feel nothing so they could rip their own muscles apart while exerting all their strength.

The next part of the plan was now moving into action; that is Jason moved into action. He was the bar's bouncer; being a troll, he must have thought that this has been the easiest job ever. As Jason strolled quickly over to deal with the man in the suit, I was sure that he was confident that this was just another drunken ass he would throw out of the bar, without incident. Jason grabbed the zombie by his arm, and then spun him around; now they were facing each other. Jason towered over the zombie, then began yelling, "Look asshole, you have two choices, one…"

Jason was a little surprised when the zombie attacked him. He swung his arms wildly and clawed at Jason's clothes. Jason smiled as the zombie attacks bounced off of his huge body with no effect. Even with the extra strength, a zombie couldn't hurt a troll.

Jason grabbed the zombie by the shoulders and lifted him into the air; he was squeezing the zombie while smiling. Jason was having a good time; if that dumb brute had paid close attention to his adversary, he may not have played into our trap so easily, but that's why our plan will work, because some people do exactly what you expect them to do.

Stage two kicked in as Jason carried the zombie toward the door. The zombie's head fell off, landed on the floor bounced twice, rolled a few feet more, and came to a stop.

Now at this point there were a lot of patrons at the bar watching Jason carry this guy off. The looks on all their faces, including Jason's, was priceless.

Jason dropped the body on the ground, took two steps back. Then he spread his arms apart, and started saying, "I didn't do that... it just fell off, I didn't do it."

I found myself laughing out loud; of course the music was still so loud, I doubt anyone could hear me. Half the bar was in shock; the other half was clueless, still drinking or watching the girls dance.

Stage three began; instead of blood pouring out of the body; a green cloud of gas started to ooze out. The head began to smoke too, I took a deep breath; the gas was poison. It wouldn't kill me, but it could still make me sick and slow me down. I didn't need to breathe; in fact, the only reason I took the breath is so that I could smell, talk and make a whistling noise if it became too quiet.

The music stopped as the lights went off; the emergency lights came on, but half of them didn't work. You have to love old night clubs, no one checking up on the safety lights. If this would have been a normal power outage no one would have freaked, and the little bit of light would have not been a big deal, but this was no normal night. The screaming and people trying to rush out lead to disarray, and the smoke was deadly as people coughed and fell to the ground.

Jason was trying to keep order with help from the bartender, but it was a fool's errand. The bartender started to choke on the smoke. It had no effect on Jason and me, and David had known this.

The next part of this plan was in effect as the undead were now pouring in through the doors. They were pushing the strippers and customers back into the bar. The smoke filled the air, and the humans were dropping like flies.

Of course the humans that were dying from the smoke were starting to get up, get up as zombies. The zombies rushing in the doors were biting any customer trying to escape, so they too would soon join the ranks of the undead. The poison smoke carried the disease, and David could weld the undead with his power.

I had stood up and was getting ready for my part, when a male stripper stepped out in front of me coughing. His back turned to me, so I thought... why not? I grabbed him, pulled him to me, and then sank my fangs into his neck. I drained him dry and tossed his body to one side, then wiped the blood off of my mouth.

Across the room Jason was smashing and tossing the undead zombies. It was time, time for Jason to die. I flashed over to him, and then slashed him a few times. I ripped his clothing as my nails dug into his flesh, but the slits in his flesh closed, with no blood to boot.

Jason swung at me as I slashed at his skin; I was too fast for him to hit. After I was sure I had his attention, I jumped into the air, then spun into a back flip and landed on the bar without a sound.

Now Jason was about thirty feet in front of me, the zombies were still grabbing at him, but it was no more than just a small nuisance to the troll. He eyed me trying to figure out who I was, then he said, "Little vampire, give me your name… then I'll know who I killed."

I smiled a wicked smile as I stared at him still perched on top of the bar. "What name would you like? The name I go by now, or the name I went by when you killed ME?"

Jason looked confused, "I don't recall killing you… wait, you do look like… nope… I don't remember you, but I'll tell you what little vampire, after I finish killing you tonight, I will try harder not to forget you."

"Name's Melabeth, and I don't care if you remember me; I remember you, and now you will pay for what you have done."

Jason smiled as he threw off some more zombies, and then he yelled, "Let's see what you're made of."

David had come back into the bar; his eyes were green, and he was surrounded by his zombies. He was standing behind Jason, and Jason was too busy watching me to notice David coming in. David held up his arm, and in his hand was the sword. He threw it through the air, over Jason's head; I caught it with my right hand.

This was not a normal sword; I haven't had a chance to see it before this very moment. I had practiced with swords with Ezra. The sword was similar to the one I had been practicing within size and shape, but that is where their similarities ended. The sword was a Viking style sword; it was considered a one handed sword, but I could fit both of my hands on the handle. The hand guard was small, but it was made out of one thick piece of steel. The blade was only about three feet long; it was straight with a slight taper to the blade and sharp on both sides. The metal of the blade really caught my eye; the blade looked like the grain of wood. One grain was the color of light gray and the other was black with strange green lights flowing through the grain. It looked like hundreds of green boats going down dark rivers.

I quickly brought my attention back to Jason; he was grinning at me like this whole thing was amusing to him, and I flashed forward.

I popped out right in front of him; he swung at me, but I was ready for that. I dropped down and rolled right under his swing; I came up to my feet and spun my sword around in an arc.

Jason was already swinging the same arm back at me; he planned on backhanding me, but my sword was ready. I took his hand off at the wrist.

I flashed a few yards back as Jason yelled in pain.

The sword made a sound, kind of like the ringing of a bell. It was strange, but I wasn't worried about it. David had told me that this was a magic sword, and it would not break.

Jason bent over, picked up his severed hand. Troll wounds were strange. There was no blood; instead, his skin was wrapped around what appeared to be red jelly, or maybe Jell-O. And in the center of the Jell-O I could see white where his bone was. Jason put his severed hand back on, and, in seconds, it melted back onto his arm.

Jason laughed, "You may not know, but I am a troll, little vampire. You can chop me up all day, and my body parts will pull themselves back together."

"I know that; there are other ways to kill a troll. Chopping them up just helps me feel better." I said this, and then smiled as large as I could.

The look on his face changed from smug confidence to uneasy. He hadn't thought I knew what he was, and therefore he wasn't afraid of me. He decided to try to play it safe, "Another time little vampire." With that he tried to head toward the exit, but the undead surged to meet him. He grabbed the first few zombies and threw them out of his way, but he was a fool, because now his back was turned to me.

I flashed the distance between us; as soon as I came out of the flash my sword flew through the air and sliced through his left knee. I cut his leg in half, causing him to fall to the ground with a crash. He immediately pushed himself up using his arms and then swung at me.

I jumped straight up and spun upside down at the same time.

I had learned some new tricks from Charlotte since I had learned how to fly. It was more like floating; changing the way gravity pulled on my body. I landed on the ceiling with my feet then ran a few feet forward, pushed off of the ceiling spun around and returned gravity to normal.

I landed behind Jason and with a quick slash of my sword; I took his arm off right at the elbow.

Jason screamed and it sounded like it was between pain and rage. He had managed to pick himself up on one foot, and his other leg that had been dismembered, now moved on its own to reattach back onto the troll.

The leg never made it.

Two zombies jumped on the piece of leg and dragged it away; at the same time, some more zombies grabbed the dismembered arm and carried it off into the crowd.

"Bring that back," yelled Jason at the zombies. He turned his eyes upon me, "What do you want? What have I done to you?"

"Still don't remember me? Let me give you a clue. The last time you saw me it was 1975, and I was still alive. Ring any bells?"

Jason looked confused, and then his eyes narrowed as if he were looking at me for the first time. His face went slack, and then the troll stuttered out, "The girl, the girl in the movie... the one we killed, Alex killed."

"You raped me; you sat there with a beer in your hand while Alex raped and killed me. You talked about how you'd rather have the money than my life... ALEX MURDERED ME, ALL OF YOU MURDERED ME... and now I will set things right."

The troll fell to his one knee, and looked as if he might cry. "I know, I know what I did, I have changed. I know you owe me nothing, but I got away from Alex and changed my life."

"LIAR," I screamed in rage.

Jason said now with tears in his eyes, "Please forgive me, I will do anything."

"Anything?" I said with a grin.

"Yes, I have changed."

I smiled, "Then do one thing for me."

"What?"

"Die... and burn in hell, you piece of shit." With that I flashed forward and attacked.

Jason caught me with his large arm throwing me through the air and against the wall.

He said with rage in his eyes, "Have it your way, vampire, I didn't have to destroy you, but I will."

I flashed forward again, only this time I sidestepped his swing from his one good arm. Then I followed through with a swing from my sword, taking his last arm right below the shoulder.

The sword rang again as the troll screamed in pain.

As fast as I could, I spun the sword into a large arc, then brought the sword fast and smooth right across his shoulders. His head slowly fell off and dropped to the floor as the sword rang even louder.

The zombies quickly picked up the head and carried it off. David motioned to a group of the undead, and they started to pick up the mass of the troll's body. A couple of zombies held out his last leg; then I cut it off so that the piece of Jason could be moved out to the trucks with ease.

"Let's go," David barked at me. All the zombies headed out of the building carrying pieces of the troll.

We needed to get out of here before friends of Jason showed up and tried to stop us. Trolls merge back together easily, and Jason was not dead, yet. I headed outside to where the truck was and jumped into the passenger seat. A zombie sat in the driver seat ready to drive. We had three box trucks, one for the head, one for the body, and the last one for all the legs and arms.

We were on our way before I knew it. I was in the second truck as David drove the first truck.

It amazed me how the zombie driving my truck and the one behind me could drive so well, but David had explained that he could control them and make them work with him. I didn't understand how these zombies David had been making were different from the undead, he had risen from the cemetery over a year ago. David had done nothing but practice his art and magic. He had been developing new Necromancer magic, and I wasn't sure how I felt about it, but Alice and the rest of the Whites had no problem telling me that David was bad news.

We had been in the city of Albuquerque, New Mexico. We were heading back to Las Vegas on I-40. I stared out the window into the vast open desert as we left the city behind. With my eyes the stars cast enough light for me to see the desert and its plants. It still looked to be an alien world with the strange shadows and colors that didn't exist when I was alive. If the moon would have been up, it would be like a day, but without the moonlight, it looked more like a cloudy day, gray and mysterious, with its own beauty. I can't say that being a vampire I miss the sun, because I don't.

We would be stopping soon, and there were only a few more hours before daylight. It wasn't long before we got off the highway, and then traveled for a little ways down some old forgotten road. The trucks found their way onto a dirt road. After another twenty minutes we came to a clearing; in less than an hour the sun would be up. I could already see the light in the sky.

I watched David get out of his truck and start to command the zombies to unload the trucks. That is when I took notice of my zombie driver. I hadn't really looked at him; I mean, who would, and it's just an animated corpse. It was Aaron Reite; just looking at him was like ripping off a scab. David was being a real dick; he had done this on purpose.

I got out of the truck slamming the door shut; I was still carrying my sword. I walked toward David and came to a stop; I was standing next to him. I didn't look at him; I just stared in front of me at all the zombies holding pieces of Jason.

The pieces of Jason were trying to come back together, but the zombies had a good hold. It was kind of funny watching the zombies sway back and forth fighting the invisible tug of the troll's body parts; it kind of looked like a strange dance.

The sun was almost up and the sky was full of light, enough to make me put on my sunglasses. They were the sunglasses Michael had given me for my birthday. I didn't wear them around David, but, after seeing Aaron the zombie as my driver, well, I didn't care if David liked it or not.

I looked over at David; he was staring at the zombies with a smirk on his face. "Looks to be a beautiful day, wouldn't you say?"

"I hate you… how could you? You know how many nightmares I have about that man."

David chuckled darkly, "All these zombies are your kills. Why cry about just one?" I looked over the crowd of faces and remembered none of them. Before I could think about it too much, the sun rose above the horizon, and two things happened at the same time.

First, my sword turned into a black cloud and quickly blew away, leaving me nothing but the hilt. Second, the parts of the troll stopped moving and a gray color washed over them as they turned to stone.

The zombies dropped the different pieces onto the ground. I walked over to the body and kicked it with such force it exploded into dust and smaller fragments. I had hit hard enough to break my leg, but my leg quickly healed. After that I took each piece and smashed it in turn, saving the head for last.

I picked up the stone head and looked into the monster's eyes that had so coldly raped me, who had watched me die, with a smile and a hard on. I crushed his head into the ground and then headed towards the truck.

David called out, "Do you need help finding your way home?"

"I know my way back." I pulled the Aaron zombie out of the cab of the truck and onto the ground. I drove away without a backward glance.

I drove to the highway, then headed west toward Vegas. I stopped at the first hotel and checked in.

I was tired and emotional; I was too tired to work through all my emotions… the rage of seeing Jason, the horror of seeing Aaron and the pain that David made me feel. I kept on thinking that I should feel some relief from all this. Shouldn't the death of Jason bring me some joy, inner peace maybe? Yet, right at this moment… I needed sleep, that's what I needed, sleep.

In my hotel room, I showered, put on some nice pajamas, closed the drapes as tight as I could, then crawled under the sheets. As I lay there quietly my mind wandered back, back to when I killed Aaron.

The memory was fresh, even though it was eight months ago. I had nightmares afterwards, reliving Aaron's last hour over and over again. David and I had killed so many Order members. David had pointed out that all the zombies were my kills, I had no idea how many. I knew before I fell to sleep, I knew what I would dream about. Damn David, didn't he know how cruel he was being.

Yes, yes, he did.

Chapter 20 The bow

弓

I awoke...

I sat in a crummy hotel room. David had been my first, my first lover, and my first friend. I wiped the tears away. I am sad for my loss.

I couldn't take anymore of this... pity party. I just killed Jason Black and was close to killing the Smith brothers. Soon I would have my revenge upon my father and Evil Alex. Once these deeds are done, I can begin my life; I can find love and keep it.

I lay back down and wrapped myself up in the blankets; after a few minutes I fell back to sleep. I was not in a dream about Aaron Reite. Instead, I'm awake inside the library. I hadn't been back here since the Island.

I'm not excited about telling Nicks about the killing of Jason Black. We killed a lot of people in that bar, and Nicks will be pissed if he finds out about it, but what he doesn't know about, won't hurt him.

I was learning my way around the library. The place was huge, and the more time I spent here the more I learned. There were books about anything I could think of, and I came to find out there were a lot of ghosts who wandered these halls. None of them would talk with me; in fact, as soon as they saw me they would run through a wall or disappear.

I decided, since I was here, I would do some more exploring. I found a staircase behind a doorway that I had never seen before. I headed up the winding set of stairs. The staircase came out in the middle of the floor inside a large room. Unlike the lower floor, there was a stone ceiling, and it was decorated with paintings of the sky and mountains.

This place didn't seem to follow the rules of space, because below me the lower floors had an open sky for a ceiling. I once thought this was a dream; now I believe this was a place of magic. There were more hallways that led away from this room; I do believe this place has no end.

As I slowly walked around the room, it took me a minute to take in all of what I was seeing. There were books of course, and two very large fireplaces at both ends of the room. Against one wall, there was something new; a table stood with a single chair in front of it. On the table were glass beakers and all kinds of measuring tools. Glass bottles of all colors and sizes sat on shelves above and around the table. On the glass bottles there were labels, but they had strange symbols on them that I couldn't identify. It didn't take a scientist to know that this was someone's lab for experiments.

On the other side of the room, I saw yet another item that I had not witnessed in this place, a full length mirror. Now that I thought about it, I hadn't seen one mirror anywhere. I walked over and looked at myself in the mirror and gasped at what I saw. There I stood, looking like a vampire; but eyes were full of light. It looks as if there was a flashlight behind my eyes, filling them with light. It was as if I were looking at my spirit. The thought sent shivers up my spine.

I walked away from the mirror and continued to take in the contents of this room. I worked my way over to the other side of the room to the second fireplace. Once again, I noticed a couple of odd things; first the fireplace had no fire just some smoke rising out of the ashes. All the fireplaces of this strange place were always lit and blazing with heat and fire, but not this one. Second, there was a stand placed on a small round table right next to the fireplace. On that stand was a violin; it looked delicate and beautiful.

I walked closer and leaned in to get a better look at the instrument when a voice startled me from behind. "I wouldn't touch that; Nicks would not like it if you did."

I turned around to find a young lady standing a few feet away from me. It only took me a second to realize she was a ghost, but it was the first ghost who talked to me; heck, it was the first ghost not to run away. She stood about my height, but she was really thin and straight with not too many curves. She wore a dress that was really dated; it reminded me of some of the outfits that Alice liked to wear; I knew that the outfit came from the eighteen hundreds or older. She stood straight as if someone had attached a steel pipe to her spine; it took no imagination at all to see that she could balance a book on that head. Her hair was brown and pulled into a tight bun on her head where she wore a little blue hat. Her face was long and sharp, but she didn't look to me much older than me.

I guess I took too long to answer her, so she spoke again, "Sorry, didn't mean to startle you, but Nicks would not like you touching his violin."

I was unsure of her, "Thanks, I was just looking... sorry, I didn't catch your name."

The ghost gave me a tight smile, "I am the Bow."

"Your name is the Bow?" I asked.

"No, my name is unimportant, but I am the Bow, I am the Bow to the violin."

I laughed as I teased her. "Oh, that makes sense; well, I am glad to meet you, Bow. I happen to be the String. In a minute my three sisters will be here and we can make some music. Of course that is assuming there is a player."

Her face went tight, "That doesn't make any sense; the violin already has strings, and I am the player."

I shook my head back and forth, "That's not the only thing that doesn't make any sense in this room, I thought you were the Bow?"

As I looked at the spirit, something seemed off besides the fact she thinks she is a bow. It wasn't that other spirits just don't talk to me. There was more to it than that. When I approached a spirit and it noticed me, they would flee. If I saw their faces before they disappeared, it was full of terror. So, I couldn't help but wonder why these ghosts were afraid of me? And, better yet, why she wasn't? As if someone whispered, her name in my ear I knew the spirit's name. I announced, "Elizabeth... that's your name."

The spirit nodded, and then spoke, "Call me the Bow, please. It is what I am; at least that is what I've become. You are so much like your father; I can see Nicks' power in you; the world will never be the same. And to think I was here while he created you, mixing the magic, as he listened to me play." She pointed over at the desk where all the science equipment was.

A lump grew in my throat when I realized what she was saying. I looked over at all the bottles in wonder. I looked back at Bow, "How did he do it?"

Bow shrugged her shoulders as she began to answer me, "I don't know. I don't believe anyone knows now."

"Nicks knows," I disagreed.

She shook her head, "Afraid not, Nicks has had many experiments in making his first child. He worked on it for... well, to be honest, I don't know how long. I have been in this place for hundreds of years, and he was deep in his work when I met him. After you didn't rise, he came up here about eight years ago in a rage; he had all he could take in failed experiments. He grabbed all his scrolls, books and notes; it was his life's work. Then he burned them all." As she said this, she pointed at the fireplace we stood next to; it had no fire but just smoked. "No fire has burned here since that day; I do not know what that means."

"He doesn't even know what I am." My voice sounded like a stretched rubber band.

Bow gave me a sympathetic look, "He knows what you are, and you are his daughter. After the day he burned his life's work, he stopped coming up here; he stopped listening to my music. After the first night you came to us, he changed, more like the old Nicks, the one I used to know."

I couldn't worry about what I was, but maybe Bow could tell me stuff that Nicks would not. "Do you know where this place is?"

"Of course," she simply replied.

"And that is..." I prompted.

She smiled, "When people die, most go to heaven or hell. Some of us get lost and its Nicks' job to help us find our way to the final death. You can do that for spirits as well; that is why the other ghosts hide from you; they hide from the judgment of God."

Hold the phone, what did she say? I was quiet for a moment as I thought of my next question. "Are you saying this is purgatory?"

"I have heard it called that, but Nicks says a better name is the Library or Conscientia. That means knowledge or place of knowledge."

"And did Nicks tell you about God?" I asked.

Bow lost eye contact with me and then looked back at me, "Nicks does not know what waits in the final death, but I have faith," She said this at the same time that she grasped a cross which hung from her neck. "I have faith, and I am ready to go to the final death; everyone I have known is dead and I hope that after all this time I can find forgiveness in the next life."

I wondered what kept her here, "Forgiveness from what?"

Bow gave me a hard look; she was holding back tears. "I murdered my husband, and I was put to death for it; I was afraid to die, so I ended up here. Nicks had pity on me, and loved how I played the violin; when Nicks believes I am ready, he will send me."

Strange, I thought; I always thought this to be some weird dream. I began to think that I might be going somewhere, maybe not my body, perhaps, just my soul, but I was not sure. With Bow here, it made me think of a million more questions, and I have no time for that. I do believe that her knowledge of how this place works is limited, but I bet she could answer another question that I have been wondering about of late.

I had come to notice that I was the only vampire that could see ghosts. I did not let the other Whites in on this at first, but I finally told Alice. She had a small freak out, and I was told never to tell anyone about this no matter what. She didn't tell me why; never seems like people will give me information; I always have to figure it out on my own.

David knew, and Alice was not happy about that, but what could she do? I now believe that my power to see ghosts has something to do with being the daughter of Nicks. I wonder if some other things I do is because of him, like my second sight.

Bow was just staring at me, and she almost looked bored, "Bow?"

"Yes, Melabeth," Bow said with a small smile.

"What kind of magic creature is Nicks?" I asked, but I wasn't sure if I should have. Everyone is always telling me that information was not safe in my head, but I was curious like a cat.

Bow laughed, "Nicks is not a creator; he's an Angel, and that makes you half Angel."

Bow said this with a very straight face; she was serious. Well, so much for getting any more useful information from her. Just as well, curiosity killed the cat, and I have been killed enough lately.

I walked around the room a little bit more; Bow followed behind me quietly, but I still knew she was there. I turned and looked at Bow, "Why not play for me?"

At this, she smiled wide, "I thought you might not ask."

Black dust swirled around her left hand; she was now holding the violin. I looked over and noticed that the violin on the table was gone. A bow came out of her right hand like some sort of cheap magic trick. She began to play.

I understood why Nicks kept her around; the way she played was indescribable. The music vibrated through my body; I felt the music from my ears to my toes. It was wonderful, magical and uplifting. I felt myself smile, and I felt some sort of release. I always loved music; I had never heard the song she played. I felt like singing, so following along with her rhythm, I sang:

When I was young I loved to play
In the grass, and in the hay
I became older and lost the way
I was sold and betrayed

Then my life fades away, fades away,
Then my life fades away, fades away,

I awoke in a brand new age
Ready to play a brand new game
New friends to help me find my way
Revenge is the game I play

Then there life will fade away, fade away,
Then there life will fade away, fade away,

Come along and be my friend
Together we will kill again
Be my friend and play with me
For the game I play, only ends when

Someone fades away, fades away,
Someone fades away, fades away,

Bow finished her song, lowered her violin, "Your voice, it's like no other. The song is a little creepy, but your voice is otherworldly."

I smiled; it was always a good feeling when someone liked and recognized your gifts in life. "Thank you, and the same thing goes for you. I have never heard your equal, or even dreamed that the violin could sound that amazing. No wonder Nicks keeps you around; I could listen to you play for hours."

Instead of being gracious about my praise, Bow looked upset; you would have thought that I just told her she sucked and needed some lessons. "What's wrong? What did I say? I meant it as a compliment."

"I know," Bow sounded whiny or about to cry.

"Then what?" I asked in dismay.

Bow looked around then made eye contact with me. "I was hoping you would not want me around. I was kind of hoping you would send me on. Nicks will not, because he likes my music and company. I am ready, even if he is not ready to send me. I will never live out my regrets here."

She wanted me to send her on, "Sorry, I don't know how. Even if I had the power, I don't have the knowledge."

Bow quickly responded, "You do have the power and it is easy; all you have to do is kill me. Choke me to death, hit me with something, or stab me, whatever. You can touch me; you can destroy me."

I had known that I could hurt Carrie, but I had never thought that I could kill her, and, if Bow was right, then all I had to do was kill her. I could send her on her way. I didn't want to kill her, not because I liked or cared for her so much that I couldn't. I didn't want to go against Nicks' will; he was going to be mad enough about Jason.

I tried to say it softly without hurting her feelings, "Nope, can't help you there, chick. If you want to die, get Nicks to do it." Well, that wasn't as nice as I meant to say it.

Bow's face went all ugly; the violin turned to ash, and then reappeared on the table across the room. Bow disappeared into the wall across the room from me.

I was becoming more powerful all the time; when I had first met Carrie, she could disappear on me, and I couldn't see her. I had come to notice that, when Carrie tried to do that, I could still see her outline; I also could feel her presence. Now that I think about it, some of my powers are very much like Necromancers. I couldn't help but wonder, is Nicks a Necromancer? That didn't add up; there was still more to this, but an Angel?

I walked back over to the table where Nicks had mixed and matched all these different bottles. Whatever was in these bottles was used to make me. I reached over and picked one up. It had strange markings on the label that I couldn't read. I popped the top and took a small whiff.

The scent hit me all at once. It was blood, but unlike any blood I had ever smelled before. I screwed the top back on and tried the next bottle. It was blood as well, but, like the first bottle, there was something different about it, something foreign. I checked the next few bottles, and each was blood and each had some new scent that I had never encountered before.

I had an idea; one of those ideas that made me feel stupid, the kind of idea that made me wonder why I hadn't thought of it before. Ever since I was turned into a vampire I had been thrust from one event to another. I had to rely on these other vampires to tell me how this new world works, but that had not been true when I was still alive.

When I was alive, if I wanted to learn something, I went to the library. It was like that recurring dream I had with me and my dad. I fixed his car by going to the library and learning from books. Of course I did all that so my dad would go to the grocery store. He never even went; as soon as I finished the car, he bragged on me, and then took off with it, with his buddies. He was supposed to go get some groceries. He came back the next day, no groceries, just drugs.

I had learned that if I need to know how to do something I could teach myself. And here I am, in a magical library, and somewhere there had to be an index that could show me the books with the answers. It was time to go exploring.

Where would you find the index cards in a place this big, or perhaps a librarian? I walked down one of the hallways from the room where I had met Bow. I came out into another small room, and, to my amazement, it was full of books. I laughed at this thought.

I picked up an old book, and it wasn't in English. I tossed the book across the room as I said to no one, "Great, I don't even know where the English part of the library is, let alone where you would find 'The Secrets of Melabeth's Life', Volume One."

"Sorry, but no book of that name can be found."

I froze at the sound of the new voice. I spun around looking for the owner of that voice but saw no one. As I looked around the room for the mysterious voice, I saw something I had not noticed when I first walked in.

Across the crowded room, there was another archway. There were books and shelves, tables and chairs all over the room; it had taken a second to take in the whole picture. Now that I had, the archway seemed to go outside. I slowly walked toward the opening. When I came through the archway, I emerged onto a balcony, and what lay before me made me rub my eyes.

I was standing on a balcony attached to what looked like a castle, and the castle sat upon a hill. Green grass and trees raced down the mountain side and down into a valley of grass. The sky had no clouds; it was pitch black and full of stars, yet it was bright as day.

What really made me shake my head is that... I wasn't sure how to describe what I was seeing. It appeared to be people moving from here to there through the trees and across the valley. The people were all out of focus, so badly that you couldn't make them out at all. They didn't look like ghosts to me; the ghosts were never that out of focus.

As I looked over this scene, it became more and more alien to me. The trees were wrong somehow and out of focus, people looked as if they walked right through them.

I felt Bow come up from behind me; it was something that I was getting used to. Just like Carrie, I had a much better feel for ghosts now. Bow materialized right next to me. She stood there quietly, looking over the balcony. I broke the silence, "What am I seeing?"

Bow answered, "Death perhaps, not even Nicks can go there. This place stands guard between the world of the living and the dead. It is the door between life and death."

"I knew this wasn't a dream," I was saying to myself.

Bow answered my statement, "Of course not."

I looked over at Bow and remembered the strange voice that I just heard. "Bow, did you just speak to me earlier when I asked for a book?"

Bow looked at me funny, "If you asked for a book, then the library would have answered you, I don't know where any of the books are."

I responded sarcastically, "Oh, the library answered me; what was I thinking... of course it did."

Bow looked at me with a small grin, "Who else could it be? Let me guess; you don't believe in magical talking castles."

I realized how stupid I sounded, and then I realized how crazy all of this was. "So you're telling me, that all I have to do is ask for a title of a book, and the castle will find it for me."

Bow smiled, "All you have to ask is for the subject matter and the castle will take you to your book. Good luck." With that, she walked away and disappeared again.

I walked back into the room and decided to give it a try. "I would like a book about vampires and ghosts."

At first nothing, then a woman's voice sweetly answered me. "Lower lever section 56473 shelf 12 Row 9B."

Wait, that's no help I thought. "Where is that?"

The voice answered me again, "Right this way."

And with that a door opened in front of me. Of course, there wasn't a door there two seconds ago, but now there was. I really feel like I am in Wonderland. I walked through the door and into pitch black. Across the empty space, I saw another door. This reminds me of the first time I came to the library, I had awakened in the black, and I had seen a door standing all by itself. This was the same thing. As I walked toward the door, I glanced behind me, and the door, I had come through was gone.

When I entered the room, I knew where I was. I was really close to where Nicks hangs out; I had walked through this area before. The roof once again was stars and there were shelves of books everywhere. Before I had a chance to ask the library for more directions, a book slid off a shelf and onto the floor.

I walked over and picked it up. The book was called, 'The Difference between Ghosts, Vampires and Ghouls', by Erick Freyman. Well, it was a place to start, so I found a comfortable chair and began to read.

I only scanned through the book; I found it too boring to read. I did learn a few things from the book, and now I had some questions for Nicks as well.

I had one more idea, "Library, please find me a pen and paper."

A drawer in an old desk slid open. I walked over and was not surprised to find what I had just asked for. I drew a couple of the symbols that I could remember from the bottles that I had found. "Library, please find me a book that can translate these symbols into English."

The library once again gave a long bunch of numbers with a shelve location, but, once again, I asked for directions. It only took a few minutes to travel across the library to the book. The book was old, and it was falling apart. I had to be very careful with it as I took it over to a desk to take a closer look at it.

I opened it up and found it was full of translations of symbols I saw in English. It took me a little while to find one of the symbols that I had seen. The symbol stood for Fairy. Great, so, in short, Nicks had been mixing magical creatures of all kinds trying to create some sort of new thing. He had burned all his records; I wonder if he would remember what he had done me with. I kind of felt a little sick as I walked away from the book. Maybe I don't want to know everything. I never wanted to be a one of a kind; I just wanted to be like everyone else. I headed to go see Nicks, and I couldn't help but feel alone.

Nicks was hanging out in a new part of the library. It was nice with a lot of fireplaces and couches; now that I thought about it, that describes most of the library in one degree or another, and a roof of stars, so many more stars than I ever saw at night. It was like I was above the planet and atmosphere. Nicks was reading when I walked up to him. I knew he knew I was here; he always did. He put a bookmark in his book and shut it. I spoke first, "So, how's it going?"

Nicks stared at me for a minute and then answered me. "It's been better; what have you been up to?"

Crap, I was hoping he wouldn't ask, "Nothing really. The same old thing really, you know."

Nicks lifted one eyebrow, "Do I? Do I know?"

"Do you?" I nervously responded.

"Why don't you sit down and tell me." He said this as he gestured to an open seat next to him.

I sat down, then decided I didn't really want to talk about it. "You know it doesn't really matter; I know you wouldn't like it, and you know it too. Let's just leave it at that."

Nicks face was stern, but he didn't sound mad, "Okay, since the killing of innocent people is not even worth talking about. What would you like to talk about?"

How did he know? The shame must have been all over my face because Nicks then added, "This bloodbath wasn't your idea, was it? What I can't understand is, why? Why would you go along with a plan that killed so many people? Is revenge so important to you?"

All I could squeak out was, "Yes."

Nicks was quiet for a second, he said in a calm, soft voice, "This must stop. There are other ways to get you justice; you can't go into a strip club and kill the entire club and call it justice. Your war on The Order has been bloody and horrible. You need to figure out how to bring some peace into your life."

I replied, trying to hold the tears in, "I know... I will find peace, soon enough."

Nicks just shook his head, "Truly?"

My emotions were always so close to anger. I looked away from Nicks and stared into the fire. He didn't interrupt me; he understood. I looked at him, "I will kill whoever I need to, to get back at the men who raped me and killed me. I'm sorry if you don't understand."

It almost sounded like Nicks was about to cry, "If I could only make you understand."

I wanted to trust in him, but I have come across a lot of my own information. I figured it was time he filled in some blanks. "I would love to understand; let's start out with why I drain life like a magic user collects manna. You know it's no secret, as soon as I got to Vegas and I was near the dead spot, then I needed to feed like the rest of the vampires. And while you're explaining that, you can tell me how I see ghosts. At first, I thought it was a vampire thing, but now I know it is not."

Nicks stood up and started to pace, and, as he passed, he spoke. "You do not pull power from dead spots. Like the one in Vegas, the one the Necromancer should know better than to screw with. I have heard they are planning on building a pyramid there."

I watched Nicks pace and then informed him, "Your information is right. They break ground soon. They plan on having it open, for business next year."

"That is an unfortunate choice."

I asked my original question, "Other dead places do not have magic or manna either. I thought I was pulling my power from manna?"

Nicks stopped pacing, looked at me, then he thoughtfully, "No, I don't believe so; I believe your power comes from death."

I was taken aback. "What do you mean death? And what do you mean you don't believe so, like you don't know for sure, or you're guessing?"

"Calm yourself," Nicks urged, "Yes, you are right; when you were made, you became one of a kind. There is no way I could have foreseen all of what you can and cannot do. First, you will find that your power never comes to you during the day; I believe that you are draining spirits. That's how you survived fifteen years in the ground; the transformation took much longer than I could have imagined, but the only reason you survived it, is from the power. A power that I had no idea you would have."

"I watched the video of my death, you did not make me," I accused.

Nicks shook his head, "Not entirely. I am afraid you are an enigma to me."

It all made sense now; I wasn't even a vampire, and no one knew what I was, or what I would become. My voice sounded empty as I asked, "And the ghosts? Why can I see them?"

Nicks looked at me as if he was hoping that this conversation wouldn't go there, "I can't answer that in full, but I will try to make you understand. I had been hoping that you hadn't even noticed that other vampires couldn't see ghosts. How did you figure it out?"

I was upset; how could he not tell me, why couldn't he tell me? I know that I should trust him, but it was hard. I told him, "Well, it was a couple of months after being in Vegas. Alice likes to come to my room at night and try to mess with me. I don't always use my second sight, so sometimes she gets me good. I know it was her way of testing me; she was trying to figure out ways around my defenses. One night when she was over I tried to introduce her to Carrie. Alice's response was that the silly ghost wasn't showing herself. Carrie had no idea why she couldn't see her. Then Alice explained to me that she didn't like ghosts and how she didn't want anything to do with my boyfriend's spirits. It was then that I explained to Alice that Carrie was not David's ghost, but my friend."

Nicks eyes widened, but he kept his voice steady, "And what did she say?"

I answered Nicks' question, "She asked me for every little detail, and then told me never to speak about it again. She made mention that I should probably kill David, or, at the very least, make sure David understood that I would kill him if he ever made mention of it to anyone. Side note, now that she has my blood in her, she not only can see ghosts, but use her power upon them. Carrie hides from her now."

Nicks sighed, "What's done is done."

"Tell me what it means?" I demanded.

Nicks eyes, that always had this red light in them, were now burning with fire. I felt three inches tall when he said with a booming voice, "It means you are my child; it means there is more to come... and it means you must find your way soon, before it is too late."

I wasn't sure what to say. I felt like I was shrinking under those eyes. I was working up a response when he waved his arm through the air. It felt as if someone let all the air out of the room. I felt myself being pulled through the dark.

As I lay in the dark I heard Nicks' voice call out to me, calmer and full of love. "Find your way, love; greatness is in you; it's up to you."

Chapter 21 The Sword
剣

After my terrible time with my father Nicks, I was glad to be awake. I hated his disappointed in me.

I looked out the hotel room window, the sky was red, and it wouldn't be long before nightfall. I wished to live in the dark; I wished to fly. Forget driving back; I wanted to feel the wind in my hair as I sailed through the sky. It would take a lot longer to return to Vegas, but I was in no hurry.

I laid out an outfit and then got dressed. I put on the same dress I had on the night before. That is after I cleaned the blood off. I had my tall boots next to the bed as I laid out my trench coat. Ezra had made this for me; it was black leather and fit me tightly around the waist when closed. It also had knives hidden throughout the garment. I was packing the rest of my stuff into a bag and half considering just throwing it away. The extra weight would affect how high I could go.

Flying was more like floating; vampires could make themselves weightless. It's kind of the opposite thing we do when we make ourselves flash. When we flash, Ezra believes that there are particles breaking apart, and that's how vampires move so fast. When we make ourselves weightless, we are so strong that, when we jump, it looks like we fly away from a human perspective. It may not be actual flying, but it is fun.

I can get at least two hundred feet up in one jump, but that wouldn't get me anywhere, so I have to jump in an arc. It's really fun when I jump off high places like buildings and cliffs. Even though I can make myself weightless, I can't make items that I am carrying weigh nothing.

I had nothing but clothes in the bag anyway; I was about to toss it into the corner of the room when I remembered I put the handle of my magic sword in there. I fished it out and looked at it; I wonder if it will turn back into a sword at night. I really don't know how this thing works, and David didn't tell me. I laid the hilt on the table; I would wait until after dark before putting it in my pocket.

I was ready to go; I looked outside, and the sky was red. I walked over to the table where the hilt laid, still no sword. Well, maybe it has to be completely dark; I mean I would hate for this hilt to turn into a sword when it was in my pocket. I guess I will just carry it, so I picked it up.

I was about to head toward the door and leave, when I heard crying coming from the floor on the other side of the bed.

I walked around slowly, a little spooked.

When I came around the bed and could see who was crying, I froze. There Carrie sat, leaning against the wall with her knees drawn up to her chest. Crying softly like she was in pain, or that she lost someone dear.

What was she doing here?

A few thoughts went through my head really quickly. First, I hadn't seen Carrie when David and I had taken on the troll. What a great friend I was. I had been so preoccupied that I didn't even notice her missing. Second, this was some more cruelty of David's; why else would she be here with me.

I came to one knee and gently laid a hand on Carrie; I tried to soothe her, "Carrie dear, it's me, Melabeth. Are you okay? Can I help you?"

Carrie slowly lifted her head; it took her a moment as if she was trying to figure out who I was. "Melabeth, it was awful, so damned awful. It was like dying again. I had no idea it would be like that, or as God as my witness I wouldn't have done it. I will tell you this; that there David, is a no good rat to talk me into that."

I asked, "I don't understand Carrie, what did David have you do? Why are you here? Is it something to do with this magic sword?"

Carrie started laughing; she was laughing so hard she was crying again. Wow, she was worse off than I thought. "Carrie, what's so funny? What's wrong with you?"

Carrie forcibly controlled her laughter and then said through giggles, "You sound like me. Twenty questions and all; then I realized how annoying that is." She went back to crying, "It's not every day you come to realize that you're so annoying, and that no one cares if they hurt you."

With that, I took her in my arms and held her to me. I understood that David was mad at me, but he has gone too far, and now I'm pissed. I moved Carrie to the edge of the bed, and, after a few minutes, she had control of herself.

I also noticed she was now wearing the same dress as when I first meet her. Without David's Necromancer power, she was weaker and could only appear as she did in death.

Concerned I asked Carrie, "Now that you are calm, tell me what's going on, and what David has done?"

Through a few sniffles Carrie explained, "He said you' all would need a magic weapon to defeat the troll in battle. You know I would do anything for you... don't you?"

I smiled, "I never doubted it for a minute, but I never wanted you to hurt yourself."

Carrie's face was sad, "Well, I really didn't either. David told me he could turn me into a spirit sword. Using my spirit, I would make a weapon that couldn't be broken, well except for during the day. He didn't tell me... that I would feel the pain of the person you cut. I felt everything, and every time you cut him, I screamed, but you couldn't hear me."

When she said that, I remembered how the sword rang like a bell when I cut the troll up. Now I realized that was Carrie's screams. I looked at Carrie, "I am so sorry."

Carrie smiled at me, "No need to apologize; you didn't do anything. It was that no good, rotten Necromancer, bless his little heart."

I felt a wave of guilt come over me, "Well, if I were honest…"

"You knew?" Carrie's eyes grew big.

Unable to keep eye contact, my admission came out in a rush, "Yes, no… maybe. David told me he was going to make a magic weapon, so I could defeat Jason. He told me that it would hurt someone to do it. I told him I didn't care; just make the weapon. I did it, so I could have my revenge. I never thought he meant you."

Carrie's face looked so hurt, "I understand… you got to do what you gotta."

I looked in her eyes, "I am really sorry, and I will make this up to you. This is entirely my fault; David would have never done this if I hadn't hurt him the way I did."

Carrie had a weak smile, "It ain't no thing sweetie. Paybacks a bitch, I think that David owes us both now."

I was walking to the truck. I decide flying would take too long, I needed to go talk to Alex McDonald. That was the detective that helped me out. He was David's stepfather's friend, and I do believe that is where David was getting his information from. I remembered the man's handwriting, it was very original and hard to forget. When David gave me that file for Christmas, it had his handwriting in it.

"Where we going?" Carrie whined from behind me.

Trying not to sound like a bitch, but not really accomplishing it, I spoke fast as I walked. "California, I think it's time that I visited the detective. So far it's always David talking to him and David is leading me around by the nose, time for me to find my own way."

I jumped in the truck and Carrie just simply floated through the cab and came to rest in the passenger seat. "It's about time girl. And since it's such a long ride, we could talk. Hanging with David has been boring me to death, well not literally. You would think since I was the third wheel, I would know a little bit more about what's going on."

I huffed as I responded, "Don't worry, I will fill you in, but meanwhile I need a little quiet time."

Carrie gave me a nasty look, "You know I don't do *quiet* time. That's one thing that ain't fair, neither you nor David like talk-in. Now here I am, crazy ghost girl talking to herself."

"Talking to herself *quietly*," I added.

I ended up talking to her until the early hours. She was a force to be reckoned with when she wanted to talk. We only stopped once at a gas station to fill up the truck and my stomach. It was easy to act like a hooker at a truck stop. In fact, I got lucky because this real perverted truck driver picked me up; he was so excited when he thought I was thirteen. I can't help but wonder what the cab of his truck will smell like when they find him.

Carrie and I talked as I drove, but I kept the subject away from Michael and me. We had got a late start, the sun rose, Carrie disappeared and I kept on driving. I had put on my dark sunglasses; I wanted to drive further before finding a place to rest. It was close to noon and I just crossed the New Mexico border from Texas. I was tired and the sun had popped out from the clouds.

I pulled the truck over at a rest station, and then I went for a short hike away from the rest area. I found a sandy spot where I could bury myself; this was the safest way to sleep. If I fell to sleep in the truck and someone tried to check on me, they would find a corpse. And if I did awake, I could attack them. I was so tired, I hadn't slept well the night before. Every time I visit the library I don't feel as rested the next day.

I finished pulling myself into the sand; it's harder to do than I had thought it would be. I remember the first time Ezra had shown me how. I just love the fact that you get sand inside every crevice and opening on your body, and I do mean every opening. I hated sleeping underground.

Why can't there be more crypts?

Chapter 22 Alex
殺人者

I hate working late.

I better give my wife a call and let her know not to wait up. Since the death, or should I say murder of my best friend Tony, I have been up to my neck in supernatural cases.

I couldn't help thinking back to when all this started for me. I was a little surprised when I was visited by members of our government. They wanted me to run a secret detective agency to keep the supernatural out of the news and the lives of the citizens.

Keeping it out of the news was much easier than I had thought. Apparently they don't print stories of people seeing witches or Bigfoot. In fact, when questioned by the reporters, it's best to tell them the truth. It brought a big smile to my face when my mind wandered back to earlier tonight, just another example of how easy it was to hide the truth.

*   *   *

The reporter asked, "So detective, what happened here? How did this guy get torn up like that?"

It was hard to hold back the smile as I told the reporter the truth, "We believe it to be a young werewolf, and the wounds on the body are consistent with that."

The reporter was agitated, "Why are you trying to cover this up? Is this a cult? Is there a new mass murderer in town? The people deserve the truth."

"They wouldn't know what to do with it… the truth that is." I said this as I walked away from the reporter. He followed me all the way to my car, asking questions the whole way. Even after I shut my door and started my car, I could still hear him shouting accusations through the window.

*   *   *

I chuckled, the truth, no one believes it. The real pain of this job was to deal with the supernatural creatures and try to serve some sort of justice. I had always been against The Order, but now that they are gone, I realized they did have a purpose. Maybe that's why I have this dangerous, horrible job, karma for what I have done.

After Tony was murdered by some of The Order members, I helped his son with information. That little shit ended up murdering and attacking The Order members everywhere. He has a powerful vampire to help him; it's my fault; I really thought he would bring positive change, but instead he brought pain, suffering and fear.

I looked at the clock it was only nine pm, it wasn't that late. I heard the front door to my office open. Beverly was leaving; my secretary would not

163

work past nine, I couldn't really blame her. I heard her yell out, "Goodnight Alex, don't work too late."

I yelled back, "Night, see ya tomorrow." The door shut and it was quiet. I had some phone calls; first I better call my wife.

*   *   *

That was my third yawn and fifth phone call tonight, and it was only fifteen minutes until midnight. So far the only lead I have on the werewolf was that it was one of the Blue Dog gang members. I may have lied to the reporter after all; this was looking a lot less like a young werewolf attack, but a planned hit.

I heard a knock at the front door, but if I ignore them, I'm sure they will go away. Great, now they're pounding, they know I'm here. Reluctantly, I got up to see who it was, and then make them go away. Checked to make sure my 9mm was in its holster resting on my hip. In this line of work it pays to be careful.

My office was in an old building in uptown Banning, CA, it had its challenges. It was more like a closet; once you came out of my office you walked directly by my secretary's desk. In front of my secretary's desk there were a couple of couches set up in a waiting room, but seldom did I have people waiting, so even though they were old, the looked new. The front of our building was only about twenty feet wide and covered with windows, the secretary had already pulled all the long vertical blinds closed. The front door was metal with a glass window. The door was covered with blinds as well.

I walked up and slowly slide the blinds apart to get a look at who was out there. There stood a girl with long black hair, wearing a black dress down to her knees. She had tall black boots. I noticed her fingernails were painted black, and she was wearing a lot of white makeup, black eyeliner and dark red lipstick. She was pretty even though she looked to be going to a Halloween dance; I never was one for the Goth look.

This was not a bad neighborhood as neighborhoods go; there is a theater across the street. There was only one pay phone out front, and sometimes it was out of order. It wasn't uncommon to get kids trying to use my phone to call their folks for a ride home after a movie. Still, something was off; there was no other movement on the street. I doubt a movie had let out, and why would such a young girl be all alone, no matter how safe of a neighborhood. I saw a big box truck illegally parked across the street, and wondered if she had anything to do with it.

Working with witches, werewolves and other supernatural creatures, I had learned to be wary of anyone late at night. This girl was out of place, but I better see what she wants, she could need help. I opened the door a crack, just enough so she could see my face. "Can I help you?" I asked pleasantly, but I kept one hand on my pistol.

"Are you Alex McDonald?" she asked quietly with a soft voice that rang like a bell.

She was a knockout, I stammered out, "Yes, what can I do for you?"

She cocked her head ever so slightly and was staring at me with huge blue eyes. She said a little louder, but still in a kind voice, "I'm Melabeth, I need to speak to you about the men who murdered me... May I come in?"

Oh shit, oh shit, she's a vampire. I've been working the supernatural cases for years, but I've yet to deal with a real vamp. Let alone this one, she killed those men at the Inland Mall in broad daylight. And how many did she kill at the cemetery in Beaumont? And let's not forget all of the reports I've seen come across my desk with her and David destroying hundreds of Order members. I had a witch years ago put protection around my office so she couldn't come in unless I invited her, but then again I would never be able to come out either. This vampire is not afraid to fight during the day, I am so screwed.

She must have read my fright, she softened her face as much as possible and with a very kind voice, "I don't want to hurt you, and I just want to talk. I just want to know what you know."

My voice sounded strained as I stuttered, "Nooot a good time, mmmmaybe later..." the last word faded with no power as it left my lips.

Her face showed no change, but her voice was commanding, "Mr. McDonald I am not going anywhere until I have a chance to speak with you. I have considered all of what you have done for me in the past as a great favor and will not bring any harm to you. Please give me a minute of your time."

I took a breath, maybe it was the please, or she might have used her mind control on me, "Okay... come on in." I opened the door and stepped back without turning my back on her.

She smiled, "Thank you."

She walked into my waiting room without a sound. The boots she was wearing had high heels on them. I had expected a sound when she entered my building, because the floor was ceramic tile. Not one sound came from her as she gracefully came through the door. I had taken a few steps back, she glided up to me and now stood in front of me.

Her smile was pleasant as she stared at me, "Would you like to stand here and talk? Or shall we go into your office?"

Bang... I jumped.

It was only the sound of the door shutting behind her. I could feel my heart trying to escape my rib cage. My vision became blurry around the edges, I was panicking.

I forced myself to regain control, I spun around putting my back to her, "Let's go into my office," I rattled off.

I hurried into my office and around my desk, the whole time the creepy vampire made no noise. I couldn't tell if she was following me, or about to rip my throat out. I spun around; she had already sat in one of the chairs in front of my desk. Damn, they move fast, I almost missed my own chair as I sat. After I situated myself, I tried to look comfortable and calm.

Trying to sound unafraid, "What can I help you with Ms. Melabeth?"

"Just Melabeth please," she looked friendly and her voice was easy and kind. "May I call you Alex?"

"Yes, that would be fine." That was the first thing I had said since she told me who she was, that didn't sound as if I were going to pee myself.

Putting her hands together in her lap, she told me, "Two nights ago I killed Jason Black. I was wondering how close you were to figure out where my other killers might be?"

I was a little confused, "I can't believe you let him live this long. He's been working at that strip club for five years now."

Her face twisted into something not so kind, I felt myself shrink in my chair. With a less calm voice, "Then why didn't you tell us earlier?"

Once again confused and a little worried over my own safety. "Look, I gave David that information a while ago. Along with where the Smith brothers can be found. As much trouble as the brothers still causes... I was thinking you would have taken care of that by now too."

Her face was still angry, but she wasn't looking at me. She was quiet and I wasn't sure what to say. I sat in the most awkward silence of my life. When she looked back up at me, she looked as if she might cry, "My father?"

Not following, I repeated her statement, "Your father?"

Still sounding sad and mad all at the same time, "Yes, my father, what have you found out about him? Do you know where he is?"

This was not good, not good at all. I slowly slide my hand down to my gun, "Well, David and I had spoken about that, a long time ago."

Her face was no longer sad, it was enraged. Her teeth were long and sharp, and her eyes were fixed upon me, wide and menacing. Her voice filled the room, "I AM NOT DAVID... TELL ME WHAT YOU KNOW OF MY FATHER."

I was in shock my hand was shaking as I clutched the handle of my gun. I was going to die; my wife was always telling me to get away from all this supernatural shit.

I didn't answer the vampire. She was looking down again, taking deep breaths, when she looked up, she looked like she was going to cry again. Okay, she's crazy; great I have a PMS vampire girl, who most likely hates men. I don't pray often, but lord if you're listening... a little help would be nice.

Melabeth spoke before I could answer her raging question, "Sorry, I'm scaring the shit out of you. I'm not mad at you; David's been lying to me. Please tell me what you know about my father."

By the time she finished speaking I could see her anger had faded away. I took some deep breaths of my own, "Okay, look... I will talk to you, but you can't do that again... okay."

She nodded her head. I took another breath, and my heart felt like I had just ran the hundred yard dash.

Trying to sound in control I spoke to her again, "Okay, I need to ask you a question first. See, a long time ago I found out about your father... Jack Dare right?" She nodded her head again to let me know that I had the name right. "Okay, well you see... I found out where he is. I did a little background check and pulled up some information on him. As I had told David, I don't feel comfortable giving you this information. If any harm is to become of this man I don't want to be a part of it. What I am asking you now is, what is your intention toward your father?"

Her eyes narrowed, but she didn't move. She was perfectly still as she stared at me. I couldn't help but twist around in my own chair. It was like being stuck in a room with a tiger. The tiger said it wouldn't hurt you, but it's a tiger. I was ready for her to start to yell at the very least, but she just sat there, unmoving, unblinking and I felt the chill run up my back. She spoke soft and kind, but I was still startled by the sudden noise after the intense silence, "Will you tell me about the Smith brothers?"

The sudden subject change caught me off guard. "Yes... in fact, give me a moment... it's here somewhere."

I pushed some files around on my desk looking for a yellow folder marked Blue Dogs. I found it under one of my stacks of paper, "Here it is. In this file there is enough information to track down those two clowns. The Blue bikers run up and down the west coast, but the Smiths are based out of San Francisco. They have family up there, including wives and children, or should I say exes and children. You will find there are several key hang out around town for the gang, it wouldn't take you long to find them."

She took the file out of my hand and thumbed through it, and then she asked, "And Alex?"

I knew she was talking about this mysterious Alex, who led the group of bikers that kidnapped and raped her. "I told David..." her look said it all, "I know, I know, you're not David." A tight smile spread across her lips. "All I was trying to say, is that you don't have enough information to hunt down this Alex. When you catch up to the Smith Brothers, I wouldn't just kill them; you will need to question them. They're the only ones who will know who this guy is, and where he might be. You have already killed Jason and I doubt your father ever knew who he was dealing with."

She considered this for a second, then with a very soft voice and a smile, "Thank you."

"No problem," was my response, but she was still sitting in front of me quiet. I knew before she spoke that she wasn't leaving without the information on her father. I couldn't just give her that; it would be like me pulling the trigger myself. I didn't mind killing the Smith Brothers or Jason Black, they were bad men, but her father was not like them; he had changed. I wasn't ready to hand Jack a death sentence.

She had a calculating look, as she began to speak, "It really is a family business. This is my father, why don't you just please give me what you have on him? You don't owe my father anything and you have no right to keep it from me."

I swallowed hard before I spoke, pushing back the fear, "I am truly sorry... I don't think I will be able to help you with anything else tonight. May I see you out?"

I had my hand on my pistol, it may not kill her, but it would put her down if I shot her in the head. It would give me enough time to light her on fire or maybe run. I couldn't worry about what I would do after I shot her in the head, first I had to hit her there; anywhere else would just piss her off. She was freaking me out; she wasn't really reacting to what I had just said. In fact, she seemed to be calm as she leaned back into the chair. She smiled as one of her fingers twisted around some of her long hair.

Calmly she asked, "Are you sure you can't help me?"

My voice cracked a little, "I'm sure... truly sorry."

Her laugh filled the room and made me jump just a little bit. With wide eyes still laughing, "You're not sorry... not yet."

I'd had enough and knew where this was going. I have never been the aggressor, the few times I have had to fight it was in self-defense, but I couldn't wait for her to make the move, she was too fast.

I pulled my gun out, but before I could even get my gun to eye level she was standing next to me. Somehow, in the blink of an eye, she had moved around my desk and now stood next to me, as my gun pointed at a empty chair.

I tried to swing my gun to meet her, but like a snake her hand sprung out as she caught my wrist. My arm movement stopped abruptly, her arm felt like a steel bar.

I moved up with my free hand to punch her in the face, when the room spun around.

I found myself slammed against the wall that had been behind her. She had picked up my two hundred pounds right out of my seat, and tossed me like a sack of potatoes. I hadn't fallen to the ground, but it was work to stay on my feet as I found myself fighting to catch my breath. I had too much adrenaline in my system to feel any real pain, but I would feel it in the morning, if there was one.

Once I caught my breath I noticed another thing. She was holding my gun; I hadn't even known that I had lost it. She dropped out the magazine, and then cleared the chamber. Flicking the pistol out of her hand it flew out of my office and clattered across the tile before coming to rest next to the front door.

I was so screwed.

I was leaning against the wall as she slowly, almost seductively walked over to me. She smiled as she slapped me real gently on my cheek, "Now, now there, there's no need for that." She turned and looked over at all my filing cabinets, then looked me in the eyes, "Are those locked? No matter, I am sure you have a key."

Melabeth walked over and pulled one open, "Nope, not locked," she chided. Then it only took her a few seconds to pull open the drawer marked with D through G. She was flipping through the files and stopped and pulled one out.

I knew she had found it for in that file was all the information I had found out on her dad, Jack Dare. I had not only doomed him, but I doubt that I would survive this myself. I had never felt this kind of self pity before, but I had never been so sure that I was going to die. As I was thinking about this she put the file on top of the other file I had just given her. With a very happy voice sounding just a little bit ditzy, "Bingo, I found it. See, that wasn't hard."

I found my voice, "You have no right to take…"

I never finished my sentence because she moved across the room and was now in my face. She had moved so fast, it looked as if she had teleported. Her eyes were challenging and through clenched lips, "Don't finish that sentence. I have the right; it's my father, my revenge. You, you have no right, none. Do you understand me?"

What use would it do to argue with her, except for a more painful death. "Yes, yes I do."

She smiled triumphantly as she reached up and touched my face, "Good boy." She beamed. Her hand wasn't cold, but it was cool to the touch. It was soft but still it felt off somehow. She stared at me as she held me pinned against the wall.

I asked her in a quiet voice, "What now?"

There was a sort of sadness in her face; she gently rubbed my cheek. She sounded like a child when she spoke, "Your choice. I am hungry, let me feed."

I deliberated for a second; I don't believe that she was really giving me a choice. If I deny her, she will kill me, but if I let her feed off me, maybe she will spare me. So I decided to try a gamble, "You may feed from me, if you don't mean to kill me."

She gave me a look like, how could I even think that. In mock horror, she started to give me reassurance, "No, no of course not. I promised if you invited me in that no harm would come to you. And even after you tried to pull a gun on me, I will keep my word."

"Thank you," I whispered.

Relief washed through my body; maybe I would see my wife again. I had never been fed on by a vampire, but what I read and heard is that it felt like sex. Most people never remembered because the vampire hypnotizes them first, but I doubt that Melabeth would do that to me; why bother.

She smiled sweetly at me, "This won't hurt."

With that, she moved her mouth toward my neck. She wrapped her body around me; I couldn't help but feel like a pervert as this young looking girl wound herself around me. I couldn't help but think that somehow I was betraying my wife.

The world slowed as she leaned in, it reminded me of waiting for the doctor to give me a shot. You knew it was coming, you just didn't know how much it would hurt. I felt a pinch on my neck, it didn't hurt, and in fact it felt good. As her lips started to suck and move it felt as if she was giving me a hickey.

I felt pleasure pulse through my body as she held me tightly against the wall. I felt ashamed as my body responded to her. I was having some kind of sexual moment with a young girl. No, I was being forced into one. It was hard to think as I gasped in pleasure.

I finished climaxing and the world spun and went in and out of focus. I think I blacked out because when I was able to see again, I was in my chair in front of my desk. Melabeth stood over me with lips smeared with crimson red, one small line dripping down her chin. She reached up and wiped away the runway drip, and then licked her finger. My stomach twisted as I watched her.

I felt dirty, like I had just been used against my will. If a man could feel like women, overpowered, pressed against ones will; I do believe I got a small taste of it. The blood loss was making me tired, but I would survive, in that I was thankful.

She smiled down at me, and in a very excited voice, "I do believe you have learned a lesson tonight. Don't you?"

I had probably learned a few, but I didn't want to piss her off, she would be gone soon, "Which was?"

She leaned in closer, and with a sinister tone, "Never ever, invite a vampire into your home. And don't even think of getting in my way."

She stood up tall, laughed a very delightful laugh. It sounded like bells to me; only I didn't find what she laughed about the funny. She gathered the files and began to leave, then stopped and turned around.

She looked at me and sadness washed across her face, she started to say something but stopped. A blank mask passed over her face and in a cold, indifferent voice, "Sorry, this is not what I had planned."

After that, she swiftly left my office, I heard the front door smack closed, and I knew that I was alone. I couldn't help but feel bad for her, I had read all the reports, and I knew what had happened to her. I was at one point eager for her to get her revenge, but now I believe something has changed. The hatred in her heart left, no room for love.

I do believe that the victim has become the villain.

Chapter 23 Flying
飛行

I was frozen on the sidewalk.

Standing out front of the detective's office feeling the effects of drinking his blood, I felt the cool air blow around my body. I had forgotten how windy it was here. Drinking blood was amazing, it was different from eating food when I was a human. Just like eating, I felt full after drinking a man's blood, but it also felt like I drank a lot of coffee. I could feel the life energy running through my body, it felt like it would push out my finger tips.

My emotions were jammed up like California traffic. I didn't hurt the detective, but I came close to killing him; my excuse is that he pulled a gun on me. Of course I was threatening him, and I had no intention of leaving that office without the information on my father. It hurts my head to even think about dealing with my father. I was afraid to even open the file and see what information the detective had on him.

When I thought of David it was like someone stabbing me in the chest, or back was more like it. It has been the first time since becoming a vampire that I felt my heart, and all I felt was pain. David betrayed me, then I had betrayed David, but when I betrayed him I hadn't known he had already betrayed me. Thinking about it was giving me a headache.

When I became too stressed, there was one thing that made me feel better. I flashed over to the box truck and grabbed the sword hilt out of my bag. I could see Carrie in the front seat of the truck awaiting my return. By holding the hilt, she became more solid. I had asked Carrie to wait in the truck.

Carrie timidly asked, "How did it go?"

I showed her the files, "He has *had* the information."

Carrie gasped as her hand shot over her mouth, "Oh… how could he?"

"I need to fly," I slid the files into the bag. Strapping the bag over my back, I jumped into the air, letting myself go weightless. Carrie knew when I went flying not to bother me, so even though her ghostly form would follow, she would be silent and invisible.

There was an old building that had been turned into a movie theater. I landed softly on top of the metal scaffolding that held a large sign that simply said FOX. The sign looked as if it were from the fifties with the large letters that lit up with tube lights, different color lights scrolled around the letters. The building was across the street from the detective's office, and it stood two stories high. In Banning, it was the tallest building.

Standing on top of the sign I could see across the valley and could tell that this spot was the highest point on the valley floor. Two mountains stood like dark shadows on either side of me. The lights of the house rolled out in front and behind me. I bent down and jumped with all my strength, the old sign screeched in protest as my body flew upward with a slight angle forward.

Soon all the cars and buildings below me turned into bright little lights as my body began its upward ascent. Charlotte had said that vampires couldn't really fly, we could float; I had learned to make my body as light as a feather. When I concentrated hard enough, I could push against the planet like we were two magnets. I could push myself higher into the air without touching the ground. Changing the way gravity pulled at me allowed me to move through the air, but this gave me very limited movement other than up and down. In fact, the wind that blew hard between the mountains had more control of where I was going than I did. Still, it was a form of flying, like a hot air balloon.

I loved it up in the sky and everything in my mind melted away as I viewed the city below, the mountains loomed to my side. The cold air rippled through my clothes and hair, but I was not cold. Some things about being a vampire sure seemed like it was worth it; of course, if I were a normal vampire, I would need to be at least one hundred years old to fly. I looked up to see stars poking out between slivers of dark clouds.

I leaned back so now that I was floating on my back as I drifted through the sky. Rolling around slowly until I was looking down at the ground. I had to grab all my hair so that it stopped whipping in my face. I had brought nothing to tie it up, so pulling it straight while holding it in a ponytail with one hand, I made my fingernails grow long and sharp with my other hand. I cut off my hair, letting it drop below me, I watched as it turned to dust and dissipated into the air.

I had learned a new trick from Charlotte about controlling my hair from growing back in seconds. This was a good trick for fighting because often my long hair would get in my way if I didn't have time to tie it up before a fight. I had to will it from growing, it was like squeezing my fist, it wasn't hard, but the minute I stopped my hair would grow back to the same length and color it was the day I had died.

I would always be the same on the outside, never growing old or changing in any way, I couldn't lose weight but then again I couldn't gain it. I've always been too thin, and would look so young; no one would ever take me seriously, they would always treat me like a child. Alice looked so much like a little girl that all the humans were always asking where her parents were. It was hard for her to do anything without controlling minds, but at least she could control them. I still was unable to make anyone see anything and it made getting around difficult, it was hard to always be treated young.

Who cares about all that, when you can fly? I let my mind go empty as I slowly spun around taking in the beauty of the night. With only the sound of the wind in my ears, I started humming a tune. The tune was a rock band I had heard on the radio. For the first time in a long time, I felt free.

I had been slowly falling to earth, it took a lot of energy to fly, like running. The longer I did it the sooner I would need to feed. Of course unlike any other vampire I could simply just wait and I would slowly recharge like a battery.

I was slowly falling toward a neighborhood with closely packed homes. I noticed a small graveyard and dropped toward the dark spot between the lights. I could still see all the graves dotted in-between the trees. I was now in a standing position as my feet softly made contact with the soft grass. I felt my hair grow, as I let it fall from my head and return to its original length. Now my hair was blonde again, but the ends were black. It looked as if I took the last six inches of my hair had been dipped in ink. I knew Carrie was with me and dying to talk, which was probably a good thing. I need to work out some things going on in my head.

That's when I saw him, standing in the shadow. He had not moved and inch as he leaned against a brick wall at the edge of the graveyard. Under a tree it was very dark even for my vision, and because he was so close to the wall my second sight had not made out the shape of his body, but none the less there he stood. And now that I knew he was there I could hear his fast beating heart as he stood without moving. He would have seen me land; what did he think he was seeing I wondered.

As I approached him, he pulled something out of his pocket, I readied myself. Then his hand went to his face I could clearly hear the sound of a Zippo lighter open as he lit his cigarette. The light from the flame of the lighter was like someone had put a spotlight on him. With my eyes all I needed was a little bit of light to see in the darkest of dark.

Now that I could see him, he looked kind of familiar. He was wearing all black even black jeans, with a black leather jacket. He had a ball cap on backwards with long curly hair. His lighter went out and he took a nervous deep drag on his cigarette, I was close enough now that I could see his hand shaking.

I came to a stop three feet in front of him, the red glow form the cigarette was all the light I needed. My teeth grew in anticipation, since I was about to feed. He spoke, and the sound startled me, it had been quiet for so long, "I screwed up… I'm sorry. I should have never let you out of that truck."

His eyes were full of sorrow and I could see his pain on his face, but I had no idea what he was talking about. I asked, "Do I know you?"

The boy stammered out, "You don't remember me? That's funny, I thought you came out of the sky for revenge upon me. Not long ago me and my brother picked you up hitchhiking and gave you a ride to a party. We never saw you again, I always wondered if we should have dropped you off there, because we knew those guys. They were F—IN creeps. As I saw you come from the sky, I thought you had come for me. You are just as I remember you, but now that I get a better look at you, I don't believe you are a ghost."

I remembered him now, "You're one of the Hood brothers. You gave me a ride in that little yellow truck. Your brother drives like a maniac... he scared the shit out of me. I forgot your name."

He simply replied, "Eric."

"So you were worried about me, Eric, how sweet." I smiled at this boy and thought better of him. Maybe I wouldn't eat him.

He took a nervous drag, and then offered me a cigarette. I took it without a word as I put it to my lips he reached over and lit it for me. Then, with a soft voice, "Are you here to kill me?"

Carrie spoke up as if it were her first breath of air, "Melabeth you never told me about hitchhiking with boys in a yellow truck."

I didn't answer Carrie, but I did answer Eric, "No, I'm not here to kill you. In truth, I don't have enough friends to start killing people who are being nice to me. If I start talking to myself, don't worry about it, I'm haunted. Your safe... for tonight."

Carrie asked with a sad voice, "Is David on that list now?"

Holding back tears, "I don't know."

With real concern Eric asked, "Don't know what?" He had not heard Carrie's question.

I calmed myself, then answered him, "Never mind. I told you I might start talking to myself... ghost. Can you do me a favor?"

He shrugged, "Anything."

I couldn't help but smile when I replied, "Really." He looked even more nervous. I held back a laugh as I asked, "Do you have a phone I can use?"

He relaxed when he heard my request. Then pointing over his shoulder, "Yeah, I live about twelve houses down. You can use my parent's phone."

"After you."

"Okay, just need to jump over this wall." And with that Eric proceeded to climb the brick wall.

I simply jumped over and landed without a noise on the other side. After a loud landing, Eric looked up at the top of the wall, I realized he was waiting for me to come over. I announced, "Ready."

Eric jumped, then spun around, I couldn't help but laugh. He shook his head, "Damn you're fast. Well, come on, it's this way."

Carrie was walking with us, even though Eric could not see her. She asked as we walked towards Eric's house, "David betrayed you, why? What would be different between y'all if he just told you where those men were?"

Until she asked that question, I hadn't really thought about it. After a second of debating, "Well, for one I would have had all my revenge. Then I could live a more peaceful… I want to be done with all this violence. I would want peace," I spoke louder as the answer came to me. "He needs my help on killing all these Order members. It might take years to take down this organization. He's afraid that once I have my revenge that I wouldn't need him anymore."

Carrie said softly, "Are you sure?"

Eric followed my thinking and added, "Not sure what you're talking about, but it sounds like he knows your heart better than you. Leading you around by your hate. Is it too much to ask, what you are?"

"What do you mean by knowing my heart? And what I am? I'm an angel, let's leave it at that."

Eric replied, "If you were him, could you trust that you would stick around? It kind of sounds like to me that once you get what you need, you're out of whatever shit you're talking about. Kind of sounds like you are blinded by anger, but I could be wrong. Oh, I have always wanted to meet an angel."

Eric's was right, I felt defeated. I put my face into my hands and stopped walking. Eric walked back to me. Slowly, carefully put his arm around me and pulled me into a slow hug, I let him. Standing in the street, I wept for my loss. For now I had lost my David, truly he was never mine. I didn't weep much, and Eric was so calm or clueless. I knew he didn't believe my angel remark. Either way it made it easier not to eat him. We continued on to his house. His house had a gate all the way around it. He had two large dogs, who knew better than to let me in. Eric wrestled with the dogs as we walked up to his home.

There he directed me into a door heading into the garage. It was a steel door with metal mesh that you could see right through. It passed through a small hallway with laundry machines. Pushing the dogs back, he shut the door. There was a second door at the other end of the laundry room. He pointed at it for me to go in. I felt the protection of his home, it was pushing me back.

I spoke softly, "Invite me in."

Like a dip-shit he said, "No need to invite, just go in there."

I turned and faced him; he looked confused because I now blocked his path. "Invite me into your home."

"Oh, yeah, no problem," He froze for a moment and eyed me. "No way, you're a vampire?"

"Please invite me."

He smiled like meeting a vampire was what he wanted. Then he really surprised me, by saying, "Come inside, you are welcome."

I felt the wall disappear, I turned and entered into the garage. To find out it was no garage, but a room built into the garage. With a new excitement in his voice, "The phone is right over there. I didn't believe vampires existed."

I chuckled, "Because they don't."

He looked confused, "Then why did I have to invite you?"

I answered him like it was no big deal, "Because it is polite."

With wonder in his eyes, "You are a vampire!" I gave him a dark look. "Wow."

He was an idiot. I ignored him and picked up the phone and dialed the number. Ezra picked up on the second ring, "Hello."

"Hello Ezra, this Melabeth. I need your help, I need Alice too."

Ezra's voice was full of concern, "Of course, where are you?"

I explained where I was and a little of what I needed. Ezra told me to hold up in a hotel room that was not far. He would meet me there in less than forty-eight hours. Ezra added, "And Melabeth, don't worry about it. We are your family."

"Thank you," I hung up, thanking Eric before he could ask any questions. I walked over to a large window, opened it, knocked out the screen and flew away. I am sure poor Eric will have trouble sleeping, but he was strange, perhaps not. I wasn't sure what to do next. Ezra was the planer, I am sure things were about to get exciting.

Chapter 24 Chasing the Smith's
チェイス

Carrie and I enjoy our time together. It kind felt like when we first met, easier. Carrie told me that she didn't mind being less powerful if it meant being with me. She had never told me before, but it had been hard to hang with David for a variety of reasons. David, ignoring her was the biggest one. Living with necromancers you would think someone would talk to her.

David was an ass, for hiding this information on my killers. It didn't take away from the fact that it was me who broke his heart. It also didn't minimize the fact that I got his family killed and now that we broke up, he is all alone. The necromancers will be his new friends; and that made me wonder how his life would have been if he had never met me.

When Ezra knocked on the door it wasn't a moment too soon. I was starting to go a little stir crazy waiting for him. He didn't come by himself, Charlotte, Alice and Michael accompanied him. After our embraces and hellos, we went straight to business. I showed them the file on the Smith brothers and shortly after that we were all piling into a van and heading north.

Ezra and Charlotte rode up front, while me and Alice rode in the middle. In the third row sat Michael and Carrie. Even though Carrie sat there, no one could hear or see her expect Alice and I. Michael kept putting stuff on her. She asked a lot of questions which were hard to answer, mainly because Alice didn't like me talking to ghost.

I had just answered a question for Carrie when Alice piped in, "Stop it already. You sound crazier than me. You haven't told us why your little friend isn't helping you? Also, why has he left you with his pet ghost? Not that I mind, he's gone, it is about time; necromancers are no fun."

I didn't want Michael to hear the reason why, "I will tell you later. Let's just say that David overheard the last conversion we had."

Charlotte turned and looked at me, "I don't recall this conversion. Alice what is she's talking about? And why aren't we talking openly?"

Alice giggled, then said, "Shh... Michael might hear it."

I interrupted, "Hey."

Michael moaned from the back seat, "I don't want to know, if Melabeth doesn't want me to hear it."

I started to say thanks, but Charlotte was much louder as she yelled back at Michael, "Son, mind your own business. I need details."

Ezra groaned, "This is going to be a long drive. Melabeth, before they get you started on your love life, or lack of one. Let me tell you something you and I care about."

Eager for the subject change, "What is it Ezra?"

Ezra explained, "Alice and I figured long ago that we might be involved in helping you rid the world of these brothers. Even without the information that detective gave you, I know about the Blue Dog Biker gang. We have many employees, and two of them that live and work in San Francisco. They are both vampires, about fifty years old. They have been keeping an eye on the gang.

"After I got off the phone with you, I gave them a call. I let them know that we were on our way, so we should have a place to stay and information on their whereabouts. The name of our informants is Bonnie and Clyde. And before you ask, no they are not the real Bonnie and Clyde. In fact, I do believe that Clyde's real name is Jacob."

Grateful for the information and the subject change, "Thank you."

Alice with great impatience, "Yes, thank you; there was no way we could have waited for that information. Now Melabeth, now that he is done wasting our time... details my doll." I gave Alice a glare, she then informed me, "I took care of that. Michael can't hear a word."

Ezra smarted in, "Can't you do that for me?"

The rest of the ride to San Francisco took forever. It took no less than three hours before Alice and Charlotte were done talking about my break up. Neither felt that I had any responsibility for breaking up with David; which by all accounts only made me feel worse. If these two thought it wasn't my fault, it most likely was.

After the conversation died away I was left with a little time to think. The minute I saw Michael, it filled me with glee. I hadn't seen him since the ship, and now we would be spending time together. Well, kind of, I was surrounded by vampires who could hear every little sound. I couldn't help but think that maybe I could find some time to sneak away with Michael... a girl could dream.

We arrived in San Francisco, pulling up to a small house on a steep hill. Bonnie and Clyde had a nice home, but very modest. Bonnie was very nice and extremely eager to please us. She stood about my height and had short brown hair that was straight with a slight curl at the end. She had big brown eyes and a much darker complexion than me. Her smile was easy and came to her face often.

Clyde was nothing like her. He was a black man that stood over six feet. He was taller than Michael, but it was hard to tell if he was taller than Ezra. Ezra was thin and tall, but Clyde was built like a steam engine. In that way he looked much larger than Ezra. He wore a beard and a knit hat with a flannel shirt. He reminded me of a lumberjack. Where Bonnie dressed like Tina Turner; she was so eighties it was hard to follow her, with all her valley girl talk.

We all sat down in the living room. Clyde had not said much to this point, but when Ezra asked for him to fill us in; we all quieted down and listened. Clyde had a deep voice, "This is what we know. Brandon and Randy, the Smith brothers, left town about a week ago. A man came to town; the only name we got was simply Alex. I think your friends were tipped off that you were after them."

Ezra asked the questions on all our minds, "Do you know where they might have gone?"

Bonnie was just settling into a chair. She had been bringing everyone drinks. She answered Ezra's question, "Washington, like we heard that there is some kind of shifter pack up there. Like they are close buds and now like hanging in the reserve."

Ezra looked at Clyde and calmly asked, "English?"

Clyde had a deep chuckle. He explained, "The "reserve" as she calls it, is the Olympic National Park. This area is over fourteen hundred square miles, with ancient glaciers on top of mountains in the center of the park. I couldn't tell you where to even start to look for someone. You all know the difference between the shifters and werewolves, so it is strange that they are working together."

I interrupted him, "Sorry, but I don't understand the difference."

Bonnie chuckled, "Like, you're serious... what rock have you been under?"

Alice cleared her throat; the room went quiet as Bonne's face lost its cockiness. Alice looked at Clyde, "I'll only say this once. My sister has a nasty habit of killing those who bother her. I won't stop her, and I doubt you two are up for the task of defending yourself."

Clyde gave Bonnie a dirty look, "Silence your mouth. Do not forget what I said."

Bonnie nodded at Clyde then turned to me, "Sorry, like I didn't mean anything by it."

I just stared at her for a second, then without acknowledging her, I asked Clyde my question. "What's the difference?"

Ezra offered up, "If you don't mind Clyde." Clyde nodded and Ezra explained, "It really isn't hard to understand. Werewolves are a magical disease spread through their bites. In many ways they are more powerful than a Shifter. They don't turn into a dog; they look like a man with a lot of hair and big claws. Half man, half wolf. A Shifter turns into whatever animal they are imitating. Some Shifters are not limited to wolves, in fact the more powerful the Shifter, the more powerful the animal. Shifters become more powerful through generations. If one were to turn into something like a bear; then they are most likely a fourth or fifth generation Shifter. Werewolves only spread by the bite; they are also out of control when they shift into a Werewolf.

"Some legends are true, some are not. They cannot control themselves on a full moon. They are not limited to that fact; they can change at other times. What you really need to know is this: destroying the heart or cutting off the head are the only two methods in which you can be assured that they are dead. Werewolves heal fast, shifters are harder to hurt period. One more thing, Werewolves and Shifters are strong, but slower, so use your speed against them."

I asked, "What about silver?"

Ezra laughed, "I told you about that. Humans made that up; in fact, you will find that silver kills a lot, according to man. The truth is that the churches used it as an excuse for needing silver to kill the evil in the world. Just stab them in the heart, cut off their heads... oh and you can burn them. Clyde, how many do you think we're up against?"

Clyde looked thoughtfully, "Well, if my information is correct. We are looking at seventeen shifters, plus the Smith brothers and the Wizard. Twenty, but there could be more."

Michael blurred out, "Twenty. Oh, this should be fun. Maybe we should wait for the Smith brothers come out of the forest."

Turning and facing Michael. I blurted out, "Why?"

Michael answered me, "At night, Werewolves, Shifters and even a Wizard are at a great disadvantage, but not during the day. The only ones in this room that can handle going outside are Ezra, Charlotte and Alice. And you can only handle a limited amount of sun."

Charlotte objected, "Don't forget about Mel, she can handle some sun."

Michael nodded and went on, "I hadn't. In fact, I left her out because she stands in a class of her own. I dare say the sun bothers her, least of all, but she's still subject to the same loss of power. No flying, flashing and your healing will be slowed. Of course, if you get cut, you will also catch on fire making for a much more difficult wound, to say the least. Bonnie, Clyde and I really won't function at all during the day. And we most likely will catch on fire if exposed to the sun for too long.

"Werewolves have been a nemesis for hundreds of years. They can smell us, so they can track us down during the day. Once they have our scent there will be nowhere to hide. Cities have always offered us a better fighting chance, with man-made undergrounds and buildings. Plus the many smells of the city can throw a scent off, but in the forest, they will find us."

Alice added, "And that is why they will never come out of the silly forest. Let's all go get them, what do you say?"

Ezra replied right away, "Sounds like fun. Count me in."

Charlotte lazily added, "No sales at the stores, I'll go."

Bonnie hesitantly asked Clyde "Is she really asking?"

Clyde chuckled, then looked at Bonnie, "No, she's not asking. Alice we'll go."

Alice chatted, "Goody… what about you Michael?"

Michael just shook his head, "This is suicide. Some of us are going to die."

Charlotte got up and walked over to Michael. She sat upon his lap, "You know you want to go. You know we will need your gift."

Michael gave her a sly smile, "It's a long drive to Seattle. And we need to pick up some supplies."

Alice jumped up, "Can I get a little tiny tent for my doll to sleep in?"

My face fell into my hands, "Oh, this is going to be fun."

Chapter 25 Olympic
山脈

After driving to Seattle we stayed in a local hotel. That evening Ezra left, but was back shortly with a Deuce in a half and it was pulling a small camper. He had the truck loaded with all things you would need for a camping trip: tents, clothes and lots of firearms. Another crate was full of knives and blades of all sizes and shapes. Michael, Ezra, and I jumped up front, while the rest rode in the back. The truck was a military vehicle painted camouflage.

It made me wonder how he could get a hold of all this so quickly, so I asked. Ezra answered, "It was easy. All you need is money; this stuff is for sale in every city in America. I love this country."

We drove west, the further we got away from the city the more green it became. It really was beautiful here with hundreds of shades of green and brown. A small mix of white laid where snow had fallen. It was night, but I could still see the dark clouds rolling over our heads, threatening to rain or snow. It took us a couple of hours to arrive at the edge of the Olympic National Park. We stopped at a campground at Dosewallips State Park. There we set up the camper, Clyde started a campfire. We gathered around to make a plan.

The plan was simple enough; we would separate tonight and feed. Then the group would get a good night, I mean day sleep. And before the sun even went below the horizon, we would head up the mountain in the truck. Once it was dark, we would arm up and hunt the dogs down.

I ran into the woods to separate and hunt on my own. It was January and the air was cold. There was no snow on the ground here, and the sky had cleared. The stars were bright and filled the nighttime sky. Only a few of the dark clouds from earlier remained. I could see the snow capped mountains looming above me. Soon enough, we would be up there fighting for our lives.

Earlier Carrie had been quiet. I knew she wished to talk now that we were away from the group. She walked with no noise until she was standing in front of me. Even though I knew where she was, I was still staring up into the mountains.

Carrie spoke hesitantly, "Whatcha thinking?"

Not even looking at her, it gushed out, "I'm a vampire. I mean those men took everything I had, or would ever have. I hate them… I'm dead. I crawled out of the ground and lost fifteen years of my life. And then the next four days were crazy… it was only four days when I met Alice. In a month I had killed how many people? I don't know; by the end of a month I had killed David's family… then living in Vegas. Then what do I do, I kill more, that's what I do. Then I betray David and leave him on his own, but do I plan to go back and make that right… no. David was the only person crazy enough to help me kill these men. Not anymore, no, no, Alice wants to help now. I found out she drank some of my blood. At first she did this to steal my memories, but she got so much more. She knows where I am, hell I know where she is. I can feel her right this moment… she can feel me, she knows how I feel. She is commanding her vampires to run up into the mountains and take on an army of werewolves. She does this for my revenge. How can we do this without some of us dying?" I dropped to the ground and stared off into space. I was losing it.

Carrie lightly touched my shoulder, "Oh hon, it's going to be okay."

I went on with my freak out, "Ten and a half months."

Carrie asked, "What's ten and half months?"

"I have been a vampire for ten and a half months. Not one year, not four hundred years… ten damn months that's how long. Every day is like a hundred, every day I push away the pain, every day I try to forget my murders and being murdered. Yet here I am, ready to rush up a mountain to kill whoever gets in my way. I want to be with Michael. For what… love? Do I know what that is? Or do I do it for distraction? Is that what David was to me? A distraction, maybe; or possibly a tool?"

Carrie moved so she was looking at me, "I was hitchhiking when I got myself killed. I was so stupid…"

I interrupted, "You're not stupid."

She smiled, then went on, "There is a lot of things I is, and some things I isn't, but I know I'm stupid. I do know some stuff, like what love is, I know that. I don't have any answers, but I will tell you what I think."

I surrendered, "Okay."

"You loved David, but he didn't love you. He loves his necromancy. He ignored you when you needed him most; he had you do-in bad, when he should have been holding your hand. The only reason your dreaming about Michael, is that David didn't keep you dreaming about him. You know what else I think? If I were you, I would have freaked out a long time ago. I'm a ghost, and I get afraid of dying hanging with you 'all."

"I think I'm stupid too."

Carrie laughed, "Yep, me and you… stupid together."

I sighed, "Should I call this off?"

Carrie shook her head, "No, if you die tomorrow night I'll be right behind you. You know this is going to be the first time I can help? Plus, I don't think you can call it off, all you can do is put it off."

I wondered, "How can you help?"

"You are stupid," She said with a smile.

I narrowed my eyes in mock anger, "Hey… watch it hick."

Carrie was excited as she told me, "Hanging with David I have learned stuff. First, I can travel far away from you, just no one can see me and I can't touch anything. It's really good for spying and such, he taught me how. And you can will me, into that hilt, and I would become your sword. That is a powerful weapon."

I was a little shocked that she offered, "Yes, but you will feel the pain of my enemies."

"Then make their deaths quick, okay." Then she gave me a wink.

That brought a smile to my face as it lightened my heart, "I can do that, and Carrie?"

"Yes?"

"Thanks, you are my friend."

She grabbed my hand and helped me to my feet. "Let's go girl, you need to eat before morning."

My little meltdown with Carrie had me feeling a little bit better. Carrie was a good friend I wouldn't know what to do without her. Too many things have happened to quickly in my life for me to take it in. I am thrown into a magical world, it's like trying to learn how to live from scratch. I couldn't help but think that with all this stuff going on that I was lucky to have someone who cared.

Chapter 26 Into The Thick Of It
それの厚いへ

I was riding shotgun again as the truck slowly climbed up a dirt road. The sun had not yet set, but we were trying to get a head start. The further we got into the mountains before night, the more time we would have to find our prey before day.

Between my breakup with David and the news that he had been betraying me had me reconsidering my life as a vampire. I remembered back when I killed the three men in the alley. David had pointed out that I had murdered the last man because I didn't have to kill him. Not long after I saw a boy trying to rape a girl and I spared his life. I had remembered David's words when I spared the boy, but they were short lived. Not long after that those words were lost to both of us as we killed many different people. Last night after my freak out I killed a man. I didn't have to, but I needed to make sure I am strong for tonight. I wasn't really upset about it, and that is what bothered me.

I had been alone after my mother died. My father was no father, and kept me away from any real friends or parental guidance. It had made me self reliant, but also I became disconnected with people around me. The drug addicts taught me that no one could be trusted and I lived my life that way. Then that life was taken from me only to be replaced with a new one. The first person I trusted has now betrayed me… I felt cold inside. If I could not trust David because he was hiding things from me, what about Nicks and the Whites? If not for Carrie I would be all alone, and I only trusted her because she was attached to me. I control her, is that trust? My thoughts were broken as Ezra brought the truck to a stop and killed the engine. He announced, "This is far enough."

We all jumped out and geared up. I was wearing my dress with the tall boots; Alice had this dress made for me and the fabric was magical. It would help protect me from fire and slices to my body; in fact everyone was wearing magical clothes. Ezra looked like he was heading to town with his black suit covered with a trench coat. He was sliding weapons into his coat and around his waist. Charlotte wore a black leather jumpsuit, with a long coat that looked the same as Ezra's. She had blades attached around her waist and chest and I was sure there were some I couldn't see. She also carried a spear; the shaft was made of steel. It would have been too heavy for a mortal.

Bonnie wore blue jeans with a red shirt covered with a jean jacket. Clyde on the other hand was something else. The large black man had on a brown leather outfit with large boots. He had chain mail wrapped around him with pieces of armor. Metal plates covered his shins and forearms, plus two large shoulder plates. He looked as if he just came out of some medieval movie. To top it off, he was holding a large double sided axe. He also had chained ammo crossing his chest; they went to an M60 which he strapped to his back. That was a lot of fire power, he looked fearsome indeed.

Alice's dress looked a lot like mine; we both looked as if we had stepped out of a twisted Gone With the Wind movie. And the fact that both of us had blades and other weapons attached all over our dresses helped with the crazy look. Alice was still cradling her baby doll in her left arm, but I knew that the baby's legs were knives.

Michael came around the back of the truck carrying two large rifles with high power scopes. He handed one to Bonnie. He was looking good, wearing skinny tight jeans with a black button up shirt. He also had on cowboy boots with a matching hat. The shirt did his chest justice as it wrapped around his chest. As his long hair whipped in the wind, he reminded me of a Marlboro commercial I had seen on TV.

I looked away to see Charlotte spinning, making sure that none of her weapons caught as she moved. I looked over at Alice and said, "Why is it that we are the only ones who got uniforms?"

Alice frowned, "UNIFORMS, as if. We look good; it's not my fault that Ezra and Charlotte think we're going to a nightclub."

Charlotte chimed in, "Or how about those two?" She pointed at Michael and Bonnie, "Ho down, perhaps?"

Clyde stepped forward and with his deep voice boomed, "I am the only one dressed for the occasion… the occasion for kicking ass that is."

We laughed as Ezra started tossing rifles out of the truck. He threw me an AK47 with a folding stock. It was shortly followed by a bag holding thirty round magazines. I strapped it onto my back along with the ammo. At our meeting last night Ezra had explained that Werewolves and Shifters had hard skin. Handguns wouldn't penetrate, the more powerful ones like a 44 wouldn't penetrate far enough. For that reason, we had to use high powered rifles. We were carrying them for two reasons, one they made it easier, two they would help us a lot if caught out in daytime. Our swords and knives could break easily upon the wolf's skin.

Ezra cleared his voice to get everyone's attention, "Remember your places. Michael and Bonnie are covering us, and will take up the rear. Charlotte guards Alice; Clyde and I will take up points behind Melabeth. Melabeth leads the way."

We all nodded as I picked up a short sword. As I walked into the forest; I could hear and therefore see with my second sight, everyone formed up behind me. It felt a little strange when last night around the fire, Ezra put a guard on Alice, but I soon found out why. Alice could only control so many minds, and if she got caught up defending herself, she would be less help to the rest of us.

I felt bad that Michael was with Bonnie. He was back there because he was much weaker than the rest of us. Bonnie was even weaker than Michael, even though she was older. They both knew how to shoot and could pick off our enemies from a distance.

The forest was amazing. As we followed the river upwards, we headed deeper into the reserve. We passed two or three waterfalls, one we had to stop so Bonnie could take a picture. Her camera was amazing, she could take a picture and it would come right out the front of the camera. She called it a Polaroid, I was amazed. She let me take a picture and I was excited to see it come to life before my eyes, but before I could take another, Ezra reminded me that this wasn't a vacation.

I responded with, "Yes, sir. Let's move it, come on men."

Bonnie added, "And women."

As we went deeper into the woods and climbed to a higher altitude, we began to walk over snowed covered ground. It was strange as we moved through the forest without a sound, not even a footprint. The animals in the forest were taken by surprise as we hurried by.

Not much longer after that the sun fell behind the mountain. Carrie reappeared next to me; she spun around confused trying to get her bearings in the dark forest. She complained, "I hate that. I'll never get used to popping into God know where, surrounded by God knows who. So, how y'all doing? Have you seen any wolves yet?"

"No, go look for me, okay," I gave her an encouraging smile.

Carrie gave me a wink, "Back faster than you can de-feather a chicken."

I could hear Bonnie from the back asking, "Who's she talking to?"

I think Michael was starting to answer when Alice pipped up, "Michael you're up. Melabeth did you send your ghost to scout?"

I nodded as I answered, "I did."

Alice replied, "Good."

Ezra commanded, "Fan out while Michael works."

I complained, "I wanted to see this."

Ezra pointed to where he wanted me to stand, "You can see in many directions. Just make sure he is safe while he concentrates."

I moved to the location he had pointed out, it stood on higher ground. I would be able to see someone approaching easily from here. I turned and looked down the hill to watch Michael work. I whistled so that my second sight would come to life, no one would be able to sneak up on me.

Michael laid down his rifle and then took a seat on a fallen tree. He looked like he was just sitting there doing nothing, a real bump on a log. I giggled at my own joke, but was hushed, by Charlotte. Michael was staring off into space with his hands in his lap. I was beginning to wonder when his power would take hold when an owl swooped by my head.

The owl was shortly followed by another. No less than twenty owls now encircled Michael, but my attention was pulled away by a squealing noise. The little squeal brought my second sight to life as the forest became a picture in my mind. I could see all the little details, no color, but still the shapes of all things filled my head. It was like a black and white movie where I could see in all directions at once. The squealing was coming from the bats.

First it was just a few bats flying around, then it was hundreds, followed by what seemed to be thousands. They filled the air and circled Michael until they became a black swirling mass. The squeal was almost a roar as they gathered. Then all at once, they flew off, flying out in all directions. They were shortly followed by the owls.

I knew that Michael not only controlled these animals, but could communicate with them. He could even see and hear what they could. They would understand what he was looking for and would send him images if they found it. The forest fell quiet as we all stood around, waiting for Michael to make contact.

An hour or more had passed, Michael had not moved and inch. Carrie floated in front of me, becoming more solid. She spoke with frustration, "I went as far as I could, but I didn't see a thing. Y'all have any luck?" I put my finger to my lips as I pointed at Michael. Carrie moaned loudly, "Oh, that's just great… more quiet time. Ain't noth-in worse than a natural yaker to be stuck haunting a bunch of stuffed vampires." I had to stifle a laugh, which brought a small smile to Carrie's face. "I guess there's noth-in to it, but to wait." And wait we did.

It was past midnight before Michael moved. He stood up and with excitement, "We got them, but they know we're here and they're readying themselves."

Ezra sounded like a general as he gave orders to Michael, "Give the information to Melabeth. She will lead, ready yourselves."

Michael flashed up to me. I was ready for him to tell me which way to go, but he did not speak. Instead, he cut the end of his finger and offered up a drop of his blood. I understood, but still I was nervous as I let him put his finger into my mouth. As he pulled his finger out I could taste the blood, it was different from humans.

Alice had been working with me to access the memories in the blood. I concentrated, and soon I was flying through the woods. Over the white snow as I whipped in and out of trees; I came upon a small group of cabins. Four of them sat in a small circle, outside I could see three, no wait, make that six large wolves. They were much bigger than normal wolves; they looked to be as big as a black bear. As I flew around the cabins one of the doors opened and two men stepped out. One was Randy Smith, one of the brothers. He still looked human, wearing blue jeans and a red plaid jacket. He was followed by Alex.

Alex was wearing a large gray overcoat; he looked like he did on the boat. He looked around and when his eyes made contact with me they stayed locked in. He followed me as I flew back and forth. Then he warned, "They know we're here, they will be here soon."

With that, he flicked his wrist; it looked as if something flew towards me... then nothing. I was now standing next to Michael, "Well, that's what it's like to be a bat. Did he kill it?"

Michael nodded, "Yes. Do you understand how to get there?"

I thought about it for a second. It was so weird; it was like remembering my way to the store. I knew exactly how to get there. I nodded, "Follow me."

With that, I turned and started into the forest. With my second sight I could see my friends taking up their positions as we moved without a sound. We moved fast, not running, but jogging. We slid through the undergrowth as we dodged limbs and jumped over dead trees and rocks. Yet none of us left tracks or even a broken twig, it was eerie being a vampire. We came upon the last hill, I knew the hour was becoming late, or early depending on your perspective. I whispered, "Over the next hill. Are we ready?"

Even a whisper I knew they could hear me. The sound of different acknowledgments filled my ear. I moved forward, but this time slower as I gripped the sword in one hand and a long knife in the other. As I crested the hill I could see the four cabins below. They were hard to make out through all the trees, but I could see them. The trees were not very dense, but thick enough, it would be hard for Michael and Bonnie to get clear shots.

The air was cold with winter's grip. From beyond the cabins I could make out movement, which soon overtook the cabins. It was a wall of fog, unnatural, for it was too cold. This was the work of magic and soon we were engulfed in a thick layer of fog. I could only see about four or five feet in front of me. That of course was using my eyes; the fog did nothing to blind my second sight. This fog would hurt the use of guns, what else Alex had laid before us was anyone's guess.

I didn't have to guess for long, with my second sight and my ears I could hear them. The wolves came at us, at the same time they were flanking us on both sides. It wouldn't take long before we were surrounded.

Before I could think of what to do, Clyde yelled out, "Aaaaa, let's get them."

With that, he flashed forward and with a mighty axe swing, he hit one of the wolves. The animal flew against a tree with a yelp and blood gushing out of its side. Ezra moved in to help Clyde. I turned to see Alice and Charlotte engaged with four of the beasts.

I was looking at Alice, but could clearly see the wolf charging me from behind. I waited and as it jumped with its mouth aimed at my head. I side stepped and with one quick swing I removed the animal's head. When the giant wolf crashed to the ground, it was no longer a wolf. There lay a young man with dark skin. His nude body was a few feet away from the head. His black hair was stained with blood as his face stared at me with empty eyes. All that remained in my hand was the hilt, the swing was strong enough to behead him, but I broke the sword in the process. I dropped and pulled out another long knife as wolves came for me, they came from every direction.

The flurry of action that followed was vicious. I cut, kicked and flashed; flipping and jumping between the trees as I fought the wolves. Gunfire rang in the air along with growling and hissing. I noticed that Alice, Charlotte, Ezra and I were working in a large circle killing the wolves. I had counted five dead men upon the ground; two of them were my kills.

I was fighting several wolves with Alice at my back; her back was to me as she fought one. Then something eerie happened, it was like our minds linked on a subconscious level. I flashed past her and next to the wolf she had been fighting and there I ran my knife into its chest. I had turned my back to the wolves that I had been fighting. One of them took the opportunity to launch at me while I was killing his friend. He leaped through the air, but he was pulled out of the air and stabbed to death by Alice.

Alice and I were now side by side and the other two wolves looked confused. Alice was messing with their heads. They moved away, but as they did, a hail of gunfire came down on them as Clyde and Ezra let them have it. These wolves had hard skin, but the high powered rifles brought them to the ground. One died from gun fire while the other lay upon the ground in its own blood. Charlotte ran up and shoved her spear through its heart and that made nine dead.

Clyde has tossed his now empty machine gun upon the ground. I noticed the wolves had backed off, regrouping in the fog. Clyde growled, "Out of ammo and the sun will rise soon."

Ezra barked, "Can't worry about that now... prepare yourselves they come again."

I noticed as the wolves encircled us yet again. I had lost track of Bonnie and Michael. I looked up at where I last saw them. I yelled out, "I am going to check on Michael."

Before anyone could respond I flashed away and literally jumped over a wolf as I headed to where he was. There on the ground was bloody and torn up body pieces. I could tell by a severed arm and her red shirt, that I was looking at what was left of Bonnie. In between, three large trees, two wolves were growling, one was pacing back and forth trying to get in. The other wolf was brown and jammed between a gap obviously fighting something inside the ring of trees.

I flashed over to the pacing wolf and took it by surprise. With my last knife, I plunged into its side, but missed its heart. The animal turned its head in rage and pain, snapping at me, I barely moved in time before losing my arm to its teeth.

The injured animal came at me; I grabbed its jaw one hand on top the other on the bottom. I twisted its head to one side while I side stepped. The heavy wolf fell to one side landing on the ground. There I kicked it in the side with enough force that it lifted the wolf off the ground as it slammed into a tree. The wolf now lay unconscious at the base of the tree.

The second wolf had not yet noticed what had happened to his friend; he was too busy fighting Michael in the tree. I noticed that Michael's high powered rifle was lying upon the ground. I quickly picked it up and ran up behind the wolf. With both hands, I shoved the end of the rifle right up the wolf's ass.

The wolf let out a sound that will haunt me to the end of my days. The wolf was now trying to back out of the trees, but I wouldn't let it. I waited just a few seconds, and then pulled the trigger. It wasn't long before a dead man with a rifle projecting from his ass lay before me. The bullet had traveled straight to his head, leaving it shattered like an old punkin.

Michael came out from between the trees. He was bloody from head to toe. His arms, both had huge gashes in them. I noticed that his left hand was missing all together. He nodded his head, "Thank you. I couldn't have thought of a better way to kill him."

I laughed, "What can I say, I am creative that way."

Michael's eyes narrowed, "Looks like you'll need to get more creative."

The injured wolf had now got back on its feet. It turned and growled, that would have not worried me, but the fact he was joined by three others did. Two of them were gray wolves like him, but not the third one.

It was one of the Smith brothers, which one I could not tell. He didn't really look like a wolf, he stood like a man. He was covered in dark brown hair, his hands had large black claws. The face was covered except for around the eyes and nose and to top it off a mouth full of yellow teeth. He looked like an older, meaner Michael J. Fox. That had me wondering if the maker of Teen Wolf had known about real Werewolves.

I smiled, "Finally, it's time to kill Teen Wolf."

I flashed forward, taking the man-wolf by surprise. I kicked him square in the chest, he hurdled backwards from the hit, but I fell under attack by the shifter wolves that were flanking him. Spinning, moving and jumping, I dodged their snapping teeth. I leaped up into the air and went weightless; I flew up to a high branch.

There I could see the injured wolf had Michael up the same tree. The other two wolves were at the base of my tree growling with anger. And teen wolf had recovered and now was heading toward my tree. Carrie was floating next to me, "I can help. I want to... plus this is my life too."

I whispered, "I know." I pulled off the strap that held the hilt to my leg. Then I held it out like it was a sword, "I am ready."

With that Carrie became a swirling cloud of dark mass. The dark cloud came to the hilt, it shrank and became dense. Once again the magic sword was in my hand, with green lines of power. I looked down to see the werewolf climbing the tree.

He jumped up to my branch. He growled with spit dripping from his foaming mouth. I calmly moved forward and with three quick, well rehearsed moves; I sliced his arm and his leg, right behind his knee.

The wolf yelped in pain. It was hard for the werewolf to remain balanced with the leg wound I had given him. Finally, I knocked him off the branch with a kick, sending him falling back first.

The two wolves moved as the werewolf crashed upon the ground. He was shortly followed by me landing a few feet away. The wolves were taken by surprise. I side stepped one of the wolves putting him between me and the other one. Running my sword sideways, I stabbed him right through his chest. With an upward pull, I sliced him open. The sword rang as the wolf fell dead upon the ground.

The other wolf attacked, but I grabbed his mouth from under his chin. Letting my claws dig into his jaw I twisted his head to one side. Then, with my sword hand, I removed his head.

With my second sight I could see that the wolf that had treed Michael had turned its attention upon me. It ran at me with its mouth open, without even turning around I dropped to one knee. The animal was about to bite upon my neck, but I thrust my sword up and over my shoulder, sending the blade into the wolf's open mouth. The blade ran straight through his head, his whole body went limp. The beast slowly slid off the blade as he fell to the ground.

As I was killing these three wolves, the werewolf had got up. Seeing me, he ran away, with a limp. Michael walked up behind me, "You are my hero."

I thought he was teasing me, but when I turned to face him, he was staring at me... like it had been the first time he had ever seen me. I laughed nervously, "Hero, really... I mean, yeah right."

Michael reached up, gently touched my face. With no humor in his face or voice, "No, really... you have saved my life... twice."

Before I could respond, Alice, Ezra, Charlotte and Clyde flashed up. Ezra announced, "Well, counting these dead wolves that make seventeen. Your two werewolves are standing next to the wizard in that clearing." He pointed to where the cabins encircled; there was a small clearing in the middle of the cabins. I could make out three men standing in the center.

Charlotte, with a big smile, "You two will have to wait until later. We have a job to finish."

Alice commanded, "Michael stays here, the rest of us will follow Melabeth."

"Where did you get that from?" Ezra asked, he was looking at my sword.

Alice answered for me, "Spirit weapon, she'll have to explain it later. Her revenge is at hand."

It truly was, there stood all the men who had raped and killed me. My revenge was close, but I had a feeling that they weren't standing there waiting to die. I moved forward, "Okay, let's finish this."

Clyde roared and yelled, "We'll drain them all for what they did to Bonnie."

We moved past one of the cabins, I was standing in front the rest of my vampire kin. They stood on either side of me, fanning back like a V. We moved forward upon their position when I ran into an invisible wall. I looked upon the ground, there laid a circle of small rocks that encircled the mage and werewolves.

Alex challenged, "I don't think I will be inviting any of you in. Do you?"

Charlotte mocked, "Is this how you plan to save yourself?"

"Not hardly…" Alex stopped answering her. He was staring at me; now he was staring at my sword. "Oh, I see, you have read the book. Well, I have read it too."

Before I could respond, the wizard lifted his staff and uttered some words. My sword started to ring and shake. I knew that the sword was Carrie screaming when the blade rang, she was in pain.

I yelled at no one in particular, "What's going on? Carrie… you all right?" Of course the sword did not answer me; instead it exploded into a pile of black ash. Even the hilt turned to dust. I screamed at Alex, "I will kill you for that." I knew that he had killed Carrie.

Alex laughed, "Oh, did the ghost mean something to you?"

Alice voice was full of wickedness, "Come on let's play."

Alex's face darkened, "Couldn't agree more."

With that the wizard slammed the bottom of his staff upon the ground, when he lifted it up the top of the staff was ablaze. I had a hard time even looking at him; I felt my skin start burning. I knew this spell, it was the same one that David's mother had used on me. It was a spell used by hunters and normally cast from across so it would seem to be the power of God was attacking us.

All the vampires took a step back, but that was not the end of Alex's attack. The ground began to tremble as vines ripped from the earth. They were trying to wrap themselves upon us, I quickly moved away, dodging the serpent like plants. I saw in my second sight as the plants got a hold of Charlotte, she fought to get free.

Alex muttered more magic words and a fireball came from his staff. The fireball flew through the air like a missile slamming into Charlotte. She burst into flames, screaming as she burned to death. Ezra yelled out, "NOOO!!!"

Alice grabbed him, "We must move away." She pulled Ezra away from the vines and his love.

Without another word we all flashed away running back to where Michael was standing. We were surrounded by the bodies of the fallen wolves, but the vines didn't look to be able to reach us. I looked over and could see Michael's face, full of disbelief. Ezra looked like a statue, it was Clyde, who broke the silence, "We must go. The sun will rise soon, let us leave, we will fight another day."

Alice nodded, "Melabeth, I know it will be hard, but it is best we try again… later."

Before I could work up a response a green blast wave of energy passed by us. Alice asked, "What the hell was that?"

"I know," Is all I could say as the dead wolves began to move.

So Alex was practicing Necromancy, damn, I wish David were here to counter this. The dead men rose from the ground and started putting their bodies back together, they also started to turn into wolves again.

I announced, "Okay, let's go, maybe another time."

We all ran into the woods, but I could hear the sound of the strange howls. Alice stopped, "Ezra, Melabeth, we must fly."

I looked at her with confusion, "But Michael can't fly."

Clyde added, "Neither can I."

Michael didn't miss a beat, "I can't fly, but we can run." He took off into the woods, closely followed by Clyde.

Ezra spoke with no emotion, "Alice and I will lead them away, and then take to the air, but Melabeth you would be better off with us; we will do what we can for them."

Alice quickly added, "I cannot use my power upon these undead creatures. Come with us."

I shook my head, "No, I will stay and help them. Just buy as much time as you can. I will see you tomorrow."

Alice gave me a big hug, "Be safe… now run." Alice still holding her doll, lifted it away from her body. The legs were nothing but handles for her knives, but they were both gone. She reached up inside her doll; her hand came out holding a pin. She talked to her doll, "One last favor." She tossed her doll in the direction of the undead wolves.

I took off, and they took off in another direction. I hurried to catch up with Michael and Clyde. This whole attack was turning into a nightmare. I heard a loud explosion from behind me, now I knew what she put in the doll's head.

As I ran, the howls of undead wolves filled the air.

Chapter 27 Hiding
隐蔽

I chased after Michael and Clyde, putting Ezra and Alice out of my mind.

I couldn't feel for Ezra or our loss of Charlotte, not now. I had to keep my mind on the here and now; I could save Michael, but not Charlotte. Clyde and Michael's path split; I followed Michael's.

I looked up and noticed a rocky outcrop on a side of the hill. I noticed a bat or two flies into a crack in the side of the rock. I yelled out, "Michael, follow me." I changed directions and as I did Michael fell into step without a word. I came to the rocks and started climbing. I looked back and saw Michael having difficulty, for he still only had one hand. I offered, "Need help?"

Michael looked at me defensively, "I got it."

We scaled the side of the cliff until we reached the crack I had noticed. I slid inside, then reached out and pulled Michael in. Within minutes the sun came out and the death dogs caught up with us. Michael worked his way back into the small cave to stay away from the sun, but I went to the edge to look down. There, twelve undead dogs growled at me; they were trying to climb up, but they just fell back down. I walked back into the cave to check on Michael.

I sat down next to him, "Thank goodness dogs can't climb."

Michael leaned back against the stone wall, "That is the third time you have saved me. I thought for sure I was going to die. I am sure glad you saw this cave, but we will be lucky if we can hold on here all day."

He was right; those death dogs sure would make it easy for someone to find us. I reassured him, "I don't think Alex will chase us down. He has spent too much time making all those protection spells at his camp."

He nodded, "True, but I wasn't worried about him. I was thinking he might send the werewolves out to hunt us."

"I hadn't thought about that," I admitted.

We sat quietly for a moment, and then I couldn't help myself. Life is too short, I thought as I crawled up on Michael's lap. His look was surprised as I took his face in my hands. Looking into his eyes, I waited for just a second… then I kissed him.

It was like nothing I felt before, Michael knew how to kiss. Soft but hard and his taste was out of this world. Even with one hand, he knew how to touch me. His hand, knew every little magical spot as it explored my dress. I reached up and started to work loose the straps on my dress, but this brought a pause to Michael.

He pulled my face away; I wanted to force my lips back with him, but I also didn't want to overpower him. He looked into my eyes, "I think we need to talk first."

"About?" my voice sounded breathless.

"Well, what do you see when you look at me?"

I was a little disappointed he wanted to talk. I answered impatiently, "You're sweet, kind and beautiful."

He chuckled as I tried to kiss him again. "Is that all you see in me? What do you know about me?"

He was frustrating me with these questions. I had dreamed of being with him for so long I couldn't hide my irritation from him, "I am trying to get to know you right now."

His face was serious, "Look, if we don't talk before we make love, I'm afraid of what might happen afterwards. I mean you don't take betrayal lightly, and I don't want to be on the other end of your anger."

"Okay, what is it that I need to know before we can be together?" I tried not to sound impatient and disappointed, but I was.

His eyes were full of pleading, "I want you. There is nothing more that I want right now. You are beautiful and wonderful. I would like to take you right here in this cave, but you are kind of immature. If you don't understand who I am now, I am afraid you'll hold it against me."

"I'm immature? How's that?"

Michael quickly tried to defend himself, "Not in all things."

I was angry now, "So, what things am I immature in?"

"Well," he paused as he searched for the right words. "Tell me what you know of my life?"

"How is that supposed to tell me how I am immature?"

Michael was stern, "Answer the question."

I tried to stare him down. After a minute I gave in, "Okay, but I can't believe you missed out on sex for this."

Michael smiled, "Neither can I, but in the long run this might be safer. Please answer the question."

I let out a huff, "Fine, I'll tell you what I know. You were turned in 1969 at the age of nineteen. Shortly after you fell in love with a human; you were with her for a couple of years. You tried to change her into a vampire, but it failed and she never rose. You were heartbroken... then if I remember right Alice made you Lea."

Michael nodded, "It wasn't just Lea. I had been a vampire for twelve years and in that time I proved to be useful to the Whites. Vampires, especially young vampires are killed often. The Whites, like most clans, are always making new vampires and if they survive to be at least twenty, then Ezra will train them. He won't train them younger because they're not powerful enough and most likely will be killed by hunters anyway. They brought me five girls that summer; Lea is all that's left. I have been with her for ten years."

I hadn't realized all that, but I wasn't sure what he was trying to tell me. I asked, "Are you in love with Lea?"

Michael shook his head, I felt myself relax. Michael started to explain again, "No, not in the way you mean. She's in love with me, but you knew that. It's just… well; I have spent ten years with her. We share the same room…"

It hit me, and I interrupted his rambling, "Have you slept with her?"

"Yes, I have had sex with her."

I asked, "Just once?"

Michael gave me a duh look, "Many times. It is not uncommon for me to have sex with her or Charlotte for that matter."

I was stunned into silence; it took me a moment to realize my hands were balled into tight fists. Michael was looking upon me with weary eyes. He did not speak; he sat quietly as I composed myself. I still sat upon his lap, but I did not move. I waited until the shock and anger washed over me. Then I asked, "Ezra… does Ezra know about this?"

He was careful with his words, "Of course. He and Charlotte has been together for centuries, but not always exclusive. You have to understand, Charlotte meant a lot to me."

I mocked him, "Oh, I can see that."

"What's that supposed to mean?"

I got up off of him, and, as I turned my back to him, I said, "Nothing, I meant nothing by it."

Michael waited a minute before he spoke. With a kind voice, he said, "This is the immaturity I was talking about. I have been a vampire for twenty-one years. I have had my heart broken and my fair share of crushes. I have been with many women and living with other vampires; well, it is part of what we are. You know… blood, sex and rock and roll."

I knew he was right; what had I expected? I was afraid to ask, but I had to know. I squeaked, "Alice?" He was quiet and I knew my answer. My voice was broken, "Alice, really, even Alice."

"She is strange, but she has needs of a woman."

My voice was hollow, "I don't know you, but I didn't need to. I just needed a distraction, and you can't even be that."

Michael's voice pleaded, "Melabeth I knew you needed to understand this, but there's more. I care about you… no, I love you. I have wanted you from the first day I met you. I was hoping, in time, maybe you would come to understand me."

I didn't answer, I walked away. I walked into the sun and to the opening of the cave. They're the twelve death dogs circled and growled. The clouds were building in the sky, and it was partly overcast. I thought about Carrie, Charlotte, David and Michael, and I felt nothing. A strange hollow feeling came over me and for the first time since I entered these woods my path seemed clear.

I was going to wait until the werewolves came to me. They could throw bombs into the cave killing us both. Alex could send a fire element into the cave or something along that line. I was going to wait, but not anymore. I didn't need the distraction after all. All this time chasing Michael, now that I caught him I didn't want him. I'll never understand why he ruined our moment? I'm not as immature as he thinks; I just wanted that glorious body.

I looked upon the undead wolves while trying to formulate a plan, other than waiting here to die. I watched the monsters turning in circles growling and something stirred in me. I felt a hunger; I was hungry, I used so much of my power. These undead wolves did not smell good; their blood was polluted with death. The hunger to devour the wolves washed over me.

I wasn't sure I understood, but I felt as if I could feed upon these creatures. I slowly stepped to the very edge. My second sight could see Michael moving up from behind me. He came to a stop just right outside the beam of light that came in the cave entrance. He was concerned, "What are you doing? You don't have to jump off a cliff for me."

I laughed darkly, then with contempt, "As if, as if you, or anyone else was worth my *life*." Michael started to speak, but I cut him off, "Bye, Michael. We'll talk later."

Then I jumped.

I was not afraid as I headed toward the white teeth below. I felt nothing, empty of emotion, but I was aware of everything. I came in fast, sliding between the biting teeth and landing in a crouch on the ground. I quickly slid under one of the large dogs, then pulled him to the ground. With his body on top of me the other undead dogs were having a hard time finding me. I bit into the animal's hairy chest and the blood entered my mouth.

The world stopped or slowed down. I felt the spirit that inhabited this creature slide down my throat. In a matter of a single gulp of nasty dead blood, I tore the remaining spirit and then devoured it. I felt my strength return as the undead wolf became a human corpse.

I came up off the ground fighting, clawing, kicking and biting.

After about the third kill, my strength became unreal; it was like drinking too much coffee. I was sliced and bitten more than once and every time it happened the sun's rays would set my blood on fire. Somehow I was able to put out the small fires and heal; lucky for me that I healed much faster than normal vampires. For not only were there cuts and bites to heal, but I had to heal burns as well.

I couldn't flash or fly, but I was still fast and for reasons I didn't understand, I felt stronger. No matter what I did to the undead dogs, tear their heads off, cut them wide open, it didn't matter since they would not die. They would not die that is until I fed from them. After I did I would feel their power flow into me as they fell to the ground dead.

Then I understood. I had fed upon weak ghosts upon the island. These wolves were raised from the dead using necromancy. In doing so they used a piece of the soul to help power the corpse. It was the main difference between wizards animating objects, their objects were animated through magic alone.

I now knew that I could feed from the dead. I was no longer hungry, and I fought with a new found strength. I fought each dog off, and then I would flip one on its back and bite it. I would slide under others to bite them underneath. The dead animals showed no fear, but they also showed no intelligence as I used the same method on each one of them.

I had kicked one away as I killed the second to last wolf. Now the last one was charging me. It was going my way, and, at last, I was down to just one. I side stepped the attacking wolf, and, at the same time, I brought my shoulder into its side. This sent the dog sliding against the ground.

As it tried to get to its feet, I ran up to the creature and grabbed its neck. That's when I noticed my hands. My fingers wrapped all the way around the large wolf's neck. I also had the strength to hold the dog with one arm. The wolf's strong legs were sliding my feet around until they became solidly planted against the cliff wall. There the wolf pushed forward, but neither I, nor the mountain would move.

I was still in shock as I lifted my free hand and took in the sight. The palm of my hand was as big as my whole face. My fingers were at least eight inches long; the whole thing reminded me of a cartoon, like my hand had been smashed. Only my hand was not flat; it was huge and elongated. That's not where it ended; my nails were black and four or five inches long and razor sharp.

"What is this?" I said to myself.

The wolf snapping at my face awoke me from my concern. I pushed the wolf back and with one quick slice of my large claws I cut its nose and lower jaw. The stupid animal still came at me like it could bite me. I bit the wolf, killing the last of the undead wolves. I was now surrounded by the bodies of shifters.

I walked away from the cliff and toward the forest. I glanced back to see Michael standing at the edge of the cave. He looked at me with fear in his eyes as he slowly retreated back into the cave. He would be safe; I was no longer worried about him.

I walked through the forest with no real emotion. The sky was still partly overcast and the sun was hiding behind a dark cloud. It didn't take long before it showed itself, I wished it hadn't. The shadows of the forest all traveled towards me. As I moved they followed, even smaller plants bent away from me as I passed by. The forest animals scurried away, and the forest went quiet; not even the bugs made a noise. A dark cloud formed around me as I headed through the forest back to Alex, The Smith brothers and my revenge.

I heard the sound of growling, I knew that it was the rest of the wolves. They were not heading in my direction so I turned and followed the sound. I walked taking in everything; the sounds grew louder as I closed the distance. It sounded as if someone was snapping branches. As I rounded a hill the wolves came into my line of sight.

The sound now made sense; the five wolves were gathered around a large oak tree. They were tearing the base of the tree apart with their jaws. Half of the mighty oak was already gone. My eyes followed up the tree to see Clyde standing upon a branch holding onto the tree trunk. He looked exhausted and past fear.

One of the undead wolves took notice of me and it brought a small smile to my face. I yelled out, "Come and get me, puppy, puppy, puppy."

Three of the undead wolves broke free from the tree and rushed towards me. The big brown wolf that I shoved the rifle up his ass was one of them. The rifle stock still projected from the wolf's ass which made me laugh.

Just as the first wolf approached, I jumped into a flip, slicing my hand downward my claws removing the beast's head.

Landing between the remaining two, I kicked one as I grabbed the other. I bit down on the brown wolf, taking his life, quickly turning to fight off the attack from the one I had kicked. It only took me a few seconds to finish him off, but that's all the time needed for the one I had beheaded to put itself back together. It was short lived as the newly formed wolf turned to face me, I reached up and grabbed its head and bit its face.

The other two wolves came upon me next, but the fight was short lived as I was fast.

I stood there; I felt a little sick, like I had eaten too much. My dress was all ripped up around the bottom, and the sleeves had been ripped back to my elbows. The fact the dress still hung on my body proved it was magical.

Clyde had dropped to the ground and was now heading my way. It was overcast, and we stood under a canopy of trees; this helped him, but he was still straining to see. I moved in his direction; as we closed the distance, he was able to recognize me, "Melabeth… is that you?"

He froze, as if there was danger, which made me react in a similar way. My second sight didn't see anything, but Clyde was looking around; he was staring at me. His face looked twisted as if he has seen a ghost. I asked, "What's wrong?"

He looked as if he were about to bolt. His voice was full of disgust, "What are you? You're the devil."

I was taken aback by his reaction to me. I closed the distance and now stopped an arm length in front of him. I demanded, "Why would you say that?"

He spoke with fear in his voice, "You look like an evil monster…"

His body went slack as he dropped to his knees. It had hardly registered that I moved one step forward and swung my hand with all my force. My hand had been flat and my fingers spread out like a large blade. I had hardly even thought about it when I swung… now he was upon his knees and as his body fell backwards upon the ground, his head rolled free of his corpse.

As I turned to walk away, the muted sunrays finally reacted with his blood. I could hear the crackling of the flames as Clyde's body burned on the forest floor. I couldn't help but think; if he really thought I was the devil, why would he piss me off? Oh well, some mysteries will never be solved.

I headed in my original direction, back toward the cabins. I came to a small pool of still water and stopped to look at my face. At once, I understood Clyde's reaction. My hands were huge and monstrous, and my teeth were even longer than usual, but that's not why he called me the devil. My eyes looked even bigger; they looked like giant blue plates of glass. Behind the blue glass burned a fire; you could see the fire burning behind my eyes. I had seen these eyes before; these were Nicks eyes. I suppose I killed Clyde for no good reason, but I didn't care.

As I walked and the shadows twisted around me, I noticed some of the shadows were now moving in a different direction. The shadows formed a large black curtain. It didn't really surprise me when Nicks strolled up. He moved fluidly toward me in a dark red robe. His hood was drawn back and hung down his back. His black hair lay untied on both sides of his head.

He gave me a small head nod, "Good day Melabeth."

"And a top of the morning to you," I said with no emotion. We looked upon each other with still faces. I wasn't even sure what he wanted, but I did know what I did. I broke the silence first, "It's time for answers. I know you didn't create me, that I was made from a spell. Who are you, and what are you to me? My eyes look like yours now, now that I have devoured death, *I want answers*."

Nicks' face became dark as clouds of dark matter swirled around him. His whole body doubled in size as his booming voice filled the air. "I am no mere mortal… watch your tone with me."

His power poured off of him as my body hair stood on end. The fear quenched my anger as I tripped over my words, "Sorry... it won't happen again... okay." I waited a second longer as his eyes flamed like two dancing fireballs. I straightened myself and said with real conviction, "Sorry, I mean it."

Nicks became normal in a blink of an eye; once again his face was full of kindness. He walked up to me, and it was natural to fall in stride with him. We walked side by side through the forest. He told me, "You are wrong and right. You were wrong about being created by the spell. You were sent to me by the spell, and then I created you, but you are right that it is time to tell you how you have become. Or rather what you may be."

"What I may be?" I asked in dismay.

Nicks gave me a kind smile, "You are full of anger right now; I can see that. Let me start as to why I have waited to tell you. I have feared that your enemies will come against you when they discover what you are. Rather, they will think they know what you are and destroy you out of fear. I don't even know what you will become, but I have hope. My wishes were that you would become stronger or rather you would come to understand what you are before anyone else could, but the time for hiding you has ended."

I kindly suggested, "Start from the beginning, I am ready."

He nodded, "Good place to begin any story. I believe the beginning of our story started the night you were murdered. Alex had stolen a terrible magic book, containing dark Necromancer magic. He found a spell which would give him and his friend's immortality, an escape from death. The spell called for a virgin to be defiled over the prepared magic circle. His spell didn't work for many reasons; one was that you were no virgin. I believe he screwed up many other things as well and in doing so he created a new spell; one that cannot be repeated.

Let it also be known who I am, for I am the Angel of Death, the Grim Reaper. It is I who reap the lost souls of this world and bring them to death. I have been called many names over the centuries, but I prefer Nicks."

I froze in my tracks as my mind tried to wrap around this information. He made sense, but it meant that I was the daughter of death. I asked the first question that popped in my head, "The Library?"

"It is the doorway to death, the entrance between this world and the next. Many people have called it by different names, the River Styx, Purgatory, that is but a few names for the library. In all my long life, it has been my job to collect the dead, and I grow tired. The world becomes more and more populated and there is never enough time to collect all the dead. I do not know what lies in the land of death, but I can tell you this much, they will not send me any help.

I longed for a child and for many centuries I searched for a way of creating such a thing, but alas, I have found nothing. That is until you... you must understand that I have a physical form like you, but unlike any creature that has ever lived, I am the only one who can travel between life and death. Spirits can travel back and forth, but they have no physical form. I can send spirits, to their final rest, and so can you. That is what you did with the wolves, their spirits were trapped and you free their souls."

"I watched the movie they killed me in, and in the end my body melted. What happened to it?" I was trying to make sense of this.

Nicks smiled, "It was the first physical body other than mine to enter the library. The night they cast the spell, I felt the call. I came to witness the end of your earthly existence. I followed your body to the land of death, and, most importantly, your soul was still attached."

"My whole body went to the land of the dead?" I remarked.

Nicks continued explaining, "Yes and every time you have visited the library, so has your body. If anyone would have checked your bed they would have found it empty. Still, there was a problem the first time you arrived in the library."

"What?"

He simply said, "You were dead."

I didn't understand the part he played or how I became a vampire, but I was about to find out. I couldn't hide my curiosity as I asked, "Then how did you bring me back?"

"Not being the first person I tried to give my gift to, I did have an idea of how this might be done. Starting with blood, I then added fairy blood and finally my own blood. Your body was too damaged and needed to be healed. Once there lived a magical creature that could heal all things, disease, injury and even aging. To harvest this power, you had to kill the creature. The magical animal was hunted down until none were left, but I had the last of the creature's blood. I added it to you and your body repaired itself."

I asked, "And what creature was this?"

Nicks looked like he was thinking about whether or not to tell me. He finally answered, "Unicorn."

"REALLY?" I asked in disbelief.

Nicks gave me a small smile, "Well, it only half worked. It repaired your body, but when I carried you back to the land of the living; you were still dead. I came up with an idea; I had no idea if it would work. I found a vampire and asked for some of his blood. He was only a little bit disagreeable, but after a small talk he donated. After adding the vampire blood, you came to life, and I had great hope. I noticed that once your body took life, it began a quick change, and I knew that you would die and rise as a vampire. I decided to take your body and lay it to rest in a quiet place, so I called upon some spirits to prepare your new resting area."

"I remembered them; I thought the girl was rude."

Nicks nodded, "She was. Still, we made you a casket, and there I lay you to rest. I was forced to kill you again, but I'd rather do that than watch you die slowly while the change happened. I had no idea if any of it would work."

I remembered something Nicks told me that night, "I thought you found me in a dumpster?"

"I had not the time to explain all things to you. You were barely in your right mind. I was not trying to deceive you, but rather give an easy explanation so that you may rest in peace. I always knew if you survived the change I would get my chance to set the record straight."

His words rang not only of truth, but of concern and love. I smiled at him, "I never think of you as someone who is trying to deceive me. I just want to understand; tell me more about the magical creatures. I obviously know about vampires and the Unicorn, but what about the Elves and Fairy?"

Nicks looked around, "I can't stay long; they will have to be short explanations. I have one other matter we must council on before I leave. The Elfin is very magical people; their ability to manipulate energy has always made them powerful. Their weakness is they live longer and produce few and over time their numbers have decreased. They mixed with man and a new race was born, Mage. Now there are many mages and only one full blooded Elf left; their race is all but extinct.

Fairies are rare, but they still exist in forests around the world. They live in self made glamour, for that is all they do. It's much like Alice's power; this is why legends of fairies are so varied."

I asked, "Do they mix with humans as well?"

Nicks laughed, "They're three inches tall. Not sure how that would work."

I laughed as well. Clearing the mental image from my head I said, "That makes sense."

Nicks added, "It also makes sense of where you get your other site, for Fairies glamour everyone, including each other. For that reason they use sonar, like a bat, so that they don't run into things."

"Is that where it comes from?" I commented in wonder.

"Before my time is up, we must speak about what you are to become."

"And what is that?"

Nicks' face held no humor, "An angel of death, like no other… but before I let such great power arise, I must know that it is good."

Defensively, I snapped, "I'm good… well, sort of."

Nicks smirked, "You have good in you, and are capable of good. On the other hand, you have evil as well. I have watched you; not all of what you have done is good. Know this, a path lies before you where this will be tested. Kill the innocent and I will strike you down."

What he said, rattled me, "Oh… okay, well, I'll try to watch out for that."

Nicks smiled tightened and his eyes narrowed, "Try harder… one more thing."

I wanted to say, Oh great, but all that came out was, "Yes."

"I love you," and with that he took me into his embrace.

"I love you too."

He pulled free, "I must go. Good luck, I am sure you will make me proud."

"Goodbye," had barely left my lips as the cloud of smoke vanished and once again I stood in the forest alone.

I turned and once again headed toward the cabins. I prayed that I might finish this one way or the other, for now I had the goodness that needed working on.

Chapter 28 Vengeance
復讐

I moved once more toward the cabins.

I moved faster now, without making a sound. It was late afternoon when I arrived at the cabins. My talk with Nicks had taken a little while. Now I wondered if I hadn't missed them all together, but my fears were gone when I reached the first cabin. On the other side of the cabin I could make out voices speaking in the clearing. It took me a moment to realize they were arguing and judging by the conversation, it had been going on for some time now.

It took ten long minutes to make sure that all three men were there. Brandon hadn't spoken nearly the whole time; his brother was still arguing with Alex on how to go out and hunt us. Judging from what he was saying it sounded as if Alex's plan was for the brothers to go out and risk their lives while he stayed behind where it was safe. The brothers weren't buying it for even a second.

Frustrated, Alex told the brothers, "If we all go out, my protective circle will fall apart. You may not kill them all, and then at night, where would you dumb asses hide?"

One of the brothers replied, "We may be dumb asses, but not as dumb as you think."

I believe Brandon spoke next, "Shut up, you're not helping. Alex, after last night do you even think they will come back?"

Alex answered, "I cannot tell, but the fact they came out into the woods against so many of us… well, I think we must plan as if they might return. Randy, can you get my bag out of the cabin? If none of us is going to hunt them down, then I better start casting some more spells."

Randy responded to Alex, "I'll grab your damn bag…" under his breath as he headed toward the cabin he added, "Lazy wizard."

As my luck would have it, he was heading toward the cabin that I was hiding behind. I looked up at the closed window. If I could kill him before the other two knew I was here, I would gain the advantage. I reached up and tested the window with my long fingers. My luck held; it was unlocked. Randy was making all kinds of noises as he slammed things around looking for whatever Alex sent him for. I slid the window up, and the wooden window frame made an awful noise. I froze, waiting for the inevitable yell that would let them all know that I was here.

It didn't happen; Randy had been making too much noise, and it covered my entrance. I quickly crawled through the window and into the cabin, landing on a small bed that was located inside a tiny bedroom. There was hardly room for the bed. I moved to the open door and watched Randy stomp to the front door of the cabin.

He held the door open as he yelled out, "I can't find your dumb ass bag."

I swiftly moved up behind him without a sound. I could hear Alex yelling at him about being useless, and did he check under the bed, but before Randy could turn around, I attacked.

Using my left hand, I buried my claws into his spine as my fingers slipped in between his ribs. My right hand sliced below his rib cage and into his lower back. I reached up and tore his heart clean out. With my left hand I held him in front of me, keeping his body from falling to the ground. His body shook as muscle spasms spread across his body. It would take a second or two for the rest of his body to catch up with the fact that he was dead.

I bit into his heart and let the warm blood flow down my throat. I could feel night closing in; I tossed the empty heart behind me like an old apple core. A smile spread across my lips as Alex approached the cabin saying, "What is wrong with you? Must I do everything myself you useless animal."

He came to a sudden halt about fifteen feet from the cabin. At this point I could hear his heart accelerate; he knew. I tossed the body to one side so I could see my next victim face to face. He stepped back, and, with a dark calm about him, said, "It is time... let's finish this, shall we?"

I smiled, "You don't have to ask me twice." I attacked.

I lunged forward; Alex ran backwards. I had just started thinking that I had forgotten something.

I remembered what I forgot when Brandon slammed into me from my side. He was already a wolf man; he clawed and bit at me as we fell upon the ground locked in combat.

The werewolf was strong, and I fought to keep him from getting a hold of me. His claws ripped into the flesh of my arms more than once. The overcast sky kept my blood from bursting into flames right away, but about the time my wounds closed my blood set on fire. I managed to put my left arm out, as the wolf's teeth lunged for my throat. I shoved my right arm between me and the wolf and at the same time my left hand was quick enough to grab his neck and keep him from biting me. The fire from my right arm caught hold on the wolf's chest hair; he jumped off of me to put himself out.

Being that it was still day, I couldn't flash, I was at a disadvantage. My large claws cut him several times as I got to my feet. Using my speed I dodged his attacks, but he caught me with a backhand. He hit me so hard that I felt my body leave the ground.

I felt the cabin wall as my body smashed into it. The wood cracked as I bounced off and landed on the ground. My shoulder was injured; I had landed on my feet. The werewolf was upon me, giving me no quarter. I slipped under his attacks and got behind him.

My shoulder kept me from using my left arm so I clawed him with my right. Four deep slashes down his back as crimson red poured freely. The wolf howled in pain as I kicked him into the wall of the cabin.

The wolf fell to the ground momentarily stunned. I used this time to see what happened to Alex. I turned to see him standing once again in his protective circle. He chanted with both hands out before him. Blue light emitted from his hands as the sky darkened. Black swirling clouds that looked no higher than the tree tops, moved in circles above my head.

With my second sight I knew that the wolf had recovered and was now on his feet. I turned around and jumped into a flip, dodging the animal's latest attack. It was hard to worry about Alex's spell when I was so busy fighting the werewolf.

I saw it with my second sight, objects falling from the sky. The first few objects hit the ground around me, and I could see what they were. Large blue, white shards of ice were sticking out of the ground, with many more on their way.

The ice storm hit all around as I dodged the large sharp icicles. The wolf was still attacking until one of the icicles hit him in the shoulder. Cutting him deeply, the wolf howled once again in pain, but before I could celebrate my victory an icicle found my shoulder.

With my second sight I could see above me and there were icicles coming down by the thousands. They were crashing into trees and smashing through the cabin roofs. I wouldn't be able to dodge the falling ice forever. The wolf was hit again, and I had an idea.

I jumped forward and grabbed the werewolf by the shoulders; kneeing the wolf hard in the gut, I pulled back at the same time. The wolf fell forward landing upon me; he growled and looked as if he might bite, but then he screamed in pain. Icicle after icicle, crashed into the werewolf's back, slicing into him as his body protected mine.

The wolf tried to break free, but I refused to let him up. His tough body was protecting me from the storm of ice. A piece of ice crashed into the back of his head and the werewolf stopped struggling. The wolf melted away; I was now looking upon the face of Brandon. His lifeless eyes stared at me as blood ran around his head.

The storm stopped as suddenly as it began. I tossed the dead body off of me and quickly rose to my feet. The world sparkled with shards of ice sticking out of everything. I looked over at Alex who was now pulling out a stone. I knew what the stone was for; it was for teleporting.

I wasn't about to let him get away. I pulled the icicle out of my shoulder, and in one motion I let it fly through the air. My aim was true as it collided with Alex's hand, sending the stone flying through the air; at the same time, Alex screamed in pain while clutching his now bloody hand. The stone landed outside of his protected circle and into a large bush.

I wasn't about to wait around until Alex cast another large spell. I ran across the icy ground to a tree that stood between two of the cabins. The tree was an evergreen about fifty feet tall with an eight inch base. I swung my claws at the base of the tree. First my right hand, then my left, each hit resulted in wood chips flying through the air. It didn't take me but a minute for the tree to start cracking and groaning and finally falling. I stepped to the side as the tree fell to the ground.

I gave Alex a grin as he looked at me in confusion. I reached down and grabbed the tree by its trunk. I held the tree out in front of me like a spear. Realization washed across Alex's face at the same time I charged him.

He wasn't quick enough to move as I hit him with the end of the tree. I pushed him across the ground with the end of the tree as he fought to get free from all the branches. The magic circle is what finally stopped me, but Alex had been pushed clean out the other side. I wasted no time by running around the circle.

By the time I made it to the other side, Alex had gotten to his feet. He said some words as he waved his arm. I was running at him, trying to close the distance, to rip his throat out before he could cast a spell. I wasn't fast enough; the spell he cast was apparent as my legs sank into the ground.

I was only about five feet away from him when the quicksand pulled me into the earth. I was sinking fast; the sand was quickly approaching my chest. Alex chuckled, "The sun is almost set."

Why he chuckled over that confused me. I informed him, "And when it does, I will have all my power."

Alex didn't answer me, instead he slowly stepped away walking backwards and never taking his eyes off me. He put his hands together and began to chant. I mumbled to myself, "Oh great, what now?"

I felt it; the sun fell below the horizon. The cloud cover and the forest hid the sun from my view, but I knew when it had set. I made myself weightless as I carefully started lifting myself from the quicksand. As I did, dark shadows formed around Alex, and then he grew in size. His hands and arms were being covered by a black liquid that moved across his whole body. The liquid dried and hardened, and it appeared to be some kind of hard black rock. As he moved, the black cracked and underneath was red, but not blood, just light. His now monster face came to life with red eyes; his mouth opened with black, yellow sharp teeth, and the same red power seemed to rise from his throat.

I had pulled myself free and floated through the air. Landing softly on the ground that had not been affected by the quicksand spell; he roared, and I hissed back.

We charged each other. I was now able to flash; my strength was greater and yet my hands stayed the same. They were large with huge claws that I used to rip at my foe. He was much slower than me, but appeared to be stronger. I wasn't about to let this fight turn into a contest of strength.

When my claws hit his new skin, they made a horrible noise. His skin was as hard as it looked, and more than once, one of my fingernails would catch a crack. When that happened, they would rip off. It hurt like crazy, but they grew back fast enough. It was the first time he clawed me that I knew this would be harder than I thought. His fingers raked across my skin, but instead of just cutting, they burned.

I had a hell of time healing the wounds. This dark spell must only work at night; no wonder he was happy about the sun going down.

We fought in the forest; I used the terrain to my advantage. I could flash and attack him from the rear or jump from tree to tree, yet the whole fight seemed to be a standoff.

He backhanded me sending me into a tree, but before he could hit me again, I kicked him with enough force to send him to the ground. He jumped up quicker than I thought he could; he came up swinging. I dodged the first two and deflected the third. I dropped down and swept his feet out from under him, and once again he landed on the ground.

As he rose from the ground, I flashed behind him. I grabbed his throat and squeezed with all my might. Alex struggled to get me off and growled with anger. He ran backwards and slammed me between him and a tree. With the sudden impact I lost my grip.

With a quick twist of his body I found myself on the ground. I was fast to get up, but not fast enough. He slammed into me, knocking me onto the ground and landing on me. His hands secured both my wrists; he pulled my arms together and was able to lock both of my wrists in one hand. Shoving my hands right above my head, he pinned me down with one free hand to boot.

He shoved his hips in between my legs. With a growling voice that was not his own, "I always thought you might come back for more. Seeing as you enjoyed it so much the first time."

I struggled and fought him not only physically, but the panic was setting in. It was strange what memory surfaced in my mind.

*   *   *

Alice was busy discussing doll history with the clerk. The clerk was utterly surprised at Alice's knowledge of dolls. I never knew there were custom doll shops that did nothing but sell dolls. There were custom dolls, antique dolls, and entire lines of clothes and accessories.

I blurred out their conversation while I looked upon the dizzying amount of dolls. It was hard to see the trees through the forest; this store was packed. The owner had them shoved everywhere on overloaded shelves. I could have been at a hoarder's house. I wouldn't have noticed the difference.

A screech of terror brought my attention back to Alice. She had the clerk in a hold with her mouth to her neck. I knew then that the clerk was the one who had shrieked, and I went back to look at the dolls. After a moment or two I heard a dull thud against the floor and I became aware that Alice was now standing next to me.

I asked, "Was she disagreeable?"

Irritated, Alice responded, "She told me I didn't know what... I... was talking about. I was there... at the doll maker's house when this doll was made. I sure as hell should know what year it was."

"The doll in your hands?" I inquired.

"Yes, this doll and she even called me a liar."

"The doll?"

She half laughed, "Shut up."

I asked, "Is that your doll?"

She smiled like a villain, "Is now. Plus, what would she do with it?"

"Because she doesn't understand the history of the doll like you?"

Alice giggled, "No silly, because she is dead."

I looked around, "Alice... stop making all the dolls look at me. I don't like it." Alice smiled slyly but did not answer, nor did the dolls stop looking at me. That is when a male Indian caught my attention. I reached over and picked it off the shelf as I said, "I like this one."

"Put that back," she about screamed it.

I was shocked by her outburst, "Why?"

Her eyes narrowed, she was on the edge of a fit, "Because it is an Indian. They come in the night and kidnap, rape and scalp... that's why."

I almost laughed, "Seriously?"

Alice hung her head and her tone was more hurt than angry. "You don't know my past. And before you say it, I know that not all Indians are bad. It's just that doll reminds me... of old memories... ones I try to forget."

I nodded and put the doll back on the shelf. Then I covered him with another doll, "Out of sight, out of mind."

Alice gave me a small smile, "Do you know my past?"

I shook my head, "No."

"Well, it's a long story, but I will give you a small piece. After many years together and after many stories, you will know me better."

"Okay," I was excited to her about her past.

"It started long ago, 1587, that was the longest year of my life. I was a part of the Roanoke colonies and the only survivor. It was led by John White a relative of mine. My mother and father wasn't even on the official list. It is believed that there were 115 colonists, but this was not accurate. Of course back then it was unusual to keep accurate records.

When we arrived, the local Indians have been already hostile to us. The last colony had turned on them because they believed the Indians had stolen a silver goblet. The Indians killed all of them, so they were angry to see us arrive. John White had decided it would be best to sail back to England for more men and supplies, but we all knew it had to do with the birth of his new granddaughter. She was the first English child to be born in the Americas; her name was Virginia Dare.

They weren't gone long before the first attacks took place. In their very first raid, they killed my Dad and mother and kidnapped me and my brother. My brother was younger than me, about twelve, if I remember right. They hadn't taken us far when they made us sit so they could rest. I couldn't understand what they were saying, but it didn't take long before they were fighting.

There were obviously two sides of this fight; finally more than half of the braves left. It was me, my brother and three Indian braves. I was about to find out what they were fighting about. The three who stayed wanted to rape me and proceeded to do so. My brother broke free of his bindings… he saved me, but at the cost of his life.

He had attacked the braves and even got hold of one of their weapons. It did him no good, but it did allow me to break free and start running. They gave up chasing me when I was in sight of the fort. Later, they found my brother's body."

I wiped away a small tear from her face. I whispered, "I had no idea how much we had in common. Did they… you know?"

She nodded, "I really didn't fight them. I was so scared…" her voice became quiet and small, "I wish I would have fought them."

"I know, but what could you have done? Did you get them later?"

Alice shrugged, "I married a man, a man with a curse, just so I could have revenge upon them. I killed lots of braves, but I never could recall what the Indians looked like, so I'll never know. It doesn't bother me anymore, for now I know there is no revenge."

"What does that mean?"

Alice smiled, "You'll see." She changed subjects without pause, "Look at this doll!"

I knew she was talking about her past.

*   *   *

Alex was trying to keep me still as I struggled under him. I reached up and bit him. With a terrible crunching sound I ripped just some of the black stones away from his throat. He yelled in pain, then roared in my ear, "I was going to give you a going away present, but you're not worth it. I think I will just kill you instead."

He pulled back his free arm about to run me through with his claws... when a steel spear came bursting out of his chest.

He screamed as a set of arms grabbed him and pulled him off of me. They're Alice and Ezra held him, one on each arm, Alice with ferocity in her eyes, "Did you forget something wizard. Melabeth stop standing around already."

I jumped to my feet, "Right, sorry. Let's finish this." I attacked his neck. I clawed with all my strength, ripping at his stone neck. At first it just tore my claws away, but, after a few more hits, pieces started to break free.

Alex was fighting Alice and Ezra with everything he had. Once or twice he almost broke free. He laughed darkly, "You can't stop me; I'll kill all of you."

Ezra grunted, "What kind of magic is this?"

Alice responded with, "I have never seen it."

Then it hit me; it was death magic. It was magic he had learned from the book; that is why he had to wait until night. I was going about this the wrong way. I stopped attacking him and my bloody fingers started to heal quickly. I could see the victory in his eyes. I narrowed my eyes at him, "Your time is up."

I bit his shoulder, but this time I didn't worry about penetrating his black armor. I put my mouth on the black substance and started to suck, I sucked in the same way I did with the undead wolves. The hard black armor started to soften around my mouth and in seconds I was swallowing it. I understood now, it was some kind of spirit armor, and I devour spirits.

Alex yelled out, "No... HOW CAN YOU DO THIS? What are you?"

I pulled back to see the man. It was easy now for Alice and Ezra too hold him. I grabbed his head, one hand on both sides. "I am death; time to go and meet my father."

I tried my hardest to savor the moment as I tore off his head.

Chapter 29 Resolutions
決議

I was on my knees, just looking at Alex's head. Alice squealed something about a celebration. Ezra didn't say anything, but I knew he was in no mood to celebrate. Ezra lifted Alex's head off the ground and started to examine it. He pulled the hair away from the ears, and for the first time I noticed how pointed they were.

Ezra spoke dryly to Alice, "Does he look familiar? You know, without the beard, and with the pointy ears."

Alice was spinning in circles, and didn't even stop to look. She was giggling when she answered him, "Can't say that I ever saw him before."

Ezra was still puzzling when he blurted out, "Richard Alexander Longaeva. I am pretty sure this is him."

I interjected with, "It's not who he is… it is who he was, and he was never shit to me."

Alice laughed at my joke, but with a more serious tone answered Ezra. "Well, if I'm right; we're all in trouble, but we can worry about that later. For now let's burn the bodies, mourn our dead and celebrate our victory."

Michael came into the clearing; he was carrying a large bobcat. He joined our conversion, "I am in no mood for celebrating."

Ezra asked, "What's the cat for?"

He answered Ezra, "It's not a cat; she is a shifter. I caught her sneaking away from one of the cabins. That is what took me so long; I had to catch her. I am glad I did, if that is really Richard Alexander Longaeva."

Alice said solemnly, "We can't leave any witness that we killed him."

Michael handed the cat to Alice. I asked, "How old is she?"

Michael shrugged, "I would guess maybe five or six."

I was shocked, "We have to kill her?"

Alice stuck her tongue out at me, "I would never kill a child. I would never allow one so innocent to be harmed. She will be my pet, and I will name her Cat." Alice sat upon the ground and started baby talking to the cat while pulling her fingers through the fur.

We spent the next few hours gathering all the evidence we could find. We put everything in the cabins and then set them ablaze. My mind was full of thoughts, and the hike back to the truck was over in no time. We were all back at our camper before the morning light.

The bobcat turned into a little girl at one point. She had dark skin with black hair. It didn't take long, with Alice's mind power, to find out that she was the daughter of one of the shifters. Her mother had passed away, and the father had no sitter, so the fool brought her along. Alice made her think that Ezra was her father, and it wasn't long before they were cuddled up in one of the beds.

I was watching the child sleep when Alice broke into my thoughts. "It would be much easier for the child if you were to blood her. Shifters make great guards for vampires, but, unlike any other vampire, all she would need is your blood once."

"I don't know," I replied.

Alice asked me, "What is your next step?"

"I plan on going to North Carolina, and dealing with my father. I will go alone; you have all done enough."

Alice smiled, "I know you feel bad about Charlotte, but Ezra does not blame you."

I responded with, "I know. She was a warrior like Ezra, and that's how warriors die."

Ezra had not been asleep; he moved his head and opened his eyes. He looked at me and then gave me a wink, and, with that, laid his head back down with the girl. He gently shifted the sleeping girl so she was lying on her back. He whispered, "Blood her now, before you leave."

I wasn't sure about this, but since Ezra asked, I did it. I walked next to the sleeping girl and cut my wrist. I put my wrist to her mouth and at first she fought it, but then she began to drink. When I pulled my wrist away the little girl's eyes sparkled as she whispered, "Goodnight mommy." She turned her head and went back to sleep.

It was a strange feeling blooding the little shifter, but it was nice to be called a mommy. I lay in bed and with heavy eyes I fell asleep.

When I awakened, I got ready to head out on my own. I had no peace, not even after killing everyone who raped and murdered me. This was not over until I dealt with my father. Alice had told me, by blooding the shifter that she would grow to protect me. It was the only way to insure that she kept the secret without killing her. The little girl was a fifth generation shifter and was powerful. I said my goodbyes to Ezra and Alice. Michael followed me out to the car. He asked, "Hey, what ever happened to Clyde?"

I flatly said, "I killed him."

Michael looked a little shocked, "Why?"

I stared at Michael then finally answered him, "Do you really love me?"

"You're dodging the question."

I disagreed, "I didn't dodge. I slammed the door shut on that conversion."

Michael shook his head with a chuckle, "You're right, I don't even care what happened, and yes I have feelings for you. That hasn't changed since the cave. Even after you turned into that scary monster girl, could you ever forgive me?"

"I thought about it, and there is nothing to forgive, but I have come to realize that maybe I should get to know you first. When I get all this revenge behind me… maybe we could go out sometime?"

"I would like that."

I smiled, "It's a date."

Chapter 30 Mindy
姉妹

I was angry as I sat there on the plane. This was the second night since the sword had been destroyed. I knew now that Carrie was gone for good. As much as the girl annoyed me... she was like a part of me. She was my first true friend. Thinking of the loss of Charlotte was making me uncomfortable in my own skin.

I have prayed to God and he does not hear me. I have killed all the men who raped and killed me. With such a price, Lizzie, Charolette and Carrie. My father lives; he had betrayed me; he sold me for drugs. He's the reason this happened to me... the murder of his own daughter no less. I trusted my dad to take care of me, to protect me, to love me.

Now he can trust me... to kill him, to take away everything he is, or will ever be.

I opened his file and looked at it; I had a nice long flight to North Carolina. Ezra had looked it over and somehow came to the conclusion I should leave my father alone. He said something about a changed man. I guess somewhere in this file there will be proof of his sainthood.

According to the file, my grandparents searched for many years for me but found nothing. My father spent most of this time in a rehab center, probably so he didn't have to deal with the guilt. A year afterward he was offered a job by a lumber mill out in North Carolina. It figures that after all those years hugging trees and telling me how men are destroying the forest, he now cut them down himself. After being in the lumber mill for a few months, he started going to some church where he met some whore. My father and this whore, whose name is Jessica Lane, got married August 14, 1977. I realized that, Elvis was destroyed by this, because he dies two days later on a toilet. I personally hold this woman and my father responsible for Elvis death.

On May 16, 1978 this whore spawns *a* child, a little *girl*. Her name fills me with rage... Mindy Melanie Dare; how dare they give her my name? I guess it makes sense; after he sold me, he probably thought, better make another one they fetch a good price when they are older.

I read further down the page; apparently the whore worked at a restaurant. Oh, how sad, the whore was killed in 1983 by a drunk driver on the way home. Now I felt bad for calling her a whore, but still, it was probably the best way out of her marriage with my father, you know before he sold her. I guess this really messed my father up because he quit his life of killing trees and became a minister of a church. Now he preaches and teaches lost people in Salisbury, North Carolina.

My half sister just turned 14 a few months ago, and what's this, she makes straight A's. That's funny; Dad never let me go to school. It looks like he's all involved in little Mindy's life; that's nice, real nice. I bet he might not sell her for drugs. I bet she's a real keeper.

The worst part about all this, when I kill him, he will go to heaven. It will be like rewarding the bastard. I happen to believe in the afterlife; I believe in God. My opinion has always been, if I am wrong who cares, but if I am right, God will care. Plus, after finding out that my new father is death himself, well, it's hard to believe in nothing. I can't help but hope I'm wrong, because I'm going to hell when I die. Still, I would like my dad to get a head start; so the question is how do I make sure he goes to hell?

I landed in Charlotte, where I rented a car; from there it was about forty minutes to Salisbury. I checked into a small motel on the outskirts of town. That night I jumped in the Impala that I had rented and went for a drive. It was a small town and not much going on after dark. I had never been to North Carolina before; I had heard this area referred to as the Bible belt. It didn't take me long to figure out why. There was a church on every corner; I found three churches within view of each other. It's kind of funny; in Vegas there are bars on every corner. I found my dad's church and parked in the lot.

I noticed there were a lot of cars already there; it was Wednesday night. Maybe they have church every night, what else would they do in this town? I didn't get out of my car, I wasn't ready. I needed a plan, but first things first, I would need a disguise.

I got back to the motel with hands full of white plastic bags. I spent about two hours at Wal-Mart, buying stuff for this new plan of mine. I noticed that there was a bar behind my motel; that's funny, I hadn't known they had a continental breakfast for vampires. The bar gets out about two a.m. That would give me plenty of time to dye my hair.

It was about one a.m. when I was finishing the last rinse on my now jet black hair. I had learned one thing about the Goth style… that it dramatically changed the way you looked. I didn't need my father catching a glimpse of me and freaking out before I was ready for him to do so.

It took less than an hour to find a couple of drunken men heading out of the bar. I followed them to their car, and then drained them. I was doing the world a favor; they had no business driving anyways. I didn't kill them, not because of my kindness, but rather I didn't need that kind of attention around the motel room where I was staying.

I shut the door to my motel room and fell backwards onto my bed. Licking my lips and tasting the blood that I had missed, I watched the room spin from the alcohol. I had a heck of a buzz going on. I kicked my shoes off and laughed as one of my shoes banged hard against the far wall.

I awoke around ten in the morning feeling good about the rest of my plan on how to deal with my father. Quickly I picked up the phone book; the first thing I needed was a location to work from.

The lady that answered at the real estate agency was southern and way too sweet, but her over the top helpfulness... well, it was helpful. I told her that I worked for an investor looking to buy up property to open a nightclub. Sounding so young, it was better to act like I was employed gathering information for someone else.

I asked her if there were any old buildings that were up for lease or purchase where my company could put a club at. I explained it would have really loud music, so it would be best if there were no homes close by.

After going over about a dozen buildings in the downtown section of Salisbury, I was starting to think this wasn't going to work. The realtor, fearing she might lose a client, hesitantly mentioned, "Well sweetheart. I don't know how some of the locals would take it... but just outside of town there is a large church. Now this church has been empty for some time. Ain't no house near, or much of anything but forest, fields and possums. Still, a church with a night club, it might not go over in these parts."

I tried to hold back the excitement from my voice, "You're probably right, still, can I have the address? Maybe my boss might want to swing by and take a look."

After hanging up, I rushed my shower, then got dressed. With my sunglasses on I hurried out the door, bags in hand, loaded the car and checked out of the motel. An hour later, I was leaving the Wal-Mart parking lot for the second time, with a trunk full of supplies.

I passed the road to the church three times. The driveway was a gravel road with large potholes. The trees grew thick around the entrance. About a couple hundred yards down the long driveway to the woods thinned out and finally opened into a clearing. The grass was high, unkempt and just the way I wanted to see it. No one had been back there in a long time.

The church itself was old looking, made up of dull red brick and a wood roof that looked rotten to me. I walked around the large building, surprised that only one of the windows was broken. The one broken window had been boarded up with plywood. The wood over the window had turned brown and black and was splitting apart; it had been a long time since anyone had done anything to this building. I worked my way back around to the front of the building where I had parked.

At the front, were two large dark stained wooden doors and for whatever reason looked to be in better shape than any other part of the building. I walked up and touched the doors; I felt no power here. I had been hoping that with no people here the power that might have protected this building had faded. The door handles had an old rusted lock and chain wrapped around the handles; with one hand, I broke the lock and slid off the chain.

With a hard tug the old door gave way and the doors flew open. The air was dusty and smelled funny, smelled like mildew and rot. The glass windows that had surrounded the church had scenes of Jesus in them. Even covered with dirt, they allowed a lot of light to come into the old church. You couldn't see through the windows, and I liked that. In fact, the light the windows let in was so bright that I didn't even take off my sunglasses as I entered the building.

What I found next really surprised me. There were two rows of nice looking pews, fifteen per side. The dark red wooden floors were dusty, but it looked as if they would clean up in no time. I walked in front of the pews; there was a raised part of the floor for the stage but nothing on it. I looked up, and there was a balcony with more wooden pews in it.

I found that there were two staircases on either side of the church leading up to the balcony. What was really nice was up in the balcony it was dark; there were no windows as the balcony sat on the crest of the roof. I brought all my stuff in from the car, and set up most of it on the stage. Then I made a little fort up in the balcony.

This place will work perfectly.

The next few days I staked out my father's church. It was located in a small neighborhood. I was walking around the church one Friday evening when I ran into the youth pastor who took one look at me and knew that I needed saving. He was in his early thirties and looked to be in shape, but he was shorter than me; he couldn't have been taller than five seven.

He stuck out his hand with a large smile, "I'm Brian, welcome to our church. Is there anything I can help you with? I am the youth pastor here."

I responded, "I don't know… I don't think I'm in the right spot."

He shook my hand, and then, with a kind but excited voice stated, "It's fine; I'll show you the way. Tonight is Youth Friday, and its movie night. The rest of the group is loading up in the van."

He started walking away, but he was still looking at me waiting for me to join him. I wasn't sure how to get out of this, so I fell in step with him, and we walked together. He asked a few questions on the way, like how did I hear about their church, and who invited me. He asked if I had a ride home after the movie because, if I didn't not to worry about it; he was giving four kids a ride and had room in his car. I explained that I had a car. We approached a small bus in the parking lot. It was surrounded by boys and girls my age.

Brian started to introduce me to everyone, I couldn't really keep up. Too many faces and names to put together, but, as if he knew, he saved the best for last. "And this over here is Mindy Dare. Mindy do you mind hanging with… I am sorry, I forgot your name."

He hadn't forgotten it; he had forgotten to ask, "Melabeth."

Soon as he heard my name he realized he had never heard it before; with a grin on his face, "Busted, I forgot to ask your name, sorry. Mindy, Melabeth, I like that name. Melabeth…"

"Melabeth White," I finished for him.

"I know some Whites who live off Jackson Rd. I think they live at Ridge Farm, any relation?"

I shook my head no, but, before he could ask any more questions, someone else needed him.

I looked at my half sister for the first time. She looked like me, I mean a lot like me. Maybe it would be better said that she and I took after our father. I was really glad I was all Goth, or we would look like twins. Her hair fell just below her shoulders, but it was the same color and thickness as my hair. And her eyes, her eyes were that crazy electric blue that I got from my dad.

She spoke first, "Hey, it's nice to meet you. Where do you go to school?"

I hadn't thought about that, "It's a secret." She stared at me with a blank face, "Home school," I added with a laugh.

"Oh, that's cool, well come on you can sit next to me," Mindy grabbed my hand and pulled me onto the bus.

The lights of the bus went off and it started off down the road. I sat next to my sister; the noise of the kids talking at the same time was hurting my head. My hearing was too sensitive for all this sound; it was like being shoved into a steel box with angry bees.

Mindy was trying to speak to me. "Backdraft," was the only word I had made out.

I yelled back, "Sorry, what was that you said?"

Leaning closer to my ear, "Backdraft," Mindy repeated. "That's the movie we are going to. Have you seen it?"

I shook my head, "Haven't even heard of it; have you seen it?"

She yelled back, "No, but I heard it was great."

We fell into silence, me and my sister that is. We could hardly hear each other anyway, and, like me, she didn't seem to be enjoying all the chatter. The youth director finally restored some order and quieted the bus down enough for us to talk to each other. Well, Mindy talked, I just sat and listened.

Twenty minutes later we arrived at the movie theater, and after filing out of the bus we all headed toward the theater like a herd of cows. I couldn't believe they had to travel to another city just to find a nice theater. I answered a few questions from other girls, but it was my sister who I ended up talking to.

After the movie started, and the talking ended, I started thinking about a few things, me and my sister had talked about. I found out my sister loved school. She liked to sing and play the piano. She also liked to paint, but her favorite thing was to go out on the lake. She liked skiing and riding in a tube and even fishing. All these things she told me, made me start to rethink my plan. Maybe I shouldn't involve her; I don't know her, but there's something about her that I like. It's as if I had known her my whole life and I felt so comfortable sitting next to her. It might be the same for her; all the other youth looked at me like I was some kind of devil worshiper on vacation. At first when she looked at me it was the same as the rest of the kids, but once we began talking she became so comfortable.

I had hardly paid any attention to the movie; it was about firemen putting out fires. I don't like fires, and this movie was full of it. Taking a vampire in a movie about fire is like taking Frankenstein to a weenie roast. By the end of the movie while everyone started talking again and going on about what they thought of it, I had made a decision, I would leave Mindy out of the plan.

Mindy was asking me a question, but I knew it wasn't the first time she asked it, "Sorry Mindy, my mind was elsewhere. You were asking about the movie right?" Mindy nodded, "Well can I tell you a little secret. I wasn't really paying attention... sorry."

Mindy laughed, "Don't worry about it; my dad does that all the time. You could swear that he was listening or paying attention to something, but he never heard a word. Don't worry, you didn't miss much; the movie was only okay."

Just at the mention of her father made me shudder. "I don't do well in big groups, but thanks for hanging with me and making me feel welcome."

Mindy smiled, she was staring at me with this intense look. "I don't know what it is about you, but it's like I know you. You remind me of my father, the way you talk and use your hands. I bet you would get along great."

I tried to hide that fact that I was gritting my teeth. I couldn't stand her talking about my father in a positive light, "So, do you get along with your dad?" Why did I ask that? The words just escaped.

Mindy spoke as we headed back toward the bus. "Oh yes, me and my father are tight. We do everything together; he's cool... for a dad that is."

I might have hurt her, but Brian startled me as he spoke to me, "Melabeth," his voice was loud and excited. "What did you think?"

"Well the movie was okay," I answered.

Brian was still smiling, "We sure hope you had a good time. Hope to see you come to our church more often. We are always planning fun things like this; in fact, Monday night we are all going to the roller rink to skate. What do you think about that?"

I gave Brian a weak smile, "Sorry, I won't be able to make Monday."

"Well, will we see you at church Sunday?" Brian asked, still smiling big.

"Well, I'll try," I lied to him.

He could see I had no intention of going to church; his smile slipped just a little, "Well, we would be glad to have you... alright, folks, let's load it up."

With that, everyone piled up into the bus and off we went. I sat next to my sister; that momentary pause with Brian was a good thing. She had upset me. Why is she worthy of my father's affections? Mindy was most definitely going to join in on the festivities.

The next twenty minutes Mindy gladly told me about her dad and how wonderful he was to her. So, by the time I escaped the youth group and was driving back toward the church, tears of blood were running down my face.

My father, who did nothing for me growing up, left me to fend for myself against other adults; who never under any circumstance was there for me. He kept me from friends my own age and even a formal education; a man who puts his drugs first, but found time to kidnap me from my grandparents, who loved me just so he would have someone to cook, clean and wash his clothes. Then he sold me for drugs, let me go to my death without even a backward glance. He didn't even say goodbye, not even that he loved me. HE LOVED HER; he took care of her and was a real father to her.

Why her? Why not me?

Mindy stole what should have been mine; she will pay, and my father will pay. I think it's time to go learn the layout at the roller rink. Monday was only a few nights off, and I had some last minute things to do.

* * *

I finished applying my makeup; I had set up a large mirror in the balcony of the old church. I stood in front of the mirror and took in my appearance. I had cut my hair so that it only hung a little lower than my chin; I had also dyed it red. It came out nice; I looked good with red hair. I was wearing a yellow sundress with blue flowers all over it, white stockings and blue shoes. I put up my hair on one side with a blue ribbon. The hardest thing about this getup was the makeup; it had taken me hours to give my face color without looking like I had a ton of makeup on. The low level lighting of the roller rink would be good; no one would notice my large eyes, and, with this getup, I would be invisible. I looked just like one of those do-gooders.

My plan revolved around getting my sister away from everyone else, without everyone else noticing. If I went as the Goth princess, everyone would be staring at me. They stared at me Saturday night, when I went to check out the place. In this getup, no one would pay close attention to me.

I went out to the car and double checked the trunk to make sure that I wasn't forgetting anything. "Check, it's all there, I'm ready," I said out loud to nobody.

It was only eleven minutes to the roller rink from the old church. I arrived early, went inside and found a booth. So far, so good; no one was staring at me like last time. All I had to do now was wait, the youth group would be here any minute.

One negative thing was that there were fewer people here on a Monday night; it would be harder to get my sister out of here without anyone noticing. Maybe it wouldn't really matter if they saw us leave, as long as they didn't follow for at least five minutes; it shouldn't be a problem. As I was wrestling with my plan, the youth group piled in the front door.

It didn't take long before I spotted my sister Mindy. I watched as half of them went to get in line for skates while the other half went to the snack line. Mindy made eye contact, but did not recognize me.

An hour later, and the group had spread out; most of the time my sister was hanging out with an unknown girl and a boy. I watched all three of them go skating and then sit and eat snacks. Finally, she got up with her friend and headed toward the girl's bathroom.

I waited outside for her; she came out engrossed in conversation with her friend. I waved my hand and said in an excited voice, "Mindy, how's it going?"

She interrupted the conversion with her friend, and looked at me. I knew from the look on her face, she didn't even recognize me, she tried to play like she knew who I was, "Oh, hey, how's it going?"

I smiled, then asked her, "I don't know if you have any time... I don't want to bother you..." I made it sound as if I was having trouble asking her a question.

Concerned, my sister asked, "What is it?"

Doing my best to act shy, "Well, your dad's a preacher, and I kind of have some questions about God. Do you think you would... or could talk with me for a minute? I mean, if you're not busy?"

She responded just as I hoped, "Of course, I have time... would you like to talk now?"

I looked around like I wasn't sure, "You don't have to."

Her friend spoke up, "Mindy go hang with her, and I'll go check up on Matt." And with a wink, she walked away.

I ushered Mindy up to a booth that was close to the front door of the building. Once we were both sitting I looked over at her, "You don't remember me, do you?"

Mindy's face turned red, "I'm sorry."

"Melabeth, last time we met I was dressed Goth. So see, how could you know who I am?"

She gasped, "Wow, you look... well you look good. I had been hoping I would see you again. I can't explain it, but I felt like we really connected."

I smiled, "I did too."

Mindy was really happy to see me; it almost made me feel bad. She stopped smiling, and, with a concerned face, asked, "So, what's going on?"

I did my best to look like I was about to cry, "Well... it's" I looked around as if there were spies trying to overhear me. "Can we go outside; it's kind of embarrassing... and I don't want anyone else to know."

Mindy quickly responded, "Great idea, then I can hear you better; it's so loud in here."

With a smile she followed me out of the booth and out the front door. There were a few guys and one girl hanging out front smoking. It was the perfect excuse to head further down the side of the building away from the smokers. She followed me without question; she trusted me.

We had just arrived at the edge of the building when Mindy stopped walking, "So what's going on?" she asked kindly.

I pointed around the corner of the building at the white Impala I was driving. "Let me grab my sweater out of my car."

She followed me as we now headed toward my car; there was no one in sight now that we were out of view from the front doors. Sounding a little confused, Mindy commented, "It's not that cold, and you're wearing a sweater silly."

I had forgotten that, but it didn't matter; the goal was at hand. We had arrived at the rear of my car; I popped the trunk, then asked, "Can I show you something important?"

Mindy looked a little unsure, "Sure... what is it?"

I opened the trunk and picked up a white hankie. Then I picked up an unmarked bottle and opened it, and poured its contents into the hankie.

Mindy inquired, "What is that?"

"Chloroform, it will help me kidnap you." A wicked smile spread across my face.

Mindy froze in shock; I was fast in cupping the handkerchief over her face. I held the back of her head with my other hand so she couldn't pull away. She hopelessly tried to push me away.

It only took a minute before she became unconscious and then fell into my arms. Then I quickly pushed her into the trunk of the car and shut it. I did one more quick check to make sure no one saw me before jumping into the driver's seat and speeding away. In ten minutes I would be at the old church, and the fun would really begin.

I got to the church without a hitch; I locked Mindy in a large cage that I had built just for her. The cage sat in the middle of the stage in the front of the church. Mindy lay quietly, still knocked out from the chloroform.

I had changed out of the do-gooders outfit. I was wearing an old pair of jeans with a worn out T-shirt. I was finishing up when I could hear movement from down in the church. Mindy was coming to; I could hear her getting to her feet and banging into the bars.

I looked over the balcony; it was nighttime outside, and, even though I could see inside the church, Mindy could not. She had run into the bars and now was feeling around the cage looking for a way out. I could tell she was coming out of her drug induced sleep. Without a sound I walked off the balcony and slowly floated toward my sister.

Mindy was still groping around in the dark, "Where am I? What's going on? Is there anyone here?"

I could hear the tears start, "Don't cry."

This made her jump, "Who's there?"

I landed next to her cage without a sound, and then lit a candle followed by another. Mindy finally must have been able to see me, "Melabeth, is that you? What are you doing... why did you kidnap me?"

I turned away from the task of lighting candles, "Yes, it's me, Melabeth. And to answer your second question... well, it's a long story, but don't you worry, I'll have time to tell it."

Mindy's heart was pounding with fear, but she was brave as she talked to me boldly, "How long do you plan on keeping me? Do you really think you will get away with this? You can go to jail for this; did you know that?"

I have to say normally I like people with a spine, but I wanted one more reason to hate her, so I was kind of hoping she would be a coward. I pushed the emotions to the side; this girl had my life, and I hated her for it. "I plan on keeping you here until I have a chance to lure our father here. Then after I deal with him, then you can go."

Mindy's voice was shaky, "Our father?"

I picked up a candle and held it to my face so she could see me. I had no makeup on and I knew my large eyes would almost seem to shine in this light. I opened my mouth and let my teeth slowly extend, "So much to tell you my sister."

My sister turned white, and then she screamed... I laughed.

Chapter 31 Reunions
再会

The next few days went by quickly. I let my sister out of the cage most of the time, except when I was sleeping or hunting. We spent all of our time talking. She wanted to know everything, every answer leads to another question. It was the third night after I had taken her from the roller rink; I had just come in from a hunt.

I entered into the candlelight and Mindy looked up from her cage, "Where have you been?"

Ever since I showed her what I was, Mindy treated me like a wild animal. She didn't act afraid, but she was never really comfortable, never sure what she could and could not ask of me. Of course that was partly because when she did ask a few questions that upset me, I hissed at her.

I answered her question nicely, "I was hunting."

She grimaced, "You didn't... hurt anyone?"

I growled, "I go around and give men back rubs. You need not worry about them; worry about yourself."

Wisely, she didn't respond, and after a few minutes I calmed down and let her out. I handed her some take out, she devoured it. I hadn't been feeding her often. Only once did she try to escape, but when I flashed in front of her and took her down like a wild cat, she never tried again.

Mindy walked around the church stretching her legs out. I had moved to the ledge of the balcony, looking down watching her in silence. She stopped and looked up at me, then started walking, stopped and looked at me again. I knew she was working up the courage to say something to me. It must have been something she knew might make me mad, because she was hesitant.

I was bored and tired of the silence, "Spit it out, Mindy. I promise I won't get mad."

She stopped walking to look up at me as she crossed her arms over her chest. With a pleading voice, "Can't you just forgive father?"

"No," I said bluntly.

She almost sounded whiny, "Why not?"

I had promised not to get mad, so I tried to keep the venom out of my voice as I answered her. "Wouldn't that be nice for you?"

"I didn't ask for me," her reply was on the edge of tears.

I floated down from the balcony and landed without a sound on the back of the pew in front of my sister. I could hear her heart speed up, but she held herself together and tried her hardest not to look scared. I smiled, but I knew it was a mean smile.

The pain was plain in my voice, "Who did you ask for? Well, if not for you… you must have asked for good old dad. And of course that works out well for you too, I can just go away, and all will be forgiven. I've got an idea, why don't you take his place?"

Mindy was mad, and, for the first time, it was stronger than her fear of me. Not yelling, but saying forcefully, "I would gladly take my father's place, but I wasn't asking for forgiveness for us. I was asking for you! You'll never find peace unless you forgive him, and if you kill him; you'll never be able to forgive yourself."

I was a little shocked to see her telling me off! I could tell she was bracing herself for my anger, but she was taken off guard with my reaction. I burst into uncontrollable laughter, and, the more I laughed, the redder my sister's face became.

She spit out at me, "Never mind, you're impossible… and evil."

The evil part brought my laughter to an end. I looked at her and with a dark voice said, "Sister, you don't know evil… not yet."

*   *   *

I arrived at my father's house close to eight. I could see lights on, and there was more than one car in the driveway. I was in full Goth, with plenty of makeup on and a black dress. I couldn't afford for my father to recognize me. I still had the red hair, but that went well with the Goth look.

I knew that he had been freaking out; it was all over the local paper. The preacher's daughter disappears from the local roller rink without a trace. Police think foul play; father in a panic. When I had been out hunting there had been a lot of missing girl flyers stuck to telephone poles.

My sister tried to tell me that after I went missing that he searched for me too. And after never finding me, that's what changed his life. He got help with the drugs and alcohol and devoted his life to helping others with addiction problems. He supposedly had many sermons where he told the congregation that he was a sinner and how drugs had taken his wife and his daughter away. I don't know how much I believed her, or thought she was just trying to save his ass.

I buried my face in my hands, "Dear God… end this… STOP this.., and help me find peace. I never found real love with David… I couldn't even love Michael… this hate is eating me alive… I need to end this; I must finish this… Oh God give me the strength to smite thy enemies." I couldn't help but smile at that last part… how dramatic of me.

I already hated myself. I wouldn't let my father get away with it; I would be brave and face the man; I could do it. I raised my head up and looked over at my father's house, then got out of the car and headed across the street and started up his driveway. That's when I saw a man come out the front door of my father's house. He walked down the sidewalk toward the driveway; then I recognized him, Brian the youth leader.

When Brian saw me, his heart rate sped up, and I could see the excitement in his eyes. I thought the gig was up, but as we closed the distance his face changed. He must have thought I was my sister; he was straining in the dark to get a better look at me.

"It's me, Melabeth," I announced with a pleasant voice. "Is Mindy in?"

I could tell Brian had been distracted, then hopeful and now his hope had been dashed. It took him a second to compose himself before he replied, "Mel… Melabeth, that's right I remember you now, movie night, right?" I nodded my head, "Look it's good to see you, but this is a bad time. You must have not heard, but Mindy is missing."

I reacted with mock horror, "Missing… Is there anything I can do to help?"

He answered me quickly, "Yeah, just keep an eye open, and if you hear anything, I mean anything at all, let us all know lickety-split. I need to go; wife's pregnant and waiting and I plan to put some flyers up on the way home."

I nodded my head and stepped out of his way so he could head to his car, "I would like to talk to Mindy's dad; is he home?"

Brian pulled his keys out to open his car, he answered me in a hurried voice, "Not right now. Some church families are inside, but he's out looking for his daughter with other members of the church."

I had planned for this, "Well, okay, sorry I couldn't have been more of a help. I haven't talked to her since Wednesday night. Good luck and…"

Brian burst out, "What?"

I acted a little confused, "I was just saying that I will help in any way that I can."

Brian interjected, "No, when did you speak with her? Was it Wednesday night? Before the movie?"

I answered him with a calm voice, "No, I hadn't met her until Friday night at the movies; before that, I had never seen her before. I talked to her this Wednesday night."

I was even telling the truth.

In a panic, he asked, "Where was she? What was she doing?"

I acted defensively, "Look, I don't want to get anyone in trouble."

Frustrated Brian scolded, "Don't worry about that; what's important here is that Jack finds his daughter."

I stammered out, "I don't know…"

Brian interrupted me, in a fit of impatience, "Do you know where she is?"

I need to get my father to come with me, so, in a calm voice, "I'll tell you what… tell Jack to come home, and I will talk to him about it. It's kind of personal; I don't feel comfortable talking to you."

Brian looked into my eyes; he had the look of an adult who knew how to impose his will upon kids. "Look, this has nothing to do with how you feel. You need to tell me what you know, and you need to tell me now."

This wasn't going the way I planned. I need to reel in the commanding nanny. "I'm leaving asshole; if Mindy's dad wants any information from me, then he'll meet me in front of the movie theater at midnight. And one more thing, he's to come alone."

"I don't understand... why won't you tell me where she is?" He yelled this as he followed me across the street to my car.

I hissed out, "Midnight... alone."

I opened my door, but before I could get in Brian grabbed my arm. He barked out, "I don't know what you're thinking..."

Before he could finish the sentence, I had broken his grip and tossed him halfway across the street. I jumped into the car and sped away. In my rearview mirror, I could see Brian get back on his feet. He stood there confused and dazed.

I wasn't worried about what he thought had happened. He would rationalize the events until the whole situation of me getting loose from his grip made perfect sense. I had bigger fish to fry, and I was losing my temper.

* * *

I had parked my car in a driveway at an empty house. From this house I crossed through a small patch of forest and into a parking lot. I was now standing behind the small mall, and, on the other side of the mall, was a theater.

I took to the sky, landing on top of the mall, and then jumped again. Gently floating landing on top of the theater roof, and here I would wait. I didn't have long. It was eleven o'clock when a silver Lumina whipped into the parking lot. A police car followed him in.

The two cars parked at the furthest corner of the lot; my father got out of the Lumina. He looked just like I remembered him, tall and thin; his hair was still as yellow as the sun. He used to keep his hair long, but now it was cut short. He needed to pretend that he was respectable; he was even wearing a gray suit. He had a blue dress shirt under the jacket but no tie with the top few buttons of his shirt undone. He looked ragged like he hadn't had much sleep.

My father hung his head in the squad car, I couldn't hear what they were talking about, but I could guess. I took to the sky again and slowly floated over a group of trees, then softly landed between them. The officer pulled away; my guess was to keep from scaring me off. I had landed in a group of trees in front of where my father and the police car were. I made no sound and it was dark in the tree line.

As my father opened his door and slid into his seat, I flashed over and opened the passenger door and hopped in looking over at his surprised face. Seeing my father this close, I swallowed and then grumbled, "I said alone."

Surprised my father asked, "Are you Melabeth?"

My emotions became too much for me; I became cold and indifferent. I stared into his eyes, "Drive, head toward the back of the mall."

My father commanded, "Tell me what you know about my daughter?"

With an authoritative voice, "Drive or she dies."

He started to ask questions, "What, are you talking…"

I didn't let him finish, "If you don't do exactly what I am telling you, she dies. Drive now," I raised my voice and the hatred seeped out, "NOW!"

He was confused, but decided to follow my directions. He asked me a few more questions as I directed him to the back of the mall. I could see the squad car following us; I was sure he was confused. It wasn't supposed to happen until midnight, and he never saw me get into the car. I had gotten in before he had a chance to park across the street. He was staying back, and that was a good thing for me.

"Stop," I ordered.

My father looked around, "Now what? Is she near?"

I rolled down my window; it was very dark in the area behind the mall. This is where the trucks delivered, I was sure the officer could see nothing but the brake lights. On one side of the car was the mall, with a few lights over metal doors. On the other side was a group of trees; on the other side of the tree, was my car.

"Don't move," I slid out the window. I moved really fast, I could tell my dad was looking around trying to see what I was doing. I grabbed a fallen branch from the tree line.

He started to put the car in park, "What part of don't move don't you understand?" He jumped because I was now standing next to his window.

He started to talk, but I hushed him. I opened his door, then jammed a stick onto the brake pedal. Using the power seat I adjusted it so there was enough pressure to keep the pedal down. "Get out without knocking the stick. Then shut the door and follow me."

Like he was in shock, he followed my directions; we were starting in the woods when it hit him. With the brake lights on, the officer would think he was still in the car. He froze and turned around; I grabbed his hand and pulled him behind me.

"Wow, you're strong for a little thing." Dad commented.

I had him in my car and was heading down the road before he spoke again. He warned, "Now, if you're involved in any way, you can get in real trouble. If you tell me now, what's going on… then maybe I can help you."

I didn't need him to fight me the whole way; I needed him to do what I wanted. I told him a story, "Okay, I didn't want to tell you, but your daughter is trying to kill herself."

He burst out in surprise, "Mindy?"

As if it was someone else, I went on with the lie. "Yes, she told me if anyone but her father came tonight, she would blow her head off; she has a gun."

I could see my father trying to process all of this. He sounded bewildered as he asked, "My gun?"

"I don't know... does it matter?" I shook my head in disbelief.

Almost crying, whispering, "Why... how did I fail her? Are we too late?"

I patted his knee sympathetically, "Don't worry, I'll hurry." I had to keep from laughing.

I pulled up in front of the church and shut the car off. I stepped out followed by my father. He was looking all around; it was a very dark night with clouds covering the moon.

A little bewildered, he finally could see the church, "Is she in there?"

"Yes, just go in the front door; I'll be right behind you." He about ran as he grabbed the door and pulled it open, then rushed inside. I closed and locked the door as I followed him in.

At the front of the church where the stage was, there were no chairs or pulpit. I had set up a cage in the center where I kept my sister Mindy. On both sides of the cage, I set up tall candle holders with many lit candles in them. There were candles lit all over the sanctuary; it was a lot of light for me, but dimly lit for the human eye.

My father was half walking, half running down the center of the church. He came to a sudden halt ten feet away from the cage. Mindy grabbed the cage bars at the sight of him.

She yelled out in panic, "Father... get out of here!"

In disarray, my father started walking toward the cage again, "Mindy? What are you doing in there? What's going on?"

Mindy took my father's outstretched hand. Between sobs and tears pouring down Mindy's face, she cried out. "Run father, run... please."

"Who's has done this?" my father cried out with anger and rage in his voice.

I was standing quietly ten feet behind my father. His head and eyes were now sweeping the church, only to find me. It took him a second to come to the conclusion that I was a threat. Even dressed up like a Goth, I was still a hundred pound girl.

My father's eyes were full of threats, as my sister was still pleading for him to leave. In the midst of her crying and panic, "It's her... she's not what she seems. Get away from her; she's a monster... a vampire."

My father was about to say something to me, but the vampire remark made him pause. Enraged, "Do you two think this is some kind of joke?" He turned and faced his daughter. "Are you trying to play a joke on me? If you are…"

Mindy yelled out, "NO FATHER… this is not a joke. That's not Melabeth… it's your daughter, Melanie. She proclaimed that she rose from the dead to have revenge upon you."

My father slammed his hand into the bars of my sister's cage, causing her to step back away from the bars in fear. My father screamed in rage, "HOW DARE YOU…" as he spun around to face me.

His face was twisted in a mix of rage and hurt. He stood staring at me with his hands clenched; I could tell he really wanted to hit me. His pain, it made me smile, and, as I did, a new emotion crossed my father's face… disbelief.

Through clenched teeth, "You think this is funny, who are you for real?"

I flashed up to his face; he didn't even have time to be surprised when I punched him in the bottom of his rib cage. He collapsed onto the ground gasping for air.

With a cruel smile I stood over him, "Goodnight daddy."

And with that I punched him in his temple and watched his eyes roll into the back of his head.

He lay before me still breathing, but out for the count; that's when it registered that Mindy was screaming at me. I would have to silence her with some duct tape.

*   *   *

I had two chairs before me. In one chair was my sister all tied up and gagged; still trying to yell at me she sounded more like a Zombie. In the other chair was my father, he was tied up as well and was starting to come to. I floated up to the balcony to get ready as my father moaned and began speaking.

I was busy washing off all the makeup. I laid out a black dress that had spaghetti straps on it; it fell to my knees. As I dressed, my father was whispering to Mindy, "It will be okay sweetie… don't be scared."

Of course he was the one who sounded scared. Mindy was still gagged so there was no reply as my father whispered encouragement. I looked in the mirror; I was back to my old self. All I had to do now was to find the courage to face my father, and end this. I tossed on my black hoodie and let my long blonde hair fall free.

Without a sound I dropped off the balcony and headed toward the front of the church. My father was busy looking at my sister and had not realized that I was now standing two feet in front of him.

I said in a very matter of fact voice, void of emotion, "Hello… father."

My father turned his head slowly, and, when his eyes fell upon me, his face froze. It was like watching wax melt as his face slipped into a mask of shock as he processed that it indeed was me.

In disbelief, he formed a question with a word, "Mel?"

A tight smiled crossed my face, "Yes, father, it's me. Long time no see; sorry it couldn't be under better circumstances, but you know the past has a way of sneaking up and biting you in the ass."

His eyes welled up with tears, "I don't understand… how can this be? Where have you been?"

I felt my half hearted smile fall, as I simply answered, "Hell. And how have you been?"

My sister moaned through her gag, but I ignored her. My father looked over at her and then back at me. He begged, "Let her go. It's me, you want; she has had nothing to do with you. It was me, who sold you to the bikers; it was me, who let you down in every possible way a father could. I kidnapped you from your grandparents. Then I exposed you to a life of hell… to be honest, I can't even remember what all I had done to you in all those years, but Mindy, she hasn't done anything to you. Why don't you let her go?"

I walked over to Mindy, my father started to plea for her again, but I hushed him. I let my fangs grow long, along with my fingernails. As my fingers elongated with growth, my face looked… more sinister. If I wanted to, I was able to open my mouth much wider than any human could. I leaned down behind my sister's chair. I was now looking over her shoulder and at my father; I gave him a big toothy grin. My arm reached over her shoulders as I stroked her face with my long fingers and sharp claws.

My father was shaking his head in disbelief, "What are you?"

I opened my mouth and bit down upon my sister's neck. She jerked in surprise as my father screamed in horror. I pulled my mouth away full of crimson blood dripping down my cheek. I laughed at my father's cries to the almighty.

I licked my sister's neck so the wound would stop bleeding; I wasn't ready for her to bleed out, yet. My father was struggling against the ropes and his chair scraped back and forth on the floor as he attempts lead him nowhere. He was praying to God and yelling at me, almost in the same breath.

I wiped some blood away from my mouth, and then smiled, "Calm yourself… we're just getting started."

My father stopped as he gasped for air; it took him a minute to gather himself. His face was covered with sweat, as he looked up at me, "You're not my daughter. You're a demon, and you have no power over me."

I let out a giggle, "Oh come on; you're tied up. Your daughter is ten feet away, and I'm killing her... can you stop it? No, you can't; of course I have power, and I am no Demon. You created me; do you remember?"

My father spit with anger as he spilled verse after verse from the bible. I let him go on for a few more minutes, and then I grabbed his chin with one hand. My grip was like iron; he could not move as I spoke softly to him, "Father, it is me. Look into my eyes; it's me, the same girl who fixed the car just by going to the library and reading a book. The same girl who took care of you when mother died. The same girl you sold for drugs so you could feed your habit. The same girl who... was taken away and was turned into a snuff film, the same girl..." tears fell from my eyes; my voice was shaking. "Who, rose from the ground, to find... no one."

The bloody tears fell from my face as I let go of my father. He was crying as well. He didn't know what to think, and then he asked, "Snuff film, what is that?"

I closed my eyes, walked a few steps and then sat down on the first row of pews. Then gathering my voice and wiping away the tears, "Well, glad you asked. See they take a girl, or maybe a boy, then they make a movie. The plot is not hard to follow; first a group of men rape you; then for the grand finale, a man rapes you while he chokes you to death. Then he finishes with your dead corpse."

My father was still crying as he whispered, "Dear God. I had no idea, none at all."

Practically yelling, "Well that makes everything so much better. What do you say, time for a family hug?"

My sister was crying, I flashed over to her, and, using my sharp nails, cut off her gag. Then, barely even trying to hide the cruelty in my tone, "Got a question for you. I am sure you heard me just say how I fixed my father's car just by getting books and reading about it. Well, let me tell you some more about that. Good old dad hadn't bought any food in the house for some time. Being on drugs and drinking all the time, good old dad could go days without a meal. I hadn't eaten anything for days, and good old dad kept saying he couldn't get a ride to the store, and the car was broken down. I got the idea that I would fix it, and fix it I did. Dad was so proud of me; it made me so happy. He jumped into the car and off he went with the promise to get some food. Mindy, could you tell me what happened next?"

Sniffling and with a shaky voice, "I don't know."

I turned to my dad, and in my best show host voice, "And what about you, father... could you finish that story for my sister?"

His face, full of shame, he said in a low voice, "I left for two days. I went across town to score some dope, but ended up getting high in the dealer's house. By the time I had returned, you wouldn't have eaten for at least five days, but you were always a survivor. You broke into the old lady's house across the street; she caught you stealing food. She ended up taking pity on you. After that, she fed you, and I let her." His voice was almost a whisper; he spoke slowly as he added, "I let her feed you many times after that."

Mindy squeaked out, "Really dad, that's awful."

My father's eyes rose to my sister's face and in an empty voice said, "I know. Mel is right, I was cruel to her, and I am responsible for her death." His eyes turned to me; his voice took on authority as he spoke with purpose. "I get it; you're here to have your revenge on me. And after you take it, you will still be a monster. You'll find no peace in it, for I am a child of God, forgiven by Jesus and washed in his blood. Let her free, for she is innocent. This is between God, you and me."

I clapped my hands together loudly as if I were taken aback by his speech. "That was inspiring; I should have come in one Sunday and watched you preach. Then again sitting with hypocrites and listening to you preach, is not my idea of a good time. Let's get to the heart of the matter concerning little Mindy here. Let me start by saying, you're right. Mindy here is innocent."

My father yelled out, "Then let her go."

I growled, "Don't interrupt me…" calming myself, I went on, "The heart of the matter concerns your daughter. See, there are three things to consider in this matter. One, she has taken my life, the life I should have received, and the love of my father. Unknowingly yes, but, none the same, she is a thief. Two, she knows too much about me, and maybe it's best the family line dies with me."

My sister whispered in a small voice, "I didn't mean to steal from you; dad and I wouldn't tell a soul… we swear."

My dad quickly added, "Mindy can keep a secret."

Mindy protested, "Dad…"

My father understood that I wasn't even close to letting him leave. He hushed her then consoled her, "Shhh… don't worry about me. I need you to be strong, the Lord will watch over you."

I interrupted their little pow-wow, "Yeah, he's been doing a real bang up job." I tapped my finger on my chin and acted like I was thinking real hard. The silence built, until I suddenly spoke, startling them both. "Well, let's say I let the first two things go. She didn't realize she was stealing, and I bet she could keep a secret. Still, there is one more little problem."

My father had hope in his eyes, "What's that?"

I smiled wickedly, "I don't want you to go to heaven."

My father's hope faded to confusion, "I don't understand."

My sister chided in, "He is already forgiven."

I turned around and smacked her, I hit her so hard blood poured out of the side of her head, and the chair almost fell over. I screamed in rage, "He is not forgiven; I don't forgive him!"

My father cried out, "Don't hurt her; she doesn't understand. Hurt me, hurt me, I am the one you want to hurt."

My sister whimpered in pain as I gave my father the death stare. I walked up to my father. Grabbing his ropes I picked him off the ground as if he weighed nothing. My father's eyes opened wide as I spoke in a menacing voice, "If I want her dead… she will be dead, but that would be the easy way out. Denounce God… or watch your little Mindy suffer. I will kill her slowly."

I dropped my father and the chair; it made a loud crash as it rocked from leg to leg before settling once again. My father clenched in pain from the sudden impact. I stared at him waiting for a reply, waiting for him to denounce God. He cleared his throat, "How does someone give back forgiveness? If I could give it back, I would have never been forgiven. There's an old saying, some bury the hatchet leaving the handle sticking out of the ground. God doesn't leave the handle sticking out, so how do I denounce him? How do I stop believing? Tell me how to return my faith, and take my sins back from God? I will… if it would save Mindy, I will… I would do it for you, if I could."

I couldn't look at him, "If you could for me, you would. Are you saying you would go to hell for me?"

He simply said, "Yes."

He wasn't lying, and I knew it, and he was right. How could I insure his trip to hell? I had been foolish, no, twisted into thinking that I could send him to hell. I had been wrong about my sister too; there was no way to make her pay for what she had taken from me. I knew that she really hadn't taken anything from me, but I must have my revenge. In my revenge, there was peace; there just had to be. My heart hurts, this was the only way I knew to make it stop. My hope lay in my revenge.

My father suddenly broke the silence, "Mindy, Mindy are you okay?"

Chapter 32 Innocent
無邪気な

I looked over at my sister; her body lay slack in the chair. Her head hung to one side as her mouth hung open with drool coming down. Blood dripped slowly off the side of her face from where I had hit her. I walked over and lifted her head and looked into her eyes.

I had hit her harder than I thought; her breathing was erratic along with her heartbeat. I may have given her brain damage. My father was now scooting his chair toward me and my sister.

He said in a broken voice, "No, no, this can't be happening. Is she…" he never finished his sentence, staring at his dying daughter. He burst out in tears and prayers.

I slowly walked away; what have I done? My father broke into my self-pity with, "Untie me, and call an ambulance."

I replied with no emotion at all, "You won't need an ambulance, and don't worry; you'll be joining her shortly. It's time to end this."

"Untie me, so I may hug her," his plea made my heart ache.

I did untie him. He immediately untied Mindy and took her in his arms. Laying her gently on the ground, he began to pray over her. A tear slid down my cheek; okay, I am not this big monster. She is fourteen and my half sister, and has done nothing but been nice to me. She appeared to have stopped breathing. I bent down to eye level with my father and on the other side of my sister. I came to my knees, then gathered myself.

I interrupted my father's praying, "Okay, here's the deal; her life for yours."

My dad stared at me for a second, "You can't save her… you killed her."

I had a hard time looking him in the eye, "I can try… my blood has healing powers. She might get a little addicted, but it will pass as long as I don't feed her anymore."

Without hesitation, he pleaded, "I would gladly give my life for her. I would give my life for yours for that matter."

My eyes narrowed, and I stared at my father, "Yeah, right."

I slit my wrist, then put it to my sister's mouth. My blood flowed into her, and, at first, nothing happened. She lay lifeless as my blood slowly dripped into her mouth. My sister's eyes came to life as her heartbeat started. Her hand shot to my arm so she could pull my arm to her mouth.

She sucked at my wrist as if it were the nectar of the Gods. I didn't need her to drink too much; I pulled my arm away with some protest from my sister.

She sat up quickly, looked at me and in a wildly excited voice, "More please."

I grinned, and then shook my head, "You've had enough. Now I will replenish that blood."

I stood up and moved around my confused sister, then picked my father up off the floor. He didn't fight me; instead he hugged me. I was too surprised to react; I was frozen.

Then my father softly whispered in my ear, "Thank you, thank you. Please let her go after you kill me. After you kill me, know this; I love you and I forgive you. Somehow, before you meet your end, find God so we can be together in peace, in the kingdom of heaven."

I replied, as I embraced my father's hug, "Sorry father, that will never be, for I am going to hell for all the things I have done… and what I'm about to do. Forgive me for I am *Sin*."

And with that I bit into my father's neck and began to drain him.

The closest way I could describe drinking blood, was having sex. It was hard to drain my father and enjoy it. I opened my eyes to see my sister staring at me with hate in her eyes. I realized she was yelling at me to stop. She looked as if she was about to try to stop me but then froze.

The look on her face was enough for me to stop drinking. She was shaking in fear, eyes wide open, mouth slowly opening as if to scream, but no sound came. I came to the understanding that she wasn't looking at me; there was something behind me.

I whistled to see who was there, but in my second sight there was no one. I turned to check… and saw what my sister had been freaking out about.

In a cloud of black smoke that lingered on the pews and only floated a few feet above the floor a hooded figure stood with a black cloak shrouding him. The only visible body parts were his hands; they were white as chalk. Two red eyes poked out of the blackness of his hood. In one of his white hands he held a scythe.

He slowly moved from the back of the church toward us, and as he did, he became more solid. His hands were white because they were made of bone, and now I could see his face; he was a skeleton.

I knew his name, Grim Reaper, the Angel of Death, Nicks.

My sister was standing behind me; she made no noise other than her ragged breathing. My father was on his knees before me, still conscious and holding his neck in the place where I had bitten him. My dad had his back to Death and had not reacted to him yet.

My sister was innocent. He had warned me about hurting the innocent.

Death's free hand rose into the air, then his boney finger pointed at me. I heard a dark, haunting voice, "I have come for you… Melanie Elizabeth Dare. For even you knew she was innocent."

Death moved forward, lifting the scythe with both arms. The scythe came swinging at me; I was frozen in shock and fear. The blade flew through my body, but it did not cut me. It simply passed through me.

I fell to the floor, since I couldn't feel from the waist down. It was as if that scythe had cut me in half. I looked down at my body; it was intact. What trickery was this?

He became solid; I could see him in my second sight becoming the shape of a man. The black smoke slid across the floor toward the figure, gathering into him; as the smoke cleared, the black cloak melted away.

And there Nicks stood above me. He looked like he did in the library with his long hair and handlebar mustache. He was wearing a white shirt with black trousers, and a dark red robe, which he wore open in the front. His eyes were beautiful and full of fiery tears, for it matched the look on his face, heartbroken.

Nicks' voice was full of pain, "How could you? Your own sister. I have stood aside for too long. It has been my duty to free spirits trapped on earth and to help them to death. I have longed for a child, and finally my prayers were granted. I praised God for you, but you have done nothing but kill.

"I have tried to teach you, I should have never used the blood of a vampire. I suppose this is my fault as much as yours. I let you chase your vengeance hoping that, when you had killed the men who had wronged you, you would come to your true calling. In your search for vengeance, you started taking the lives of the innocent, and I warned against such actions, but your heart was hard and full of hate.

"Now you have come against your father, a good man, a man who has made life changes to atone for what he had done to you. You tortured and killed a fourteen year old girl, not any girl, but your sister. And you even referred to her as innocent as if my warning meant nothing. I know you fed her your blood to bring her back, but you know as well as I, that she will have a price to pay. Your blood doesn't die; it must be destroyed. Did you even think about what you have done to your sister? No… of course you didn't; you had no choice; she was dead. What do you have to say for yourself?"

His words burned like red hot pokers. I pushed the pain away and went to that empty place in me; the place where nothing hurt and I cared for no one. Looking up at my father, I said unapologetically, "He must die; he deserves it for what he has done. I will kill him."

Nicks slowly shook his head, "Sorry to hear that, but I won't allow it. I must take responsibly and end this no matter how much it grieves me." Nicks looked at my father then to my sister. "If you have any last words for Melanie before you go, have them now. Then be off with you, for you are free to go."

I hissed out, "It doesn't matter if you let them leave; I will catch up with them again."

My father stared at Nicks, then at me. In a shaky voice, "Melanie I love you, and I forgive you."

My sister helped my father to his feet, "Come on dad, let's get out of here." She stopped, then asked Nicks, "Are you going to… is she… you know."

Nicks nodded his head, "Yes."

She answered in a small voice, "Thanks for saving us. Melanie, I am so sorry… we could have been sisters. I hope somehow you find a way to forgive our father, for I know I will find a way to forgive you." I growled at her; she looked at Nicks then back at me, "Bye, Melanie."

With a menacing voice I replied, "Bye, see you soon."

I did not believe Nicks was going to kill me.

My sister helped my father out to the front door of the church. I looked up at Nicks as tears fell freely from his face, and for the first time, I felt afraid for my life.

I whined to Nicks, "Father, you can't kill me. Your own daughter, come on now."

Nicks shook his head, then turned and started walking away. He stopped and turned back to me, "You brought this upon yourself. I love you."

Anger erupted in me, "YOU CAN'T KILL ME… I swear to you I will have my revenge; do you hear me? My father will not…"

Nicks walked out the front door; as he did, black smoke rose from the cracks in the floor, and in the smoke there were ghosts. They didn't look like people, more like Casper's or people with sheets over their heads. I wasn't afraid because I knew ghosts couldn't hurt me.

Then they pushed over all the candles… fire would hurt me! I still could not feel my legs and they would not respond.

The old church caught up in flames immediately, and the red flames hurried up the walls. I started to use my arms to pull myself to the doors to escape the flames. The ghosts wrapped themselves around my dead legs.

I clawed deep into the wood floor and pulled with all my strength, only to come up with hands full of splinters. The flames were now burning up in the ceiling, and the whole church was filled with smoke, but I had no need to breathe.

I had an idea, I would dig myself out, and I would make it out of here. I heard loud noises of wood snapping. The roof came crashing down, bringing fire and flames to the floor and to me.

A giant beam landed on my back, as if the spirits weren't doing a good enough job to hold me down. Then I felt it, the searing pain of the fire, first burning my back and then my legs; I clawed hard, trying to rip the floor apart.

The balcony broke free on one side, spilling all its contents before me. The large mirror I had up there landed in front of me. The glass was full of cracks. I could see myself, the fire engulfing my back. The pain and fear in my own face.

My efforts did me no good for now my body was burning, and I was screaming in pain. I didn't scream for long, for my face was on fire, and the pain left as fast as it came. As I looked into the mirror, I watched in horror as the fire engulfed me.

Then the world went from bright colors of orange and red, into darkness...

Chapter 33 Hell
地獄

I had awoken.

I have always wondered if there was a heaven or hell. If there is a hell, I am sure of where I am. Still, it felt more like I just came out of a bad dream. My head was hazy, disconnected… I tried to reconnect, but I just couldn't.

I couldn't find my hands, arms, feet or legs. I was not breathing, but I was used to that. Not breathing was one thing, but I couldn't take in air even if I wanted to, for I had no mouth. There was no sound, not even the smallest of noises. I strained, but heard nothing, like I had no ears as well. If I had eyes, there was nothing to see, for the world was the blackest of nights.

I could remember once long ago. I had gone caving with my father, and he had turned the lights off. That was the first time I had experienced true darkness, but not the last. The next time I experienced it, I found myself in a coffin. This was different, for there was a complete lack of any feeling. The only sounds were my thoughts as they bounced around inside my head.

For a while it was just me and my thoughts, but it was shortly followed by flashes of light, not flashes of light that I was seeing from my eyes but memories. The longer I sat in this state of nothingness, the clearer my memories became. It wasn't too long before I was outside sitting in a field, with the sun shining brightly around me. The details of the memory were amazing.

It was an older memory from my life before I became a vampire. I was in a field with a group of hippies. Father wasn't far off talking with some friends while I sat next to my mother; she was braiding my hair. As my mother worked, she was talking about love and life and how we should never hurt another person. She was speaking to me; I had gotten into a fight earlier with one of the other girls, for there was a camp full of hippies, and we all traveled from place to place. I was eight so this would have been 1968.

In the memory, I could clearly see my father heading toward me. He was coming to talk to me about the fight I had just had. This was my old father, before drugs and alcohol turned him into a monster. This was a man full of love, with kind eyes.

This was the man I tried to kill. The drugs had destroyed him, filled him with wanting and greed. The drugs took his love, and left him with nothing but wanting. He wronged me, and I wronged him. How could I have done that? Why did I hurt the father that had found his love, his heart? Was I now the monster? Blood, revenge, and no love left in me?

My father smiled as he sat next to me, "Mel, are you all right?"

I was still angry, "Yes." My arms were tightly folded across my chest as I answered him.

My mother added, "You need not be so difficult Beth. It's good to be independent, but do you not see that you can't hurt others. You must learn how to respect others and love without boundaries."

"And control your anger," my father added. "You may be independent like your mother says, but you need others; we all do."

"Why?" I didn't feel that I needed anyone.

My mom laughed, and then turned my face so I was looking into her deep blue eyes. "You need me... right?"

I felt my angry face crack under my mother's gaze. Her look was full of love and deep kindness, "Yes, but I don't need Willow."

"Willow again," my father shook his head. "You two need to learn to get along."

"I second that," my mom added the last part with a hug.

The memory faded away, and the next scene was much darker. I was twelve and it was 1972. It was only a few months before my mother overdosed on drugs. The house was dark, and the only light came from the glow of the TV. I wasn't watching it; I lay on the couch trying to sleep. The wind howled outside as it battered against the side of the house. The house would fill with light about every five minutes, followed by a crash of thunder.

I was trying to sleep; my room was too scary from the shadows coming in through the window. My mom and dad were fighting; not even the storm would drown out the yelling. The house went black as the power went out. The sudden loss of light had quieted my parents down; now the storm seemed even louder, it was the dominant sound.

Followed by a loud crack of thunder was my mother falling into the living room. My father was right behind her. She screamed at him, "Why didn't you pay the power bill? You useless son-of-a-bitch."

My dad yelled back, "Power outage, it's a power outage. Storm... there's a storm."

I sat up just in time, for my father dropped onto the couch. My mom was in the kitchen looking for a flashlight. She was unable to find one, so she stumbled into the dark living room. I scooted over as she sat on the couch; now I was in-between my parents. I started to get up, but they both yelled at the same time, "Where are you going?"

"Sorry," I said, as I sat back down.

My father reached up and felt my face, "Oh, it's Mel."

My mom yelled, "What the hell are you doing out of bed?"

I started to explain, "Well..."

She screamed, "GET BACK INTO YOUR ROOM." She slapped the back of my head.

With that, I ran back to my room with tears in my eyes. They were both high, and I knew it. I felt so alone, as I sat upon my bed, pulling my knees to my chest. I pulled my blanket over my head as the storm crashed, my parents yelled, and the darkness overwhelmed me.

I became aware of a noise. The memory faded as the noise began. First the noise came and went like a passing car. Then the volume was loud, then quiet, but the noise had very little change in rhythm. It sounded like a drum, thump, thump, thump, and the sound bounced around in my head. After a while, the sound slowly became louder. It was hard to think with the constant noise, but what else could I do? It was either the memories or the beating of the drum.

The next set of memories was me killing my first boyfriend, Chris. At the time I told myself it was the only way to stop him. He had become such a monster and I was afraid of him raping me again. Even at fourteen I knew I had other choices. I did it to protect my dad, but why? He did not deserve my protection. I could have called the police and not killed him. I would have ended up back with my grandparents. My father would have most likely killed himself on drugs. That's why I did it… I believed that it was my job to watch over and save my father. Even at the expense of my own life, I regret that line of thinking.

More memories came to mind, such as awakening in the coffin and digging my way out. The first day of my life as a vampire was truly magical, but marred with the ugly memories of my death. I can remember killing my second person; in this memory I did it because I was hungry. He was sitting in front of his TV drinking a beer; he never saw me coming. I didn't do it with hate or revenge; I was not covering for another. I simply wanted to eat, and I have no idea whether or not he was good or bad. I didn't feel as bad for this kill; I was a tiger, killing for survival.

Like the switching of the channel, I recalled hitchhiking and being picked up by two men. They ended up being monsters themselves. They had murdered Carrie and countless other girls. Killing them filled me with pride. Later, Alice and I became good at this, the predator, of predators. It was truly justice; they got what they had coming to them. In turn, we stopped them from hurting others and fed our needs.

When the memories surfaced of me and David killing men from The Order, I was filled with regret. After killing Aaron Reite, I had learned that not all members were evil men that needed justice. Some of them were just the opposite, trying to serve and protect others. They understood that if they didn't deal with evil magic users that humans would turn against them. I had learned this, but I did not change my course of action. I hunted them down and killed them; I helped David murder countless men and women.

The night that David helped me kill Jason Black, I watched him kill an entire bar of innocent people. I did nothing to stop it. In fact, I helped, all for my revenge. The memory was harsh, watching the people fall upon the floor and scream in pain, their bodies bent as they died from the poison gases only to rise again as zombies. I didn't try to save them; I didn't even care. In fact the only thing that upset me that night was David being mean to me. I couldn't stand these memories; I hated thinking about my own selfishness. My hate could not devour enough people.

Trying to think of happy thoughts, I couldn't, not with that drum banging in my ear. If I could have screamed, I would have. The noise just kept on banging over and over again, with no end. In this endless black world the memories could not be held back.

I found myself on the Atlantic Sun. This curse of nightmares is where I first met Peter Lionheart traveling with Alex. Once again, my revenge consumed me, as I battled to kill Alex. It was my need to kill him that led to such craziness. It was hard to deny that the fire that was later created may not have happened if I hadn't been so gung ho about killing Alex. And how many people died on that ship? I don't know, but I do know of two children and their mother… I do know that their deaths are partly my fault. I knew that I did not directly kill them, and Alex was the one who started the fire, but I was not innocent.

It was also my fault the book escaped. I don't know what that book was, or what it did, but I knew it was bad. How many people might die because of that?

If I had eyes, I would cry.

The pounding noise continued as the memory I most dreaded came to my head. It was the fresh memory and I knew without a doubt the most condemning. After I had kidnapped my sister, I had held her for a few days while my father looked for her. Why did I do this? So that he could suffer and learn to hate God. During this time with my sister, I spent a lot of time talking with her. Mostly it was her asking questions about me. I told her everything; I covered my entire life… well at least a good overview.

Before I tricked my father and brought him to the church. I had let my sister out of the cage; we walked around the church as she asked me questions.

"Alice sounds crazy," my sister added as I finished another story about her.

I defended Alice, "She is crazy, but there is so much more to her. In many ways she is my sister and my only friend… now that Carrie is dead, or gone."

"I would have liked to meet Carrie, but I probably would have been too scared. I have never seen a ghost before."

My heart hurts for Carrie, "You would have liked her. I'm sure that Carrie would have liked you as well."

Mindy saw my feelings and exploited them. She asked, "What do you plan to do with father?"

Lost in my thoughts of Carrie, I half answered her, "Kill him, and finish my revenge."

"I know what he did was awful; I don't deny that, but what will your revenge do for you?"

She had my full attention now, "What will it do for me? It will give me peace, and I will finally be able to go forward in life. I am so close to being free from the pain."

My sister was careful with her words. She cleared her throat, "I would like nothing better for you than to find your peace. Earlier you were telling me about your friend David. His family was murdered too; did you not kill the man who did it?"

"Yes," I responded. Wondering what she was trying to say.

"Did the death of that man give David peace? Did it help with the pain of losing his family?"

"I don't know!" But I did. I knew that it had not helped him one bit. He was so angry that he declared war against The Order.

My sister asked me another question, "What is justice? I mean what is it to you?"

"When others suffer for the crimes... is there another?"

Mindy shrugged her shoulders, "Perhaps."

"I'll bite, and do, what is this other justice?"

Mindy giggled a little, "Nice pun?"

I smiled, "Thanks."

Sensing that she had only a short time to explain her version of justice, Mindy explained. "Tim burned Bill's house down because of jealousy. Bill was full of anger and revenge so he burned Tim's house down. He was soon to find out that Tim did not care about his house or his belongings. Bill was still angry, so he burned Tim's family. Tim loved his wife and two children, so, of course, he looked for revenge. Bill had no family.

"Tim captured Bill and killed him slowly. Later, Tim was put to death for murder. So you see that revenge is hard, for it is impossible to make someone else feel the same pain you have. On the other hand, if Bill would have called the police and had Tim arrested for burning his house, he would have saved his family, even though Tim's arrest would have had done nothing for Bill's losses. Justice would have been served.

"What I am trying to say is that justice is not to pay back the victim, but rather to stop the villain from creating more victims. In society we try to rehabilitate criminals, not make them pay back their victims. True justice, even killing a man, is to stop them from committing more crimes."

I shook my head at her, "Then how does the victim find peace? How do I move on?"

"Forgiveness," she stated.

I was almost yelling, "What, forgiveness from God?"

"That's what God does, but you need to forgive the trespasses of others. You must forgive, so you can move on. Nothing can take back what they took from you. You had your justice with the other men; they can't hurt anyone else, but father is not a bad man. He is changed; he has suffered. Most importantly, he has learned his lesson."

"SILENCE!" I bared my teeth and hissed. I swiped at her face with my claws, but I did not hit her. My sister retreated across the church; there she hid in a corner and cried.

The memory of her crying was so loud in my head, and, as I tried to tune it out, all I could hear was that *damn drum*.

I had known she was right, but I refused to listen to her. I do believe that love and hate have the same goal, to devour others. Still the end result is night and day, for being devoured by love is wonderful, and by hate, misery. No wonder I have no relationship with David, since we both hate and have no love.

My memories shifted to the day I met David, the first day on the bus, and the boy who captured my attention. He made me feel safe, and the love in his heart I craved. He held me accountable when I killed a man in the alley. He was the reason the very next night I spared a boy who was trying to take advantage of a girl. His love for me gave me hope and peace, but my hate fought for control.

After his family was murdered, we went to Vegas; we changed. We took each other as lovers, but really there was not much love. We filled our bed with sex and hate, and that was the bond we shared. The hate destroyed the boy I knew, and it wasn't long before my need for David was for my own revenge. What did the hate do to me?

I could laugh at myself and my infatuation with Michael. He knew that I had no love in my heart. What did I want with him? Not to love, for all that mattered to me was the death of everyone involved in my murder. He knew this. Yet when my time came to have him, I didn't want him because of his lack of purity. What kind of hypocrite had I become?

My thoughts were interrupted by a new sensation. I could feel my body, first my hands, followed by my feet. At first my body was numb, but slowly the feeling became stronger. I could now tell that I was curled into a ball. I could not move and the thought came that I could be underground again.

There was a chance I was not dead. I could have been saved from the fire, and then buried. My body would slowly repair itself, and I would soon arise once more, but it didn't answer the question. Why did I keep hearing that damn drum?

I must have fallen asleep; time had passed. I awoke to the sound of the drum; it was now louder. I also came to realize it was not as constant as I originally believed. It had sped up and then slowed down. New noises filled my ears. It was the sound of the world, but it sounded as if I were hearing them from under the water. I heard noises of cars, a TV and people talking. When they spoke I could almost make out what they were saying.

After some time with sounds ever changing and my movement still severely hindered, I became bored. My mind slipped back into the memories of my past.

Even in death, I found love, first with Carrie; many times she pulled me back to reality. She wasn't very smart, but she had a heart of gold. She was also loyal and had suffered the same horrible fate that I had. She understood my pain, so when she questioned my revenge, it made me question my motives. In the end I blew her off, leaving her alone with David and finally using her to complete my revenge. She went wherever ghosts went. She did this for me. I hope she is happy and at rest; I owed her more than I could repay.

Alice was a sister to me though one could argue that her influence was worse than her friendship. I don't know how I would have made it if it weren't for her help. The same thought went to all the Whites. Ezra taught me how to fight and in many ways was a second father. How did I repay him… by killing his lover, Charlotte, and yet I knew he held no grudge against me.

Charlotte… I hadn't really had time to mourn her death. What was she to me, a sister, a mother, or a good friend? In many ways she was all of those things, and in the end she died for me. She had known what we were up against, and not once did she act as if there was any other choice. The night before we went up into the mountain to face the wolves was the last time me and she had talked. Charlotte sat down next to me in front of the dying fire. I was pretty sure she wanted to talk to me about Michael; she wanted nothing more than for us to get together. The sky was full of light, for the morning sun was cresting soon. Ezra wished us all to go to bed as soon as the sun rose. We needed to be rested before entering the mountain.

I asked Charlotte, "Is Alice, making you help me?"

She laughed at me, "No, don't be ridiculous. I am a warrior, and so are you. When Alice asked for your help to recover the book, you jumped right in. You didn't ask her why; nor did you worry about your own personal safety. Tomorrow we will go up in that mountain and face your enemies;

some of us might not come back. Then again we could all be killed. If you're asking why I'm here, I am here to fight, fight for you. We are a warrior clan, and that is what *we* do."

"You're willing to lay your life down for me, just because I asked you to?"

She gave me a small smile, then wrapped her arm around me, "If I were to ask it of you?"

I nodded, for we both knew the answer. I would go to my death for any one of them. I was afraid of getting killed, but not of dying. I whispered, "Live by the sword…"

Charlotte finished, "Die by the sword."

The memory died away since I was too distracted by a noise. I heard strange music and the world vibrated. I was still too weak to move. Where did they bury me?

*   *   *

I do believe I'm in hell.

I have been falling asleep and awakening for what seems to be months. My body would have never taken this long to repair itself, and I still feel so weak. I awaken to all the strange noises, music, TV, cars, people talking at all times. That damn drum, not only does it sound like I am underwater, but it kind of feels that way too. My body felt a little stronger now, so I was able to push and feel around with my hands and feet. It felt as if I were in a trash bag unable to find any solid surface to push against. The voices above sounded as if some of them could be my loved ones. On many occasions I thought my dad was talking to me, but that didn't make any sense.

I was bored and forced to relive my life over and over again. I begged for forgiveness from God, but I doubt he could hear me… now that I was dead. Of course, if he forgave like me, I'll be here a while.

One memory haunted me the most. It was not the memory of being raped and killed or even the terrible crimes I committed against others. It was the memory of me and my sister right before I left to pick up our father.

I was about ready to go; Mindy was in her cage. She had not spoken to me since our conversation the night before. She had angered me, as if forgiveness was my only way to peace. She believed I was a fool; that that stupid story would convince me to let our father go. I came over to her cage, "I'm off to get father, so, *cheer up!* Soon we will all be together… one happy family."

Mindy's face was void of any real emotion, "This is your moment. I have had a vision, and I now know once you walk out that door your choice will be made."

I giggled at her, "My choice was made a long time ago. In this vision, does father die? I just wanted to know, because I love happy endings."

She pleaded, "Please listen. If you stop now, you will have peace. If you don't, you will suffer. I don't know how, but I know this. I really care about you; it's not just father that I am trying to save."

I had to admit she was convincing, but I didn't believe her. I thought of something awful. "Maybe you're right; maybe I should reconsider? I wouldn't want to suffer." Her facial expression told me she wasn't buying it. I laughed, "Okay, okay, I'll make you a deal; how about that?"

"What deal?"

I grinned wickedly, "I'll let dad go, and kill you instead. Father will suffer knowing he lost you… without even making a profit by selling you. What do you think?"

In the blink of an eye, she responded, "Okay, I will gladly take his place. You must promise never to hurt father."

I was taken aback by her sincerity, "As if… I don't have to promise shit. I could kill you and change my mind on a whim, but I will not kill you. It is Father, who must die. In another world… we could have been real sisters."

As I left I could hear her saying, "You will regret this, and it's not too late…" She was still talking as the old wooden door slammed closed. I hopped into my rental car; it was time to go get dad.

The memory of my sister giving me a final warning made me regretful. For, if I could have listened, I could have had a life… friends, possibly Michael, and, if not Michael, I would have found love. As my past haunted me, my world shrank. The bag that held me became tighter and more uncomfortable. Trapped under crazy sounds I did my best to kick and push my way out.

In and out of sleep, I was always awakening to the feeling of my body being squashed. I now knew that I was in Hell, for I knew that I was not stationary. Not only was I moving through the land of the dead, but I could feel others pushing up against my bag.

This went on forever, or at least that is what it felt like. One day something changed… it felt as if my bag was pulled from out of the water. I was still in my bag, but now I could tell that I was lying on my back, since I could feel gravity. The bag constricted me, pushing and squeezing me. If I could have screamed, I would have.

The bag pushed my head into what felt like a steel pipe, only the pipe was not wide enough for my head. No matter, the bag pushed harder. I thought that I could hear my screams until I realized that they came from someone else.

The noises did not matter for my head hurt like no other; the pain was so great it was all I could think of.

I didn't care about living or dying; I didn't care where I was. All I cared about was stopping the pain. My head was being squashed… hurry and kill me… please. This lasted for what felt like forever.

The pain was so great it took me a second to realize what I was seeing. A light far in the distance, and I was getting closer. The light was becoming bigger and brighter; it was hard to care because of the pain. Somewhere in my head, I knew that I was finally heading to my final destination. Heaven or Hell, I wasn't sure I cared; I just wanted the pain to end.

The light became so bright, and before I knew it, I was engulfed by the light. The light was pure white and so bright I could see nothing. First, the light, but foremost was that my head didn't hurt as bad. Second, was that sound exploded into my ears, so loud that I couldn't make it out; it was overwhelming, shortly followed by what felt like being thrown into icy water.

I was freezing, and screaming for air… wait… I was screaming, breathing and falling through the air. Too many things were happening to me in the bright light to understand. The cold air, the fact I could breathe, and now I felt as if I had come to some sort of landing upon a hard stone. I couldn't help but cry as my senses were overwhelmed.

Something was wrong. HANDS… that is what I am feeling, hands feeling across my body… I hadn't enough strength to push them away.

At first I was totally and completely freaked about the hands, but then they wrapped me in blankets. I was so cold my mouth chattered. I don't know whose hands were touching me, but I was thankful. I was thankful for the blanket, and thankful that my head was no longer being squeezed with a vise.

I was so tired… the pain and the light… I felt mentally and physically exhausted, and I even felt another sensation, hunger. It all went away when I realized that I was now being held in someone's arms. It must have been a large man. The light was still bright, but the world was starting to come into focus. The noise became more manageable. I realized this person holding me was speaking to me. The voice was kind, but sounded feminine.

My vision began to clear a little more, and I became excited, for I think God himself was holding me. The face came more and more into focus, but as it did, I could tell it was a woman. I had guessed that God might be a woman. The woman's voice was soft and kind, "My little girl."

Her voice was familiar, and something was off. I was making out others talking in the room. I heard the word *nurse*; what was going on? I strained my eyes to see the face of the woman holding me.

She was… Oh my God… wait… she spoke, "My little Molly." She was my sister… my blood… it was my sister. It all came together for I could hear the drums, her heartbeat.

All I could do was… SCREAM.

Chapter 34 A New Beginning?
初心者

Two weeks…

It had been two weeks since my re-birth. Two of the longest weeks of my life, but of course that is not counting the last nine months I spent in Hell. I couldn't freak out, and I can't freak out in front of my sister. She has no idea, and she deserves better than this; it is as if I have stolen her child. For her sake, I have to act as if I am a baby. Of course, I don't have any experience with babies and I have already made mistakes. I spoke once; I didn't mean to; it just happened.

I was still in the hospital when my sister woke me, "Proud grandfather."

I opened my eyes to find that my father… or wait, my grandfather was holding me. Without thinking I said, "Father."

Mindy spoke quickly, "Did she say father?"

"No, she's just baby talking," I didn't know this man who now spoke, but it didn't take long to find out he was my new father. That would make him my third father; first there was Jack, then Nicks and now John. Boy this was going to be hard to keep straight.

I wanted to play it off so I made baby noise, to try to throw them off. That's when some stupid nurse started in, "I have never heard a day old baby make such strong vocal sounds… amazing."

All I could think was, *great.*

My father, Jack announced, "That's my girl; she's already a genius."

The next two weeks were horrible. I couldn't decide what was worse, feeding from my sister's breast, or bathroom time, and what was I to do with my waking hours; I was always glad to sleep. It would be good if someone would leave me within sight of the TV, but that hasn't happened yet.

I was hungry as I lay in my crib; I decided to try to get more sleep before I cried. I really hated feeding time, unless my father did it. I enjoyed his voice and the fact he used a bottle. I stared at my mobile waiting for sleep.

*　　　*　　　*

I was moving without a sound through a neighborhood that I was not familiar with. My body moved without effort; I knew this feeling. I knew that I was a vampire; I also knew that I was excited about something. After I traveled down an alley I came to realize that this was not me. I was in someone else's body and had no control. It was like watching a movie. Only this was the best movie ever; I felt what they felt, smelled the air, I had all five senses.

I also knew this was a vampire, and even though I didn't know who, or what they were thinking; I knew how they felt. It was a female, and she was excited about where she was heading. I didn't understand what was going on, but I didn't care. After two weeks of lying on my back, I was really enjoying this. I pushed the fear to the side.

The vampire moved swiftly through the neighborhood. It was a nice looking middle class neighborhood with lots of tall trees. It looked a lot like North Carolina, the same place where I died and was re-born. The vampire came to an older part of town. The house here looked to be from the earlier part of the nineteenth century. She came to a stop in front of an old home that looked like it needed a lot of T.L.C. It was two stories high with a widow's peak off to the right.

She moved to the right of the house, then traveled into the yard and down the alley. The vampire floated into the air coming to a stop in front of a window. The window was not locked, but why would it be, it was on the second story.

After opening the window, the vampire whispered, "Invite me in." There was no response, so she requested again, "Invite me in."

The second time she spoke it was in stereo... I awoke with a start.

I was lying upon my back looking at my mobile. What a crazy dream. A voice softly spoke, "Invite me in."

I froze; who was this? It took me a minute, "Come in."

Barely a moment had passed when arms came down into my crib and scooped me up. Without a sound she carried me to a rocker. Rocking me in her arms Alice smiled down upon me. She pulled out a bottle and began to feed me. The fact she was here was so amazing; I was happy she had found me.

I had been hungry, so I started to devour the liquid in the bottle. Alice started humming a song as she rocked me back and forth. After a little time passed I was still feeding from the bottle like it was the first meal I had ever had. The milk was amazing, like nectar of the Gods. And I began to wonder, where did she get this bottle from?

I couldn't wait to finish the bottle, for it had been months since I was able to speak to anyone. It was still dark in the room; I strained my eyes looking at the bottle. The liquid was black and moved with an eerie slowness. The taste was divine, the best thing I had tasted since... Oh, my.

I reached and pushed the giant bottle out of my mouth; it was gigantic from my point of view. I asked, "What are you feeding..."

Alice interrupted me by shoving the bottle back into my mouth. "Shh... babies don't talk!"

A Story by Nicks

My brother was an aspiring writer before he passed away. He only finished one short story, but still managed to leave a legacy. I felt lead to take up where my brother left off and write the stories we used to tell each other. In doing so, not only am I keeping his memory alive, but also sharing a vision. The character Nicks in my book is my representation of my brother and my cherished memories of him. I would like to share his one finished story. I am proud to add his story to the end of my book. I dedicate this to you, Nick.

The Dwarf And The Basilisk
By: Nicholas B. Hood

Once there was a creature known only as the Basilisk.

It was a monster easily over a hundred feet long, its head towering twenty feet above the ground. It most closely resembled a gigantic snake, but looked much like a dragon with its massive jaws full of ivory sabers. A spiny black crest like a reptilian wing, adorned its head. Its back was covered in bright warning colors of red green and yellow. Its belly was like shinning black obsidian with scales as hard as stone. And its eyes, they were horrible, lidless black holes with an eerie glow from somewhere within.

The Basilisk did not slither upon the ground like a serpent, but rather moved lofty and upright, holding his head high with evil pride. He left a path of destruction where ever he went; shrubs and trees would wither and die at his passing. Rocks in his path would split before his will, and water through which he passed became polluted and foul. Any man or mortal creature who looked upon the Basilisk would be filled with horror and immediately die, such power of evil was there in him.

It is on one such path of destruction that this story begins.

He arose at dawn having no fear or respect for the sun. Rising from a hole of his own making in the face of sloped rock carved smooth by a once great river, whose rushing water from that half unearthed rock once fell. Now the water from that river, which once flowed clear and strong, was thick and gray. Water that was once cool and pure was now steaming hot and foul. It slipped and oozed its way down the rock face, gathering at the bottom where it moved sluggishly down the riverbed, carrying with it the dead victims of its poisonous vapors.

All around the vegetation was shrunken and dead. The trees were dry leafless shambles of lifeless wood. No birds were chirping, no cock did crow, and nothing stirred. For all creatures big and small there in that place were among the dead. All murdered by the abyss filled eyes and poisonous breath of the Basilisk.

With his head already above the trees, he looked down upon his carnage. He lifted his nose to smell the air and as he did his crest, which was folded down against his back in sleep, unfurled and crowned his magnificent head.

Now fully rested, the Basilisk left his temporary dwelling to seek further destruction elsewhere.

He traveled with speed greater than that of birds and left a path of decaying vegetation twice his own body width as he went. After long he came upon the foothills of snow capped mountains. His eyes beheld their desolate peaks and he thought to turn and seek more populated areas when his nose caught a familiar scent. It smelled of burning iron, of a metal working forge.

The Basilisk's eyes flickered like burning embers in a dying fire. His jaw lowered revealing razor sharp teeth and his mouth salivated sizzling acid with the thought of humans. In his mind he could hear their screams and see them running in horror before his great evil.

The smell led him to a pass through the mountains and into their hidden places. His way was blocked by sheer walls of rough black stone where mountains melted into one. So strong was his will that the rock cracked and split and the Basilisk wormed his way through.

At that same moment, in the valley below, the dwarf swung his wood ax, splitting yet another log cleanly into. The day had grown long and Hamfast was growing weary of his daily toil. He stopped a moment whipping his brow with a handkerchief from his pocket before chopping a few more logs for the evening cook fires. From the west, just below the mountain peaks, the sun was casting tall shadows across the valley when the dwarf had finished.

It seemed to Hamfast that he had been doing this kind of last minute wood chopping a lot of late. There was never enough time for wood chopping with all the endless work in the forge below. Yawning, Hamfast leaned on the handle of his wood axe to rest a moment before he would have to haul the wood to the cook fires.

As he rested, his eyes wondered upon the Titan Peaks, they completely encircled the valley, cradling it, standing like sentinels against time. This was his valley, all of it, the Valley of Shadows. And his pride, his inheritance, venting from a crevasse in the valley floor, laid Thrawldains Forge. The forge where jewels were made deep in the earths secret places. It was the ultimate form of dwarven expression, the art of catching and forming light. It was the dwarves' greatest gift to this world; that of gleaming gem stones.

Hamfast Goodnfat was an average looking dwarf, only slightly taller than four feet and quite plump with a long curly black beard streaked with gray. He dressed plainly, even for a dwarf, and you would hardly know he was lord of the land but for his shining mail shirt and a set of large golden keys hanging from his belt. But he was a rich man and he knew it, or at least most of the time he did. Sometimes he thought that between his nagging wife, his idiot children, his lazy workers, and their lazy wives, it was a wonder they didn't all starve.

Hamfast's rest was interrupted as something strange caught his attention that made the hairs on the back of his neck stand up. The dwarf was blinking franticly. He could not believe his own eyes as their gaze beheld a gigantic snake winding down the side of the mountain, its body waving like a flag in the wind. He nearly fell over his ax from the shock of it.

Rubbing his eyes, he could see that it was moving rapidly towards his orchard. Some of the precious fruit trees were turning black and withering away. The dwarf could watch no more and he sprang into action.

The Basilisk reared up instinctively at seeing the dwarf rushing towards him, waving an ax and screaming franticly. The Basilisk was so bewildered that the dwarf was upon him before he could react further. Hamfast struck furiously, his ax thudding harmlessly against the Basilisks armored scales again and again. The Basilisk was so dumbfounded that he simply watched as the dwarf rain blow after blow.

Hamfast was tiring, swinging his ax slower and slower when the Basilisk roared in an exasperated tone, "Excuse me?"

The dwarf was so shaken he nearly leapt out of his own skin. He stepped back nervously, his eyes tracing their way up the Basilisk's scaly body. When his eyes finally met the Basilisk's gaze, his ax dropped from his grip and he stood paralyzed with fear. "Well?" said the Basilisk. Crooking his head and showing his teeth, he almost appeared to be grinning.

"Well, eh…beggin yer pardon sir, but eh…" the dwarf stammered. "Would ya mind not destroying me orchard? I wouldn't mind if ya was hungry er somthin, but I just can't stand ta see good food go to waste. I mean just cause ya don't like fruit don't mean ya can't let other folks enjoy it. I mean eh…Well where's the sense in that?!"

The Basilisk was laughing now, a sound that was like rumbling from deep in the earth's volcanic center. "You really are bold dwarf." The Basilisk mused. "Very well, just point me in the direction of the nearest human settlement, and I'll be on my way."

"Humans!" the dwarf spat. "Why ya won't find none of their kind round here. What would ya want with their scum any how?" Hamfast seemed to forget whom he was talking to. "Why if ya ask me, every last one of them should be hunted down and skinned alive like the filthy animals they are. Those lolly lay about no account sons of…"

"I'm not interested in your racism dwarf." The Basilisk interrupted. "I like humans, their flavor is exquisite. Which is more than I can say for you. You have a nasty fairy stank all over you."

The dwarf made a funny face. "Yuck! I like meat an all, but there's no way I'd ever eat anything that lives in its own filth the way humans do. I'm having a feast tonight, but sorry no humans on my table."

"Is that an invitation?" asked the Basilisk.

The dwarf was confused. "Invitation to what?"

"To your feast of course," offered the Basilisk.

"Well it's not feast per say, it's more like a…" Hamfast managed before the Basilisk interrupted again.

"Then it's a deal. I'll stop destroying your orchard and you'll feed me. So lead the way. Oh, and call me Basilisk." The Basilisk didn't ask for the dwarf's name.

"Yes of course Mr. Basilisk, sir." Hamfast didn't know what else to say. He couldn't figure out how it had come to this. What would his wife say? But with nothing else to do for it, he led the way.

The Basilisk was far too big for the front entrance to the forge, so Hamfast led him around to the back door. The rear entrance was very large and the storerooms beyond dwarfed even the Basilisk. They passed through room after room, each one containing enough stored food to feed an army for a lifetime.

Even the Basilisk had to be impressed when they reached the dining room. The walls and ceiling sparkled with the light of countless gems. Six pillars of spiraling silver and gold ran the length of the rectangular room. A long wooden table surrounded by ornately carved chairs stood gracefully upon clawed feet. Immense candelabras of gold and platinum made a shinning row along the table's surface. Two fireplaces and twelve sconces painted the room with colored light; the effect was something like magic.

"Wait here while I…" Hamfast paused for a moment, struggling to think of an excuse to leave the room. "… Ah, check on dinner." The dwarf then rushed out through another door way and disappeared through the hallway beyond, yelling as he went. "Gretchen, I'm home, and guess who's coming to dinner!"

The smell of cooking food permeated the air as the Basilisk made himself comfortable, coiling his length in one corner of the room. He could hear Hamfast and his wife arguing from somewhere in the caverns beyond. "I can't believe we live in a constant state of famine and you're inviting guests to dinner!" Gretchen was saying.

"I saw him through the window; he looks big enough to eat this whole place."

"It's not like I had a choice, Gretchen!" Hamfast answered angrily. "He sort of insisted."

"We could have been happy living back home, and you could have taken that job with my father, but nooo, you had to drag us out to this god forsaken wilderness, for crying out loud!" Gretchen moaned. "Why I ever married you is beyond me!"

Hamfast sounded really angry now. "Now don't start that again, Gretchen, and I mean it! You always say that when things don't go right, but this guest situation is only temporary. I'll think of something. I always do."

The Basilisk could hear Gretchen stomping off. "You better! You better, or you'll be sleeping alone!" She threatened as she went.

The Basilisk knew she was long gone when he heard Hamfast saying, "Hmph, like I care!"

Dinner got under way without much more delay. Before long the food was on the table and everyone was seated. There were twelve of them in all, including the Basilisk: Hamfast; his wife; his two sons, Twillin and Dillin; his daughter Mhim; his three indentured servants: Burbeer Butterblack, Pikey Potterwheel, Furwhin Firejewl; and their wives: Applecake, Rose, and Tofu.

The table was filled with food, so much food that the Basilisk wondered when everyone else would arrive. There were six sides of beef, twelve turkeys, thirty meant pies, a hundred other pies, ten kegs of beer, fifty different plates of vegetables, a large bowl of assorted fruit, cakes, cookies, truffles, pudding, noodles, stacked loaves of bread, five potatoes as large as men, and a barrel of gravy to boot.

The dwarves said no grace and gave no etiquette; they simply dug in, eating like hungry pigs. There was no conversation and for a long while the only sounds was that of rampant chewing.

Hamfast nearly choked when Twillen asked the Basilisk to "please pass the salt." He smacked Twillen in the back of the head and called him an idiot under his breath. Twillen just looked confused, and Hamfast sighed as Gretchen threatened Twillen with a wave of her long wooden spoon.

Amazingly, at the end of the meal, all of the food was gone. Twillin and Dillin actually fought over the last meat pie which Hamfast took and ate greedily. The Basilisk was stuffed, and he had to admit to himself that the meal was pretty good, but he told the dwarf that he preferred his meat spoiled. A full belly always made him sleepy, so the dwarf led him to an empty storeroom, where he slept for hours.

It was early morning when the Basilisk awoke. The dwarves had just finished mid breakfast, that's between first and third breakfast, and were preparing to return to the forge. Since the Basilisk was awake, and there never were many visitors, Hamfast offered to take him on a tour of the forge its self. Perhaps out of morbid curiosity the Basilisk accepted.

The forge was not close at hand, the way was a good hours journey. Hamfast led the way with the Basilisk following closely behind him, while Furwhin, Burbeer, Pikey, Dillin, and Twillen all lagged far behind. They traveled down a wide tunnel that spiraled steeply towards the forge below. Along the way there were many wondrous examples of dwarven art.

The tunnel was dimly lit by strangely luminous crystal rods, held by iron hands, jutting from out of the stone walls. These crystal rods came in pairs, one on each side, every few feet. A little less frequent were white marble archways that resembled the ribs of whales. Before each archway came a set of statues depicting dwarven heroes, the shinning plaques on their bases told the stories of their brave deeds.

Though the presence of the Basilisk was like a blight upon their world, nothing could break the dwarven spirit, and they sang with pride an enchanted song of dwarven lore to pass the time.

A long long time ago,
In days so long
Come and gone:
The sun so bright,
The sky so blue,
The earth was young,
The earth was new.

Silvin Thistlestar
An elf from afar,
He traveled the world
To see the sights,
He found our home
Upon the heights.

Silvin thought dwarves quite queer.
And he did jest and he did jeer:

Your legs are short,
Your voices are gruff,
Your wives have beards,
Your manors are rough,

You live like moles with faces like trolls,
You work all day and never play,
Gold and jewels your only love
You've none for trees or sky above.

Silvin thought dwarves quite queer.
And he did jest and he did jeer.

Boren Boneaxe held his tongue.
The ax he bore
Would settle the score.
He cut Silvin down just like a tree,
Hacked off his legs at the knee.

Silvin thought dwarves quite queer.
And he did jest and he did jeer.

The taller you are the farther you fall,
And that's what you get fer flappin yer jaw! "

The air grew warm as they descended and a low rumbling could be heard from somewhere below. When they finally reached the forge, the heat was intense and the source of the rambling became apparent. A stone dragon, which was part of the far wall itself, dominated the huge rectangular room. A steady stream of lava was flowing out of the dragons gaping jaws, and spilling into a giant stone goblet below. The detail of these stone monuments was a testament of dwarven craftsmanship. The dragon, carved of red stone, was incredibly convincing. Its clear-jeweled eyes gave the dragon a presence of life, glowing with a distorted image from the lava flowing behind them. The angle of the spewing lava made it seem as if the dragon was using its fiery breath weapon, and the sound of it reverberating against the cavern walls, was as the dragons roar.

The goblet was of gray stone, with scenes of battles engraved upon it. From a peculiar round hole near the bottom of the goblet, it could be seen that the lava actually ran through the goblet and into somewhere unseen below. The rest of the forge was very plain, the walls were smooth and bare, the floors dull and dusty. All about was strewn the clutter of hard work. Stones littered the floor. Carts filled with various minerals road on tracks that crisscrossed the floor and ran through tunnels leading in and out of the forge. Everywhere with no semblance of order was scattered things like; racks holding tools, anvils of varying size, small tables and chairs, and most notably was a rack, near the goblet, cluttered with hundreds of bottles containing mysterious substances.

The dwarves wasted no time and proceeded right to work. Hamfast went straight to a small table in front of the rack with bottles and began laying out an assortment of small tools, bags, bottles, and other strange implements. Furwhin, Burbeer, and Pikey began putting on aprons and goggles. Twillin and Dillin began rolling a cart full of rocks along its tracks towards the table where Hamfast was working.

"No,no,no…" Hamfast was saying while examining a rock from the cart. These just won't do. You boys know what to look fer by now, so stop bringing me this useless rubble." Hamfast tossed the useless rock back in the cart.

"Ah, but we can't find anything else." Dillin moaned in frustration.

"Ya, and we looked everywhere!" Twillin added in a pleading tone.

"Don't give me that boy." Hamfast directed his gaze at Twillin. "You've got the whole of the earth to explore. Now get to it." Hamfast motioned his hand as if to slap the boy, though Twillin stood several feet away. Twillin smiled, and with his little pudgy face, his rosy little checks, crooked teeth and that silly little wispy yellow beard, Hamfast couldn't help but smile back.

Dillin, who was a little older with dark hair like his father, just shrugged saying, "Fine." And with a scowl on his face he grabbed a couple of pick axes from one of the racks and tossed them carelessly into an empty cart. Twillin grabbed a strange lantern that illuminated when he touched it. Then the larger stouter Dillin pushed the cart as fast as he could along its tracks and they sped out of the forge through one of the tunnels.

"Are we ready?" Hamfast asked.

Furwhin and Burbeer, who were standing on opposite ends of an anvil, held up their hammers in answer. At that Pikey used a long metal instrument to thrust a rock about the size of a mans head into the round hole on the side of the goblet. He pulled it back out after only a short moment and the rock was red with heat. He than placed the glowing rock on the anvil where Furwhin and Burbeer were waiting. Hamfast poured a vile of blue liquid on the rock, which resulted in a cloud of shimmering steam. He took a few steps back and yelled, "Strike!"

Furwhin swung first, his hammer striking the rock in a shower of sparks with a sound like thunder. Burbeer swung his hammer with equal might, and after they both had struck many times, little remained of the rock. It seemed nothing more than a lump of black powder, but when Furwhin brushed it away with his hand, what was left was an emerald about the size of a dwarven hand. It was rough and somewhat square shaped, but with a little cutting and polish it would be magnificent.

Throughout the day they made many jewels of many hues, and all the while the Basilisk watched in silence. There was no discernable expression on his face, but he was impressed. He could not appreciate the beauty of these rare gems though, for beauty he could not see. Jewels were nothing to him, but he knew of the great value that humans placed in them. From now on the humans would come to him. He would make a trail of gems for them to follow if he had to, but in any event, once the humans knew the jewels were there they would come, and he would be waiting.

He could claim this place as his own, the dwarves could not stop him, no one could. Many heroes had tried; they tried and failed. The more time he spent with these dwarves, the more repulsive he found them. He would have liked nothing more than to kill all of them then and there, but they could prove more useful alive. Instead he would weave a spell to make them his slaves. They would resist, but overtime his will would over power them. Once enslaved, the dwarves would keep the gems coming, and thus keep the humans coming as well. Though it would take some time for the Basilisk to implement his plan, he was content with the certainty of it.

Hamfast was in deep thought himself. He had to come up with a plan to get rid of the Basilisk. He couldn't possibly afford to keep feeding the Basilisk, besides if he didn't get rid of the Basilisk soon, Gretchen would kill him. All the while he worked, Hamfast thought and thought and thought and finally he had a plan.

The next day when the Basilisk awoke the dwarf was waiting for him. "Are you hungry?" Hamfast asked. "Cause if ya are, a couple of cows fell through a vent and into the lower caverns. I think they've been down there fer days. They may have been diseased or somethin."

"Disease!" The Basilisk spoke excitedly. "Is it anthrax? Please say it's anthrax. Oh how I love anthrax!"

"Well, I don't know, but we can find out." The dwarf answered.

They traveled through cravens deep in the earth, through tunnels that had only recently been excavated. When they reached their destination the Basilisk had to squeeze through the entrance. Sure enough they entered a large cavern with sunlight spilling in from an opening hundreds of feet above their heads. The Basilisk went straight for the three cow corpses while Hamfast tried to slip out.

Just outside the entrance, Twillin and Dillin came out from their hiding place. "Okay you know what to do," Dillin began. "When Hamfast comes out we smash these rocks with our hammers and collapse the entrance."

"Now?" Twillin asked.

"No, not now you idiot!" Dillin snapped.

Twillin pushed Dillin saying, " You're an idiot."

"That's it!" Shouted Dillin and he tackled Twillin sending them both sprawling on the ground. Something must have been knocked lose during their struggle because the entrance began to collapse.

Hamfast panicked and ran for the exit yelling, "Noooo!" He stopped just short of being smashed by falling rocks.

"What's going on here, dwarf?" The Basilisk rose up from his meal in anger, moving threateningly towards Hamfast. "Those cows weren't dead for more than a few hours and now this. What have you gotten me into?"

Hamfast cringed as he spoke, expecting the worst. "No, no, it, it, was just an accident. A cave in, don't worry I'm sure my people will dig us out soon."

The Basilisk moved towards the collapsed entry, his eyes shone brightly and a breeze began to pick up as he challenged the very rock itself with the power of his will. He should have been able to force the entrance open, but his attempt was blocked. Among the ruble of the collapsed entry were clusters of quarts crystals that somehow reflected his gaze back upon him. This was the first time the Basilisk had ever been exposed to his own power, and it proved too much even for him. For an instant he was faced with his own evil, and he truly understood the horror that his victims felt. The sensation was exhilarating, but also exhausting. He was filled with a renewed since of pride at seeing his great evil, but he was angry that he could not force his way out.

So, they waited, the Basilisk peering up at the hole in the ceiling wondering if he could get out that way, while the dwarf paced back and forth. On the other side Twillin and Dillin worked furiously to clear the rubble, but they knew it would be hours before they would reach the other side. They were just sure the Basilisk would be doing terrible things to their father, so they worked at an exhausting pace.

After a while Hamfast began moaning, "I'm so hungry. We've been here for hours, we'll probably starve before they get us out!"

"Dwarf," the Basilisk spoke in an exhausted tone. We've been in here for twenty minutes."

"I can't help it," Hamfast admitted. "I'm sooo famished. I feel like my stomach is turning inside out."

The Basilisk signed deeply. "Put it out of your mind and think of something else, or better yet, just shut up."

The silence lasted just a little while when the Basilisk said, "I'm bored. Let's have a contest of riddles."

Hamfast smiled a crooked grin. "I love riddles."

"Good, then you make the first one," said the Basilisk.

Hamfast scratched his beard for a moment and then said, "Lives like a mole, not in a hole, in dark it lies, growing eyes?"

The Basilisk had to think about it for some time and then it hit him. "Damn Dwarf! I told you to stop thinking about food!"

"I'm sorry Mr. Basilisk, it won't happen again," Hamfast insisted.

They were both silent for the next few hours. The Basilisk was concentrating on finding a way out in case the dwarf's kin never came through but he was distracted. The dwarf was staring at him whenever he wasn't looking, and whenever he turned to look Hamfast would look away quickly.

The Basilisk's patience was wearing thin, and he was determined to put the dwarf in his place. "Stop that dwarf! Stop your games now, or that's it!"

Hamfast looked crazed, his eyes were bulging, and he was shaking visibly. "Stop what? I wasn't doing anything Mr. Bas-K-delish."

"What did you call me?" The Basilisk shouted.

Hamfast staggered back in fear, "Ah, nothing Mr. Baskdelish, I mean Basilisk, Basilisk!"

"That's it!" And with that the Basilisk swallowed the dwarf whole.

That will be the end of that, he thought, and he settled down to take a nap. Before he could fall asleep, he began to feel a sharp pain in his stomach. It got worse and worse, until he cried out in pain and agony. He fell to the cavern floor twitching violently, and then he died.

After about four or five hours, Twillin and Dillin finally broke through. Seeing the Basilisk sprawled out with his tongue hanging out they knew he was dead. Still, they approached cautiously. Hamfast was nowhere to be found.

"Look it's moving!" Twillin shouted, pointing at the Basilisk.

A lump began forming on its body and it was moving up and down. Suddenly, Hamfast burst out of the Basilisk's body. He was covered in its blood and licking his fingers. He looked over at Twillin and Dillin, who were standing in awe, and said, "Hmph, needs salt."